Now to Forever

ASHLEY MANLEY

WILDFLOWER
BOOKS
LLC

Identifiers:

979-8-9899682-8-2 (paperback) | 979-8-9899682-9-9 (eBook)

Cover by Elise Stamm, Blue Heron Graphic Design

Interior graphics from iStock

First edition: July 2025 | Wildflower Books LLC

Editors:

Victoria Straw (developmental)

Kaitlin Slowik (copy edit)

Ciara Lewis (proofread)

Dear Reader,

Once again, out of all the books in the world, thanks so much for choosing this one to read. As a reminder, *Now to Forever* is part of a duet. If you haven't read June's book, *Forever and Back*, you can absolutely read this one as a standalone, just be prepared for a few spoilers about June's story.

Before you continue, please know Scotty has a sharp tongue and foul mouth. The F-word is used a whopping 77 times in these pages. I tried to control her, but as you'll find out, there's just no reining that girl in. Along with explicit language, there are also on-page scenes of romance found in chapters 25, 33, and 40, and heavy themes of addiction, self-harm, and domestic abuse throughout the book.

Thanks for being here. I hope you love Scotty as much as I do.

XO, Ashley

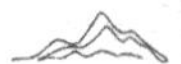

To my tribe on Instagram who laughs with me and believes in me, and to every reader who has slid into my inbox and DMs, telling me to keep writing. You are the cheerleaders I didn't know to look for, but I'd never be here without. This one's for y'all. If you hate it, blame yourselves.

ONE

"I'm Gary. I've been watching videos of dirty maids for three years."

A murmured response of *hey Garys* echo as Gary's shoulders droop. Standing at the front of the room, his familiar face sighs as he shifts his weight between his feet.

In any other circumstance, hearing that sentence would make me laugh so hard I'd piss myself, but in the din of the stuffy Methodist church basement, I nod sympathetically from my back-row seat. We all know his story—Gary shares the details of his porn addiction nearly every month.

Someone clears their throat, a few metal chairs scrape across the linoleum floor, a phone dings with a text, and I take a sip of coffee that tastes like it was brewed at the dawn of time—same as it does every month. I wince the second it hits my tongue and spit it back into the Styrofoam cup in my hands. *Disfuckinggusting.*

"And, I don't know," Gary continues, "I was doing so good. Didn't watch a single video for a month. But then—" His eyes widen. "I couldn't stop myself."

His nubby fingers scratch the beard covering his face like the fur of a mangy dog as the paunch of his belly is barely contained by the oil-stained Ledger Motors & Notary shirt. It begs the question: Does anyone ever need a notary while having their tires rotated?

"I caved," he admits. "And it wasn't just one video. I watched my favorite cleaner—Sally Scrubs—she's so thorough with the rag. The way she uses a toothbrush . . ."

His voice trails off as his breathing becomes labored, fists clenching and unclenching at his sides. Gary's desire to rub one out is as obvious as it is traumatizing. He shakes his head with a start, as if he just remembered he's in front of a room full of people and not wherever he watches Sally scrub.

"But then there were more—hours. And—I couldn't stop myself."

Poor Gary looks like he wants to cry.

"And my wife, Deb, she found me watching and . . ." He clears his throat, eyes darting around the room. "And, well, that didn't end too well."

Mel, the meeting leader, stands at her usual position behind the podium next to him, her slender face filled with sympathy. "Gary, I'm so sorry. And how did that make you fe—"

"Have you always been into porn?" I ask, my voice loud enough it cuts Mel off from where I sit in the back. "When you were a kid, I mean? Or have dirty magazines? Maybe it's just who you are."

He and Mel look at me with different expressions. Gary shocked, Mel annoyed. *As usual.*

I ignore her; I've always wondered how long the signs of addiction are there and missed. How much time people could've spent doing something if they only knew where to look—if I would've known where to look, maybe Zeb . . .

"Or your mom?" I press. "Did she have a kink? I think porn addictions are less common with women, but"—I sweep the hand not holding the brewed feces around the room with a chuckle—"who are we to judge how someone gets their rocks off?"

The room takes a collective blink as Gary massages a temple. "Uh."

He looks at Mel.

"I'm not—"

"How's your sex life with Deb?" I pivot; he's clearly not interested in why his parents' issues might have contributed to his current situation. Maybe it's something happening now that's triggering his obsession. Maybe Deb needs to spice things up—*yes!* "Is it the cleaning or the outfit that gets you excited?"

His eyes widen and Mel's jaw drops.

"Maybe it's Deb?" If she's not helping, no wonder he's dripping over Sally. I can't believe I've never asked. He can't do this on his own; he needs her. Maybe he doesn't know to ask. She might have no clue. If she did more, maybe Gary wouldn't even be in this room. "Have you ever asked her to dress up? Or take a toothbrush and—"

"Scotty!" Mel snaps from the podium, stopping my words dead with her could-freeze-a-fire glare. "Enough."

I frown; she softens, looking at Gary with a sincere smile.

"Gary, is there anything else you'd like to share today?"

He shakes his head, seemingly resigned to his fate of watching nude women clean other people's houses, and drops like a bag of wet cement into his chair.

"As many of you know," Mel says, sliding one hand along the edge of the podium before running it through her cropped blonde hair. "I became an alcoholic about five seconds after the phone call my daughter was killed in a car accident. A drunk driver ran her off the road on her way home from the library—she was in college down in Georgia—and her car wrapped around a tree. I had never drunk more than a glass of wine before that, but once I got the news . . ." Her voice trails off and she shakes her head. "I couldn't stop. Bottles and bottles and bottles of the stuff trying to bring her back." Somehow, she smiles. "But I'm happy to report that today makes six months since I started the Ledger's Ledgers and six months without a drop of alcohol." A wave of soft applause breaks out. "And, as you know, I have no qualifications to be up here talking about addiction other than the fact I have one. I don't share my victory to brag, more to give hope. Inspire you in those dark moments where it feels like you have no choice—no purpose—you do. It took an unexpected friend of mine explaining that sometimes a change we make can impact seven others around us. And those can impact seven more and so on. Seven doesn't seem like much when problems feel so big, but"—she shrugs—"at the end of the day, it's a lot of sevens."

The people around me smile earnestly; they have delusional hope.

Inside: I feel nothing.

Because though I have no addiction, I recognize it for what it is: a ruthless sonofabitch that takes no prisoners and holds no punches, strangling the light out of anything good. An eclipse lasting for generations. And while I don't disagree that one person can impact seven, I've never seen it do anything positive. Every ripple caused by addiction leads to a tsunami that ends in a hellscape.

When people call warm praises and congratulations, I speak over them.

"Do you think it will last?" I ask, silencing the sea of addicts. Mel looks at me from her position at the front of the room, taking a sip from her cup. "Or do you think the next time you notice she's gone you'll uncork a bottle?"

"Scotty," she says, tilting her head slightly. "I notice she's gone every damn second of my life." Before I can say another word, she looks to the rest of the room. "Who would like to share next?"

I patiently wait for the woman with a food addiction to share her problems with hiding snacks before I begin offering my suggestions.

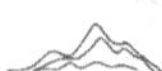

Even in the Blue Ridge Mountains, the August air is thicker than the backside of a swampy ball sack. Outside the church, rolling hills form the backdrop as the rest of Ledger's Ledgers fan out across the parking lot to their vehicles. As many people as vices. Drugs, alcohol, sex, food, shopping . . . it's a world I'd never know to believe in if I didn't grow up knee-deep in a cesspool of it. There aren't enough people in the town of Ledger, North Carolina to have addiction-specific meetings like AA, so Mel made up her own six months ago, playing off the town's slogan of *Life on the Ledge*. The addicts, no matter the vice, come together the second Sunday of each month to form an underground congregation of the damned.

"You have to stop doing that, Scotty," Mel says, taking a drag of her cigarette as she stands next to the LL sign in her usual attire of blue jeans and a Blue Ridge Blooms Nursery T-shirt. The lines on her upper lip curve toward the cylinder in her mouth like a mountain road until she blows the smoke in the opposite direction of where I stand. "You can't interrogate everyone like a damn cop when they share. It's hard enough to give problems a voice, you can't make it worse."

I pin her with an annoyed look. "That's not what I'm doing."

She chuckles, smoke puffing out of her mouth like a dragon. "I know that, but they don't. You don't share and your questions come off as judgmental."

I make a disagreeing grunt but say nothing.

"And you try to convince everyone that it's up to others to fix their problems."

I scoff. "And?"

She rolls her eyes. "And it's not. When you have a problem like this, nobody else can fix it. Nobody else can care more than you or it won't work."

This is the biggest pile of bullshit I've ever heard of, but I don't argue. She won't listen.

"Why do you keep coming to these meetings? I didn't know your parents, but I've heard stories. You're nothing like them." She raises her eyebrows. "Or your brother—the good kid who made bad choices."

Her cigarette crackles with her next drag.

I do not tell her that because of all those people she listed I'm more fucked than any person who sits in that depressing basement. Instead: "Moral support."

She scoffs, dropping her cigarette and stamping it out with the potting-soil-covered toe of her tennis shoe. "You're full of shit, Scotty," she says, waving toward a police car pulling slowly into the parking lot, friendly smile overtaking her face.

When the car stops next to us, I physically pinch my lips together with my teeth to contain the feral growl that begs to come out.

Ford Callahan. Yet another reason my life is the way it is. Only back in town nine months from whatever circle of hell he went to reign over for the last twenty years, I've interacted with him once, avoiding him ever since. As much as I've worked to ignore him—giving a wide berth to every parking lot I see his truck parked in—just knowing he's in the same town as me has afflicted my body like a flesh-eating virus. His proximity makes me itch.

"Officer," Mel says warmly. *Gag.* "Good to see you today. You know Scotty?"

"Mel." He smiles slightly—the ease of it hitting me like a sledge-hammer—then turns his head toward me. "I do. Scotty."

His elbow is casually propped on the open window of the car and his aviator sunglasses hide what I know to be bright blue eyes. In the warm afternoon light, hair that I knew to be the darkest brown two decades ago is now subtly dashed with salt. In another ten or fifteen years, he'll be considered a silver fox. I want to gouge his eyes out, scalp him, and feed his bits to the buzzards.

"Don't be modest, *Officer*," I say, turning to Mel. "I've had Ford's dick in my mouth."

Ford lets out a choked snort while Mel pinches the bridge of her nose, squeezing her eyes shut with a sharp exhale.

"Then I guess you know she only speaks in razor blades," she says to Ford.

He chuckles—*bastard*—the sound making me seethe as he looks up at me. In the lenses of his sunglasses, my own reflection scowls at me.

"Don't worry, Mel," he says, smirk tugging at his lips and making a dimple dent in the scruff of his jaw. "I'm well aware. And fluent." His chin dips—slowly. Like he's looking me over. The notion makes my blood boil so hot with rage I'm surprised it doesn't singe my cutoff jean shorts and loose-fitting shirt right off my skin. I fold my arms across my chest; he shifts his attention back to her. "Just wanted to check in. You good?"

She smiles genuinely, slight laugh in her voice when she speaks. "I'm good, Ford. Stop worrying about me. Six months sober to-day."

He grins, like he's proud. "Probably won't stop me, but I'm happy for you." Then to me, "Scotty, good to see you."

Motherfucker.

I look at him and force a smile with all my teeth. "Pleasant as a bowl of shit soup, Officer Callahan."

He chuckles with an exhale, looking me over one last time before lifting his fingers from the wheel in a slight wave and cruising out of the lot.

"I'm not even going to ask," Mel mutters.

"Wouldn't answer if you did."

Mel and I have only known each other from our six months of talking after the meetings, but these exchanges have become who we are. I don't say much; she lectures me like a Snapple lid while sprinkling in small pieces of her personal life I don't ask for. I know she was born and raised in western North Carolina and, following her divorce, moved to Ledger about ten years ago with her two kids. She works at a plant nursery and lost her daughter to a drunk driver roughly two years ago, which led her to becoming a drunk herself. According to her, if there was something at the bottom of the bottle that was worth killing her daughter over, she was going to find what it was. She never found it; now she's sober.

And, unfortunately, I now know that she knows Ford. Judging by the hokey look on her face when she spoke to him, she even likes him. Another soul lost.

We're quiet, watching cars come and go.

"You aren't going to find what you're looking for," she says. "Not here. Not like this."

Gary walks by, lifting his chin in a silent goodbye as he trudges to his truck.

"And what is it that you think I'm looking for?"

"Here's what I see—" She taps another cigarette out of the box with a muttered, "One vice for another," lights it, and takes a deep inhale before continuing. "You've been shoveling shit your whole life, and I can't imagine what that's like, but you continuing to show up here shows you are addicted to one thing, Scotty." She points her lit cigarette at me. "Being unhappy."

I make a *psh!* sound, waving my hand dismissively. "In your professional opinion?" I snark.

"What do you do when you aren't here grilling everyone?"

I run my tongue across the back of my teeth, silent.

"You need a purpose, Scotty. More than chasing ghosts. More than this. You never share—the only person you talk to is me after meetings. You told me once about a hobby, the next month you'd moved on to something else."

My eyebrows pinch in offense. "I dabble."

The truth is, I haven't *dabbled* in a while. Where I used to experiment with hobbies, my no-strings-attached free trials lost their luster when I walked into the boxing gym four months ago only to find Ford taking up all the space in it. So I've been staying home. Working. *Fine.*

"You need to do something for you." She flicks her fingers, making ashes drop from the end of her cigarette. "Chase something that excites you. Let yourself love something. *Someone*."

Some*one* is the last thing I need.

"And *your* purpose?" I shoot back. "You drank yourself stupid for—what—nearly two years? What changed? Your daughter's still dead."

At my directness, she doesn't waver, simply drops her cigarette and stamps it out with her shoe.

"You never run out of bitch, do you?"

I don't know if she's trying to be funny, but I laugh anyway. Her lips quirk into an almost smile.

"Someone pointed out if I would have died and my daughter lived, I would be devastated if she wasted her life the way I was. I was drunk for her the same way I'm sober for her. And my son who is still very much alive. Would you be doing this if your brother and dad were still here?"

The shout of a child interrupts the unwanted feelings her question provokes and makes us both look. In the nearly vacant lot, next to my Bronco, a minivan parks. Little arms flail from the back windows and a frazzled redheaded driver in the front seat smiles, slightly confused as she looks through her windshield at me, Mel, and the church.

The hell is Joo doing here?

I smile toward the circus in the parking lot with a wave before giving Mel a smug look. "I'm fine. See? My best friend is here." I do not tell her she's also my only friend. "I'm a social butterfly."

"Scotty," Mel calls as I walk toward the screams. I pause to look over my shoulder. "Fine isn't the same as living."

I debate telling her I would be *fine* if everyone left me the hell alone, but she breaks our gaze by turning to a woman exiting the church and I revert mine to the familiar minivan.

"Aunt Scotty! Look at this!" Twin five-year-old voices shout from the back seat before I fully make it to June's driver's side window.

When both boys flip me off, I bark out a laugh and return the gesture.

"Scotty!" June snaps, glaring at me from the driver's seat before she blows out an exasperated breath and turns to the boys in their booster seats. "Hank. Ty. Don't do that. We talked about that finger."

They start to whine, she rolls her eyes, looking up at me then glancing around the empty lot, lingering on the LL sign before Mel picks it up and carries it inside the church.

"What are you doing here?"

"What are *you* doing here?" I retort, lifting my chin.

"I was driving by and saw the Bronco—at a church—and thought the world must be ending or you must be dead, so I pulled over."

I shift my weight between my feet and cross my arms over my chest.

"Praying."

She squints at me, her curly red hair framing her not-convinced face.

"Lost cause. What else?"

I say nothing. The truth is, I don't know how to answer. I don't know why I'm here. Six months ago, I was on my usual Sunday drive, saw the sign as I went by, and decided to go in. Like maybe a basement full of people like my entire family might give me some insight, direction, or answers. I've gotten none, yet I keep showing up.

"You're a pain in the ass." One of her kids shouts about her use of *ass*. "How long?"

I shrug, annoyed. "Not as long as you harassed my clientele with your problems."

She glares at me, no doubt reliving the time that lasted until just months ago when her marriage was crumbling, and she could only find solace by sharing everything she felt with those who couldn't respond . . . because they were dead.

"Was that Ford?"

I scuff the toe of my sandal against the ground, stretching the silence between us.

"I'm worried about you, Scott."

I sigh. "It's nothing, Joo." She opens her mouth to argue but I raise a hand, silencing her. "I'm serious, it's nothing. I'm fine. I'm just . . . I don't know. Restless or something. In a rut. Maybe this is my midlife crisis."

"What else have you been doing? I hardly saw you all summer."

"Pilates," I lie.

She rolls her eyes. "We didn't even hang out for your birthday."

"Forty-one isn't a big deal."

She puts her hands together like she's praying, pressing her fingertips to her forehead and blowing out a slow breath before looking at me again. I've seen her like this before—usually when she's trying not to go apeshit on her kids. "You're always working or in that sad apartment."

My jaw drops. "That's fucking rude, it's not sad." June winces, and the boys start shouting about swear words again. "We went boxing. That's something."

She scoffs. "That was four months ago, and we both turned into psychos."

I chuckle; she's not wrong. She unloaded on her husband, Camp, and I attacked Ford. Not that he didn't deserve it.

"Talk to me, Scott. You live alone, above a crematorium in an apartment with one window and—"

"Two," I correct, holding up two fingers. "The bathroom has that round one."

"Fine." She closes her eyes, as if trying to keep herself from snapping. "You know what I mean. Just—" She looks at the church. "Are you dating?"

Why is she pushing this?

A car drives through the lot around us, loud music vibrating the windows with a rattle. "I like being alone."

Her look says she doesn't believe me. "There's a new teacher at the school. He's a coach—Camp said he's single. Has two kids—" I frown. "And he's nice. And cute."

"He's cute?"

She nods too many times. "Like, so cute, Scotty."

I squint at her.

"Seriously. *So* cute." Her tone is eager. *Too* eager. "Hot, really. And-and-and funny. Think about it. And promise me you'll tell me if something is going on. Let me help?"

I soften toward her, my best friend that's been by my side through every dark age on the timeline of my life. "Fine." I squeeze her arm through the down window. "But my apartment is cheery as unicorn shit."

She snorts and the boys scream.

The engine of the minivan hums when she turns the key, and her eyes search me like she's looking for a gunshot wound before shifting the gear. "You're a pain."

I grin. "I know I'm not."

As she drives away, I know in a million years she'll never understand what it's like to be me. She ended up with the family, the house, the photography career that sets her on fire. Once upon a time, I thought that would be me: a woman who would smile easy surrounded by people who loved her. But it didn't work out that way and I've made peace with it. When you live a life filled with ghosts and defined by loss, alone is easier. People alone don't come home from a hike only to find out everyone they love is gone, forced to spend the rest of their lives with a hole in their chest. They don't go to college thinking one day they might become a lawyer only to drop out and spend their days cremating bodies.

June and Mel don't get it. They can't. Nobody can.

When I start down the road, it's the same out-of-the-way drive I've been making every Sunday for nearly twenty years: past the run-down trailer park on the edge of town, over the river by the wooden cross nearly smothered by the tree line, and to a two-story house in a cookie-cutter neighborhood where a family of three washes a car, pickup truck, and SUV in the driveway.

The mom sees me, pausing mid-scrub with a sponge to wave when I slow down. I smile slightly, only giving myself a few seconds of watching—the husband and son oblivious of my presence.

When I get home, I start a record by The Black Crowes, pour whiskey in a rocks glass, and turn on all the lights. Dark shadows from the lampshade reach across the ceiling as lyrics about talking to angels play like an anthem. When the last sip burns my belly, I convince myself my apartment is as bright as the damn sun.

Two

"Wanda?" I call from my office. "Today's send-off is for Archie Watkins. He ready?"

"Of course he is, honey," she answers, her thick southern twang bouncing down the hall. "Wheeling him up now."

I double-check his paperwork as I walk from my office to the cremation room—all accounted for. Archie was eighty-two and died from complications following heart surgery.

Though I mostly keep to myself aside from a few random dates when the spirit moves me, Ledger's small size means most names are familiar to me. Archie, however, had become enough of a presence in my life for sadness to wash over me at the thought of him being gone. His brother owns the gas station across the street from Happy Endings, and, for a reason I never quite understood, this translated to him becoming a regular visitor. I got the job; he showed up the next day.

And the next.

And the next.

He'd go to the gas station every morning, meet his brother and a group of retired men for a cup of coffee, then shuffle across the street and ask, *"Now, Scotty, who we lightin' on fire today?"* At first, his visits annoyed me—part of the appeal of working with the dead is not having to be social—but annoyance grew into something else. Something comfortable. After twenty years, enjoyable.

After I'd tell him who was on the docket, he'd give me a piece of gossip about the deceased. Usually affairs, though there were a couple murderers, one cross-dresser, and a bank robber who all had their secrets spilled while we stood over them in their cardboard cremation containers as their favorite music played through the speakers.

Archie also never tired of taking a tour of the old brick building. Happy Endings isn't big; there's one big room with the retort—what most people know as a cremator—with exposed brick walls, concrete floors, a stainless-steel worktable, and one large window that looks into the witnessing room. More like a living room than anything, the witnessing room is painted a deep shade of green with eclectic furniture, a coffee station on an antique table, and a shelf of urns and mugs made by a local potter from a couple towns over. The home-like atmosphere is why many people opt to watch family members go into the retort from there. More than once, Archie commented, *"Never thought it'd be so comfortable to watch someone you love burn up."* But it was the back room that fascinated him the most—the place he dubbed Wanda's Workshop. This is where nearly everything happens: a garage door for body intake, a large cooler for body storage, all the tools needed for body preparation, and tables and equipment for processing the remains post-cremation.

Archie would watch Wanda at the table, his old lips in a tight line as she dragged a magnet through the pan of cremains, turning almost giddy when she'd pick up a medical pin that didn't get incinerated. *"Never knew he had a bad hip,"* he'd mumble as he watched her work.

At the same time I hang the clipboard of paperwork on the hook next to the dials and buttons of the retort, Wanda wheels in Archie in his cardboard casket. As always, my eyes are drawn to her first. Ridiculous coif of blonde hair, line of cleavage a mile long, and clothes so tight and bright they should require a warning sign and special eyewear.

"You're conspicuous as ever," I say, regarding her blue spandex dress over neon-green fishnet stockings.

"Makin' sure they see me in heaven, honey," she says with a bright white smile and bloodred lips as she maneuvers Archie to line up with the opening of the retort door. Her chunky wedged boots clomp against the concrete floor as she smacks a piece of gum. "Plus"—she blows out a frustrated breath—"you know that apartment I've been renting above my sister's garage?"

I nod, glancing at her before turning my attention to the stereo system, finding a Lynyrd Skynyrd playlist—Archie's favorite band—and playing it low.

"Well, my nephew is coming home and wants it—you know moms, always wanting to help their kids." She gives an annoyed huff; the sentiment is lost on me. My mother has never once *wanted to help.* "So now I have to find somewhere else to go."

She gives me a wide-eyed look which is enhanced by the three gallons of mascara she must wear.

"And, you know, Wanda the Wicked ain't a name people forget in a few years. I can't find a pot to piss in around here."

"That's too bad," I say, recalling the headlines in the small newspaper when she was arrested a few years ago.

She shrugs, smiling slightly as she takes the clipboard from the hook and flips through the paperwork to fill in her required lines.

"I'll figure it out, just a pain in the tush."

Then, like she didn't just say she's getting kicked out of her house with nowhere to go, she hums along with Lynyrd Skynyrd while I look Archie over. Wanda, despite the insane colors and makeup she wears into work every day, is a master at making the deceased look naturally alive. Like at any moment they could pop their eyes open and start talking.

Archie looks exactly as he did the last time he came in to see who was next for the fire. Black button-down shirt, blue jeans, and a living warmth to the skin of his round face and bald head.

"You miss this part?" she asks as she glances at me before returning the clipboard to the hook.

I shake my head. "When I had your job, they never looked so alive. More dead than they really were."

She grins and blows a small bubble with her gum but doesn't say anything else as she moves dials. The pep in her step as she works is emphasized by the jiggle of her chest.

I hired her two years ago, and despite her unorthodox style that leans more toward forty-seven-year-old stripper than cremation technician, I've yet to regret it. On the contrary, it's been one of the best decisions of my life. Before, I did it all. I picked the bodies up from the morgue, bathed and dressed them, sat with the families, and worked the cremation process all in the name of saving money and doing it the same way the owner I bought it from did before me. Then, one day I was standing in line at the Walmart and there was Wanda, eyeing my basket and telling me the eyeliner I had picked out wouldn't suit my hazel eyes. When I tried to tell her to go fix someone else's face, I couldn't get a word in edgewise; she refused to shut the hell up and in turn talked me right out of arguing with her and into buying a different color. Once she got over the eyeliner lecture, she noticed my Madonna shirt and jumped right into every iconic look she ever had. *"Weren't those cones one for the record books?"* There was a sort of whimsy to her voice as she made twin conic gestures at her own chest.

She just kept talking, and for whatever reason, I kept listening. It turned out she was a beautician out of work who needed a job, and I was a funeral director who needed a break.

"Why'd you lose your job?" I asked her as we stood by my Bronco and loaded my bags into the back.

"I got arrested—charges dropped—for attempted murder on my ex-husband," she said with a shrug, slipping a piece of gum into her mouth as she squinted thick mascaraed lashes up toward the sun.

Then I recognized her from the paper: Wanda the Wicked.

"You do it?" I asked, eyeing her outfit and trying to determine if she could murder someone. She was wearing skintight purple pants, a crocheted black shirt over a bright pink bra, and had more makeup on her face and hairspray in her hair than I'd used in my life. I had no way of knowing how old she was by looking at her—she could've been eighteen or eighty.

"Don't matter much in a town like this now does it, honey?" she asked with a wry smile. I knew what she meant—I lived in the same small town where my reputation was decided by the trailer park I grew up in and the family whose shit was the opposite of together.

Before I knew what was happening, Wanda reached over to me and maneuvered my hair around my head. *"You should wear your part to the side. Makes you look less tired."*

I hired her on the spot and never asked about her ex-husband again.

"Is Dondi coming in today?" I ask, smoothing my "Free Bird" shirt under my blazer.

Dondi is the body removal attendant and brings bodies to either the crematorium or the town funeral home, Tranquil Departures, in a refrigerated van he's dubbed the Ice Pop.

"He said no deliveries scheduled for today when I saw him last night."

My eyebrows pinch. "You saw him last night?"

She pats the bottom of her coif, chomping her gum. "Yesterday, last night. Same difference."

Something flitters across her face as the front door opens and Archie's wife appears on the other side of the window in the witnessing room.

I look down at Archie and a pang of sorrow burns in my chest. "Time to get lit on fire, old friend."

Mrs. Watkins dabs her eyes from our spot in the witnessing room as we watch Wanda through the window, sliding Archie into the retort. The stainless-steel door closes and the process of Archie turning from the man we loved to ashes begins. The sound of the retort hums like a high-powered fan, but in our position on the opposite side of the glass, it's so quiet and unobtrusive it's as if it's not even happening at all. Like the life that was once intertwined with so many others isn't even in there turning to dust.

"He loved you, Scotty," she says as she peers through the glass and "Sweet Home Alabama" plays softly through the speakers. "Loved the life you brought to death. He always said that when he spoke of you. We both—" She looks at me, her mouth open in her extended pause. "Thought he loved you."

I swallow several times uncomfortable with both her compliment and the delivery. She's probably in her seventies and beautiful in that way older women are. Her silver hair is cropped but curly, and she's wearing a simple white button-down shirt with almost trendy blue jeans. There are gold studs in her ears and a gold necklace around her neck with a small clock hanging from it that she's sliding along the chain. When she catches me watching the movement, she stops. I wonder if it belonged to Archie.

"I had him fooled, Mrs. Watkins," I say with a slight smile.

"Please," she says, batting a hand through the air as she sniffs. "Call me"—she pauses, looking at me with an unexpected intensity—"Lydia."

I've never met Archie's wife, but she's odd. Despite how put together she looks, she's awkward compared to Archie. Maybe it's the grief. It's rare to see anyone smooth when a piece of their heart is being cooked in front of them at sixteen hundred degrees.

I force a smile. "Lydia."

She clears her throat several times before finally asking: "Did you know your grandparents?"

My head whips toward her at the unexpected personal nature of the question.

She blinks, with a curious tilt of her chin and shape of her eyes. I roll my lips between my teeth, considering how to answer.

"My dad's parents, a little," I finally tell her, skirting around the details. The truth: a little was far too much. My own dad, a wreck of a man, was raised by people who fell to the same blight of bad decisions as the rest of the bloodline. Apples don't fall far from the family tree because he got both his love of liquor and short temper from my grandfather. On nights my brother and I had the unfortunate privilege of being dumped on them, our only goal was to stay out of the way and not get screamed at or spanked.

"And your mom's parents?" Her warm eyes stay steady on mine.

I shake my head, looking away from her to the cremation room, clearing my throat to mask my surprise at her inquisition. And still, because it's Archie's wife: "No. My mom moved out and married young . . . I never asked questions. She told me they were no good." At sixteen, my mom had my brother, married my dad, Lyle Armstrong, and dropped her Joplin name. The rare times someone brought them up, she said she left that name and the people tied to it where they belonged. "I had enough no good, you know?"

"I'm sure that's not true," Lydia says, twisting a tissue in her hands. "That's nonsense."

At this, I laugh.

"Mrs. Watkins—" She frowns. "Sorry, Lydia." I clear my throat once again. "I appreciate that. But . . . I know you and Archie had kids—they got lucky. I got . . ." *Fucked.* Her crisp white shirt makes me think this word would not land well. "Unlucky."

She stares; it's analytical. Same as every time my history comes up to anyone who hasn't been through it. My mother's parents were nameless, faceless villains in a long line of them. She never talked about them; I never asked. I had enough repossessed vehicles, threats of eviction, and someone slamming a door before leaving for days without bringing more shitty people into the disastrous mix.

Abruptly, Lydia crosses the room to the coffee table where she fishes a small album out of her purse and hands it to me. "We have a lake house—did you know?" I shake my head as she nods for me to open it. "I say we, it was really just Archie's." She chuckles. "We bought it almost fifty years ago. Spent most summers there."

At the first image, I snort a laugh. "An A-frame? Never would expect ol' Archie to fit in a triangle." Yet there he is, black button-down shirt and blue jeans, sitting on a large porch in front of a triangle-shaped wall covered in windows.

"It was new back then, but he didn't care what it looked like." Her lips lift in amusement. "It could have been a dirt-floored shack, and he would have wanted it. Told me it was his place to escape even though it was less than thirty minutes from where we lived."

I flip the pages. Random snapshots fill the sleeves of the extremely dated and mostly hideous A-frame. Lydia cooking in a kitchen, wearing denim overalls and surrounded by mustard-yellow appliances. A strange looking black-and-white dog lying on burnt-orange shag carpet by a woodstove and tube television. Archie reading the newspaper on a floral couch. When I get to a picture of a little kid taking a bath overflowing with bubbles in a puke-green tiled bathroom, she chuckles and says, "Our grandson."

I smile and flip to a photo that was taken outside: people sitting on the large porch, kids floating on tubes around the small beach. Tall pine trees. Archie fishing out of a canoe in the distance. A brief punch of sadness hits and I think of my dad. Despite his flaws, he loved fishing. We never had a boat, but he'd sit on a riverbank with a cooler of beer all day long, even if he didn't catch a thing.

The last page is more faded than the rest. Archie and Lydia are young—much younger than they were in the rest of the photos—holding a baby they're looking down at with proud smiles. Their love is evident. The face of the baby isn't visible, but it's easy to imagine the gummy smile curving its mouth and drool coating its chin.

"Our oldest grandchild," she says.

I close the album and hand it back to her with a smile. "It looks like you had a lot of great memories there."

The lines on her face deepen as she seems to be considering what to say next. She rubs one palm over the brown leather cover of the album—slowly—like it's something sacred.

"I'm sorry you had such a rough go at childhood," she says. "It should have been different. I wish"—I raise my eyebrows. *Where the hell is this going?*—"life wasn't so complicated."

Okay.

I press my lips together and say nothing.

"We all make choices in life we have to live with," she continues, face filled with distant resignation. "Fight battles we shouldn't have fought. Skipped battles we shouldn't have skipped." She laughs softly; it's empty. "Regrets are the hardest thing in the world to reconcile when you get to be my age." Her voice is sad; her hand is back on the clock around her neck, zipping it along its chain. Her gaze remains steady on the working retort. "I guess that's being human, hard as it is to manage sometimes."

Though I don't disagree with the sentiment, my smile is half forced and fully confused.

"You do something special here, Scotty. The way you play this music and wear your T-shirts. Archie saw it. Everyone does. And they"—she looks at me, lines on her face deepening as she struggles to find words—"are so proud."

Lydia is either on drugs or has dementia; it's the only reason she'd babble like this.

I shift my weight uncomfortably between my high heels, smile feeling wooden on my face. "Somebody has to do it."

"Archie wanted you to have the lake house," she blurts.

My reaction would have been the same if she had ripped open her white shirt and revealed a bald eagle tattoo covering her chest. I look at her and let out a loud, abrupt "HA!"

She chuckles; it's genuine.

"He said you'd do this. 'Can't take a compliment, that girl will never take a house,' he told me. It was the only thing he wanted changed in the will at the end." She sniffs, fresh line of tears lining her eyes, and she hands me a key, pressing it into my palm as if trying to make sure it stays. "He told me, 'You tell her there's more than bodies in this life to light on fire.'"

I look at the key in my hand like it might vanish.

"Why?" I ask, my tone thick with skepticism. "You have kids. A daughter and a son, right? Archie told me."

"My son doesn't want it—he's grown and gone. Too busy for Ledger."

"Your daughter?" She shakes her head. "A grandkid? That one in the photo has to be old enough for a house." My chest tightens. "Give it to them."

"He said *you*." Before I can argue she adds, "You deserve to be happy, sweetheart. Have some goodness and beauty in your life."

This odd woman lets this hang as my mind reels. I think of June calling my apartment sad a mere twenty-four hours ago. Mel, asking me if I'm happy. Both of them essentially telling me to get a life.

And I'm happy . . . *ish*.

I think I am.

Do I even know? I know the last months have left me feeling like I'm going backward. Like every choice I've made and every bad thing that's happened is hitting me with the steady beat of a drum, over and over. For twenty years I've been alone, and I've been fine with that. Fine with my life. Then came a shift—seemingly out of nowhere—where I've found myself wondering if things could have been different. As much as I don't want to admit it, I know part of it's Ford. A big part. Since I learned he was back in town nine months ago, Ledger has shrunk. Time has stopped. And seeing him outside the LL meeting . . .

"Can I pay you for it?" I ask, flipping the key around in my fingers. "I have money. Contrary to the habits of the rest of my family I have a savings account like an actual adult."

I've saved. Other than the loan to buy the business and the expenses that come with it, my bills are minimal.

She waves a hand through the air, smiling kindly. "I believe you do, Scotty, but it's a gift. No strings. It needs a lot of work. And if you don't like it"—her eyes flick back to the window and the small door that separates her from Archie, as if she's waiting for him to crawl out of the opening and wrap his arms around her—"sell it."

Sell it? A house on the lake, even if it's as dated as it looks in the photos, would be worth a small fortune.

It takes a split second for a brand-new thought to slam into me: I could pay off the crematorium and I could leave. *Leave.* Maybe the root cause of this whole funk I'm in isn't me being alone, it's the town. It has to be. I need to get out of Ledger. Away from the memories and the ghosts. Ford. I could take this house, sell it, and would have enough money just to go. Anywhere. To the ocean—no, the desert. I could move to the desert: a landscape so harsh only scorpions and prickly plants survive. That would suit me. Nobody will bother me there. Pester me about the brightness of my apartment. I'd miss June, but she'll understand. She'll visit with her camera and take pictures. This house could be my fresh start. My new life. My happy. Could it be that easy?

"I don't think I can," I say, offering Lydia the key. "People will probably think I stole it."

I want her to take it back as much as I want her not to.

She wraps her hand around mine, her skin soft and gentle as she presses it closed, and the key digs into my palm. "You think too little of people, Scotty. And who cares if they do?"

Hope fills me so quickly it makes me lightheaded.

Our gazes are steady through the window as the retort works. "I'll miss his daily visits," I admit.

A small smile tugs at her lips. "I know the feeling."

We're quiet a beat; me lost in what this house could mean if I kept it, her probably drowning in the idea of a life without her husband.

"It needs work," she finally says, breaking the silence. "I'm sure you noticed it's outdated. But I've paid for the power and water, so it should be on. I haven't been there in over a year, but I know there's a canoe." She chuckles softly with a shake of her head. "God knows what else."

I squeeze the key in my hand until I feel the teeth bite into my skin, confirming it's real.

"I'll think about it," I finally say. "And thank you."

"Ah." She rubs a palm on my back. "Thank you, sweetheart."

For the rest of Archie's cremation, she's more relaxed and less strange, telling me stories of the two of them, some involving the A-frame on the lake, most not. She cries at some of the songs that play, leading to stories of them at a Lynyrd Skynyrd concert before they had kids . . . where they *made* one of said kids.

Two hours later, when she's gone, she leaves me with paperwork to sign for the deed and a few notes on the house. Though she hasn't been there, a family friend checks on the place every couple of days. "He keeps the critters fed and makes sure the place hasn't burned down," she said with an amused shake of her head.

For the first time in years, I'm almost giddy.

THREE

"SCOTTY! WHAT CAN I get for ya tonight?"

The familiar bartender smiles, round face and shaved head seemingly widening with his mouth.

"Hey, Ben," I say lightly. He wipes the bar as I slip into my usual stool at Liberty Tap. "The usual."

He winks, smile not fading. "You got it."

I peruse the menu for as long as it takes for him to pour my drink—whiskey neat—closing it and handing it to him after he sets the glass down.

I take a sip, warmth coating my throat as it slides to my belly. "Good as ever." I grin. "And I'll have the trout."

"You got it." He doesn't move to leave, eyes lingering over me. "It's good to see you tonight. You look nice." His cheeks redden just slightly as he looks at me for something he absolutely won't find.

It's awkward; I'm not sure what to say. I could flirt, but it would be cruel. Almost as cruel as what happened a few months ago after too many whiskeys. There's no need for me to respond because he reads me for what I am—an emotional black hole—and taps the bottom corner of the menu on the bar before giving me a tight smile and leaving to enter the order into the computer.

I blow out a breath and take another sip.

The afternoon was busy, but Archie's house sat like an intrusive triangular thought through it all, poking at me. Even though it's only a quick five-mile drive from the crematorium, I couldn't bring myself to go look at it. Like I needed to mentally prepare for what it means to walk into a house—on a lake—that is technically mine. A house that will set me free.

"This seat taken?" a man's voice asks.

I answer without looking, rolling my eyes as I unroll my silverware from the napkin. "Don't see a sign on it."

He slides the stool out from under the bar and his smell overpowers me—a masculine scent I can't name—before I glance his way.

I groan at the sight of Ford Callahan's stupid face. "Explains the smell."

He doesn't react, merely drops into the seat like it's no big deal looking way happier than I am.

Like I haven't been avoiding him for the nine months he's been back.

Like every time I see him patrolling in his cop car or cruising in his truck, I don't consider ramming him off the road.

Like he didn't make me believe in something better for myself before taking off with it like a thief in the night.

"Scotty," he says, blue eyes twinkling before he directs his attention down the bar and lifts his chin toward Ben. "Hey, man."

Ben smiles and pulls a rocks glass off a shelf.

"Ford, good to see ya. Where's the boss?"

Boss?

Ford grins. "Mom's."

Without prompt, Ben fills the glass with ice, club soda, and . . . nothing else? He tosses a cocktail napkin down and sets the drink on it in front of Ford before busying himself with another order. Ford's eyes latch on to mine like bloodthirsty leeches. He picks the glass up, swirls it around, and takes a slow sip before sucking a piece of ice into his mouth and then crunching it between his teeth.

That baby-faced, blue-eyed, broad-shouldered, life-destroying sonofabitch.

He smirks; I roll my eyes.

My hand wraps around my fork and I squeeze it so tightly my knuckles go white.

"Good to see you, Scotty."

I drop the fork in my hand and exchange it for my whiskey, taking a long sip. When he adds, "You look good," I finish it.

My eyes cut to his. "Your *boss* know you're out trolling for women?"

He raises his eyebrows, amused. "You jealous?"

I drop my forearms on the bar and straighten my spine, looking him square in the eyes that always seem to be smiling. "Fucktose intolerant, actually." Before he can respond: "Are you following me? I see you everywhere."

"It's a small town, Scotty," he argues through a laugh. "Of course you see me everywhere. I'm a cop. It's part of the job. You want me to give you my schedule so you can avoid me forever?"

I force a too-big smile. "Actually, yes. Thanks for offering."

He fixes his gaze on me, expression teetering between solemn and hopeful. "Would it fix what I did?"

At the absurdity of his question, I laugh, loud. Like there's any way to *fix* what he's done or change his lifetime role as a silent star in the Scotty Armstrong shitshow. "Unless you plan on getting hit by a bus, Ford, there's not a shitsicle's chance in hell to *fix* what you did."

A laugh-like *pah!* puffs out of him. "So you're going to hate me forever?"

Our history hangs between us like a thick fog in a mountain valley.

"That's the plan," I tell him as he takes a swig of his club soda, his eyebrows raising as he watches me watch him. Pissing me off. "Why are you here?"

"To eat." He crunches on another piece of ice.

Crunch.

Crunch.

Crunch.

"I mean in Ledger," I huff. "Why are you back? You were gone for over twenty years. Why don't you crawl back to whatever hole you came from and go back to sucking souls like a good little dementor?"

He snorts. "Still got the tongue of a viper, I see. And there weren't enough birds." He looks at me, sizing me up, before adding, "And the company wasn't nearly as good."

Even though his lips aren't smiling, one of the many annoying qualities about Ford Callahan and his now slightly bearded baby face is that his eyes always are. His mouth always curving just enough to make you wonder if he just finished laughing. Like he can't not be happy.

If I were a cat, I'd claw his pretty face.

"And, what, you get clean and become a cop?" His smug look is replaced by a slack jaw. *Ha!* "Guilty conscience, *Officer Callahan*?"

"What?" He slowly sets his drink down. "The hell you talking about, Scotty?"

I snort a non-humorous laugh. When I first ran into Ford a few months ago, it was fortunate for me it was at a boxing ring where I hit him until my arms hurt. After that, I always imagined we would unload all this on each other, but Liberty Tap was not where I pictured it. Actually, the fiery pits of hell seemed more fitting, but as I'm not one to shy away from any battle, the most popular restaurant in Ledger will do just fine.

I fold my hands on the bar, looking at him with steely determination. "As I recall, you and my brother decided to burglarize a house—for drug money—and when the cops showed up, you let him take the blame while you blasted out of this town and never looked back. Meanwhile, he died—along with my dad—and you were nowhere to be found."

The hurt on his face would hurt me if I harbored a heart or shred of sympathy.

"That's not what happened."

Liar.

"Oh, really?" I say, raising my glass toward Ben who grabs the bottle and pours a refill, eyes pinging between me and Ford. "Spin me a tale, Golden Boy. Tell me how it all went down."

Our gazes clash and hold like lightning to an electric rod in a storm.

All he says: "Not that." After a weighted pause he mutters, "And I hate when you call me that."

It's true, he always had. Once the *Ledger Times* wrote an article about him after a high school football game and called him Ledger's Golden Boy, I never let him live it down.

"Well," I say, holding my glass toward him in a mock toast, "I hate that your dad found the need to inseminate your mom, so I guess we're even."

He shakes his head, lips twitching just slightly as we study each other, the silence broken up by Ben sliding my food in front of me and refilling Ford's club soda.

"You on the clock or something?" I ask between bites, eyeing his drink.

He crunches another piece of ice. "On the wagon." My chin jerks back and he chuckles. "Nothing like whatever you're imagining. Between the job and . . . some other things . . ." He shrugs. "Just seemed like it wasn't helping matters."

I nod and chew slowly, studying him as he takes another sip. He has the nerve to look comfortable. His arms in a T-shirt have the nerve to be muscular. He just . . . has the nerve.

"Heard Archie left you his place on the lake. He a little sweet on you?" he asks with a tease.

There are no secrets in this damn town.

"He didn't care that I was born to rot, if that's what you mean."

"That what you think?" His eyebrows raise. "That you were born to rot?"

"I think everyone I love is either dead, didn't show up, or doesn't belong to me." I let those words sink in. "Not so different than a rot."

He stares at me for what feels like the same twenty years he's been gone with an intensity too big for any one moment.

"You moving into it?"

A pressure starts to build in me with the question. Not just the question, at Ford asking it. At the shade of blue of his eyes and the foreign yet familiar look of hope swimming in them. At him being in this town after so long of not. I think of what Lydia said. June. Even Mel. *Chase something that excites you.* And like clouds parting in the middle of a Cat 5 hurricane, my path forward becomes crystal clear: "I'm selling it," I hear myself say. "And leaving Ledger."

He slowly lowers his glass, a line forming between his eyebrows. "Leaving?"

"Yes." My body tingles with the promise of freedom. I'm excited—it feels good, right even. Like it's what I've needed to do all along. "Leaving."

"Why?"

Before I can answer, a woman—blonde, mid-thirties, and wearing a navy-blue dress—sits on the stool on the opposite side of him. I don't recognize her, but it's not too surprising since I prefer the company of my lifeless clients over those with an actual pulse.

"Hey," she says to Ford, breathless quality to her voice as she rubs a palm across the spot between his shoulder blades and pecks him on the cheek.

"Anna," he says in a velvety smooth voice that makes her smile a swoony shape that nearly makes me vomit on the bar.

When she notices me, I raise my glass and her smile falters slightly. She gives a curt, "Hey."

I blink to Ford. "A boss *and* a bitch, how fitting." My eyes flick to *Anna*. "And I see you've moved on to blondes. Aren't you full of surprises, Golden Boy."

Ford pins me with a look as Anna's chin pulls back slightly.

"Don't mind her," he says, licking his lips, looking at me sideways before giving her all his attention. "Bark's worse than the bite."

I resist the urge to snap my teeth.

"How do you know each other?" Anna presses, leaning into him territorially.

"We—"

"Please, Ford. Let me," I interrupt with a too-perky tone and tilt of my lips. "It's the darndest story." I shift my voice to a stage whisper. "When we were young, he couldn't keep his fingers out of my—"

"Scotty," Ford snaps, hard edge to his voice. "Enough."

I give him an innocent look and he turns his entire body, making his back form a wall separating me from them.

Chickenshit.

They fall into conversation, and I push my plate across the bar, appetite gone. I take my wallet out of my purse and wave a credit card to Ben who takes it.

At the back of Ford's neck the familiar star-shaped birthmark just behind his right ear catches my eye. When Anna laughs, for a split second I wonder if he kisses her thumbnail like he used to kiss mine.

Then I remember: I don't care if he does. I *hope* he does. I hope she shoves her whole damn finger down his whole damn throat.

As they keep talking and laughing, my annoyance is replaced by peace. Maybe even glee. I don't have to deal with this, I'm leaving. I didn't know it before but I sure as hell do now: I can't breathe in this town because I can't stay in this town. I've served my time. When Lydia offered me the house, my mind went to the desert, so that's where I'll go. Start over. Be excited. Live in the land of eternal sand, sunshine, and sexy cowboys.

I stand and slide my stool under the bar.

"Good catching up, Scotty," Ford says.

I sign my bill, flicking my gaze to Ford as Anna wraps her hand around his bicep; there's a challenging look in her eyes as she stakes her claim. *All yours.*

"Sure."

"Friends?" he asks, eyes searching mine. A shade of blue still so distinctly and catastrophically him.

"Ha!" I shout too loudly as I sling my purse over my shoulder and throw back the rest of my drink, slamming the empty glass down harder than necessary. "I'll make you a deal, Ford. You change the fact you ran off to live your best life while I spent years—" *Nope.* Not giving him more than he deserves. "You change that you left, without so much as a goodbye, and we can be *best* friends. Hell, you change that, and I'll get your pretty little face tattooed on me." He says nothing, but his eyes stay locked on mine. "And, sweetheart?" I look at Anna, leaning slightly over Ford so she knows two can play this game. "As the woman he fucked first, you won't do it for him."

She gawks; I give her a pouty smile.

I start to leave but stop, leaning in so close to Ford my mouth brushes against his ear as I lower my voice to a whisper. "Go fuck yourself, Golden Boy."

His jaw pops; I grin.

I hate that man.

June

Do you know what it means when I find out my best friend got a house on the lake from my mother-in-law who heard it at the grocery store from Archie Watkins's sister-in-law's niece?!

Scotty

I'm selling it and moving.

You are not. To where?

The desert. I'm thinking Arizona. Still researching.

Not allowed.

And we're renovating our kitchen and it's going to take a while.

Over four months.

I need you to host Thanksgiving. I've been meaning to ask you.

I can't host Thanksgiving! And this house needs a shit ton of work. So. I. Can. Sell. It. And. Move.

Move later. You can and you will. I need you to do this. Please.

You're dead to me.

My ashes as a centerpiece will be a great conversation starter on Thanksgiving. That you're hosting. AT YOUR LAKE HOUSE.

Give the cute coach my number.

Camp did yesterday.

Four

THE HOUSE RESEMBLES A ridiculous pyramid constructed in the seventies and smells like the walls are insulated with mothballs. The photos did not do this place justice: it's worse. All ridiculous lines and wallpaper and outdated everything.

The downstairs of the house is both open and cramped, the angles of the walls seemingly stealing square footage. A U-shaped kitchen and small living room bleed into one another, and down a short hall there's a bedroom, bathroom, and a utility room with a washing machine one spin cycle away from falling apart.

Other than the pristine view of the lake out of the one solid wall of windows, it's ghastly.

My heels click up a steep spiral staircase that leads to the master loft. Behind the clunky headboard of the bed is a smaller wall of windows, framing in a thick hedge of trees. The closet has a few of Archie's shirts, fishing gear, and a lone pair of suspenders. The

Pepto-colored tile master bathroom has a full-sized bathtub, grimy grout, and carpeting on the toilet.

Through the entirety of it all, above me is the exposed, wood-planked apex of the roofline.

I lean on the spindled railing that overlooks the open downstairs, wondering if I can do this. If I *want* to do this. If it can possibly sell for enough money to get me out of here.

Straight ahead, the lake and the town's namesake rock ledge fill the windows like a painting. While most of the lakeshore sits down at water level with a gentle slope, there's a long section—directly across from me—that's bordered by a slick granite rock face that drops straight down. At the top, a rock ledge where the first people settled and declared the town Ledger. Way Archie told it, his great-great-grand something was the one who led the Ledger-naming charge.

Light from the mid-afternoon sun makes the ripples on the water look like sparkly confetti.

The house, though burning my retinas, vibrates with a kind of energy that begs to be noticed. Like it's only ugly because nobody thought to make it shine.

And, dammit, something in that grabs my throat and squeezes. Like maybe all my ugly and all the ugly in this stupid triangle can become something less ugly together.

I push off the railing and start toward the steps, stopping when I catch my reflection in a gold-framed mirror leaning against the wall, its old age evident by the wavy glass.

Everything about me looks abstract: my dark, brown-haired bob is big and wild, my hazel eyes are more wideset, and my lean build is Wanda-like curvy. I tug on the lapel of my blazer, tilting my head. My reflection is always a mind fuck; it never shows what's there, only what's not. Even though I've come to accept it, every time it happens it's a deep bruise being pushed on. This mirror might be the most accurate one I've ever looked at.

Down the stairs, across the shaggy carpet, by the tube television and floral everything furniture, I emerge onto the large porch and take a deep breath of the hot summer air.

At the wooded corner of the property sits a shed resembling a kill room. I make my way toward it, clusters of pine needles making the points of my heels wobble with every step. Unkempt grass and piles of leaves slope gently down to a sandy patch of beach with a canoe resting bottom up, two paddles next to it. In the middle of the yard, a bird lands at a half-filled bird feeder hanging from a hook.

I spent my entire childhood on this lake, laughing with June and being chased by Ford. Pretending I belonged here instead of the run-down trailer park I grew up in and with the worthless parents that bred me. Standing on the familiar shoreline, I feel just as fraudulent all these years later, and it nearly knocks the wind out of me.

Ripples caused by a small boat kiss the shore as I let the idea of me in this house—a place of my own on the lake June and I used to dream we'd live on—be the thing to cut the shackles that have tied me to every person I've lost—dead or alive—and set me free.

At the cedar-shingled shed, the door sticks the first time I try to open it, swinging open the second. No dead bodies, just a wooden workbench with tackle boxes and tools. There's one window letting light in and a single dusty bulb hanging from a beam in the center with a string.

I open a tackle box and chuckle: Between the hooks and lures, there's a plastic bag of rolled joints. *Archie, you sneaky bastard.*

In the first cabinet: dried up cans of paint. In the next: a small box I pull from the shelf.

A loud bark rips through the air and a shot of terror makes the box fall from my hands—metal sinkers and plastic bobbers scattering across the floor—as my head snaps to the doorway.

There, sitting with a tilted head and another loud bark, is a dog.

Hand to my chest, heart pounding, I let out a breathy laugh. "Shit, dog."

Its tongue lolls out of its mouth as it barely lifts its ass off the ground, wags its tail once, and sits back down with a whimper before barking again.

I wince at the noise, studying the strange pattern on the fur—I recognize it from one of the photos Lydia showed me. It's mostly black with random yet bold streaks and splatters of white. Like a zebra and a wolf got drunk at a party and banged a new species into existence. "The hell did you come from?"

Another whimper, but it doesn't bark this time. I look around the shed, keeping my distance from the creature but noticing the details I hadn't before: metal bowls on the wood-planked floor, kibble in a container, and, much to my dismay, a doggy door. Archie had a dog.

Fuck.

We stare at each other, me and the strange animal, some kind of sizing up like we aren't quite sure what to make of the other.

Out of nowhere, it barks again—loud—and leaps like a kangaroo toward me until its front paws land on my thighs. I stumble back as the thing licks my face between barks.

"God," I grunt. "Get the hell off me."

"Molly!" a female voice calls from outside, making the dog pause and ears perk. "Molly!" she repeats. "Here, girl!"

Instantly, the creature drops from me and takes off out of the shed at a sprint.

I mutter, wiping the dirt from my pants and follow. There, dropping a bike in the middle of the driveway, is a teenage girl, crouching as *Molly* licks her face.

She stands, cocking her head to the side as dark brown hair hangs over her pale face and raccoon-inspired eyelinered eyes squint at me.

"What the Wednesday Addams fan club are you supposed to be?" I ask, crossing my arms over my chest as her black-edged eyes widen. The rest of her outfit is just as ridiculous. Black combat boots, black leggings, and a black sweatshirt, sleeves so long they nearly swallow her fingers.

"A human," she says, eyes wandering down to my shoes before snapping back to my face. "What in the stick-up-my-butt pantsuit are *you* supposed to be?"

I snort a laugh, studying her. "What are you doing here?"

"Feeding Molly."

I eye Molly and the teenage goth queen, noting they resemble one another, but am unsure of what to say to any kid other than June's. "Hm."

"Who are you?" she demands, borderline rude.

I look at the house and lake, every reason I have to leave both behind flashing before my eyes. "The new owner. Does this dog just free-range it or something? There's no fence or leash."

"She's trained to stay. She's trained to do a lot, really. Archie let her in when he was here, and when he wasn't she just kind of . . ." She looks around the property. "Did whatever."

I look at the dog again, seemingly harmless as the girl pets her.

"It's trained?" I ask, suspicious.

"*She* is." She pins me with an annoyed look then holds her palm out and looks at said trained dog and says, "Sit."

Molly sits.

"Down."

Molly lays down.

"Porch." Molly runs across the yard, around the trees, up the four steps of the porch and lays by the front door, a sort of pride in her pant.

"Impressive," I admit.

The girl smiles in a way that translates to *I told you so*. "Do you have kids?"

"No."

"Husband?"

My eyes narrow. "No."

"Why not?"

"Didn't your mom tell you that it's rude to ask so many damn questions?"

Her expression remains neutral as we start toward the porch. What little bit of her eyes I can see stay fixed on me.

"My parents were shitty," I tell her.

Something like disappointment flitters across her features. "So because you had bad parents you can't be one?"

"Would you go to space without going to astronaut school?" I ask, eyebrows raised.

She looks back to Molly, not responding.

"How old are you?"

"Fifteen."

"Where do you live?"

She scoffs. "I can't tell a strange woman where I live."

"Ah. But you can come to a strange woman's house and interrogate the shit out of her?"

"You swear a lot."

I lift my chin with a smirk. "It's part of my *stick up my butt* appeal."

For the first time, she almost laughs, and we stop at the porch, leaning against the edge. Molly whimpers from her spot by the door and the girl gives a firm, "Here," prompting the dog to do a kind of army crawl across the porch until she's beside us, earning a scratch behind her black-and-white ears.

I study the girl's weird features again; she'd be pretty if she didn't wear so much makeup.

"Your mom teach you to wear eyeliner like that?"

She shrugs.

"Your parents know you're here?"

She holds up a wrist, barely pulling up the sleeve of her sweatshirt to show a chunky watch with a screen. "My dad makes me wear this so he can track me."

I puff out a laugh at the annoyed expression on her face. I can't relate: I've never been tracked in my life. "And your mom? She okay with you going to a triangle house hanging out with a dog by yourself?"

At this, she pushes herself off the porch, dusts her hands off, and looks at her combat boots. "She's out of town. She's a poet."

"A traveling poet?"

She rolls her eyes. "So?"

I don't care enough to push it. "Fine."

"I usually come by in the afternoons and feed her if you want me to keep coming."

I look at her ridiculous eyeliner and the dog who could be her twin sibling; I have no clue why she'd want to keep showing up here. "Fine."

"Well, I just have something I need to get out of the shed, and then I can get going."

She starts walking and I hold a palm out stopping her. "Is it in a little plastic bag?"

Guilt writes itself all over her face. *Busted.*

"Yeah, that's not happening."

She blows out a breath. "What are you going to do with it?"

I shrug. "Smoke it. Flush it. Sell it on the street to a stoner in need. Either way, it's not yours."

She rolls her eyes—again—and starts toward her bike with a muttered, "Whatever."

"What's your name?"

"Wren," she says, turning to look at me as she picks up her bike. "Yours?"

"Scotty."

"That's a boy's name."

"Better than a bird."

She swings a combat boot–clad foot over the bike and positions herself on the seat and shrugs. "Not my fault."

Wren takes off down the driveway, and I chuckle. Little weirdo isn't wrong about that.

When she's gone, I turn back to the house. A triangle in the woods, not making a lick of sense with its big front porch and wall of windows, a subtle reflection of the trees and water on the glass.

I close my eyes and take a deep inhale. It's clean. Crisp. It's still warm, hot even, but fall isn't far away, confirmed by the slightest yellow tint on the tips of trees across the lake when I open my eyes. Even just one fall here would be more than I'd ever imagined for myself.

I'll live here, renovate it, sell it, and get the hell out of this town. I said it to Ford last night in a moment of spontaneous verbal combustion—even when I texted June I wasn't sure I actually meant it—but I see it all so clearly now: Everything I've felt these last months is because Ford waltzed back into town, reviving thoughts of what was and what-ifs. Even if I wasn't leaving, houses like this belong to people with babies in bathtubs and families who sit on porches—things I'll never have or want.

Molly barks, bringing my attention to her at my feet. "Fine," I say, petting her on the head for the first time, surprised at how soft her fur is beneath my fingertips. "I'll keep the house. For now."

She barks—again—making me wince as she looks up at me with a doggish kind of smile.

"You chew my shoes and you're fucking fish food."

FIVE

"WHAT'S HAPPENING, SCOTTY?" DONDI asks with a gap-toothed smile and a fist in my direction that I meet with my own.

Just shy of thirty, Dondi's half Native American, half white with shaggy dark hair, a lanky build, and an oddly charming gap between his front teeth. He talks and moves with a kind of drawl that belongs on a surfboard in California more than driving dead bodies around the mountains of North Carolina, yet here he is.

I met him at a bar where he was wearing a ridiculous hibiscus-covered shirt and telling some friends he couldn't find a job because he has a weak spot for weed and a rap sheet of petty crimes a mile long. *How do you feel about driving dead bodies around?* I asked, interrupting the conversation he was having. He looked at me, as if really pondering the question, then said thoughtfully, *"The Dondinator would consider it an honor and privilege to chillax with those heading on to what's next."*

I looked at him, wondering what the hell *The Dondinator* was, but something about him was oddly disarming. A sweetness of sorts. Like a three-legged dog. *"I'll give you a chance,"* I said, his friends looking at me like I was a guardian angel with twelve heads. *"But if you fuck it up, that's it."* The next day, I convinced the town's funeral home, Tranquil Departures, to partner with me to hire him. In the year and a half since he's been here, he's been amazing. Not only does he pick the bodies up in his beloved Ice Pop, he's also gone through trainings so he can service the retort and the rest of the machines we use in the cremation process.

"Dondi," I say, noticing his Hawaiian shirt is less wrinkled than usual and, due to the belt he's wearing, the sag of his pants less severe. "You have a hot date or something?"

He drops into the wingback chair in the witnessing room, glancing at Wanda as she sashays in wearing fitted black pants, a low-cut red shirt, and hooker-blue eyeshadow. "The Dondinator is starting to realize life is a date, is it not?"

I pinch my lips at his ridiculous Dondinator, which I now know is his third person name for himself, but don't miss the look him and Wanda exchange as she sits on the couch with a small smile.

"Noted," I say. Then to Wanda, "Morning."

She smiles, but it's worried as her eyes bounce across my clothes—plain shirt, yoga pants, and rubber ankle boots I haven't worn in years. "You sick or something, honey? That what this meeting's about?"

"I got a house," I tell them, matter-of-fact as I lean against the window. "And I'm going to live in it while I renovate it." I ignore their shocked expressions. "Like one of those people on HGTV without the dumb drama of needing to take down a load-bearing wall."

June's request of me hosting Thanksgiving and the overall state of the house forced me to come up with a plan. She's never once asked me to do something like this, and I couldn't say no. For as long as we've been friends, I've been the forever single, basically orphaned third wheel. I owe her. I'll renovate the house, host the godforsaken feast, and then list it. I immediately emailed a realtor who responded with a list of comp properties and the speculation that with its location on the lake—and if fully updated per the list of items he included—it could net nearly a million dollars. I almost fell over. I could repay Lydia for the house, pay off the crematorium and sell it, and have plenty left to start over somewhere else. Even the massive to-renovate list he sent didn't seem so scary in the scheme of the freedom it would give me.

I clear my throat.

"Wanda, you still need somewhere to live?"

She nods, seemingly stunned into silence.

"You can have my apartment—while I do this—rent free if you take on some of the responsibilities that come with that."

She brings a hand to her mouth, thick lashes fluttering.

"And, Dondi," I direct at him. "Your job will stay the same unless Wanda needs help with something and I'm not around." He opens his mouth, but I talk over him. "Unless that's a problem, there's a lot of work that needs to be done at the house, and I need time to do it."

They stare; I clear my throat.

"What I'm saying is, I'm moving out of the apartment and spending less time at work. I'll be at every send-off, of course, but the in-between things I'll be—I'll need to—I won't be here." I huff, annoyed by how they're looking at me like I'm performing a miracle. "Will that be a problem?"

"You're moving out of the crematorium?" Wanda asks, hand to mouth as she rises from the couch and takes short steps toward me, face filling with emotion.

Here we go.

"To work," I correct.

"Whoa!" Dondi says with wide eyes. "The Dondinator would never believe this if he wasn't sitting here. The Ash Queen leaves the fire. What's next, you selling to Tranquil Departures?"

I puff a slight laugh. "Not today." *But soon.* The funeral home has been trying to buy me out for years—like they need to be the death conglomerates of Ledger—and I've always shot them down. Once I know the house isn't a complete waste, I'll call them.

Wanda hugs me with a squeal, making me grunt. "This is amazing, honey. Anything you need, Dondi and I are here to help. Aren't we?"

"You know it," he pipes in.

"And we can do any of the send-offs too," Wanda adds, dabbing at her eyes with the pads of her fingertips.

"No!" I snap too loudly, taking a breath before adding in a more even voice: "No, I can't pawn all the work off. It'll go to your head."

They chuckle, but they also know the truth: I do the send-offs because the send-offs are why I'm here.

"I never thought I'd see the day you move out of this place," Wanda says, her red lips shaky with emotion. "Thank you for this, Scotty. You've given me more than anyone else in my life, and I mean that."

Something claws at my throat with the looks on both of their faces, but a loud knock banging on the back door saves me. We look at each other—the door is the service entrance that leads to the back of the building and only used by us. My eyes narrow. "Stop looking at me like your eyes are made of pudding and get to work. I'll see who it is."

I don't wait for them to respond, and in my short walk to the back, another knock bangs. "I'm coming!" I shout.

When I push the heavy door open, warmth from outside mixes with the coolness from inside at the threshold.

"Can I help yo—"

My words die, replaced by pure hatred for the face in front of me.

There, with smiling eyes despite the flat line of his lips, stands Ford Callahan. In his police uniform.

I groan, moving to pull the door closed.

He grips the edge of it, swinging it open. "Five minutes, Scotty."

"No."

He holds the door open, filling the space around me like a bear on a country road. "Please."

I cross my arms over my chest, leaning in the doorway. "Why?"

"You caught me off guard the other night, and I don't like how it ended."

"So you're here for a happy ending?" I quip.

A smile tugs at his lips, but he neither moves nor says anything.

I stare at him, debating. He looks so nice and normal; it's hard to believe he's an emotional terrorist under that uniform. I eye his belt. They even give this menace a gun.

"Everything okay, honey?" Wanda calls, wedged heels clicking behind me.

When I catch her gaze over my shoulder she halts, eyes wide, before adjusting her chest with her hands and smiling something sinister, tone shifting to pure lust. "Well, hello there, Officer Callahan."

I snort, looking back to Ford who dips his chin toward her. "Wanda, good to see you. Scotty asked me to stop by. Just fulfilling my duties to the fine citizens of Ledger."

I roll my eyes; he winks.

I can't wait to get out of here.

"Fine," I grit out.

Without another word, I step out into the sun and let the door close with a heavy slam behind me. Ford looks at me, long and wordless, making my entire body burn like feet on summer concrete.

"Any day now," I say, bored.

"It's about Zeb."

I groan, turning to walk back into the building. He wraps his hand around my arm, stopping me with his strength.

"I'm not doing this, Ford, let me go. I said all I needed to say about my brother."

I tug at the handle, remembering it's locked from outside and groan again in frustration as Ford keeps a grip on my arm with one hand and something makes a clanking noise.

"Sorry, Scotty"—metal clicks as he twists me around and press-es me belly-first against his cruiser parked behind the building, keeping my arm bent and pinched to my back—"I knew you were going to be a stubborn pain in the ass about this, and I need you to listen."

"Handcuffs?" I shout furiously as I try to pull my arms apart. The metal digs into my wrists as I wriggle my torso against his car with a grunt. "Are you fucking kidding me, Ford?"

He turns me around to face him and I spit in his face; he wipes it, as unfazed as if it were a raindrop.

"Let me go, you bastard," I demand, more arm pulling and more getting nowhere.

"You going to listen or keep hissin' like a damn viper?"

"This is illegal," I snap.

He chuckles. "Call the cops."

Heart pounding in my throat, I feel trapped. I *am* trapped.

"You knew as well as I did Zeb had gotten deep into drugs," he begins, voice calm as he leans against the cruiser while I struggle to break free with grunts and swears. "You and I talked about it, but with both of us gone at school, I don't think we knew how bad it was."

I look away from him as he talks, focusing on the cuffs and not the searing pain in my chest the memories bring. Because yes, I knew Zeb was in deep. His calls had gotten erratic, talking in circles and barely making sense. He'd ask for money—which was laughable since I was a poor college kid at a nothing school on scholarship. Every single night I'd lie in bed, feeling the anxiety like a vise around my chest and throat, convinced the next call I got about him was going to be the worst. He'd be in jail or dead. Little did I know how accurate all my late-night worst-case scenarios would become. Little did I know how much more I should have been doing to help.

"I tried talking to him about it, but we were just kids," he continues. "Twenty-one. And I'd been off at college—we'd drifted a little—but every time I came home it was like more and more of him was gone. He was playing music at the local bars—" He pauses, eyes toward the sky as he chuckles softly, dragging a hand down the side of his face. "He loved that guitar, didn't he?"

I look at him but don't say anything. I don't need to. We both know how much Zeb loved music. From the guitar that was always with him, to the music notes tattooed down his spine, to the late nights he spent in dive bars playing songs he wrote. I have two things from my brother: his Bronco and his records he played constantly. When Ford realizes I'm not going to say any of this aloud, he keeps talking. "I drank, smoked a little pot, but the things he was into . . ." His voice trails off as the vessels of poison fill my skull like they filled my brother's body. Pipes. Needles. Pills. Powder.

Every destructive thing I couldn't stop him from doing.

Ford steps toward me, lifting a hand to hold my chin so I'm forced to look at him. "The day he got arrested, I was home for the weekend, helping my parents on the orchard. The tractor broke down on the last row of trees—stupid detail to remember, but I do. I picked him up at his apartment to go grab a beer, and he asked if we could make a stop. I never—I didn't know."

My chin held in place by his thumb and forefinger, we stare at each other, and I see in his eyes the same hurt that lives in me. I hate him more for it. Hate myself more for it.

"And what?" I demand. "You just stop at a random house and let him out? No questions asked?" I scoff. "Was he high?"

He drops my chin, blows out a breath, and closes his eyes. "I didn't know what he was doing until I watched him walk up to the house, and instead of knocking on the door, he broke a window. And . . ." He looks at me again, a battle in his eyes. Like he's at war with himself.

"The cops were there," I supply, not bothering to hide my bitterness.

He says nothing.

We're quiet as the story gets slightly rewritten in my brain, but only just barely. Because though he didn't know what Zeb was doing, he still left. He told me he loved me then he disappeared, leaving me to deal with every single hard thing that came next. Alone.

"Where have you been?" I ask, less heat in my voice as I lean against his car. "You just vanished."

"Atlanta. I finished school in Raleigh, went to the academy. Moved to the city. Worked for the Narcotics Unit for years."

Ironic. Ford loses his best friend to drugs and spends his life putting people in jail because of them.

"Why'd you come back?" When he hesitates, I add, "And don't tell me some bullshit line about birds."

"Redemption, for one. I have a lot to make up for—to a lot of people. And . . ." He swallows, opens his mouth, closes it, swallows again. "I have a kid. Thought it would be better here. Closer to my parents. Slower."

"A kid?" I whisper, the idea of it sucker punching me to near speechlessness. "Who you raise?"

He chuckles with a slight nod and a soft voice. "That's usually how it works, Scotty."

It takes all of my energy not to drop like a sandbag down the side of the cop car. "Girls in Atlanta must be hard up to procreate."

He doesn't take the bait.

"That the boss you were talking about?"

He chuckles. "One and only. Ben says that because kids call the shots."

My eyes find his left finger. Empty. "The mom?"

He says nothing.

I click my tongue; his silence frustrates me way more than I like. "Boy or girl?"

He shakes his head. "Not sharing that one."

I snort, shifting my cuffed hands behind my back. "Scared of what I'll do to your kid, Ford?"

He puffs out a breath, slightest of smiles creeping onto his eternal baby face. "Scared of what you'll do to *me*, Scotty."

"Explains the cuffs." I tug my hands away from each other and the chain clinks.

"So, you and Kid Doe move back to Ledger for a slow life on your parents' orchard. How perfect for y'all. I hope you eat apple pies until your shit smells like cinnamon. Bet your mother loves that."

He chuckles but doesn't make a move to release me. "How did you end up doing this?" He nods toward the crematorium.

"Ah." I study the back of the old brick building. "Seemed like a good place to get rid of the bodies of men who handcuff me. Which"—I rake my gaze over his uniformed body—"I've had better."

He laughs; it tickles like a feather in my belly. "You're as much of a pain in the ass now as you were twenty years ago."

I grin. "Thank you."

The door of the crematorium swings open, and Wanda goes wide-eyed as she takes in the scene. "Scotty? You okay, honey?"

"Just peachy," I reply, gesturing toward Ford with my chin. "Trying to figure out what size urn would be required if we cremated someone with such a small dick."

"Wanda," Ford says without missing a beat as he spins me around and pushes me harder than needed against his car. I grunt as he presses against me and works to unlock the cuffs. He stays that way, him against me. The warmth of his breath at my ear, the spice of his cologne in my nostrils, his fingers working at my hands.

I look at him over my shoulder, and his eyes meet mine. I could swear his breathing stops. Could swear mine does. He steps back, giving Wanda his attention. "Would you believe me if I told you she begged me for it?"

He slips the cuffs off my wrists and hooks them back onto his belt.

"Well, I can see why," Wanda replies with a wink to Ford before looking at me.

"I'll be right in," I tell her as I rub my wrists.

She disappears back inside, keeping the door slightly ajar.

Ford and I regard each other, a tension in the air.

"Friends?" Ford asks, hopeful lilt to his voice.

"With benefits?" I ask with a smirk, taking the few steps toward the door, turning to face him as I wrap one hand around the knob.

He shrugs. "Depends on the benefits."

My eyebrows raise, unable to get a read on him. What he wants or why he's here. "Fine," I relent. "Friends." Then a caveat: "In public."

"And in private?" he says it smooth and with a smile. Like he's teasing. Maybe even flirting.

I open the door fully and turn to look at him one last time. Ford Callahan in a police uniform. His dark hair is a little longer on top, familiar face somewhere between clean shaven and scruffy, and bright blue eyes are so very appealing yet wasted on the man I once loved who once left.

"I have no intention of ever seeing you in private again," I say. "And I have a feeling you wouldn't know how to handle me anymore if you did."

I step inside and the door slams behind me, shutting him out of my life—where he belongs.

Six

"WHAT'S THIS?" WREN ASKS, nose scrunched and eyeliner-at-tacked eyes narrowed as she holds up a book. With a fish-man. And a half-naked woman. Called *Hookered.*

"A book," I say, snatching it out of her hands and picking up the box she got it from—even I know she doesn't need to be exposed to my nightstand box of tricks—and set it at the base of the spiral staircase. "Are you not familiar with the concept?"

"What is it?"

"Monster romance, what does it look like?"

"You read books about monsters?" Her eyes narrow. "Why?"

"They're funny."

Her face maintains a skeptical expression as she eyes the box. "Are they supposed to be?"

"I don't care if they're *supposed to be.*" I take several of Archie's fish knickknacks off the shelf in the living room and put them into the box I'm packing. "Plus, it's always a fun surprise to see where their dic—" She stares at me, hanging on every word. "—tionaries are."

"My mom says you should feel something when you read," she says, shifting her focus to pulling dishes out of the cabinets in the kitchen. Despite how hot it is today, she's wearing a grey sweatshirt. "That's why she writes poetry."

"Yeah, well, that's why she's a mom," I explain, picking up a decorative plate showcasing a painted little boy fishing with a cane pole and putting it in the donation box. Molly sniffs around the room, stopping when she gets to my box of tricks. "Your aptitude for parenting can be determined by what you read. Monster romance? No parenting skills. Poetry? Supermom."

When I smile, she doesn't, staring blankly at the mugs on the tiled kitchen counter.

The only sound between us is the Weezer record playing as I empty the bookshelf. When the last song ends and the musicless clicking starts grating on my last nerve, I ask, "So what kind of poetry does your mom write?"

"Acrostic."

The laugh that bursts out of me dies when I realize she's serious. "I thought acrostic poems were for, I don't know, second graders."

"Some people write more complex ones," she explains, fidgeting with one of the mugs. "My mom writes the kind that tell a whole story. Some poets write them so the first and last letters of the lines spell something."

"Impressive." I don't know if I mean it, nor do I know if it sounds more or less interesting than the sex authors can manage to think up in my monster books, but I let her traveling poet mom have her moment. I put two birding books into a box then turn my attention to the furniture. The coffee table—made of wood with an etched glass inlay—seems like a good place to start. I slip a pair of work gloves on.

"Are you ever going to get married?"

"No." I grip the edge of the rectangular table, giving it a push—ugly thing is heavier than it looks. The first step of renovating a house, I learned after hours of watching the internet, is to empty it. And while there isn't a ton in here—a couple shelves of books and tchotchkes, dishes in the kitchen, and a few paintings and pictures on the walls—the furniture is an obstacle. It's all so old and heavy, it's as if the wood has been petrified.

"Why?" she demands. "Because you had bad parents?"

"Again with the questions—you should be a cop." I push the table toward the front door; she mutters something under her breath. "But." I grunt as I start to work the table across the threshold of the door and onto the porch, noticing Molly's head now fully in my box of fun at the base of the steps. "Hey! Out of there, dog! Sit! Run! Go live somewhere else!" She ignores my shouts, continuing her deep dive. Fucking dog. She listens to nothing I say.

I turn my attention back to Wren before giving a final shove of the table. "And I don't think I would be a good wife. Or that I know how to find a good husband. Or that I care to find out about either."

"Maybe you would if you didn't read about monsters."

I pant out a tired breath and look at her through the doorway, narrowing my eyes. "Don't yuck my yum, She Who Applies Eyeliner with a Paintbrush." We exchange tit-for-tat looks. "If you're going to talk shit about my monsters, I'm not paying you to help."

"You're not paying me."

"You're not helping."

She studies me, like she's not sure what to make of this conversation, but when a small smile tugs at my lips, the same happens on hers. She walks over to the record player sitting on the floor in the corner of the living room and digs through the box of records next to it.

"Why do you have these?" she asks, examining one record before exchanging it for another then another.

"They were my brother's." She decides on one and slips it out of its sleeve and onto the player before settling the needle in the groove. I chuckle when Aerosmith starts rocking through the speaker. "He loved music. He was a musician. Acoustic stuff with a guitar. He had one of those voices that was kind of rough and kind of smooth. Worn velvet."

Her silence encourages me to keep talking. In a rare moment, I want to.

"No matter what he sang about, it all sounded sad. Like the music itself needed a high dose of antidepressants. I'd tease him about it—try to get him to lighten up. Thought maybe he was trying to be some kind of moody hipster. But now I think maybe . . ." My thoughts drift to Zeb—dark hair long enough he could tuck behind his ears and haunted eyes. I knew he was using—Ford nailed it when he said it—and I fought him on it. *"Are you high?"* I'd demand when he called, talking in tongues of nonsense. *"Come stay with me. I can find you a meeting or something."* He'd dismiss me. *"Nah. I'm fine, Scotty. Just having a little fun. Taking the edge off."* And then I'd drop it. Because the truth was, what did I know about drugs? I'd only ever drank and smoked weed; I wanted to believe him. Desperately. Wanted him to be *fine.* And even more, I didn't want to push him away. Between our mother being what she was and our dad being a timebomb more gone than home, Zeb was all I had.

"Maybe what?" Wren asks.

"Maybe that's just who he was," I finish. "Sad."

"What happened to him?"

I shimmy-shove the table to the side of the porch.

"The sadness won."

Steven Tyler's voice belts out "Dream On" in our silence, and for once, Wren doesn't press me for more. Based on the barbed-wire lump in my throat, there's no more to give anyway. He died a death I didn't stop and don't understand.

She thumbs through the box of records again. "Which ones are yours?"

I blink.

"Like which music do you like? You can't only listen to stuff someone else picked your whole life."

My chin pulls back. "Why?"

"Because it's weird."

In my silence, she raises her eyebrows.

"I like Miranda Lambert," I finally tell her, grunting as I start pushing a chair toward the door.

She thumbs through the records again. "I don't see any."

"I don't have any." Her judgmental mouth opens to say more teenage bullshit, but I shut her down. "I'm on a budget. You done in the kitchen?"

On the porch with the chair, I put my hands on my hips, blowing out a winded breath as I look through the doorway at her.

"The cabinets are empty, most fit in the box," she says, moving from the records to pat Molly, who has taken a break from rummaging to nap in a sun-painted puddle on the floor. "And I should go."

She breezes by me down the porch steps and to her bike.

"Good riddance," I mutter.

Over her shoulder as she pedals away, she calls, "See you tomorrow."

I watch her until she's out of sight, not sure what to make of her. The makeup, the clothes, the poet mother, and the weed in the shed. She doesn't swear and speaks like a straight A kid yet looks like she might run off with a circus full of emo clowns. A complete paradox.

And not my problem.

Over the next hours I pack up the rest of Archie's belongings. I finish the kitchen—the few pots and pans Wren couldn't fit in the box. In the downstairs bedroom covered in wood paneling, I take down creepy framed art of Norman Rockwell–style paintings of kids fishing, their skin so creamy white they look like little ghosts in every scene. In the closet, there's a stack of old sheets and blankets. Most of it I pitch, but there's one quilt that looks like it has a history. I keep it, along with one framed photo: the same one that was in the back of Lydia's album of her and Archie holding a baby. I don't know them—not really—but the smile on their faces as they look at the child feels like home. I'm not the sentimental type, but I can't get rid of it; maybe I'll call Lydia and give it back to her. After all, it's her family, not mine.

A tap on the window pulls me from the photo; on the other side, a mostly bald man with a combover and wild eyes smiles and waves before stepping to fill the propped-open front doorway. I note the gigantic pit stains on his light blue button-down shirt and the bright white shoes that peep from the bottom of his navy dress pants. *Who in the sweat-soaked hell is this?*

"Scotty?" He grins. "Vince Allers. We emailed about listing the place." His eyes dart around. "What a diamond in the rough!"

Recognition strikes: the real estate agent.

"Hi." I set the framed photo in the Keep box and close the distance between us. The sweat glistening on his forehead makes me wonder if he ran here from another continent. "I wasn't expecting you in person."

"Who can resist?" He pulls a handkerchief out of his pocket and blots his forehead. When he notices me watching, he waves it around like a flag before shoving it in his pocket. "Hyperhidrosis," he explains. "I sweat like a whore in church."

Okay.

"Anyway, I had to stop by. I knew your grandad. What a guy!" I frown at the mention of my deadbeat relative while he claps his hands and rubs them together quickly, the shape of his eyes nearly morphing into actual money signs. "This place could make us a fortune."

My eyebrows raise, and he chuckles, waving his palms toward me. "Mostly you, but, hey—" He rubs his index finger and thumb together. "Guy's gotta pay the bills, right?"

I force a smile "Sure." We look at the boxes I've been working on. "I can show you around . . ."

He bats a dismissive hand.

"No need." *Thank God.* "You're busy. Just a few minutes of walking around will be good for me to get a good grasp for some firm numbers. Any bodies I should know about?" He chuckles; I don't know if it's because he knows my profession or just tells shitty jokes, but when I don't laugh, he clears his throat. "That work for you?"

On one hand, I'm concerned his sweat situation is going to cause water damage anywhere he walks, but on the other, I appreciate his eagerness. I want this thing sold yesterday.

"If you don't mind mothballs and hideous décor," I tell him, gesturing with one hand to the house. "She's all yours."

He chuckles. "I've seen worse." Then, with a whistle and phone in hand, he starts examining the house, opening kitchen cabinets, closet doors, and the box of tricks at the bottom of the steps. As he pries the lid off, Molly's head fully dives into it.

"Sex toys help with resale value, Vince?" I ask from across the room.

He jerks to a stand with a sheepish chuckle. "Never know." He gives me a wink before pulling the sweat rag from his pocket and wandering down the hall.

Nosy bastard.

I lift a box labeled Donate to take to the Bronco. Through the open front door of the house, I hear tires crunch. The banging of a tailgate. The dumping of something pebbly.

When I peek my head out, there, with a bag of birdseed, stands Ford. Feeding the birds in the middle of the yard.

"Can I help you, Officer?" I ask, descending the porch steps.

He turns with a smile. "Scotty."

I prop the box on my hip when I'm beside him. "What are you doing?"

"Feeding your birds." He hangs a filled feeder on the crook and fills another one before tossing the empty bag into the back of his truck. He's wearing athletic clothes; there's sweat around the neck of his grey T-shirt.

"You still going to that boxing gym?"

"Depends." He smirks. It suits him. I notice. "You looking for a fight?"

Not touching that one.

I glance from the feeders to the few birds flittering around a nearby tree. "They don't look hungry."

He looks at me, his eyes as bright and blue as the sparkly water around us. "I did it for Archie."

Ford is the one who's been looking after the place. *Of course.*

"Archie have some kind of army looking after this place?"

He laughs through a puff of breath. "What do you mean?"

"You're here with birdseed, and some gothic princess likes the dog." Said dog lets out a loud bark from inside that makes me roll my eyes. "I didn't know I inherited house guests."

He nods, slowly, then looks out at the lake. "Who's the girl?"

"A mystery. A teenager. I don't know. Horrible makeup and bad clothes on a bike. You know her?"

"I've seen her."

I study the water and the rock ledge; a boat sputters by and a fish jumps.

"All done, Scotty," Vince calls as he emerges onto the porch, acknowledging Ford as he approaches us and shoves his phone and sweat rag into his pocket. "I think everything I sent you in the email checks out."

"Good."

"It's as ugly as you said," he says, chuckling, loosening the already loose knot of his tie. "But the bones are good. Should get what I thought. You thinking December?"

I nod.

"December?" Ford asks.

"Scotty's selling the place," Vince says with a proud grin. "We're business partners."

No, we are not.

Ford says nothing, eyes glued on me.

"Well," Vince drawls, clapping his hands and rubbing them quickly once again. "Let me know when it's ready, and we'll get her listed. Bet this place will go fast. Look at that view." Another whistle.

Despite how annoying this faucet of a man is, I grin at the good news.

He says goodbye, whistling as he gets into his black Lincoln Town Car and cruises away.

"You really selling?" Ford asks.

I shift the box on my hip. "I'm really selling."

"Why?"

"Get out of Ledger."

I can't read his expression, not the way I used to be able to at least.

"Why?"

"Why not?" I say, bristling. "You left. People don't always live in the same place forever."

In the too-long silence, the box feels heavy in my arms. I shift it to my other hip, then opt to hold it in front of me with both hands, putting a barrier between us.

"Where are you going?" he finally asks, eyes bouncing between mine.

"I'm thinking somewhere out west." *Far away from you.* I swallow, glancing at the lake. It's revoltingly perfect. A feeling too big for my body starts to grow under my skin. "Somewhere with a better view."

At this, he laughs softly, attention going over my shoulder where Molly is making a series of growling noises I've been trying to ignore. "What's Molly got?"

I turn to find Molly the Menace on the porch with a bright-pink petaled device in her mouth. I groan, annoyed. "Little bitch is eating my best vibrator." Ford booms out a laugh and I shrug. "There goes my sure thing. That dog hates me."

He shakes his head, studying me with an amused tilt to his lips. "That's your sure thing?"

"You offering to fill the void, Officer?" I tease.

He doesn't hesitate: "Void need filled?"

"Hardly." I smirk. "I have backups for times such as these."

We watch the dog eat my beloved, battery-operated boyfriend. I wonder what Ford's thinking—if standing so close to me feels like digging up old bones to him as much as it does to me. If watching a dog chew on my sex toy makes him think of us putting hands and lips and the full weight of our bodies on each other.

"I've missed you, Scotty."

Right there in the middle of broad daylight, those four words clothesline me, nearly causing me to drop the box I'm holding.

All I can manage: "Yeah."

In our stare, an ache consumes me. The kind that hurts the roots of my hair and ends of my teeth and tips of my fingernails. The only man I've ever loved looks at me like the last twenty years didn't happen. "Well, I gotta go kill the dog over future orgasms I'll never have and keep packing up Archie's haunted relics." I gesture with the box I'm holding. "You need anything else?"

He shakes his head, but it's me that moves first. I put the box I'm carrying down—right in the middle of the yard for no reason—and swipe the birding books from the top. My retreat to the house is with quick steps and my breath held, only stopping to pick up my gnarled vibrator before I slam the front door.

Inside, Molly jumps around like a jack-in-the-box on crack as I press my back against the door. I don't take a full breath until I hear the crunch of Ford's tires leaving the driveway. When he's gone, I throw the vibrator across the house with a yell.

The dog never stops barking.

SEVEN

"Tell me about what you do, Scotty," Dean says with an eager expression from the booth across from me.

I force a smile. "I burn bodies."

He laughs, the light reflecting off the lenses of his rectangular glasses as he swipes his hand across the grey-streaked swoosh of hair across his forehead. And while June's physical description of Dean wasn't that far off—he's attractive enough—he's also a math teacher. And the team he coaches? Something called Mathletes. He's wearing a sweater-vest, has a scholarly-looking goatee, and sips sherry out of some little wineglass I didn't know Ledger had access to. Other than being human, we have absolutely nothing in common. "That's right. Camp told me. Fascinating. How many bodies you burn in a week? Just an estimate?"

Right. Dean also loves estimates. He asked me to estimate the number of people in Liberty Tap when we arrived and the number of cups that could fit on a tray. I, on the other hand, would rather eat a rhinoceros testicle than talk about estimates. "Five hundred."

"Really?" he asks, stilling his sherry midair as his stormy-grey eyes widen behind his glasses. "Five hundred?"

"No." I take a long sip of my whiskey. "I was trying to be funny. Maybe five. Maybe ten. Sometimes less, sometimes more." I feel the slightest bit guilty for being so short, so I force myself to fill the dull void. "The retort"—he blinks at the word—"what most people call a cremator—can do around three a day. Some people cremate their loved ones to have a ceremony later, those we do anytime, but a lot of families that come to us like to be there, and we make it a ceremony—kind of like a funeral—that's what we're known for. Send-offs, I call them. Anyway, those take longer. It depends, I guess, on who we have that week and what they need from us. That's my estimate."

"Variance." He grins, raising his glass toward me. "Keeps things exciting."

"Sure." I take another sip of my drink. "So how did you get into . . . math?"

He swallows his sherry with a loud *Ah!* and sets his glass on the table. "I've always been a numbers guy. My parents will tell you my first word was a number—can you believe that? Counted blocks and cars and it just never stopped." He gives me a look that conveys how amazing he thinks this is.

I press my lips in a tight smile, eyes scanning the crowd of the restaurant. Looking for a magical portal I can jump into to get the hell out of here. "I bet."

"Let me guess." He props his elbows on the table, smirk slanting across his face. "You were burning leaves in the backyard as a kid?"

"They didn't like outdoor fires at the trailer park," I tell him, watching the door of the restaurant and wondering how long it would take Dean to notice if I went to the restroom and never came back.

"Oh," Dean says, seemingly stumped by this answer.

My eyes ping around the room, desperation clawing at my chest as the familiar restaurant suddenly makes me claustrophobic. The door opens and my head turns as if pulled by a string. Ford walks in . . . with Anna. His eyes meet mine and hold, and it feels tangible. Like an actual rope forms between us that I could grip onto and pull myself toward him on. Anna gestures to the bar and he turns back to her, cutting our tie and walking with his hand on the small of her back. He's in jeans and a T-shirt, she's wearing an oversized cream-colored cardigan over a floor-length, casual, striped dress. Her blonde highlighted hair bounces as she laughs at something he says then they slide into two open stools. She's disgustingly perfect, and I feel personally victimized by how good they look together. The whole scene makes my throat barricade itself closed and refuse to let oxygen enter my lungs. All the while, oblivious Dean contin- ues. Something about estimating the number of house fires caused by leaf burning.

"Let's sit at the bar," I blurt, already sliding out of the booth. "The drinks will come faster." He looks at the bar as if he's consid- ering the logistics of this decision as I smooth my dress. It's black and fitted and was chosen before I knew Dean was a mathlete.

Along with the stilettos. And the expensive lingerie. "And the number of drinks I have is directly proportional to the probability of me putting out."

I pulled that line out of my ass and it does what I need it to.

He chokes on his sherry and his face goes red. "Wow. Okay. Bar it is."

No longer in control of my body, I beeline it to the bar, taking the stool next to Ford, pushing the one next to me out for Dean with the toe of my shoe.

"Scotty," Ford says, amused smile on his face when I look at him. "Didn't know you were here."

"I could say the same." I raise my eyebrows. "Anna."

She smiles, but it's not friendly. More like she's hoping I have a stroke.

"Who's your friend?" Ford asks.

Dean sits on the stool next to me and adjusts his glasses before extending a hand toward Ford. "Dean Simmons. New math teacher at Ledger High."

Ford introduces himself and they shake hands across me. "This is Anna."

Dean waves and she smiles. "My son is in your class. Miles McIntire?"

"Ah!" Dean says, excited look on his face. "He's an algebraic wizard!"

She smiles, proud and wide like a doting mother. "He just loves your class!"

They fall into conversation across Ford and I, animated as they careen toward one another.

Ford and I both lean back in our seats to give them space to talk. I sip my whiskey and look at him.

"So."

"So." His lips twitch as he gestures toward Dean with his chin, leaning in slightly and using a low voice to ask, "A math teacher, huh?"

I fight a smile. "Seems to get Anna all hot and bothered."

He chuckles and sucks a piece of ice from his glass, chewing it with a lazy smile. "I remember math homework getting you all hot and bothered."

His blue eyes are hot; he's flirting.

"That wasn't the math, Golden Boy."

"I know."

In the background, the sounds of Ben making drinks, hums of laughter and conversation from nearby tables, and even the math-motivated conversation happening across us seem to silence. As if an invisible volume knob lowered everything but our conversation.

I say nothing, busying my mouth by taking another sip.

"He your sure thing tonight?" Ford asks so only I can hear him.

I don't shy away from the challenge nor the sexy edge in his voice.

"If I say yes?"

He's quiet but doesn't look away. On the contrary, he leans closer, our arms fully touching, his mouth at my ear. "I'd tell you I'd rather he not be."

I clear my throat—an attempt to hide how his closeness makes my body start to throb—and take another sip. "And what would you rather me do?"

"Use one of your backups."

"Ah." I cock an eyebrow. "I get a second-rate sex toy, and you take her home for the real thing? Doesn't sound very fair to me."

Dean and Anna are talking about something that happened at school with the printing of report cards. Her eyes are wide; his hand not holding his sherry waves in outrage.

Ford brings his club soda up to his lips but doesn't drink, just waits. We look at each other, my mind flying around like a tumbleweed in a windstorm. I couldn't pinpoint one thought if there was a gun to my head.

"And if I'm not taking her home?"

"Aren't you?"

"Tell me you don't want me to."

I give him a flat look.

"I mean it, Scotty," he whispers. "Say the words, 'don't take her home,' and I won't."

I can't control the sharp breath I suck in nor the way my mouth opens. He sees, pulling the glass away from his mouth and licking his lips. And then I feel one thing stronger than the rest: longing. Despite all the hurt and time apart, there's still a physical pull I can't deny; even all these years later, I want him so badly it makes my already tight dress nearly smother me.

"I don't care who you fuck," I say with a flippant tone and another sip.

"I think you do."

"I don't."

He pins me with a stare I return.

"Maybe I do."

I chuckle softly. "Do what?"

"Care."

I straighten, the same fire flickering in his eyes that's burning up my whole body. "About?"

He leans in until his mouth is at my ear, whispering, "Who you fu—"

"Anyone need a drink?" Ben asks, bending the moment right in half. Dean and Anna return to their respective spaces, and Ford shifts away from me, all contact lost. All the while, my heart pounds so hard in my chest my ribs might crack. *What just happened?*

I raise my glass instantly. "Yep."

Ben winks then grabs the whiskey, pouring to his usual mark. I gesture for more, needing it to drown the memory of how Ford was just looking at me, and he nearly fills the glass to the top. I down it like a college kid on spring break in Myrtle Beach: in a single gulp, all eyes on me.

"So, Anna," I say, putting my empty glass down with a too-loud thud as she takes a delicate sip of her white wine, "see this guy conned you into another date. He must be a better lay than he used to be."

Beside me, Dean chokes. However, unlike last time when Anna was shocked to silence, she straightens, resting one hand on Ford's thigh. "I actually wouldn't know because he stopped dating such easy women." She smiles like she's been practicing that line in the bathroom mirror. *Cute.* "We're focusing on building a strong emotional foundation before letting anything physical distract us."

When I realize she's serious, a loud laugh bubbles out of me. I laugh so hard I smack the bar with a loud *thwack.*

Dean clears his throat next to me. "What's funny?"

A muscle pops on Ford's jaw. Any want that was in his face earlier is being replaced by anger. *Good.*

"Sweetheart," I say, leaning into Ford's space. "That means he's soft for you. Did he tell you he had me handcuffed and pinned to his car just days ago?" She flicks her eyes to him; he cuts his gaze to me.

"Scotty," he growls, tension ticking at his neck.

I click my tongue. "And"—my eyes drop to the glass of wine she's white-knuckle gripping—"I don't mean to shit in your chardonnay, but when he pushed up against me, it was anything but emotional. Or soft. On the contrary, I thi—"

"You know what?" Anna stands, downing her wine and grabbing her purse. "I'm not doing this." She looks at Ford. "Your psycho ex-girlfriend will not ruin this night. Ford, let's go."

I look at him, surprised to see a coldness in his eyes. Surprised I care. *Wasn't this what I was trying to do?* He stands, pulls cash out of his wallet and tosses it on the bar, scowl on his face. "You happy now?"

Surprisingly, I am not.

"I—"

He doesn't wait; he's gone. Following Anna. "And I wasn't his girlfriend!" I shout at their retreating backs, neither of them turning to look.

I look at Dean, who's now standing too, slipping his wallet out of his khakis. "Where are you going? We just got here. I *estimated* this would last longer."

He shakes his head, small smile on his face as he drops a few bills on the bar. "Do I need to answer that, Scotty?"

"*That*?" I ask, gesturing to the door with a disbelieving snort. "That was nothing. That was someone who was something before but isn't now. And that woman is a wimp. She was begging for it! She should actually thank me for toughening her up!"

I laugh, but he doesn't.

"It's fine. You don't need to explain. But I'm not sticking around for it." He dips his chin. "It was nice meeting you."

"Right," I say softly, watching him leave.

I sit there, alone. It shouldn't feel different than any other night, yet it absolutely does. At the familiar crowded bar, my solitude feels like it's been put under a microscope. Magnified. I drink another drink with my chin lifted, imagining myself sitting at a dusty bar in the desert, wondering if a new solo stool surrounded by different strangers will feel any different. Why I hated seeing Ford walk in here tonight as much as I couldn't stay away from him. Wondering why I haven't felt this alone since the day I came off the trail and found him not there.

And with my final sip, I wonder if loneliness gives two shits about geography, and if me leaving will only ever lead to new places filled with the same kind of empty.

EIGHT

Wren shows up every day for a week and it's always the same: dark eyeliner, hair hanging in her face, combat boots, and a dark-colored sweatshirt despite the sweat on her forehead. Our exchanges have been the opposite of revealing. After asking about Zeb, she hasn't asked anything else about my family. Like I scared her straight by simply existing.

In return, I've asked very little about her.

She shows up, lobs me a few angsty remarks and eye rolls, helps me with whatever project I'm working on, and pets Molly.

Fucking Molly.

The dog does nothing but eat the things she shouldn't and bark so much I think I've lost hearing in one ear. Yet today when Wren arrives while I'm in the middle of taking cabinet doors off the kitchen cabinets, Molly sits quietly and performs tricks like a circus pony.

Bitch.

"Looks like a crack house in here," Wren says, as I pull a door from its hinges and stack it on the floor with the others.

I eye her. "How do you know what a crack house looks like?"

"I do." She gives me a challenging look. "Got a problem with that?"

"You're snippy." I unscrew another door with two quick zips of the screw gun. "When's your poet of a mother get back from her trip? I think you need a hug."

Eye roll.

Something's wrong. I have a negative number of maternal instincts, but I know a pissed-off kid, and she's standing right in front of me. "You in trouble?"

She shrugs and toys with the hem of her sweatshirt. I take the last two doors off the cabinets and lean against the now doorless kitchen, studying her.

"I got in trouble a lot," I say casually. "Let me rephrase that: I got in trouble a lot compared to my best friend, but not that much compared to kids from the wrong side of town. Half empty, half full, that whole thing."

"My dad found weed in my backpack," she finally admits, her gaze down on her shoes as she scuffs a toe against the linoleum. "He's pissed. It wasn't mine, but—it's—he didn't care. Gave me the company-you-keep speech."

"Ah," I say, walking to my toolbox and picking up two hammers, proffering one to her. "Guess we shouldn't tell him about the stash in the shed," I joke. She doesn't laugh, taking the hammer. "He know you're here?"

She half shrugs, gesturing with her watch. "I'm being tracked, remember?"

"Hm. Well, here's what I think in my monster-romance-reading opinion: Your dad is probably right. If your friends aren't willing to carry their own weed, they're lazy assholes. Nobody needs friends like that." She almost smiles. "And I can't have you stoned on the job, so . . . it would be better for me if you didn't get arrested or grounded or whatever happens to fifteen-year-olds, so there's that."

She laughs softly. "Yeah," she says. "Okay."

I bump her with my shoulder, feeling oddly affectionate toward her. She looks fragile. Like a girl made of glass. "Okay."

We turn to the kitchen. I hand her a pair of safety glasses and work gloves, already slipping my own on. "Put them on."

She does as I say, eyeing the openings of the cabinets and holes where the old appliances used to be.

"Why do we need these?"

"The countertops," I tell her, tapping my hammer against the yellowed tile. "I watched a few videos on how to do it, but I can't find the screws, and the tile makes them too heavy for me to carry myself anyway."

"So . . . ?"

"So"—I hold up my hammer and grin—"we're going to beat the shit out of them."

She's skeptical; I don't hesitate. I raise the hammer over my head and pummel it down with an oddly satisfying sharp *crack!* Squares of tile crack, shatter, and spew bits of dust the second the hammer hits them.

I grin; she gives a half-assed swing, not even cracking the surface.

"Wimp." I take another swing, shattering four of the squares at once, making me shout *Ha!*

She swings again, harder this time, and splits a tile in half.

I elbow her. "Fun, right?"

She laughs—reluctantly—and swings again, harder.

Another one breaks, then another, chips of archaic porcelain flying into the air. I put a record on—Red Hot Chili Peppers—and turn it up as loud as it will go.

We go through the entire side A of the album without stopping the work. I flip to side B and the smashing and random bubbles of laughter continue.

Molly barks, loud and high-pitched—we bust the tile.

There's a knock at the door we don't notice—we bust the tile.

The music stops abruptly and someone asks, "Y'all having fun?"—we stop.

Look.

Ford. Pinching the needle between his fingers with an amused smirk on his face.

"Wren," I say, my attention on Ford as I peel my work gloves off. "Close your eyes so you can't be a witness to what comes next."

"Scotty, I need to tell you something . . ." she says, voice hushed, as she grabs my elbow. I do a double take; her eyes are wide and panicked.

"Jeez, I'm not really going to kill him," I tell her, taking my eyewear off.

He moves to the opposite side of the now-demolished kitchen counter, wearing athletic shorts, a sweaty T-shirt, and tennis shoes. His eyes go from the destroyed tile, to me, and then to Wren. Molly whimpers as she steps over rogue pieces of debris to settle next to him, angelic as he pets her head.

"Officer," I say, with a too-sweet tone and smile. "You still need a warrant even though your girlfriend couldn't handle my jokes."

"Jokes?" he asks, knowing look on his face. But his eyes don't linger on me; they go to Wren. Where they stay.

His demeanor shifts. He squares his shoulders, crosses his arms over his chest and looks like a TV cop deciding what angle he's going to run a case.

"Wrenny," he says, voice more stern than I've heard it.

Wrenny? My eyes bounce from her to him. *Is this about the weed?*

I look back to Wren, confused. Her gaze is down, scrubbing the toe of her ridiculous combat boot through the rubble of tile, avoiding eye contact with him or me. Her fingers pinch the cuffs of her sweatshirt. Finally, she lifts her chin and looks at him, shoulders sagging. In a voice so soft I can barely hear it, she says, "Hey, Dad."

Shit.

Nine

"So that's Kid Doe?" I ask as we watch Wren ride her bike down the street toward what I now know is Ford's house.

Two blocks away.

Where she lives with him.

Because he's her dad she was supposed to meet at home thirty minutes ago.

"That's Kid Doe," he parrots as we step up onto the porch. "How's she seem?"

I lean against the doorjamb; he stands at the top of the steps with a wide stance and arms folded over his chest.

"Like a judgmental little shit."

He chuckles. "What else?"

"She told me her mom's a traveling poet." I cock a skeptical eyebrow.

A heavy sigh drains from one side of his mouth. "And what did you think about that?"

"At first, I thought it was an interesting lie to conjure up." I pause, waiting for him to deny it. When he doesn't, I add, "Now I'm wondering how you ended up with a poet."

He laughs softly, but it's hollow. His gaze goes to the lake. "Didn't end up with a poet. An addict though. In prison." He lets the words land, and they most certainly do. Right in my sternum, crushing my chest.

My "What?" comes out like a gust of wind.

"I met her at a bar—only saw her a couple of times. Definitely didn't know about the drugs." He puffs a sound sadder than a laugh and looks off toward the tree line. My brain feels like a snow globe filled with shards of glass being shaken. "She was high and drunk when she hit another car, killing the other driver—just a college kid—instantly. Part of the reason we're here."

"How long?"

"Accident was about two years ago. She went away last year. Sentenced to ten to twenty."

"Shit."

"Yeah."

A heavy silence follows. *Wren has a mom in prison.*

"How'd your night end with the math teacher?"

I give him a *don't be a dumbass* look.

He chuckles. "Right."

"How about Anna? Did my little pep talk encourage her to let you get to second base?"

"Far from." He raises his eyebrows. "She wanted to *talk.*"

"That's very grown up of her," I tease. When he doesn't smile, I more seriously add, "And how did that go?"

"Well . . ." he says, glancing out over the water and scrubbing his hand across the back of his head. "She said you and I have unresolved issues we need to work out in order for me to become more emotionally available."

I bite back the laugh that begs to come out. "And do we?"

He blinks.

"Have unresolved issues that are keeping you from being emotionally available?"

"Do we?" he asks.

It's a simple question but the way he spins it on me sends me back to the barstool where I was all but ready to rip my clothes off as our dates stood right next to us.

My neck heats.

I swallow.

Force a smirk.

And lie.

"I'm resolved."

He looks at me so long I wonder if he's trying to count my eyelashes.

"So," he finally says, putting his hands on his hips and peering around me into the house. "What's your plan here other than beating the hell out of the countertops to the tune of 'Scar Tissue'? You hire a contractor?"

"I'm doing it myself."

He laughs, incredulous. "You?"

"Yes, Ford. *Me*. In case you didn't notice while you were palling around with my idiot brother and sneaking out with me to get naked on back roads, I didn't exactly grow up having things done for me. I've been on my own a long time, I can figure it out. I have a toolbox with tools." His amused expression almost makes me smile. "Plus, I'm trying to save money since I'm selling it. God knows Vince wants his full commission check." He regards me for what feels like a full minute. "More important," I add, "breaking shit's cathartic."

He smiles fully, white teeth and perfectly curved lips making his face more attractive. "I would say if anyone can do it, it's you, Scotty."

"Careful, Ford, that sounds like a compliment."

"Might be."

I hate every inch of myself that still feels like that naïve teenager that got swept up in make-believe twenty plus years ago.

"You know Wren was coming here?"

He nods. "I wasn't sure if you'd met, but then figured you had when you described the girl feeding Molly."

"She told me about the weed." I squint at the water, the late afternoon sun making it blindingly bright.

"And?"

"And she said it wasn't hers; I believe her. I also said I agreed with her overbearing dad. Too bad I didn't know it was you, would have told her about the time we got stoned and naked under the bleachers after your game."

He drops his head back with a booming laugh, scrubbing a hand across his hair to make the longer strands on top stick up on end. "Damn. That was another lifetime. Parenting is hard. Hell, life is hard."

I have so many things I could say back, but instead: "Yeah."

Molly trots across the yard and a pontoon boat cruises by with Jimmy Buffett music blasting.

"Birds were hungry." Ford eyes the nearly empty feeders.

I snort a laugh from where I'm still leaning against the doorway. "You really turn into an old-man bird nerd, eh, Golden Boy?"

He shakes his head, lips twitching as he fights a smile. "Had to fill my time with something that kept me out of trouble."

I look at him. His face is the same as it ever was, just a little more grown into. His short and seemingly accidental beard has subtle strands of silver and slopes across the once bare jaw of his youth, failing to hide his now-deeper dimples. His eyes are still bright as ever, just bordered by lines that suit him. With the afternoon sun shining, he's him amplified. Who he was the last time I saw him when I was twenty and who he became.

It unnerves me.

He works his teeth over his bottom lip, shifting his weight between his tennis shoes on the bottom step of the porch. "I have a favor to ask. An exchange really."

I don't hesitate: "No."

"I haven't asked!"

"You have nothing I want, Ford. You actually have an excess of nothing I want."

"Can you just hear me out?" The desperation in his voice intrigues me. I've seen men at this point before: so pliable. "It's about Wren. I think you can help her."

I scoff. "How?"

"Spend time with her. Let her help you. See if she talks." He shrugs. "She won't talk to me—not about the big things—and she dances circles around the counselors we've tried."

Something about that visual pokes at my heart like a needle in a pin cushion. Her ridiculous eyeliner, oversized sweatshirts, and combat boots. And now: the mom in prison.

But he doesn't know that.

"Take off your shirt," I say coolly, not moving from my easy stance in the doorway.

His eyebrows pinch. "The hell, Scotty? Why?"

"You want something from me, I want something from you. Take. Off. Your. Shirt."

To my surprise, he does, annoyed look on his face once his shirt is over his head and balled up in his hands. His body is as annoyingly good as I expected it to be. Muscular, not ripped, subtle dusting of hair on his chest but not enough to be offensive. Familiar and new.

If I was interested, I would be very happy with the sight before me.

He holds his hands out to the side, as if asking *what the fuck,* but I don't budge from my position nor react. "Now your shoes. And pants."

"What?" His eyes widen.

"Unresolved issues. Do it."

He mutters under his breath before reluctantly dropping his T-shirt on the porch, toeing off his tennis shoes, and dragging the athletic pants down his legs, scowl on his face as he steps out of them.

I smirk, bored.

"And the rest."

"Are you kidding me right now, Scotty?" He looks around like someone could be watching him.

I scoff. "I don't know, *Ford*, were you kidding me when you handcuffed me and forced me to talk to you?" Nothing. "That's what I thought. Strip and beg or I'm not playing."

To my surprise, he does. He bends over, slides his boxer briefs down his legs, and when he stands, both hands are covering his crotch, and his face is flushed.

Victory.

My eyes drop to his hands and linger as I say, "I'm listening."

He clears his throat. "As I was saying—dammit, Scotty, will you look at my face?"

"No," I say, keeping my eyes on his crotch until a couple kayakers on the lake pass by, gawking at Ford's bare ass that's facing them. I smile—wide—and wave enthusiastically.

"Ledger's finest, y'all!" I shout. "Here to serve and protect."

Their laughter dances across the water in a wobbly echo.

Ford turns, gives what I imagine is both a humiliated and apologetic smile before looking back at me with clenched teeth. "I was thinking," he grits out. "Maybe Wren could keep coming back.

And, I don't know, you can talk to her. Tell her about your life. She needs help, and she won't talk to me or anyone."

"You want me to help your kid?" I laugh, unamused, the irony of the situation neither lost on me nor missing the chance to karate chop me in the throat. "I grew up in a dumpster fire, Ford, I don't know the first thing about kids."

"But you know about dumpster fires, Scotty. Her mom is an addict. In prison! And doesn't give a shit about her!" When his voice raises, he takes a steadying breath. "She told you she was a poet. Please."

I look him over. Naked as a jaybird except for a pair of socks.

"I'm leaving. As soon as this place sells," I remind him. "I'm fixing this place, selling it, and leaving Ledger."

"Okay," he says. "Fine. You're leaving. I'll take whatever you'll give."

I pick at my fingernails, disinterested. "What's in it for me?"

His knees bend with a kind of anxious bob. "You'll have help with the house. Wren. Me—I'll help."

"Hm." I don't really want anything. And yet, I walk toward him—slowly—keeping my eyes locked with his for the four steps it takes for me to get less than a foot away from his naked body. I rake my gaze down him before kneeling to scoop up his clothes. "These will do."

I turn, stroll to the house, toss the clothes inside on the floor, and let the door slam behind me without looking back.

"Scotty!" His shout of my name is muffled through the door where my back is pressed. "Are you kidding me right now?"

He knows I'm not. If I knew where a lighter was, I would have set the clothes on fire in front of him.

Another muffled shout: "Give me my damn clothes!"

I peel myself from the door and stand at one of the many windows that fill the wall. His panicked eyes flick to mine. I smile and wave through the glass, mouthing, *I can't hear you*, cupping a hand around my ear and shooting him a helpless grin.

Molly wags her tail from her position next to me. In her mouth, a destroyed pillow.

Bitch.

For a second, Ford's pissed-off scowl makes me think he might bulldoze the door down, but instead, he does the last thing I expect: He drops his hands and smirks when my eyes slip to the prize between his thighs. *My, my.* I didn't think he had it in him. Hands on his hips he shouts, "You could have just asked, Viper."

Despite the heat crawling up my neck, I laugh, but when he turns to walk away, it dies. Along with my ability to breathe.

Because it's not the news that Wren has a mom in prison, or the fact that Ford stripped naked with a body like that I'll be thinking of when I lie in bed tonight. It's not even how absurd it is he thinks I'm at all capable of helping his kid. It's the single strip of music notes he has tattooed down his spine that I'd recognize anywhere.

The exact same ones my brother had.

TEN

WREN RETURNS A MUTE. She pets Molly, sits quietly on an up-side-down five-gallon bucket, and watches me like a creepy owl while I struggle to rip up the shag carpet. She's wearing an over-sized sweatshirt. In a T-shirt, I'm sweating like Vince the real estate agent.

As much as I want to, I don't force conversation. I sat with too many counselors and people "trying to help" after my parents were so predictably them and my brother started blasting off the rails, I once thought of sewing my lips shut. I get how she feels: people who don't know, don't know.

June, as it turned out, was the only one who took a hint, which is why our friendship has lasted. When we were kids and I was in stained and secondhand Bongo jeans and ate free school lunches without a parent in sight, she never asked. Even now, when I don't want to talk about it—which is ever—we don't talk about it.

I struggle to get the carpet up; Wren's quiet. Tom Petty's voice sends an echoed "I Won't Back Down" through the house; she leaves.

It's the same the next day.

And the next.

And.

The.

Next.

I don't talk to her; she doesn't talk to me.

When Wren's in the house, Molly lies beside her with her chin resting on her crossed front paws. When Wren leaves, Molly chews everything that isn't nailed down and barks like she wants my ears to bleed.

I'm peeling wallpaper off the living room wall when she walks in, silent yet again as she drops her backpack and claims her usual perch. Contrary to the home renovating blog that called this *a job so easy it's more relaxing than work*, I'd prefer getting a pap smear with a meat cleaver than doing it a second longer.

Vince told me in his email this wallpaper had to go for *us* to get the biggest bang for *our* buck, so it's going.

I drag a wet sponge across the wallpaper, wedge the blade of a scraper under a corner, and pull. Praying for a big satisfying piece like the peeling skin of a sunburn, I swear when it's only a sliver. The size of the ridiculously sloped wall seems to multiply with every too-small piece.

"Fucking wallpaper," I mutter, wiping my forehead with the back of my arm. Wren watches me from her upside-down bucket as she pets Molly. She's quiet, staring at me with big blue eyes—which I now see are very much Ford's—through a ridiculous curtain of hair as I chug water. She looks so much like Ford's kid it stings like saltwater in a cut. Like I always imagined it would.

I roll my eyes, turn the music up, and get back to work, trying my best to ignore the fact that she's sitting there like some kind of paralyzed mime. And while it's the kind of conversation I usually prefer with most people, after an hour of me scraping and swearing and her staying silent, I'm a twig ready to snap.

I can't do this.

Climbing down the two rungs of the stepladder, I drop the scraper, sponge, and gloves to the floor. With a pen on a yellow legal pad, I scribble a note and hand it to her.

Wallpaper
Ruins
Every
Nice day

She reads it and gives me an uncaring look.

"I wrote an acrostic poem with your name." She rereads it, softening slightly but staying quiet. "You want to go for a drive, or just sit there and mope all day?" For the first time in days, her eyes light up. "Text your dad on that dorky watch and tell him I'm taking you out to get a tattoo."

She pounds away at her wrist then follows me to the Bronco, Molly right behind her.

"Aren't we the trio of bitches?" I ask with a smile as I start the ignition.

Wren cuts her eyes to me, a silent scolding for calling us *bitches*, but her lips lift slightly enough I know she's coming around. With Molly's head out the rear window, Wren rolls hers down and props her elbow on the opening. I pick up the speed once we're on the main road and her hand reaches into the air, dancing in the breeze the way people seem just drawn to do. As her palm rises and falls with the force of the air, the fabric of her sweatshirt flutters like a kite in the wind and her brown hair whips around her face.

"What kind of music do you like?" I shout over the wind.

"Lindsey Stirling," she says, without looking at me, hand riding the waves. My eyes catch on her arm. Two Band-Aids slash across her forearm. She sees me looking and pulls her arm in the car, pinching her sleeves in her fingers and glueing them to her lap.

At the next stop sign, I fumble with my phone to find the unfamiliar musician. "You get hurt?" I lift my chin toward her arm.

"Just a cut."

I look at her. She looks at her hands in her lap. I drop it.

When the music fills the speakers, it's an explosion of the unexpected: Chords of a violin rip through the air without a single lyric. I can't tell if it's lovely or lonely, but by the second song, I realize it's maybe both.

At a red light, the familiar downtown and the colorful town mural welcoming summer tourists to the lake with obnoxious cheer greets us. *Life on the Ledge.* I almost laugh: *mission accomplished.*

The buildings run into each other in two parallel strips as we cruise through town. Faded bricks that are now home to modern shops, cafés, and even an art gallery line the street. It's as small as it was when I was a kid, just newer. A little more sparkly, a little less sleepy. One thing untouched: the timeless mountains painting the backdrop.

Out of town and away from the lake, the views are magnified. Summer's refusal to relent to fall is evident by the still mostly green rolling hills around us. The roads wind by picturesque farms until the houses get farther between and more dilapidated; the music seems to know. Shifting from sharp riffs to something more subdued. Melancholy.

When we get to the lane that hasn't changed in the years since I've lived there, I pull onto the edge of the road and cut the engine, letting the abrupt silence envelop us. In the absence of the music, the droning buzz of cicadas is thick.

In the distance: a door slams, a kid laughs, a motorcycle revs.

A faded sign for Mountain Acres sits at the front, a row of run-down trailers in a staggered line behind it. The lane running alongside is littered with cans, bottles, and one lone Dollar General bag skirting around in the breeze.

"I grew up here," I start, staring out the windshield and feeling like I'm looking at a picture in a banned book. "In that second one"—I point in the general direction and she angles her head to see—"the greenish one with trash and boxes on the porch? That's where I did homework—or didn't do homework." I chuckle softly and a faint smile lifts her lips. "My mom—Glory—didn't want the job of raising kids—or any job for that matter. Sometimes she was there, most of the time she wasn't. She'd stay out at the bars all night doing God knows what." I heard rumors, of course. Kids never can keep a secret about what the parents of their peers were doing. I heard my mom had boyfriends, but her infidelity was the least of my concerns. All I knew was she never showed up when I asked her to. When I needed her to. "My dad was a trucker, Lyle was his name, on the road more than home. Probably better that way."

The dynamic always shifted for the worse when he was home. Glory was around more, and the results were unpredictable. Them in that tiny trailer was like two sticks of dynamite being held to a match. They'd drink, they'd fight, they'd fuck. It was the epitome of toxic.

"I spent a lot of time at my best friend's house. June's her name. And with your dad. Though I'm pretty sure your grandma didn't love that."

Her expression stays unreadable.

At the trailer I once lived in but still pay the rent for, the rickety door opens and out walks a woman in cutoff jean shorts and a spaghetti strapped tank top, so thin she could pass as a skeleton wrapped in skin with stringy dark brown hair. She drops a bag of trash on the small porch next to the one I put there last time I visited. She pulls a cigarette out of her pocket and pinches it between her lips.

There's an old-model, blue SUV in the driveway. If it's hers, I have no clue where it came from or how she afforded it.

Our gazes hook, hold, and I start the ignition as she cups a hand around the lighter at the end of the cigarette, tilting her chin skyward to blow out the smoke.

Wren looks from the woman to me.

"Yep," I say, reading her mind as I shift the Bronco into drive. "That's Glory."

Without another word, I turn up the volume of the blaring violins as loud as it will go and floor the gas, causing an abrupt jolt that jerks us back as the speed climbs to a number higher than Ford would approve of.

As the wind rips through the windows, Molly barks, head out the window, and Wren lets out an unexpected laugh.

We don't talk the entire drive home, but the tension that filled the air in the house all week has lessened. When we pull into the driveway, Ford's there, filling up the stupid bird feeders, and we watch him through the windshield after I park.

"Your car is old," Wren says.

"It's not a car," I scoff, bristled by her first words after days of none. "It's a Bronco. And it's not old, it's a classic. 1989—it's older than you!"

She looks at me like this does not impress her, eyeing the tape deck and wind-up windows. Though I had it reupholstered and added a Bluetooth option to the stereo, there's no hiding the fact it's vintage. "Where'd you get it?"

"It was my brother's."

"You only listen to your dead brother's records and drive his car?"

I blink, my silent *and get to your fucking point, you little shithead.*

"Well, do you even like it?" Even her eyeliner fails to hide the disgust in her eyes.

I scoff defensively as I look around the dated interior. Sure, the seats are uncomfortable and it's a bit bulky, but . . . "Of course I like it," I snap. "And I like you better when you don't talk."

She rolls her eyes. "I'm just saying, it doesn't look like something you'd drive."

"Noted," I mutter, turning my attention back to Ford, blissful amongst his birding equipment. "He always this weird about birds?"

"Yep." She waves at him as we start to open our doors. "He's obsessed. Apps on his phone, guidebooks everywhere."

She makes her way to the bird feeders, thumping one before giving him a half-hearted hug. He says something that morphs her face into a reluctant eye-rolling smile then scrubs a hand in her hair. Glancing over her to me, he smiles with his whole face. He's a good dad. The way some people know a house is solid by simply knocking on a random wall, I can tell by watching Ford that he's the kind of father any kid would be lucky to have. It's a one-two punch to my solar plexus.

By the time I get to him, Wren is lifting her bike out of the grass. To me: "Your poems need work."

"So do your social skills."

She shrugs, almost smiles, and pushes her bike a few steps before riding away, zigzagging freely down the street.

"Hey," Ford says, stealing my attention. "How was the tattoo shop?"

I raise my eyebrows. "Never thought I'd have a matching ass tattoo of a dragon with a fifteen-year-old, but here we are."

He chuckles. "How is she?"

"Well." I sigh. "She wasn't talking to me for the last few days, so I decided to add some more trauma into her cocktail of life and show her where I grew up."

His eyes widen. "How did that go?"

"Glory was on the porch. You can imagine what Wren thought. But"—I shrug—"she talked to me before she left. Actually, she told me what she thought about the Bronco." I give him a *stupid-ass kids these days* look. "I guess it worked."

He looks toward the lake. "You see your mom much?"

I follow his gaze; a swimmer with effortless strokes cuts across the water followed by a boat pulling kids on a tube. Laughter mingles with the hum of the motor.

"Every month. Keep the lights on. Make sure she's not dead and has something to eat other than beer and Slim Jims."

"I'm sorry," Ford says, falling into step next to me as I head toward the house.

"About Glory?" I say with a slight chuckle. "You didn't make her."

At the bottom of the porch steps, he shakes his head. "Not about that."

"Okay. Then you're going to have to be more specific because I got a list of grievances about a mi—"

"That I left," he says, eyes searching mine. "That I never called. That I—that I loved you and ran."

His words deliver yet another sharp jab straight through me.

"Water under the dilapidated bridge," I say with faux indifference, stopping in the middle of the porch. "I love you means something different when you're a kid anyway. It's all hormones and hard-ons, you know?"

He doesn't laugh.

A palpable silence follows. Like it has a pulse and power over the situation. Like it's required for whomever stands in it to drown in thoughts marred by missed opportunities and mistakes and godforsaken maybes.

"Right," I finally say, leaning against one of the pillars on the porch and shoving my hands in my back pockets.

"You want to get a drink tonight?" he asks.

A loud laugh spills out of me. "Why?"

"Talk. Laugh. Pretend I didn't fuck up and you don't hate me for it."

"Unresolved issues you're trying to deal with, Golden Boy?" I tease.

His hands settle on his hips and a boyish grin consumes his face. "Something like that."

I will not be able to sit with him and not get all swoony. I know it by the way my hands itch to move and my throat burns when I look at him too long.

"When did you get that tattoo?" I ask. "The one Zeb had?"

"Hm." His tongue bats around the inside of his mouth. "Wondered if you saw that. Day after he died."

I had no idea my brother was gone, and Ford was already memorializing him on his flesh.

"I'm moving," I remind him, more of my weight pressing against the wooden post.

He blows out a sharp breath. "I know."

"In months." My pulse pings in my throat. *Why is he doing this?* "As soon as Thanksgiving is over."

"Well, it's August." His lips twitch like he's fighting a smile. "Seems like enough time to get a drink." My nostrils flare as he adds, "Unless you were planning on the drink lasting three months."

My fingers curl in the back pockets of my jeans. His amusement makes his face more punchable than usual.

"Fine," I say, eyeing a bird at the feeder I think to be a chickadee based on Archie's old guidebooks I've been studying. "I'll have a drink."

His grin is so fast it's like it's been waiting in his lips. "Yeah? Six? Liberty Tap?"

"Fine."

I don't move from my position on the porch, hands still tucked in my back pockets as he retreats to his truck.

Window down, his face is perfection. All smile lines and warmth.

As he drives away, my chest hurts. Like each pump of my own heart is killing me. I won't show up—I can't. Because I loved him once and he left. Because I loved him once and my life fell apart after. But most importantly, because when I look at him, it's like none of those things matter. And as much as I want to be the person he thinks he sees when he looks at me, I'm not. Probably never was. And I'm leaving. One drink with him will make things more complicated. More painful.

Instead of getting ready, I put a Matchbox Twenty record on, pour a plastic cup of whiskey, and spend my night ripping the rest of the shag carpeting off the floor of a house that will never really be mine.

The fucking dog barks the entire time.

June

The weirdest thing happened. Camp went to Liberty Tap tonight.

And he sat next to Ford.

Who was waiting for you.

And since you aren't responding, I'm guessing you know that you forgot to show up.

Please know, I just screamed at the phone.

Eleven

Despite the fact the new bed I bought is on back order and Archie's old mattress rivals a torture device, morning in the A-frame is the best part of living here.

Light pours through the angular windows, sandwiching me between rays of silky warmth, making my mostly ruined back worth it. When I sit up, there's no way to ignore the view straight ahead. Framed by the short hall and slightly obstructed by the spindles of the railing, it's all tall trees, rock face, and lake water. Like waking up and being in a dream instead of leaving one.

Except the dog.

At the foot of the mattress, Molly grunts and growls, one of my shoes in her mouth.

I groan.

"No!"

She doesn't react.

"Stop!"

She growls louder.

"Die!"

She looks at me, shoe pinched between her paws, barks twice, and resumes chewing.

I throw a pillow at her with a grunt.

She stands—shoe in mouth—and trots downstairs, nails clicking as she goes. I can't help but wonder if the real reason Lydia gave me the house was because she didn't want to deal with this stupid mutt asshole.

I drag myself out of bed, go to the bathroom—washing my face and brushing my teeth in the middle of a sea of still Pepto-colored tile—and make my way downstairs, ignoring the chewed shoe in the middle of the ripped-up floor as I cross the living room. In only an oversized T-shirt, I step outside and Molly sprints around me with a bark, making me stumble and swear before sniffing her way around the yard to do her morning business.

The cool morning air sends a shiver down my spine but soothes me like a salve.

On the old porch swing, I push my bare toes against the boards to make me sway. The water is calm, the birds are loud. Molly barks; a car appears. A police car.

Ford.

My chest tightens from guilt or regret or want or all of the above.

In full uniform, he gets out, pets Molly, and starts toward me, carrying a drink caddy with four coffees.

He stops at the edge of the porch, which hits him at hip level, and his eyes roam over me—doing a slight double take when he notices my shirt—then gestures with the drinks before setting them down. "Morning," he says, his voice still holding rich hints of sleep.

I look at the coffee. "You expecting more people?"

An amused sound rumbles in his chest but doesn't meet his lips. "I didn't know how you take it anymore, so I brought you options." I stop swinging. His attention goes to movement at the bird feeders. "You got a few finches this morning."

I do not give a flying fuck about the birds.

"You bought four coffees for me?"

His eyes slide back to mine. "Three." He lifts one out of the caddy and smiles around a sip. "I figured whatever happened last night to keep you from showing up meant you'd need coffee today."

Damn him.

Guilt pokes me. "I forgot I had better things to do."

The look on his face tells me he's not buying today's bullshit.

"I have to get to work," he says, massaging the back of his neck and looking at his patrol car before looking back at me. He sets his coffee down, places both palms on the edge of the porch, and hinges at the waist as he drops his chin before lifting it. He blows out a breath then pins me in place with his eyes. "Maybe I'm misreading everything here, but when I look at you it's like everything in between hasn't happened. Like you and my hands are still opposite ends of a magnet because all I want to do when I see you is touch you. You feel that? Like your heart can't keep up because it's beating so fast?"

I cannot breathe, let alone answer him.

"I can't stop thinking about you, Scotty. Anna was right—I didn't even care that she ended it. That night, I didn't sleep wondering if you were in bed with that guy. If he got to kiss you and touch you and know you in a way I've convinced myself only I should get to even though all this time has passed." He pauses to swallow, gaze staying locked on mine like wet to water. "And, showing up here, seeing you with hair like this and in that shirt—it takes my damn breath away."

My stomach drops fourteen floors.

"You feel any of that?"

Without hesitating: "No."

His lips roll inward between his teeth and his eyes flick to my shirt again—the one I stole from him when I made him strip. "You wear that every night?"

For the week I've had it, I have. The first time was an accident, I grabbed it blindly from a pile of clothes. The rest . . .

"I don't pay much attention to what I wear at night," I say, annoyed by the transparency of the lie in my voice.

My heart is pounding so hard I wonder if he can feel it vibrating the porch. The ground. The molecules of the atmosphere.

"I have to get going."

He swipes his coffee from the porch, dips his chin, and walks to his car.

I shouldn't say anything. I should keep my mouth closed and let him drive away, praying he takes a hint and leaves me alone like he did twenty years ago, but when he opens the door, I hear myself shout, "Black."

He stills, looks at me.

"I take my coffee black. With a shake of cinnamon."

"That's the one with a number one on it," he says, almost smug. "Guess some things never change."

I hate how right he is almost as much as I hate the hope blooming in my belly.

When he drives away, Molly barks.

TWELVE

"WHAT IS IT WITH people and dogs?" I ask, annoyed at the cremation box holding a golden retriever. "The dog that came with the house is a royal pain in the ass."

Wanda chuckles. "Dogs match energy—I saw that on a TV show once. They get a vibe or something—like a sixth sense. Aura reading, maybe." She looks at me thoughtfully. "That's what the pet psychic said. She said there are no bad dogs, just owners that don't know how to lean into the partnership and accept they rely on the dog as much as the dog relies on them." She looks at the ceiling, lips moving without sound as her head bobs back and forth, as if repeating the words to herself, then she smiles. "Yep, that's what she said. I'll never forget it because I thought that was so insightful it must be true."

I take the clipboard from her, skimming the paperwork. "I need that dog like I need a rosebush shoved up my ass."

Wanda shrugs, rolling the dog into the retort. "I'm just saying, the pet psychic said the dog knows."

"Knows what?"

She huffs, annoyed as she pushes the button to start the machine, steady hum filling the air. "What you need. What you're missing. That you're out of balance. Keep up, honey."

I give an annoyed grunt and head toward my office.

"What's the dog doing?" she asks, chomping her gum as she follows on my heels.

"For one," I say as I drop into my chair, "barking like a banshee."

She considers this, blowing a bubble, cinnamon scent of it wafting toward me from her position on the other side of my desk. "Probably means you need to talk more."

I scoff.

"What else?"

"Chewing my shit to smithereens."

"Hm." She blows and pops another bubble. "What kind of shit?"

"My vibrator for one," I say without looking at her as I sift through a pile of mail.

"You need a blood-pumpin' piece. Next."

I give her a look that doesn't need translation. "And everything else. She eats whatever I don't want her to."

Wanda makes a contemplative sound and says, "Probably means you need to go have some fun."

I hate everyone.

"Thanks for your analysis." I open my laptop. "Anything else I can help you with?"

"That apartment is a dream," she gushes, propping a hip against my desk and clasping her long-nailed hands together. "Even though it's right in town, it's so quiet. And what a nice break from hearing my sister and her husband yelling about whose turn it is to take out the trash." She smacks her gum with a smile. "How's the house?"

"Aside from the dog that's a menace to society? Slow." I click open my email. "Those DIY bitches made me think I'd have a flipped house in an hour, including commercials."

She chuckles, pushing off my desk to stand in the doorway. "Well, if it makes you feel any better, all the true crime I watched and my ex-husband still walks around breathing oxygen without a care in the dang world." My head snaps to her, and the smile on her face is so nonchalant I must have misheard her. She shrugs. "Everything seems easier on camera."

I blink. We have never talked about what did or didn't happen with her ex-husband and her arrest.

"Anyway." She waves a dismissive hand through the air. "When Dondi left this morning, he was saying that the Sellecks were asking about you selling again."

"Of course they were." I scroll through my emails. I've always resisted the Sellecks' offers. Partially because I had no idea what I'd do if I sold, but mostly because of Zeb: He was burned alone. No matter how many bodies I watch become ashes, no matter how many T-shirts I wear or favorite bands I play, I can't shake the thought or the guilt. Now, with a one-way ticket plan, I fully intend on taking the Sellecks up on their offer so I can get out of here—even if I have to carry the guilt along with me in a U-Haul across the country—just not yet. I haven't said anything to Wanda and Dondi because the house hasn't convinced me it's worth two pennies. Other than the view, it sucks. "Did he tell them to suck a tit?"

She laughs, loud this time, her prominent bust bouncing with the shake of her shoulders. "I'm sure he said, 'The Dondinator will ask the Ash Queen.'"

I can hear that.

But—I check the clock, and it's only eight a.m. and Dondi doesn't usually deliver any bodies from the morgue until after nine.

"Why was Dondi already in this morning?"

She presses her heavily hair-sprayed hair with a hand, knowing look on her face. "He helped me move the rest of my stuff in."

My eyebrows raise; her painted lips form a heart-shaped pout. There it is: Dondi and Wanda are fucking in my bed.

I'll be cremating that mattress.

"Don't look at me like that, Scotty. We're humans." She pauses to shimmy. "We aren't all like you."

My chin jerks back. "What is *that* supposed to mean?"

She shrugs, smug look on her face. "I don't know, honey, maybe you should ask that dog of yours."

At my glare, she strolls away.

THIRTEEN

"WERE YOU AND MY dad a thing?" Wren asks, peeling a strip of wallpaper.

"Hm." I swallow my initial response of *piss off* due to not wanting her to slip off into another silent hole and drag a sponge down the wall. "I'll make you a deal, every time you ask me a question, I get to ask you one."

Her eyeliner makes her look like an extra in a scary movie as she looks at me. Nearly three weeks of her showing almost daily and I still don't know much about her. If she needs me to talk to get her to talk, I'll play.

"Fine," she mumbles.

I wedge a scraper under a lifted corner of wallpaper. "We were a kind of thing," I start, choosing my words carefully. Not sure how to explain the kind of thing that consumes you mind, body, and soul. The kind of thing that makes you see forever only to find it was a mirage. "We were never anything official. But I never dated anyone else as long as we were together—which was years—I don't think he did either. Of course, I never gave him the satisfaction of asking."

"Why?"

"That's two questions," I say, raising my eyebrows. "But I'll answer because I'm feeling generous." She rolls her eyes. "I always thought labels were pointless. Everything I witnessed showed me a title never guaranteed happiness or love." I shrug. "My parents were married, but it never made them happy. I never wanted it. I thought if it was meant to be it didn't need a name, it just was. I think it drove your dad crazy how untethered I was." I laugh softly. "Probably still does."

"And now?"

"I draw the line at three questions," I deflect. Because what happened was, after years of him chasing me around, my brother died and Ford ran away to start a new life that didn't involve me, leaving me to pick up the pieces of how much damage that caused—how broken he left me—alone. "My turn." I desperately want to start with a heavy hitter. About her mom, her eyeliner, hell, even her sweatshirts that make no sense in the weather, but I have a feeling she'll shut down. So instead, I go easy. "Why do you like Lindsey Stirling?"

A smile curves her lips as she peels a section of paper from the wall. "I like that there's no lyrics. You can decide if the song is happy or sad, you know? If it's about love or loss or . . . dandelions and marshmallows."

"Aren't you an insightful little sh—" She looks at me. "—ell-fish."

She almost laughs.

"My turn again. Do you want to date my dad now?"

I debate slapping her.

"That's . . ." I stare at the ugly plaid wallpaper, searching for a word both meaning *so bad it hurts* as much as *over my dead body*. "Complicated." When she starts to open her mouth, I add, "We're nothing. And I'm selling this place and moving."

She makes a disbelieving sound. "Where are you moving to?"

"The desert." I point to a stack of real estate magazines at the base of the steps. "Arizona maybe. I'm still thinking. Maybe New Mexico. Or Utah."

She stills, pinching a piece of wallpaper between her fingers midair as she looks at me. "Why?"

The simple word irks me. Moving is about me leaving more than any actual destination. The truth is I don't care. It's about being somewhere else where I can breathe deep and not constantly be reminded of every wrong thing I've done or failed to do. Maine or New Mexico, I just don't give a shit.

"Because I want to," I snap. "And no more questions about me and your dad." She opens her mouth. "Or where I'm moving."

A noise outside takes my attention to the window. Ford backs his truck down the driveway, stopping just shy of the bird feeders.

Wren and I stand at the wall of windows, watching as he gets out of the truck. He's wearing dark pants, duty belt, and an army-green T-shirt with a black bulletproof vest over it, lacking the uniform shirt that's usually over it. He drags a bag of birdseed to the tailgate and rips it open then fills each feeder before tossing the empty bag into the back and slamming the tailgate.

Molly gives a loud bark and he waves, easy smile on his face.

"Nothing, my ass," Wren says. "My dad's feeding your birds."

"Don't say ass." I don't look away from Ford as he starts walking toward the house. "And I'm not into birds, only monsters. His efforts do nothing for me."

"Whatever," she mutters, going back to her patch of wallpaper as Ford climbs the steps of the porch and enters the house through the propped-open door.

"Officer Callahan," I say. "Back for more punishment, I see."

"A glutton for it," he says with a quick wink before looking around the house. "Looks good in here."

"Liar." I shake my head as I accept the truth: It's a wreck. The carpeting is out of the living room, but the cabinets still need to be demoed out of the kitchen. As well as the heavy pieces of destroyed countertops. And the linoleum floor that covers that half of the house. And the appliances that are so heavy I could only get them to the middle of the downstairs before nearly dying. "I was hoping to get everything out and start painting next weekend but that feels . . . ambitious."

"Want help?" he asks.

Dear God, yes!

"I'm good."

"Done!" Wren shouts, proudly showcasing a large strip of wallpaper between her fingertips. "And I'm leaving." She peels her gloves off and jogs to Ford, her combat boots pounding against the floor until she stops to give him a hug. "I have that study group at the school. Lily's mom is picking me up."

He kisses her temple. "Have fun. Text me if you need anything."

"Sure." Sweat mats her hair to her forehead and she rolls her eyes—which she might do more than blinking—before we regard one another.

"Thank you for helping," I tell her. "You're more useful than you look."

"You're shockingly less useful than you look," she says, devoid of emotion.

I feel a smirk tug at my lips. "See you tomorrow?"

"Is that a question?"

"Only if that's yours."

She shakes her head, but there's a pep to her movements as she trots down the porch steps. "Hey, Dad?" she calls, lifting her bike in the driveway and walking it a few steps. He steps in the doorway. "I think Scotty still has the hots for you."

"Hey!" I shout, shoving Ford out of the way so I'm standing on the porch. "I was trying to forge a relationship by being vulnerable, you tattletale. And I never said that!"

She ignores me, already pedaling down the road.

When I look at Ford, he's smug, and I feel my neck heating—I'm flushed. This kid is the absolute worst. "I didn't say that."

He fights a smile. "Explains why you made me strip."

"That," I explain, flustered, "was because I wanted to see if your dick sprouted feathers."

He barks out a laugh, eyes roaming the disaster of a house. "This the better thing you had to do the other night?"

"Maybe."

"Okay then." He breezes back to his truck and returns with a duffle bag.

My eyes narrow. "What are you doing?"

He tugs at the Velcro straps at his sides, slipping the vest over his head and putting it by the door.

"I'm getting changed." My *why the hell would you do that* look prompts him to add, "So I can free up some of your time."

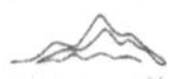

Ford is annoyingly useful. Mere hours after he arrives, the entire kitchen is in pieces at the curb and all the appliances are out of the house. It would have taken me four hundred years to do that job alone.

We barely spoke as we worked. I cranked music, and other than grunting and chuckled swear words, there wasn't much else. Now, on the porch, it's quiet as we sit with our legs dangling off the edge eating delivered sandwiches for dinner.

It's nearly seven, but there's still plenty of light. Early September is warm enough that boaters and kayakers linger on the lake.

"Wren seemed happy," he says between bites. "Today go good?"

I nod, wiping my mouth.

"She likes you."

I chuckle between bites.

"I think she's more intrigued about why you trust me with her." Molly sits in front of me, making whimpered begs for food until I toss her a piece of bread. "What has you so worried anyway? She seems normal to me. Granted, the only teen I've ever spent time around is June's daughter."

"Nothing. Everything." He blows out a weighted breath. "She's moody—and I know that's a teenage thing—but some days it feels more than that. She'll shut in. Go silent for a few days at a time. We never argue until we do." He's quiet a beat, and I consider what he's saying. Even though I don't know what it means, I try to piece it together. "I never knew her mom was pregnant—didn't even know Wren existed until she was three. Because her mom, Riley's her name, was arrested for possession and I got a call to get her." My eyes widen, a combination of shock and guilt churning in my gut. He chuckles. "My reaction exactly. Had a paternity test but I didn't need it—she was the spitting image of my baby pictures. I got custody easily, but Riley didn't lose all her rights. God knows what Wren saw in those first few years, or even on the few overnight visits she had after. But when she killed that girl . . . I don't know. The trial dragged on for nearly a year. Took a toll on Wren. There was a shift. Her moods, her clothes. The makeup."

I have no answers, so I stay silent, chewing and thinking and chewing and thinking. Of my own childhood, my own reactions to the shit thrown my way. Of all the decisions I've made that have led to where we are. Him having a kid he didn't know existed morphing the blood in my veins to a slow-moving sludge.

A red bird lands on the feeder. "That one of your girlfriends?" I ask around a mouthful of food.

His laugh nearly turns to a choke on his sandwich. "A cardinal," he says, wiping his mouth with a napkin. "A male. Most males have brighter colors. Some say they're a sign of lost loved ones looking after you when you see them."

Another bird lands, blue and white with a little mohawk. I look at him.

"Tufted titmouse."

At that ridiculous name, I laugh like a fifth-grade boy.

"How did this happen?" I ask as I ball up my trash and shove it into the bag. "This has a very *listens to NPR and plays online chess with strangers* vibe."

He takes his last bite and balls up his trash, collecting the bag as we stand. "The job—especially in Atlanta—is a lot. The things cops see—the things they can't change or unsee—it's . . ." He takes a deep breath and exhales it slowly, eyes closing like he's reliving the worst parts of his past—the parts I know nothing about—before reopening them. "A lot. I was drinking more than I should, pretty pissed most of the time, but when I got Wren"—he shrugs—"I just quit. We spent a lot of time sitting on our back porch, just for fresh air, you know? I imagined she'd lived through a lot of chaos, so I tried to make things calm. She'd color or play with blocks. The birds started landing, she started asking questions. And, with her name—it just happened, I guess. I became a sober-cop, bird-nerd anomaly." He grins, and it's as proud as it is contagious.

"Well, it suits you," I say, studying the nuances of his face as we stroll toward the water. There's a faded white scar on his jaw, noticeable because the maybe-on-purpose, maybe-not scruff doesn't grow as thick there. A mole on his neck I remember touching with my index finger when we were young.

"You staring at me, Viper?" he asks, the look in his eyes knowing I damn well am.

"I am," I admit. "Trying to see what it is I ever found attractive about you."

He laughs softly as we stop at the canoe.

"What about you, Scotty Armstrong? What are you into, if not birds and illegitimate children?"

"Ah," I say, feigning deep consideration. "I'm into ashes. And monster smut. And sometimes I renovate houses."

He chuckles and shakes his head, corners of his eyes crinkling when they meet mine. "Still elusive as ever."

"Not really," I tell him. "That's all I got. I've been in Ledger." I raise my eyebrows. "Same shit, different decade."

His eyes on mine feel gravitational, like if I look at them long enough they'll suck me right to him. I force myself to look at the water, both of us quiet until we reach the shoreline.

At the canoe, he flips it over and kneels next to it, rubbing his palm along the bottom then looking up at me with a grin. "What are you doing the rest of the night?"

"Taking a bath in an outdated bathtub. Reading a book about a devastatingly handsome lizard." I wiggle my eyebrows. "Why?"

He stands, holding out a paddle. "Let's see if she floats."

Every warning alarm in my body goes off as I look at the paddle wrapped in his fingers. The way I immediately want to. The speed at which the instant shot of warmth and excitement zips through me. How my heart immediately pounds at an unusually fast rhythm.

"I shouldn't," I say, not convincing either of us as the lake sits feet away, painted in gold, looking like a scene made to be in.

"Ahh." There's a teasing quality to his voice. "I get it now."

My eyebrows pinch.

"I got old and ugly," he says with a knowing smirk. "But you, Scotty Armstrong, got boring."

He's goading me; it works.

With a glare, I snatch the paddle out of his hand. "I hope a bird shits on your head."

With a victorious smile: "Some things never change."

He pushes the canoe into the water and tosses his keys and phone onto the shore. I step in, taking a wobbly seat at the front.

He chuckles from the seat behind me; I wave a middle finger in the air without looking at him.

I have no doubt he knows I'm also smiling.

FOURTEEN

I'M IN A CANOE with Ford. It takes thirty minutes of us being on the lake and him pointing out birds to me like a nature guide for this to sink in. Every sound synonymous with the lake—birds, bugs, and boat motors—mixes with the soft splash of the paddles cutting through the water to form a surreal and soothing sound-track.

The sun is low, the lake has emptied. It's peaceful. I'll never admit it to Ford, but it's better than a bubble bath and any book I own.

"Tell me how you got the crematorium," he says from the back of the canoe. "And the name."

I tuck my chin to my shoulder, not fully looking back at him. His paddle cuts into the water; I rest mine on my lap.

I hesitate and think of him being so open about Wren. Himself. His job.

I take a deep breath in, forcing the words with my exhale.

"The police told me when my dad got the call about Zeb, he told them to burn him." A bird cuts through the sky; I wonder if Ford knows what it is. "So they sent the body to the crematorium and did just that. I was on that trip for college—you remember it. Two weeks hiking the Appalachian Trail with that earth science class. Seems stupid now." I pause to watch a bass boat troll by, knowing I didn't need to tell Ford that part. I had talked to him on the phone just before I left. *"I'll miss talking to you,"* he'd said. *"You'll find some boy and live in those woods forever, I bet,"* he teased. Then the ones that lingered the longest and hurt the most after he was long gone: *"You know I'll still love you even if you do."* I laughed then. I'd never once called him my boyfriend, never once told him I loved him, but he had to have known both those things were true. *"Yeah, yeah, Golden Boy. Have fun with my brother this weekend, and I'll see you when you pick me up if I'm not shacked up in a tent with Sasquatch."* That was the plan: he'd be there at the trailhead and pick me up. While my brother stayed in Ledger working a job putting up fences, Ford and I went off to college. Him at a big state school in Raleigh, me at a small college close to home. Only an hour away from each other, we were together nearly every weekend.

I clear my throat. "Anyway, I didn't even know he'd died—June couldn't connect with the teacher in charge. Cell phones were shit then, and the group SAT phone was down, but it didn't seem that important. What could go wrong, you know? Little did I know as I was eating beans from a can and laughing around a fire, my brother was being burned alone, not a soul there to say goodbye to him or play a good song." I laugh softly, but even to my own ears it sounds sad. Like a cry from the bottom of an empty well. "My dad went to get the ashes a few days later—after spending God knows how long pouring liquor down his throat—and Zeb was in a glorified trash bag and cardboard box. My dad was so wasted he drove right off the bridge into Crow Creek. Sometimes I wonder if it was on purpose—not that it matters. Dad drowned. Zeb's ashes washed away."

Giving those words life is all it takes for me to viscerally relive every moment of that story like it was the day it happened. The way I dropped to my knees and my muscles seized when I saw June's face at the trailhead. She was bleach white, crying as she spoke. *"Zeb died,"* she blurted through her sobs. *"And your dad."* I was dirty, smelled like I hadn't had a shower in two weeks, and couldn't even get my backpack off before I vomited on her shoes.

I went into the woods for two weeks and the world fell apart.

I happily hiked on day one; Zeb got arrested.

I signed a logbook with a smiley face at a trail checkpoint on day two; Zeb somehow got released on bail.

I stacked rocks in a creek with my classmates on day four; Zeb lost his job, shoved one more needle into his arm, and took his final breath.

I finally figured out how to start a fire with a piece of flint on day nine; Zeb was getting cremated. Alone.

I couldn't stop thinking about Ford on day thirteen; my dad got drunk, picked up Zeb's ashes, crashed into the creek, and died while Zeb's cremains wash away.

Somewhere in that timeline I never quite placed, Ford left; we never spoke again.

When I came out of the woods, the only things waiting were guilt and grief. Ford was gone, my brother was gone. I refused to go to whatever sham of a funeral my uncle planned for my dad.

Ford clears his throat, cutting his paddle into the water and bringing me back to the canoe and him.

"Anyway, after that, I came back to Ledger, hellfire in my veins, and went right to the crematorium. I sat on the front steps until he told me exactly how my brother was treated. I nearly punched him in the face when he showed me the process. *'Bodies without directions are sent in naked and with a sheet,'* he told me. You can imagine the words I had for him."

I turn around in my seat to fully face Ford now. His intense expression is wholly fixed on me. His paddle is on his lap; any movement of the canoe is now a drift.

"Turns out, I'm annoying enough, because he gave me a job. He said in that uppity voice of his—you remember him? Mr. Garth?"

Ford lets out a soft laugh. "I do."

"He said, *'Ms. Armstrong, if you think you can do so much better, why don't you do it?'* So I did. I dressed them so they looked like who they were and started playing music they liked. Did it the way Zeb would have wanted, ya know?" Ford nods again. "And then I just . . . never left. What would I have done, anyway? Only a year and a half of college credits on my resumé. I couldn't bring myself to go back to school. Seemed pointless. The next few months . . ." There is so much to say, so much Ford has no idea about, but the narrowing of my throat tells me not today. Not yet. "The next few months were difficult. And Glory—" I blow out an incredulous breath and give him a look that explains that shitshow. "That woman had every excuse in the book for what happened and why she didn't try and find me. Mr. Garth gave me the apartment over the crematorium and paid for me to go through crematory training. I did that for years. The Death Liaison, he called me." I smile fondly. I annoyed the hell out of that man, but he was good to me. "He retired about ten years ago and I took out a loan and bought it from him." I shrug. "I changed the name to Happy Endings for shock value." Ford chuckles and puts the tip of his paddle in the water, steering us away from the tree line. "And here we are."

Stories like mine never get easier to tell, but in that canoe, for the first time, I feel a hint of relief. Like a deep breath after being under water for too long.

"I didn't know," he says as I start paddling again, steering us toward a floating dock in the middle of the lake. "That nobody could reach you. June and I talked. And I called you—not that it matters. It went to your voicemail, and I didn't know what to say—didn't know how to explain any of it—so I didn't leave a message."

"And never called again for twenty years," I add.

"And never called again for twenty years," he echoes, voice quiet.

At the floating dock, Ford ties off to a cleat with a small rope, and we climb onto it, taking in the lake around us in silence.

"After that, everything crumbled," I continue, the words falling out of my mouth like a line of dominoes. "It's like I had tried to escape who I was, and this town and the universe felt it—sucked me back in like a damn vacuum and reminded me of my place. Like God got pissed I was trying to act too big for my britches. Had the nerve to hope for a better life. If I never would have gone on that hike—or gone to college at all—maybe it wouldn't have happened." Three ducks fly by; we both watch them. "Anyway, twenty years seems like a good amount of time to try again. Get out of here. Nobody left to get wrecked if I'm gone except Glory." I laugh an unamused laugh. "Way that woman bitches she'll probably throw me a party."

He stares at me; I stare at the water.

"You're different," he finally says.

"Well, I'm forty-one, so, that's a given."

He shakes his head. "Not that. You . . . you used to have this look when I'd pick you up from your house. Almost smug, you know? Defiant. Like, where you came from and what everyone else in your family did had nothing to do with what you were. Like it was the least interesting thing about you."

"And now?"

His eyes squint just enough that lines web out around them as he looks at me like he's seeing every truth that lives inside of me. "Now it seems like it's the only thing you think of."

I scoff. "It's not."

"Really?" He takes a wobbly step toward me as the dock bobs in another wake. "Why didn't you show up for a drink?"

At once, anger starts to swirl and collide against itself within me, and I don't mask it in my voice. "I told you I was busy."

"Why are you still single?" he presses.

"You're single!" I argue, louder.

"Why are you alone?" He doesn't wait for my answer before rapid-firing his next questions: "Why is there nobody in your life? Why do you want to sell the house? To move to the damn desert? Why won't you look at me? Why are you dating guys like math-man Dean? Why can't w—"

"Because you left!" I shout, silencing him as the angry words bounce around us and ricochet off the water. "Because you left," I repeat, voice lower and more controlled. "And when you did that, you took everything with you, whether you knew it or not or meant to or not, you did it just the same. So stop the investigation, *Officer*, there's your answer. I am the way that I am because I gave everything away a long time ago and never got it back."

My heart slams beneath my ribs. He has the audacity to look ruined.

"I left because I thought you'd blame me," he finally says. "Because I blamed myself." He's close enough to me now that we could touch but don't. "Because *I* didn't do enough to save Zeb. Because *I* let him go into that house. Because—" He stops suddenly, as if there's more, but he's not ready. The only sound I hear is my own blood rushing in my ears; the tension between us is strong enough to produce electricity. "Because I thought you'd be better off."

Despite the burn that blisters the space between my throat and chest, I force myself to look at him. And he looks back. We stare at each other as the dock bounces like a ship lost at sea with whatever the water decides to do in a silence as heavy as our history. When my eyes feel like they might burn out of their sockets, I blink away, forcing a deep breath, then another, his words invading every curve and corner of my body.

"Well you thought wrong," I tell him.

I scan the shoreline to distract me. I count four boats. Seven roof peaks. A single cardinal, bright red as it floats through the air. I think of what Ford said earlier.

"You go to church?" I ask.

"Not since I was a kid," he says, head tracking the movement of a nearby kayak.

"I once heard a preacher say that if you commit suicide, it's a guaranteed one-way ticket to hell. You think that's true for drug overdoses?"

He makes a thoughtful sound. "I think people like to pretend they understand God more than they actually do, and I think God sees people in a way we never will."

His perspective makes it hard to not wrap my arms around him; I focus on the ripples of the water from a jumping fish.

"Remember swimming out here as a kid?" he asks.

A million memories of us on this lake flash at once. "Best days ever."

"Zeb was always finding the highest thing to jump off." Ford chuckles. "Can't believe he didn't die out here."

"I don't know why you were ever his friend." I can't help but smile. "He was an idiot. Beginning to the end."

"He was a good time." Ford bumps me with his shoulder, the subtle movement enough to make the dock teeter. "And he had a pretty sister."

A soft laugh builds in my chest, but I clear my throat to hide it. When I brave another look at him, there's so much affection in his eyes it nearly pushes me into the water.

Too fast for me to react, he takes my hand in his. His blue eyes are so serious—so sincere—panic thrums through me. He lifts my hand to his mouth and kisses my thumbnail.

He remembers.

It's so beautifully simple it nearly brings me to my knees.

He pulls his lips from my thumb and rubs the tip of his nose against my nail before lowering our hands and pinching my thumb with his. "I want us to try."

The sound that comes out of my mouth is something between an insane woman's laugh and a pained woman's cry. I stare at our hands; his so big—so warm. *Wrong for mine.* "Try what?" I ask, yanking my hand free. "To be fuck buddies like we were in high school? Did you not listen to a damn thing I just said?"

His expression crashes, usually smiling eyes filling with hurt. "That's not what we were, and you know it."

My skin wraps around my bones like heat during cremation with the way he's looking at me. Like he sees someone that doesn't exist anymore. That hasn't existed for over twenty years. How dare he show up here and do this. How dare he show up here at all.

I crouch down, my hands trembling with fury as I untie the knot on the cleat, pushing the canoe away from the dock and hopping in as it starts to float away. I can't breathe. I can't think. I can't do this—whatever it is. The feelings, the looks—the fucking looks that threaten to drown me high and dry without a single drop of water.

My hands shake as I pick up the paddle, digging the blade into the water with angry strokes.

"Scotty," he pleads. When I don't respond: "Scotty!"

I look over my shoulder at him. "Don't ever look at me like that again."

Then I'm gone, paddling away and leaving Ford Callahan on a dock in the middle of Lake Ledger as he shouts my name and angry tears drip down my face.

After he spent an afternoon ripping out a kitchen with me.

After he looked at me like he wanted to keep on looking.

After he ran away once and left me broken.

"Dammit, Scotty, don't do this." I can barely breathe over the sound of my name on his lips. But I don't stop, and I definitely don't look back.

Not when I hear the splash behind me.

Not when I hit the beachy shore and drag the canoe into the grass and drop the paddles next to his phone and keys.

Not when I march inside, toss his duffle and vest onto the porch, and lock the door.

Not when he's on the porch, shouting my name and pounding on the door, apologizing for something I'm not sure I understand.

When he's quiet, I peel myself from the door and look out the window. He's standing fully clothed, soaking wet, and taking jagged breaths like he just swam across the lake. Because he did. Because I'm as broken and busted as this disaster of a house.

He stands directly in front of me, only the glass separating us, looking as wounded as my whole life has felt.

I want to smile, flip him off, and tell him to go to hell, but I have neither the words nor desire. Water drips down his face, clinging to the short stubble on his jaw and chin before dropping to the splintered wooden planks of the porch.

He presses one palm on the window and drops his forehead next to it, not breaking eye contact as his skin spreads against the surface of the glass like he's been spilled there.

I stare at his hand. At his face. At him. I press my thumb to the glass opposite his palm. For a split second I wish I could be who he seems to think I am. That I'm at all capable of trying whatever this is.

Instead of going to him, apologizing, and telling him everything like I should, I drop my hand from the glass and walk away, hoping he sees that whatever he's trying to do here is a waste of time.

June

How's the house coming? Need help?

Scotty

How can you help? Isn't your kitchen in shambles too?

Right. Well how is yours? When can I see it?

Fine. Knocking out the list the realtor sent me to get it sale-ready. You can see it then.

I got some real estate magazines for Arizona. Desert yards don't have grass. Weird, right?

I think I finally got rid of Ford once and for all.

That idiot can't take a hint. And he has a thing for birds.

And he just disappeared after Zeb . . .

AND! He's a cop, I'm pretty sure they're all kinds of fucked. And I'm leaving . . .

Even if I wasn't leaving, what would that look like? Me and Ford? Has he not seen the trailer I grew up in?

Blink twice if the twins have tied you to a tree.

Do you really want me to answer?

Because if you do, I'll tell you that you loved that boy when we were kids, and he hurt you when Zeb died because he was as young and heartbroken as the rest of us. I'd also tell you that you put more stock in where you came from than anyone else does. You read books about alien sex, birds seem like child's play. And don't you hate the desert?

I like you better when you're tied to a tree.

FIFTEEN

"GLORY, YOU IN HERE?" I call, pushing the rickety door of the trailer open with armfuls of groceries. The unfortunate scent of cigarette smoke and too-strong air freshener assaults me the second I step inside and set the bags on the floor.

"Where else would I be?" she snaps, making her way down the short hall, muttering a swear under her breath as she eyes me before dropping into the worn recliner. Her jeans and shirt are both a size too big for her skinny frame. "Dressin' up like that make you feel better about where you came from, Scotty Ann?"

I roll my neck, tugging at the lapel of my navy blazer as I force a sweet smile. "Now why would I ever need to recover from this cozy corner of Satan's crotch, Glory?"

She scoffs. "You look ridiculous in that jacket and those shoes. Polyester tryin' to be silk."

I sort through the groceries. "Noted."

She rolls her eyes, taps a cigarette out of a box and brings it up to her mouth, lighting it with her bony fingers as I take the groceries to the kitchen and start putting them away. Despite the dilapidated appearance of the exterior and the overall depressing tone of the trailer park itself, the inside is tidy. Dated, worn, and certainly dreary, but it's clean enough. Everything is original from when we moved into it when I was a kid, and even then, it belonged to the people who lived here before us.

"You bring beer this time?" she barks.

Out of her line of sight in the kitchen, I raise both my fists, middle fingers flying as I pantomime a scream. It's only once a month, but every second in these nicotine-soaked, wood-paneled walls pushes me one step closer to the nervous breakdown she's gunning for me to have. In the couple hours I'm here, I check my best interest at the door in order to make sure she's alive, has food in the fridge, and the place hasn't completely fallen apart.

June has told me I'm insane for continuing to show up here. Maybe I am. Part of me wonders if I'm simply delusional enough to still have hope we can have a normal relationship while another part of me thinks it's simply knowing I didn't do enough to help Zeb, and now I'm all she has. Either way, I show up fully prepared to scrape every bit of shit she spews off myself when I leave.

Instead of telling her to go buy her own beer and fuck off, I say nothing, putting milk, eggs, and orange juice into the fridge and twenty frozen dinners with broccoli and grilled chicken in the freezer. She may have left me out to dry my entire life, but I refuse to do the same. Refuse to be her. Plus, I'm leaving. I can endure this for a few more months. I check the calendar on my phone; it's September second. Thanksgiving is less than three months away. Even if I list December first and it sells right away, it dawns on me that there will still be thirty more days of closing procedures. I can't leave until January. *Four months.*

I take a steadying breath. I've dealt with her a lifetime; I can handle four more months.

After that, she's on her own.

"Saw you out there with a girl the other day. She yours?"

I walk to the doorway and glare at her but don't dare tell her it's Ford's kid. That will prompt her mouth to start a downpour not an umbrella in the world could protect me from.

She scoffs and takes a drag of her cigarette, tapping it on the edge of the ashtray next to her. "You've been spreading your legs for a long time, how am I supposed to know? It's not like you tell me what's going on in your life. You could have a whole family out there I don't know about because you're too ashamed for people to know who I am."

I look at her, unamused. "I've been meaning to tell you, it was a relief you didn't show up to my high school graduation—which I invited you to repeatedly—because I didn't want anyone to know who I really was. Happy now?"

Her cheeks hollow out with her next deep drag of her cigarette and her hazel eyes, cloudy from age and a life filled with complete disregard for real food and clean air, hold mine in an icy stare. When she exhales, she picks up the remote and mutters, "Thought so." With a click of the button, *The Price is Right* fills the TV screen.

Four more months.

I buzz around, putting the groceries away and starting a load of laundry.

Back in the living room, she stubs out her smoke, watching me as I collect a few bags of trash from wastebaskets, tying them up and setting them at the front door to take when I leave.

"All my friends have grandkids."

Here we go.

"What friends do you have, Glory?"

She snorts. "I'm not an invalid, I have friends. And why do you have to keep calling me Glory? I'm your mother. I gave you life! You're disrespectful—always have been. It's no wonder I didn't show up at your graduation when you treat me like this. Like I'm some kind of-of second-class citizen." Her puckered lips make her skinny face look like a beak. Ford could name the bird.

I clench my teeth, going to the bathroom to collect the last of the trash and stopping as I tie the bag in the hall and study the collage-style picture frame that hangs. There are a couple school photos of Zeb and I from elementary years with wild hair and missing teeth, a few photos of my dad's rotten parents and his brother, and one of Glory, my dad, and me and Zeb on the beach, thirty some years ago. It was the only vacation we ever took. Only time I saw the ocean until I went with June's family in high school.

We drank Slurpees and ate crabs; my parents never fought once in those three days.

I wonder if life would have been better if we had just stayed there and never came back from that trip. Lived on that beach or had a house at the lake. Dad would have fished—maybe would have been happier—and maybe Glory would still be Mama. Maybe we could have been happy. Normal. Maybe Zeb would still be here.

It was after that trip things took a nosedive. Like going on vacation showed us a good life we'd never have. Only weeks later we were at a playground, and I fell and skinned my knee. *"Mama! Mama!"* I wailed. She got to me, jerked me up, and said with a frustrated voice, *"Stop shoutin' Mama in front of all these people."* I looked at her, confused as my knee bled and snot came out of my nose. *"My name is Glory. That's what you'll call me."*

From then on, I did.

"You lost?" Glory barks, shaking me from my trance. "I said, you and your brother never cared one bit about me. Look what he went and did. Used them drugs until they used him." I look at her as I tie the last bag, wishing it was her head inside of it instead of empty toilet paper rolls and used Q-tips. "My family was no good—turned their backs on me when I needed them. Lyle was a worthless husband and daddy." We agree on at least one thing. "Now all I'm left with is you treatin' me like a burden."

I drop the bag of trash at the door and give her a deadpan look. "The nerve of Zeb to become an addict and die without considering the fact you'd be stuck with me."

She drops her head back with an incredulous sound then taps another Lucky out of the box, lighting it with a long drag.

The truth is, in the hardest days when I miss Zeb the most, I'm furious at him, but not for the same reasons as Glory. I'm pissed he wouldn't let me help. Pissed he couldn't see all the people he had who wanted him here. Who would have done anything so that he'd still be here. Pissed that as much as Glory's stuck with me, I'm stuck with her, Zeb nowhere around for me to call and commiserate with when I leave here after every visit.

And at my very lowest moments when his absence is the loudest, I hate him. For all of it.

"What have you been doing?" Smoke leaks out of her mouth with each word. "You have cuts on your hands. That part of your ridiculous job burning all those bodies? You should hear what my friends say about that. They think you're a freak."

"Can't wait to meet them." I pick up my purse and open the door, tossing the bags of trash onto the porch in hopes she'll eventually get them to the trailer park dumpster. "I got a house. On the lake."

"On the lake?" She stills mid-drag. "How'd you afford that?"

"It was given to me." I roll my shoulders. "By a friend."

Her eyes narrow.

"Archie Watkins and his wife Lydia," I explain. "You know them?"

She jolts upright in her recliner and snatches the cigarette from her mouth, glaring.

"Never heard of them." Her voice has a harder edge than usual. *Okay.*

"Well, Archie died, and he wanted me to have it."

She says nothing, staring blankly at the TV as she nibbles on her lip, smoke from the ass end of her cigarette swirling into the air.

I don't know what she's thinking. I also don't care.

"Go figure they'd give you a house on the lake while I'm stuck here," she finally says, resettling into her recliner. "What you wanna live on that lake for anyway? Mosquitoes are as big as bald eagles." I roll my eyes. "Figures you'd live there though. Fancy clothes. Fancy job. Hoity lake house. It's like you live your life tryin' to make me look bad."

"Got me," I say dryly.

"Figured as much." She looks at me, gently rocking in the over-sized recliner as *The Price is Right* blares a winning bell. "It won't work, you know."

I frown from the doorway. "What won't?"

"A fancy new house. Won't change where you came from. You could run away as far as your legs could carry you—an island, a desert, a damn igloo on the top of the globe. Can't outrun where you come from, Scotty Ann. Can't hide from it neither."

Her words slam into me like a wrecking ball, but I refuse to argue. Refuse to let her worm her way into my head and bore holes into my plan. I can get away from this place; I will. "Good to know."

Cigarette wobbling on her lips, she regards me once more. "The Callahan boy is back in town. Got here earlier this year. Maybe if you weren't such a bitch he'd take you back. You remember him, don't ya?"

The urge to laugh in her face then smother her with a pillow is hard to contain.

"Barely." She opens her mouth to say more, but I'm done. I've reached my Glory quota of hearing what a disappointment I am, how hard her life is, and God knows what she wants to say about Ford. "I'll see you in a few weeks. Call me if you need anything. Get your own beer."

Before I drive away, I smack the steering wheel and scream until I can't. When the sound of fast violins fills the air, I match the speed by flooring the gas. The only thing keeping me from having a complete come apart is knowing in four more months, I'll never have to make this trip again.

Sixteen

"You and Dondi are leaking body fluids onto my bed."

Wanda blows and pops a bubble with a loud smack, not looking at me as she takes the long-handled broom off the rack in the cremation room. "One, it's my bed right now. Two, and?"

"And?" I ask, incredulous. "That's a bit—"

Dondi walks into the room with a whistle, winking at Wanda and smiling his gap-toothed grin while giving me an exaggerated bow. "The Ash Queen is in the house, and The Dondinator is here to serve"—he cuts his eyes to Wanda—"by any means necessary."

I roll my eyes, taking a clipboard from him to sign for the body he's brought before handing it back. He smacks Wanda on her ass, and she giggles as he walks out.

"Jesus. I spend less time here for a few weeks and you two are . . ."

"Happy?" she fills in, perfectly arched eyebrows raised as she bats her dark eyelashes.

"Horny," I correct, tone clipped.

She huffs a breath, eyeing me sideways as she drags the broom from the back of the retort toward the front, directing the cremated remains to a collection funnel. "What crawled up your hiney and died?"

I scoff, adjusting my Billie Holiday T-shirt.

She leans the broom against the wall then kneels to pull the bin of cremains from its cubby, giving it a little shake. "You're grumpy, what's going on, honey?"

"Do you think I'm a bitch?"

She cackles, loud, before stifling it when she catches my annoyed expression, tops of her boobs bouncing like Jell-O in a bowl. She clears her throat. "I think that you can be a little . . . harsh . . . when you feel uncomfortable." She sets the bin on a table and rests her hands on my shoulders, sliding her palms down the dark blue sleeves of my blazer. Her big hair moves like a solid mass as she tilts her head. "When people in here thank you for what you do, how you handle each person with such care even if you didn't know them. You say something funny, self-deprecating about how you have them fooled. Hell, you told me I could stay in the apartment, and when I thanked you it was almost like you wanted to jump out of your skin. But you have a heart of gold. Sometimes you hide it, but everyone still sees it, honey."

I rub my tongue behind my teeth. My mother's words don't usually hang with me—and it was by no means the first time she's ever called me a bitch—but hearing it yesterday in relation to Ford after making him swim across the lake stuck with me.

"Do you ever, I don't know, think because of who you are you're trapped?"

She must. Wanda the Wicked, unable to get a normal job in her field or an apartment with her name, can't possibly be happy in her life in a town like Ledger.

"I think," she says, adjusting the ruffled hem of her shirt so somehow more cleavage appears at her neckline, "that I was trapped in one situation, so I did what I had to do to get out of it." She raises her eyebrows with her maybe-confession. "I'd rather be where I am now than where I was. I know what people say about me, but I don't care. And you don't seem to care. And based on what Dondi does to me with his tongue in your bed, he really doesn't care."

At my grimace, she giggles, picking up the cremains-filled bin and starting toward her workshop, me following.

"All I'm saying is, we're damned if we do, damned if we don't. If I'm going to be damned, I'd rather it be on my own terms. I decided long ago that I'd stop worrying about what was and worry about now."

"Now," I repeat, considering, as she sets the bin on a table and drags a magnet through its contents, nothing sticking to it.

She glances at me before dumping everything in the cylindrical canister of the cremulator, putting the lid on, and starting it. The hum fills the room as it works to turn the cremains into an even consistency.

"Now to forever," she clarifies, "that's what matters. What happened before?" She shrugs. "Ain't no changing that, honey. Ain't no point dwelling on it neither."

"Hm." I watch as she moves around the room to take makeup out of a drawer in preparation for the next body. Like a broken spigot blasting water, the last couple of days flood me. Ford's words from days prior calling me scared. His face against my window after I made him swim. June's annoying-ass texts. And Glory. Just . . . fucking Glory. "You just, what, pretend it didn't happen?"

She snorts a laugh. "Can't live through that and pretend it didn't happen, honey. One piece of life doesn't have to determine the rest is all." In my silence: "You ever had bad sex?"

I laugh at the segue. "Haven't we all?"

"You have sex again after that?"

She pops a bubble with her gum, and I nod. "Sure."

"Well, think of it like sex. Just because it's bad once, don't mean it has to be bad forever. You find someone else, someone that knows what you need. Life ain't no different. Who cares about the bad lay, you think about the now. The good one that's comin', if you catch my drift." She winks. "Learn from the past but don't dwell on it, you know?"

"Now to forever." I let her slogan roll around on my tongue, unsure about its flavor. About the idea of just living today and looking at the future like all the shit that came before isn't relevant. Like I might not be damned because every Armstrong that came before me was.

She raises her perfect eyebrows, looking at me as she rests one hand on the door to the body cooler. "Now to forever, honey."

The linoleum I'm attempting to pry from the kitchen floor is clinging to the wood beneath it like it's adamantly opposed to being removed, and I hate everything about renovating a house.

Molly barks and I scowl. The dog is my nemesis. Aside from eating my vibrator and shoes, she has acquired a taste for the wooden handles of tools and my best underwear.

Wren walks in—cutoff shorts, dark-blue sweatshirt with a mountain design on it, a whole stick of eyeliner smeared on her lids, and combat boots—and drops her backpack inside the door. Molly trots over to her and obediently sits, acting the opposite of the little shit-bitch she is.

"Hey," I say without stopping my work. I push the large floor scraper like a push broom with a grunt, wedging up a mere millimeter of flooring with my efforts. "Haven't seen you in a few days."

She blows out a breath with a loud puff. "We had stuff with my grandparents. I had a big essay that was due and some social studies thing."

"Ah." I shove the scraper in vain. "I'll be sure to dock your pay."

"By all means."

She watches me work until she seems to decide she wants to help, grabbing the other scraper and prying the linoleum with me.

"You and my dad got a lot done in the kitchen the other day."

I grunt.

"And he came home in wet clothes . . ."

"He went swimming," I say, scraping harder.

"And he was in a bad mood."

"Fine," I add, more aggression in my movements. "He went swimming against his will."

"Why?"

"Jesus, Wren," I snap, driving my scraper into the wooden sub-floor making it splinter. I glare at her. "Drop it."

The truth is, I feel like shit about it. The truth is, every word Ford said to me was true. The truth is, since I don't know what to do with any of it, my current plan is to pretend it doesn't bother me even though the visual of him pressing up against the window has lingered in my periphery ever since it happened.

She mutters something under her breath and rolls her eyes. But, to my surprise, she keeps scraping.

Not another word is spoken until the linoleum is peeled up and dragged outside. I grab us two bottles of water from a mini-fridge in the middle of the living room.

"It's my turn for a question," I say after a long sip. "Why do you wear the sweatshirts?"

"I get cold," she says, defensive as she pinches the sleeves in her fingers.

"You're sweating, but okay." I take another sip, studying the way her long bangs are matted to her forehead.

"What happened to your brother?"

"Going right for the jugular today, huh?" I huff. "He died."

She raises her eyebrows, like *really?*

"Fine. He liked drugs and they didn't like him back. He got arrested for breaking into a house—I'm sure your dad told you that much—and after that he spiraled. Fast. Lost his job, seemingly lost his mind. Someone found him with a needle in his arm—a concerned neighbor or something—and"—I shrug—"as they say, the rest is history."

"And your dad died?"

"Yes. Went on a little bender of his own." I give her an empty smile. "And that's two questions, by the way."

Another token eye roll.

"Why did you tell me your mom was a poet?"

This earns a thoughtful look. "My dad and I used to read a book of poems when I was little. I always wondered what the people were like that wrote them—women I imagined. Mother Goose energy. People asked me about my mom, poet sounded better than what she really was. Nothing. Awful. A train wreck. All of the above." She smiles but it's sad. "And I like acrostic poems."

I get it. Completely. "Even though everyone knew my parents, I introduced myself as an orphan."

She laughs softly. "I'll try that one sometime." She screws the lid on her water bottle. "And your second question?"

I grin. "Wanna write an acrostic poem?"

She smiles fully.

And we do. All over the now-revealed subfloor of the house with black markers. Hers are better than mine. More soulful and wordy. I use small words like *sky* to write *Sometimes Kites Yank*, but hers are more thoughtful. More heartfelt. Just more.

My favorite is with home:

However long it takes
Over days and weeks and months
My spirit will live in these walls
Even on nights when it's hard.

"Your mom might not be a poet," I tell her, rereading her words over and over. "But you sure as hell are."

She looks at me with a rare soft expression. No eye roll. No smart-ass response. She takes my words for what they are: a compliment.

The wood, tarnished with old glue and scrapes is now also covered in words and bold letters. It's pure magic. I can see the people that end up living here shuffling sock-covered feet over a floor that floats just above it. If they stand long enough over the right ones, some of that mystical energy might shoot right up into their toes and make their bones tingle.

As Ford's truck pulls into the driveway, I barely notice the person I imagine standing in the socks is me.

SEVENTEEN

"THERE IS A CHANCE I handled the canoe situation poorly."

Ford gives me a *go to hell* look as he fills the bird feeders with seed. "That some kind of apology?"

He tosses the empty bag into the back of his truck with more force than necessary before opening a box of birdseed bricks and cages. He unwraps them, puts the bricks into the cages and hangs them up with the other bird feeders. *Weird.*

"Something like that."

He grunts. "Needs work."

"Fine." I clench my teeth. "I'm sorry that you found the need to put me in a situation where I needed to make you swim across the lake."

He tosses the empty box in the truck bed, slamming the tailgate closed. "You know what your problem is, Scotty?"

"I have a feeling you're about to tell me, *Ford*."

"You let the shit in your life ruin every good thing."

I suck in a sharp breath. "Don't you dare even pretend to know what I do or don't do. You've been gone. You don't get to strut back into town and start psychoanalyzing me like a shrink. You left. You. Left."

"And you let me," he shouts, hands in the air. "You ever think of that?" he demands, standing close to me as his chest rises and falls with his angry breaths. "I messed up, but you weren't exactly breaking my door down finding out where I went."

"Oh," I huff in a near shout. "Oh. Don't even do this. Don't put this on me."

He shakes his head with a disbelieving laugh. "You're so full of shit!"

"Better than anything you could fill me with."

He glares at me. "If you let me get in this truck without apologizing, I won't come back. Not as a friend. Not as anything."

"Well, leaving me in the dust is your specialty, so I'm sure you'd have no problem with that."

"I'm sorry!" he shouts, shocking me to a mute stillness. "I don't have a problem saying it and I have—over and over. I'm sorry I let your brother go in that house. I'm sorry—" He shakes his head, swallowing as if needing to regroup. "I'm sorry I didn't go hunt you down in the woods to tell you when everything happened. I'm sorry I let you carry this alone. I'm sorry I loved you and I left you and it took twenty years for me to come back here and try to make up for all this. But I *am* sorry. And I'll say it as many times as you need to hear it. But you don't get to do the things you do and play your fucking mind games and not apologize. So, right now, say it or I swear to God, I'm gone."

Despite the desperate look in his eyes, the fact my insides feel too big for my outsides, and the way his raw honesty peels the skin right off my skeleton, I say nothing.

Resignation fills his eyes and his voice drops. "Okay then."

He walks to the front of his truck, opens the driver's door and—

"Wait!" I shout. He stills, looking at me but keeping a hand on the door. My throat is so constricted it's a physical feat to get the next words out. "I'm sorry," I rasp. He slams the door and turns to me, waiting. "When you look at me that way you look at me—I don't know what to do with it. Making you swim was probably not the best consequence."

He walks to where I'm standing at the back of his truck. "What way do I look at you?"

"Like—" He steps so close to me I can feel the warmth of his breath and smell the mint. I pull my head back, trying to find more air to breathe, but stand firm. "Like you want to keep looking. Like you think I'm . . ."

"You're what?"

I swallow. "Worth it."

"You are."

Instead of gouging his eyes out like I want, I stay completely calm and still, trying like hell to ignore the ridiculous dance my heart and breath and belly are doing. "Keep saying things like that and you'll be back in the lake."

He drops his chin to his chest, shaking his head as he puffs out a laugh. "That was shit as far as apologies go."

"Noted."

"I want to keep looking at you," he says, tucking a strand of hair behind my ear. "Like you're worth it."

"And if I say no?"

His tongue darts out and swipes across his bottom lip. He's got scruff on his jaw. The dark hair on his head is slightly disheveled. "You going to?"

I bite back a smile, looking away from his face. I should tell him I don't care what he does with that ugly mug of his. That he needs to leave me the hell alone and fix his kid himself. That I can feed my own birds and demo my own house. That I'm leaving in months, and this has nowhere to go but over. I should say all these things, but before I can, Ford runs his knuckles along my jaw and stops them under my chin, lifting just enough my eyes are forced to meet his. He leans in, so close I could lick him like a lollipop if I stuck my tongue out. My body responds like a damn turncoat. All heat and trembles in places I should definitely not be heating and trembling. "Maybe."

"Ah," he says, voice low and a whispery breeze across my skin as his knuckles drag—slowly—down the side of my neck. "And if I said I've been thinking about kissing you?"

"I would say your thoughts do nothing for me." Translation: Your thoughts are making me hot and bothered as hell in my front yard next to these stupid bird feeders.

I'm no good for anyone, but God I want Ford—desperately. I don't know how to let someone get close, but every single time he gets vulnerable and lays it all on the line, he excavates everything I've ever felt for him, and despite all the hurt and heartache, I want to be as close to him as a second layer of skin.

If he kissed me, I would melt. If he said he wanted to slam me like a hammer, I would let him. Until I splintered. Repeatedly.

Stroking my skin with his thumb, he leans in close and says, "Good thing that's not what I'm thinking." He drops his hand, cool as a cucumber as I choke on air. "I barely know you. I need you to ask me to ask you out on a date."

"Ha!" I take a step away from him for more oxygen. "Is that your way of asking me out?"

A faint curve pulls at the edge of his mouth. "Not this time. I'm not doing all the chasing this go around."

My eyebrows pinch; he laughs.

"You heard me. I want us to try, but it can't be like it was before. You pushing me away and me ignoring it. I know you feel what I'm feeling—know you want me to keep showing up—but I need to hear it."

"A date with the Golden Boy," I say, pulling my shoulders back to compensate for the wanton-quality of my voice. "Would ruin my reputation."

"Good to know, Viper." He smirks. Like he knows what's in my head. "I'll wait. You just say the words." We look at each other a beat longer, then he takes another step back, pointing his thumb over his shoulder into the house. "Show me what you and Wren did today."

He follows me inside, not bothering to hide his amusement when he sees the marker-covered floor. "Wren and her acrostic poems. Hand me a marker."

I do; he writes the letters S-C-O-T-T-Y down in a line. I take another one, writing F-O-R-D.

I'm still writing when he stands to leave. "I have to get home."

I walk him out, disappointed as I lean against the door. "Thanks for the birdseed cages."

He chuckles, crossing the porch and turning at the bottom of the steps. "They're suet cakes. Woodpeckers like them."

"Anything to keep your harem happy."

He doesn't respond, merely strolls to his truck and lifts his hand in a wave before disappearing down the road.

Inside, I scoop up his marker, stopping when I see what he'd written.

Someday I'll tell you the
Color of your eyes is my favorite shade
Over every feather of every bird
Then you'll know you're worth it
Tomorrow I'll be back and I hope
You'll let me look at you without making me swim

When I reread mine—*Fuck Off you Royal Dick*—it doesn't seem near as funny as it did when I wrote it. Mostly because I don't mean a single word.

EIGHTEEN

WHILE EVERY DIYING MANIAC on the internet made me think I'd be done with my house in a weekend, a month in and it looks worse than it did the day I moved in. Bare floors, bare walls, no furniture. All that remains in the gutted downstairs is the wood-stove, a mini fridge, and a microwave. Other than the bathrooms I've decided out of sheer exhaustion to hire out, it's a blank slate if a blank slate was wood paneled and triangular.

Even with the delays, the house will still be ready by Thanksgiving for June's ridiculous feast and, per the weekly emails I get from Vince reminding me of all the money we're going to make, will be listed on December first.

And yet.

The more I move forward, the more complicated my feelings get. The more I start to imagine myself here beyond a single season. Despite the lack of people in my life to fill the house, I wish I had enough money to load it onto the back of a truck and take it with me to wherever it is I end up going.

"We just scraped all that wallpaper and you want to put more up?" Wren asks with a groan, glaring at the floral printed material in my hands. "What the hell is wrong with you?"

"Don't swear."

"You swear all the time."

"Fine, I'll quit." She looks at me like I can't do it, and I give her a silent look that says *watch and fucking learn.* "As I was saying, this is just a little wallpaper for that weird-shaped wall under the steps. See the greenish blue in the flowers? It will go with the paint." I hold the paint chip out, and her neutral expression confirms my decision. "Told you I'm *clucking* smart." I grin; she rolls her eyes. "Anyway, we should technically do the wallpaper last, but I'm worried I won't like it—and it's small—so let's start there and we'll paint the other walls after."

"Your pyramid, your rules," she mutters.

A Third Eye Blind record plays as we get to work, rolling the paste on and lining up strips. "How's school been?" I ask, holding the ladder as she smooths the paper near the top with a wide-bladed scraper.

She shrugs, her oversized sweatshirt hanging off her shoulders. "Fine. My grandma homeschooled me for the last few months of school when we moved here in the spring, so I'm still the new kid, but it's not bad."

"And"—I trade her scraper for another strip of wallpaper, and she works to line the pattern up—"do they know about your mom?"

"I'm not a psycho," she says, smoothing bubbles out of the paper. "The kids at my old school knew, that's why my dad wanted to move here. Fresh start." She rolls her eyes. "Adults always think a fresh start is the answer."

I almost laugh at how ironic the statement is: her here because Ford was chasing a fresh start, me leaving because I'm doing the same.

"And it isn't?"

"My mom's still in prison, still killed someone, still wanted to do drugs and whatever else she did more than she wanted me." She smooths a palm along the wallpaper. "Doesn't seem like where I live matters that much." *God, she's smart.* In my contemplative silence, she adds, "But I'm fine."

Fine. I know that word and know it never means what it's supposed to. Fine is the word used to make everyone else more comfortable. It means falling apart but hiding it. When parents choose something else—something poisonous. When there's loss. Heartbreak. When I watched my brother spiral like dirty dishwater draining from a kitchen sink. Me spending the last twenty years making decisions in hopes of actually being *fine.*

Fine: Pretending to be someone else at the lake when I was a kid.

Fine: The desperation I felt after things fell apart and left me hollow as a dead tree trunk.

And then it hits me: Maybe I'll never be fine. Maybe she's right. Maybe fresh starts don't exist for people like me. Maybe the constant red thread that's always connected me to where I came from will never end, not a pair of scissors in the world strong enough to cut it.

And most terrifying: Maybe leaving won't change a damn thing, just like Glory said.

I clear my throat.

"It's okay not to be fine, you know," I say, passing her another strip of wallpaper. "I don't know if anybody I trusted told me that when I was younger, and maybe you and I aren't so different. I acted out after . . . everything. Drank more than I should have. Dated some real winners. And it's taken a while for me to be fine."

"You're fine now?" she asks, brows pinched in skepticism as she looks down over her shoulder.

"Of course, I am." I hold my palms up. "Fine as a f—" She raises her eyebrows. "—isherman on a bass boat."

She smooths the last strip. At the top, in the corner where the wall meets the ceiling, excess paper droops down. I frown. "Let me get a razor blade to clean that up."

She holds out her hand. "I'll do it."

I pass her the blade; she drags it along the corner.

"Crap!" she hisses, stopping abruptly to suck her finger. "The blade slipped."

She comes down the ladder, blood bursting at the tip of her index finger.

"Bathroom," I command, guiding her with a hand on her shoulder down the hall.

At the sink, she rinses her finger, blood mixing with water down the drain of the puke-green sink. "I don't think you'll need stitches." I try to examine the cut. "Let me look for Band-Aids."

"It's fine," she says, jerking her hand away from me.

"Okay, nice try. Your dad will arrest me if I send you home bleeding. Let me look." She tries pulling away from me, but I slide the sleeve of her sweatshirt up on her forearm, high enough it stays dry so I can get a firm grip.

"Scotty! Stop!" she yells, trying to pull her arm away again.

"Jesus, Wren. What the hell is wrong with you?" I squeeze my fingers around her arm, wrestling to still her.

Then I look in my hand and see her arm. Covered in white lines. Scars. At least a dozen.

I look at her; her black-rimmed eyes are desperate and filling with tears as they bounce back and forth between mine. Frantic.

No.

I push her sleeve all the way up, heart pounding in my chest as every tally mark of grief is revealed between her wrist and her elbow. "You've been cutting yourself," I whisper. Two are newer. Red and still healing. "Jesus, Wren."

At her other arm, I touch her skin like I'm not sure if she's really there. Like maybe my eyes are lying. She doesn't fight me as I slide the sleeve up revealing the same marks all the way up to her elbow. My chest feels like it's been dug out with a shovel and filled with lead.

"Take off your pants," I demand. I had a college roommate who cut herself. All over her inner thighs and across her stomach. "Now."

Tears drip down her cheeks. "They aren't anywhere else."

"Dammit, Wren, let me see." She pulls her leggings down, just to her knees—I see her inner thighs are clean. "Now your stomach." She hesitates. "Now!" I shout, emotion burning my eyes and throat.

She lifts her shirt; her stomach is unmarked.

We look at each other, both quiet and unmoving.

"Okay," I whisper. "This is all going to be okay."

With a sharp inhale, Wren drops her face to her hands and lets out a loud cry. My response is reflexive: I wrap my arms around her, and she leans into me with all her weight, sobbing. Her screams and cries highlight the lie of fine—it never is.

We drop to the tile floor, her in my arms. "I'm so sorry, Scotty," she sobs. Over and over and over. Her cries turn to sniffles and mix with my *shhh*s.

All I can think: I'm in over my head.

I have no clue what to do, how to help her, or why I'm the one sitting with her on this hideous bathroom floor. She deserves someone better. Smarter. A mother who didn't fuck her whole life up.

Hugging her knees to her chest, she sits up, her smeared eyeliner painting her face.

"Does your dad know?" I ask, resting my back against the bathtub.

She shakes her head, sniffling. "He might suspect, but he hates when we fight. He'd never bring it up unless he knew for sure."

I nod, shell-shocked and heartbroken.

"Are you going to tell him?" she asks with a sniff.

Once I realized she was okay, it's the only thing I've been thinking of. If I tell him, I lose her trust, which is what he wanted out of me spending time with her. If I don't tell him . . . I can't even think about that. I bite a nail. "I don't know." I chew until my finger bleeds then move on to the next one. "When was the last time?"

Through sniffles: "A few weeks ago."

I'm not sure what the protocol is for this. "Why?"

"Because"—she starts to cry again—"my dad found the weed and got mad at me." I pass her a roll of toilet paper and she blows her nose. "And I knew about you before I met you. He told me about you. And your brother. So"—she exhales a shaky breath—"I don't know." New tears follow, and she says something garbled that I can't understand. "And I should have just told you he was my dad, but not many people want to hang out with a cop's kid."

"Especially that cop." My joke flops; neither of us laugh.

She blows her nose again.

"Why do you do it?" I ask. "What does it feel like?"

Her eyes widen slightly, caught off guard by my directness. "I started after my mom went to prison. A kid at school knew, called me a convict baby. Even though my dad's a decorated cop and zoomed around Atlanta like a superhero." She scoffs as she shakes her head, wiping her eyes with a wad of toilet paper. "I accidentally cut myself doing dishes on a glass that night, but instead of it hurting, I felt relief. Like I had so much pain in me it needed to be bled out. It's just—some days I'm fine, and then all the sudden I remember my mom killed someone's daughter, and I don't know what to do with that."

I go dizzy at the visual.

"Are you mad at me?"

Despite the mental health crisis exploding in my ugly bathroom, I laugh. "I'm the furthest thing from mad, Wren. I'm . . . sad. Scared. Completely clueless." I blow out a long and weighted breath. "This is why people who read monster romance don't have kids." She almost smiles. "Text your dad, tell him I'm dropping you off."

She punches at her watch, then stares at me.

"I don't know," I tell her, answering the question we're both thinking as I stand from the bathroom floor. "What I'm going to do or not do, I just—I need time. And, if we do this—if I keep it between us—you listen to everything I say, got it?"

"Yes. I swear." She sniffs as she stands. "Please, Scotty."

"If I see a new cut, I'm telling him."

She nods.

"Are you—" I swallow, scared to finish the question. "Do you want to die?"

Her eyes go as wide as baseballs. "No."

"Okay." I have no way of knowing if she's telling the truth, but I hope she is. Desperately.

Then it strikes me right between the eyes how hard this is. How royally fucked-up parenthood must be. One minute you're scraping wallpaper and laughing, the next you're in an outdated bathroom, everything falling apart without a soul to tell you what to do. Nothing to guide you but panic and a prayer that feels too small. You inhale without a care in the world only to find your lungs collapsed on the exhale.

I'm not made for this; I don't have a clue.

I study Wren in the Bronco, her gaze out the window, and a deluge of doubt washes over me along with a twisted feeling of confirmation. Because if I can't handle one hard moment with a kid, I know for certain my choice not to be a mother was also my best.

NINETEEN

"I'm Winter and I'm addicted to winning."

Winter's rhinestone-clad shirt faintly sparkles under the overhead fluorescent lighting of the basement as she chuckles softly. Mel gives her a look from the puny podium but stays quiet.

"Right. Anyway," Winter continues. "It just started out as a hobby, you know. I was bored one day. My husband watches football every Saturday, Sunday, Monday, Thursday." She ticks the days off on her fingers and sticks her tongue out, as if to emphasize how annoying this is, but her pink lips are smiling. "So I just thought, what if I had my own fun—bet on the games so I could be more engaged. Like marriage therapy or something." The familiar sounds of the LL meetings occur in her pause: the sliding of the metal folding chairs, a cough, someone texting, a crunch on a stale cookie. I look at the coffee in my hands, the thought of tasting it nearly makes me gag.

Winter lets out a long sigh, toying with her dark ponytail. "Well, after that, I just couldn't stop. I'd win; I'd fly. I'd be clapping and hollering. And I mean, my husband loved that I was watching the ball games. It was only ten dollars here or twenty there. Then I'd lose." Her eyes widen. "I got even more frantic to win again. Like, just one more bet. And, you know, they make it so easy—right on your dang phone and linked to your bank account!" She says it with a tone that implies *can you believe this?* "I read once it has something to do with the dopamine—why it's so fun, you know?

"It was fine, and then, over the summer, it was the Olympics and"—a breath whooshes out of her like air deflating from a tire—"I got us into some trouble." She picks at one of the rhinestones on her shirt. "I drained our savings account, and now here I am. Trying to fix my mess or something. So, that's my pitiful story." She smiles, but it's sadder than before. "Now football season is here and . . ."

"What if you took the apps off your phone?" I ask, cutting the silence.

Winter tilts her head as Mel mutters, "Christ, Scotty. Here we go."

"Well," Winter says thoughtfully. "I'd still know it's there. Out of sight don't mean out of mind when I know how good winning feels. I didn't bet on a single game last weekend, though." She beams at this.

"What about another hobby?" I press, sitting up taller. "When your husband watches football, you could knit or something."

"I—"

"Do you even want to quit?" I snap, Winter's cheery expression crashing. I've never understood why people don't just stop. Why my brother never stopped. I never said it out loud, but deep down I wondered if it was as simple as him never wanting to. Like drugs gave him something nothing else could despite the damage they were causing. Like he simply didn't give two shits about what anyone thought. Maybe Wren's mom was no different: using because she wanted to. Because she was selfish. The sentiment makes my blood boil with rage. "It doesn't even sound like you're trying." I'm shouting now. "What will your kids think if they see this? Do they know about the money?"

Winter looks like she's on the verge of tears.

"Scotty!" Mel shouts, the entirety of Ledger's Ledgers staring at me with wide eyes, gaping mouths, and Styrofoam cups of shouldn't-even-be-called-coffee in hand. "Enough!"

My mouth snaps shut, and I sag back in my chair. Mel redirects the meeting to an alcoholic taking their turn to share; I don't bother asking him any questions.

I was harsh, sure, but it's not like it matters. Months of me saying what I say—trying to help them—yet here they all are making the same stupid choices, me not making a lick of difference. While I normally sit in here and stew about my decayed family tree, everyone today has made me think of Wren. Her mom choosing everything else over her, leading to where she is now: sad, scarred, and shattered to pieces.

And, of course, there's the fact that I didn't tell Ford, which has been festering in me like some kind of world-ending plague.

It's been nearly a week, and though I've seen Wren nearly every day—examining her body for fresh cuts like I know what the fuck I'm doing as she rolls her eyes—I've avoided him.

He fills up the birdseed; I wave and pretend I have somewhere to go.

He comes by to check on Wren; I tell him she's fine.

He looks at me the way he looks at me; I threaten to throw him in the lake.

"Well, that was quite a show," Mel says as we stand outside, meeting attendees scattering toward their cars around us. She takes a long drag from her cigarette followed by a smoke-filled exhale. "Even for you."

"I aim to please," I say dryly.

"You ever hear insanity is doing the same thing over and over hoping for a different result?" I nod. "Addiction feels like that. Least for me it did. If I get drunk today, maybe I won't notice she's gone. It didn't work, so I'd try again the next day. And the next."

"You're insane," I quip. "Explains so much."

Her brows lift. "As insane as the woman who continues to harass others so she can keep shouldering the blame for something that has nothing to do with her."

I give her a deadpan look. "I think my brother dying because I didn't do enough to help him has a little bit to do with me."

She drops the half-smoked cigarette to the ground and stomps it out before picking it up and tossing it in a trash can.

"Life is filled with tragedy, Scotty. People leave, people die. We feel hurt deeper than we imagine possible. Deeper than we think our bodies can bear. It's on us to decide how we respond, for better or worse."

I scoff.

"Listen," she says, annoyed. "You and your brother grew up in the same house—same parents—but what happened to him isn't on you. Hell, even your parents can't claim full responsibility. Somewhere along the way, you made a choice, he made a different one."

I . . . have never once considered this.

In my silence: "You need to let all of it go. Live for you. He doesn't have now, my daughter either, but you do." She gives a weak smile. "I do."

Wanda's *now to forever* flitters through me.

She waves at someone across the lot; my attention stays on her. "What if I don't know how?"

She flicks her eyes to me for a split second. "You do." A smile overtakes her face as she looks away from me and coos, "Officer Callahan." *Ford?* The one and only takes his final steps to us across the nearly vacant parking lot wearing his uniform. He smiles at me—it makes my veins itch—but it's Mel he hugs. "To what do we owe the pleasure?" she asks, patting his chest.

"Just thought I'd say hi. Check in." He grins at her then faces me. "Scotty."

"Officer." I look at my hands, wishing I had a cigarette, cup of coffee, or yo-yo so I had something to do with them.

"Well, I'm just fine, Ford," she says warmly. "You've done enough. You don't have to babysit me. This one though." She tilts her head my way. "Watch out."

He chuckles, his hands resting on the belt of his uniform. "Believe it or not, I think she's been avoiding me."

She gives me a pointed look.

"Sounds like something she would do."

"She thinks," I snap, "you both should stop talking about her like she's not standing right the hell here."

Mel rolls her eyes, picking up the LL sign and waving a hand through the air as she walks toward the church. "Good luck with that one, Officer."

He rakes his gaze over my fitted jeans and casual plum-colored V-neck shirt, big enough it drapes low on my chest and slightly off one shoulder. He doesn't move or say anything, but the simple act of his eyeballs moving the way they are makes heat trickle up my neck. When our gazes collide, I look away first.

Damn him.

"So," I say in the tense silence. "You got something to say, or you just here pretending to be sexy?"

He smirks, smug. "You think I'm sexy?"

"*Pretending* to be sexy; I know better."

"Noted. I'll work on it." His blue eyes smile bright, and a dimple carves into his cheek before his expression turns serious. "Something happen with Wren?"

"What?" My throat constricts with guilt. "No. Why?"

"Because you've been avoiding me for days." I don't bother arguing. "Figured it's either her or because you're nervous to ask me to ask you on a date."

At this, I laugh, some of the tension dissolving. "Hardly."

"I can see how that would be the case." He steps toward me now, opening his mouth just enough I see his tongue work across his lips as he hooks two fingers in a belt loop of my jeans, tugging my compliant body toward him. "Me pretending to be sexy can be pretty intimidating."

"Ah." I shove my hands in the back pockets of my jeans to keep from climbing him like a sin-stepped ladder in the church parking lot. "You see right through me."

"But I'm here now, Scotty, and I can assure you there's nothing to be nervous about." He's smiling fully, and its impact on my insides is stupid. Tugging my belt loops again, my hips bump into his. "And I think you've been waiting for the perfect moment of you standing outside an LL meeting—which, I can't wait to hear the story behind—to ask me."

"Really?" *Why am I playing along?* "And what would you say, should you find me standing outside an LL meeting, and I said I wanted such a thing as a date with you?"

"I'd say—" He leans in close to me, his lips grazing my ear when he speaks, sending a shiver down my spine, "Let me pick you up Friday."

Maybe it's what Mel just said, but I don't hesitate: "Okay."

"See," he says, grinning as he releases his hands from my jeans and takes a step backward, my body noticing the space the second he pulls away. "Wasn't that easy?"

I pinch my lips tight to hide my amusement, saying nothing as I watch him walk away, knowing smirk angled across his face. A breeze whispers against my skin, and he waves across the parking lot before slipping into his car. Next to my Bronco, June's minivan is parked. She's leaning against the hood, raising two coffees in my direction, grinning.

"What are you doing here?" I ask as I step next to her, taking a coffee she offers.

"Whatever you are," she says, eyebrows raised nearly to the messy red bun on the top of her head.

I give her a look as I take a sip from my cup, relishing in the flavor with satisfied moan. "Thank God. I think there's a demon in that church out to steal the tastebuds of Ledger."

"And Ford?" she asks, opening the back of her van so we can sit on the bumper.

I take another sip of my coffee. *The only man that I've ever loved who won't stop saying all the right things and I can't stop fantasizing about when I'm using my B-squad vibrator?* Not going there. "Complicated."

"Okay," she drawls, blowing out a sharp sigh. "The house coming along? Your moving plans?"

The house that I'm renovating to sell but am actually starting to like? Not touching that one either. "Hm," I say with another sip.

"No," she snaps. "You don't get to *hm* me."

My head whips to face her. Her typical creamy skin is red and her usually kind eyes are wide and filled with seven different shades of pissed off.

"What is *that* supposed to mean?"

She guffaws with a somewhat maniacal tilt of her head "What is *that* supposed to mean?" she shouts. "You *hm* when you're fortifying your walls. You *hm* when something is uncomfortable. You *hm* when you're deciding to move to the damn desert without rhyme or reason. You don't get to *hm* me when we're talking about Ford or your new house that you haven't let me see yet. Don't you dare fucking *hm* me, Scotty Armstrong."

She blows out an angry breath, glaring at me and clutching the cup of coffee in her hands like she's trying to crush it. In the entirety of our years of friendship, she's never once yelled at me like this.

"Fine," I say, looking at her like the psycho she's being. "Ford asked me out. Again."

Her eyes widen. "And?"

"And I said yes." Her eyes widen even further. Before I chicken out, I add, "And Wren's been cutting herself and I haven't told him."

She chokes on her coffee; I tell her everything. And like the wonderful friend I know I don't deserve, she walks me through solutions—complete with a lineup of podcasts I can listen to should I need more information—and helps me formulate a plan.

"She's lucky to have you," she says as we hug goodbye and she props her chin on my shoulder. "Why do you want to sell the house? You could just live there, Scott. Spend your life looking at the lake like we dreamed of when we were kids."

"What am I going to do with a house, Joo? I have no family. You're my only friend. And this town . . ."

"First"—she pulls back from me—"I come with Camp and three kids, so that's five friends." She grins when I roll my eyes. "And second, even though I don't agree with you, who cares if that's true? *This town* loves you. *This town* doesn't care about any of the stuff you're talking about. That's all you."

My eyes narrow.

"I'm serious. Rich single men live in mansions all the time. You in an A-frame with two bedrooms—which I can't confirm because you haven't let me see it—isn't so far-fetched."

I hate how right she is. Hate that some nights I lie in bed and think about what it would be like if I didn't sell it. If Mel and Wanda are right, and all I have to do is start doing what I want right now, maybe I could stay. Choose this house. Hell, maybe even choose Ford and Wren if they'd choose me.

She squeezes my cheeks with her palms. "And you hate the desert."

I frown, face smooshed between her hands. "Says who?"

"You." She drops her hands from my face and takes a step back. "When you went to Vegas for some cremation conference and a sixteen-hour marriage ten years ago." We exchange a look. I went to learn about new cremation technology but ended up drinking too much tequila and marrying a Swede named Sven by a preacher dressed as Elvis. "I asked how the desert was, and you said, *'That place is worse than a sand-filled pile of petrified shit. All people do out there is cry about water and slather on lotion. My nose bled more in two days than my uterus during a week-long red tide."*

Her impression is good; it sounds like something I'd say.

"I've turned over a new leaf and it's a cactus needle," I say in a dismissive tone.

She rolls her eyes, opening the door to her minivan.

"I don't know, Joo . . . who has a whole house without pictures to hang on the wall?" I challenge. "Seems like a waste."

"Well," she says as she slips into the driver's seat. "Turns out, your *only* friend is a photographer."

She smiles up at me before driving away.

My whole route home—by the trailer park, the forgotten cross, and the two-story house with no cars in the driveway today—I can't shake the feeling that my best friend might have a point.

Twenty

"Your dad asked me out on a date," I say as I roll a line of deep-blue paint onto the wall.

"And?" Wren dips her roller in the pan then drags a diagonal line across the wall.

"And I said yes." My mouth goes dry. "Because he's so ugly I figured I'd take one for the team."

She rolls her eyes. "Right."

"And," I continue, recalling my conversation with June and the plan that followed, "first, I wanted to know if that bothers you. Someone like me going on a date with him?"

"You're asking my opinion?" she asks, dumbfounded. "Why?"

"Duh. You're his kid. You're part of this whole weird thing. And, I'm not a poet, but I want to, I don't know, make sure you won't be mad or lash out or something. I'm not trying to be your mom or anything—not that I should be anyone's mom, right?" I laugh; she doesn't. "I just want to make sure you're good with it."

"I'm not going to cut myself because you go out with my dad," she says.

I give her a look. "Not funny. But, I don't know, you've had a lot of stuff happen. I just—I don't want to be another thing, you know?"

Her roller stills on the wall, and she looks at me, unreadable expression on her face making this feel more . . . more. Nobody around me ever asked how their actions made me feel. My dad never consulted me before he went apeshit then AWOL; Glory never asked how I felt about her downing a six-pack then disappearing all night; Zeb sure as shit never got my opinion on the pills he dumped down his throat and snorted up his nose. Everyone always just did whatever they wanted, letting me deal with the leftovers like a picked-over dinner party in hell.

"All I'm saying is that I don't want you to look back and think about me going out on a date with your dad and it be something bad. Like you-you—I don't know, you'd rather he-he—" I'm stuttering like June under pressure, and I want to pound my head against the wall.

Wren puts me out of my misery. "Scotty, I don't mind," she says with a small smile. "I think you'd be good for him."

"Yeah?" I ask, relieved.

She smiles fully, resuming the movement of her roller. "You think I want a dad that's married to birds? You're, like, a full step up." She flicks her eyes to mine. "Plus, a kid would maybe be lucky to have you as a mom." I still, mid-dunk of my roller in the pan, looking at her. When she notices: "You know, if they were desperate."

I laugh softly, ignoring the weird flippity-floppity feeling in my belly. "Aside from you basically calling me mommy-of-the-year material," I tease, "I know you don't want your dad to know about what's going on, but the truth is, even though I don't have a fu—" Her dark eyelinered eyes narrow. "—nnel of knowledge of how to deal with a kid, not telling him is even screwing with my less-than-moral compass."

She nods, resigned look on her face as she sweeps another blue streak across the wall.

"I want you to go to therapy."

Her head snaps to me, eyes wide. "What? No, Scotty. Please."

"Yes." It was June's idea. Actually, June's idea was to tell Ford right away, but when I explained why I couldn't, she said I needed someone more equipped. "I looked it up. I can take you without being your guardian. I made an appointment for next week at a place over in Rocky Ridge. Nobody should recognize us."

"Do I have a choice?"

"You do," I say, dragging my roller across the wall. "We can tell your dad."

She lets out an ugh-like groan.

"Fine." She sloshes the paint around the pan too aggressively with her roller, making it splash over the edge and onto the acrostic-poem-covered floor. She looks at me, like she's daring me to say something; I look right back, daring her to tempt me.

I put my roller down and grab a gift bag, offering it to her.

She sets her roller in the pan and wordlessly takes it, pulling out a bag of rubber bands, a fidget spinner, and a journal. Her eyes lift to mine.

"I read these might help," I explain. "The rubber bands are for your wrist; you snap it when you get the urge to . . . When you hurt. It helps, I guess. I read. The rest are self-explanatory." I bat my tongue around my mouth, uncharacteristically uncomfortable as her eyes go from me to the things.

She opens the bag of rubber bands, pulling out two before setting everything else to the side. She offers me one.

My eyes narrow.

"For when you hurt."

I can't make the words *I don't hurt* come out of my mouth, so I take the rubber band, emotion clogging my throat as we slip them onto our wrists.

She picks up a roller from the pan. "Anything else you want to use my self-destructive behavior to blackmail me into doing?"

I snort a laugh but consider the question. When we finish the wall we're painting, the walls will be done. And, because I'm not a complete sociopath, I've hired people for the next steps so I don't burn the house down or kill myself. It will be expensive, but at this point, I'll take the financial hit—I'm mentally spent on doing all this work. Electrical, plumbing, kitchen cabinet install, flooring, and trim have all been outsourced. Next comes buying furniture and décor. Other than doing the backsplash for the kitchen—which is weeks away—I need to think of something else for us to do together.

She pushes the roller of paint across the wall, her black-encircled eyes looking at me like she's waiting for some kind of sentencing. The way her long hair hides her face and awful makeup hides her features, it's like she can't even be seen. Like she doesn't *want* to be seen.

"Yes," I tell her as I pull out my phone and fire off a text. "Let's finish the wall, and then there's someone I want you to meet."

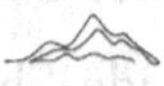

"You have skin like porcelain straight from China, honey," Wanda says with a smack of her gum, ample cleavage inches from Wren's nose as she leans over her, running her fingers through her hair. "And such a thick mane! Like a prize-winning derby horse!"

Wren looks from me to Wanda's neon fitted shirt, purple leggings, and cheetah heels, to the stainless-steel details of the room. Her stool sits smack dab in the middle of Wanda's Workshop next to the corpse of a man Wanda had been working on before I texted.

Wanda steps back, as if sizing her up, before putting her hands on her curvy hips. "Who's your inspo?" she asks.

"Inspo . . . ?" Wren asks.

Wanda pops a shoulder along with a bubble. "You know, who do you look at and think, 'That girl's got it goin' on!'?" She pats her hair sprayed mass of hair. "Mine is Dolly Parton. That woman wears a wig and a set of tits like nobody's business." She shimmies, making her own *tits* jiggle.

Wren shifts uncomfortably on her stool, eyes down, sleeves of her shirt pinched in her fingers. Despite Wanda's Wandaness, my heart crumbles.

My childhood was fucked. I hid from a lot and pretended a lot—hell, I still do—but the lengths she's gone to . . . it's like every slash I found on her arm was branded into my own skin the second I found them. The visceral way I felt her pain was almost as unexpected as seeing the cuts themselves.

"She likes Lindsey Stirling," I say.

"Lindsey Stirling . . . ?" Wanda's eyes squint and she taps her chin, as if trying to imagine such a woman.

Wren shakes her head. "Scotty."

"You don't have to be embarrassed," I tell her gently. "Look at her—Wanda, of all people, is a judgment-free zone. We can look up a pic—"

"No," Wren says, more sure this time, looking at Wanda. "When I look at Scotty, that's what I think."

My mouth opens slightly, and Wanda claps her hands, face lit up like a Christmas tree. Like this is the best news of her day. "Well of course you do, honey. She's a knockout."

When Wren's eyes meet mine, she shrugs, slight smile tugging at her lips. Wanda wraps a cape around Wren's shoulders then pulls a pair of scissors out of an apron tied around her hips.

In my forty-one years on this earth, it's the nicest thing anyone has ever said to me. And while my knee-jerk reaction is to laugh and tell her she's set her standards too low, I stay quiet, tucking the moment into a secret pocket inside me.

Wanda says something to make Wren laugh at the same time she takes the first snip with her scissors.

An hour later, Wren's hair is cut, her beautiful face visible. Gone is the dark makeup, and in its place a subtle line of brown eyeliner, peach blush, and clear lip gloss. Before I take her home, we stop by the boutique in town. She doesn't want to part with the combat boots, but she does let me buy her five new sweaters, none of them black.

At her house, she looks at me through the rolled-down passenger window, bags of clothes looped around her arms.

"I have to ask you something." She takes a sharp inhale, as if she's about to jump into a frigid pool. "Did Wanda use the same makeup on me as she does on the dead bodies?"

I laugh—loud.

"Don't ask questions you don't want the answers to."

She smiles, barely recognizable as her blue eyes sparkle just like her dad's. "Thanks, Scotty."

It hangs between us until I shift the gear into drive.

"I didn't do anything."

It earns an eye roll. "Either way, I'm really glad you said yes to my dad."

Then she's off toward her house, bounce in her step as she climbs the porch. The front door opens and there's Ford—still in his uniform, shocked and doing a double take as she walks by. She pauses to give him a hug before disappearing down a hall.

I wave but don't wait, not sure I'll be able to keep my emotions in check if he tries talking to me.

When I get home, there's a text from him. *If you were standing in front of me, I'd be looking at you like you're worth it.*

Even I can't ignore the way butterflies flutter in my stomach with one thousand tiny wings.

I respond the only way I know how: *Then I guess you'd also be in the lake.*

TWENTY-ONE

"So this is a date with forty-two-year-old Ford Callahan?" He drops the tailgate of his truck parked in a spot surrounded by at least a hundred acres of cornfields. "Pretty sure this was how the date went where you robbed me of my virgin morals."

Ford chuckles.

"You definitely led that heist." Very true. "And I'd like to think I've improved slightly with age." He pulls two blankets out of a bag and lays them across the bed of the truck. Out of the back seat, he grabs two pillows, placing them where the bed hits the cab, and a small speaker. The horizon line is painted with every shade of orange, yellow, and pink that only seems to exist when the sun sets.

I did not give Ford the satisfaction of gaping at him when he picked me up, but now that he's preoccupied by turning the bed of his truck into some kind of love nest—complete with a string of lights he's plugging into a portable battery pack—I treat myself to a good old-fashioned eye fuck.

Ford was good looking when we were young, but it's as if he grew into himself. He's in jeans and a T-shirt with a shacket over it and unbuttoned. The cuffs of his sleeves are rolled up, hitting his forearms midway. His neck is sexy at the collar, his wrists are sexy out the sleeves. Ford is a cop that boxes for sport and he looks it; I'd happily eat every piece of him with a fork. However, his body could be a soft potato because tonight it's his face that has me salivating every time I look at him. The perpetual five-o'clock shadow is gone; he's shaved smooth. The scar on his jaw is more visible as are his dimples and every curve of his lips and angle of his jaw.

His eyes, of course, are his patented shade of bright blue.

"You staring at me, Scotty?" he asks, with a smug smirk as he sets a cooler on the tailgate.

"Recording content for a mental porno I'm producing, actually."

He booms out a laugh, vibrating my chest through my sweater, and pulls out a bottle of wine, working the cork free with a corkscrew and a swift *pop!* before pouring a glass and handing it to me. He corks the bottle and grabs a bottle of Coca-Cola—made of glass—out of the cooler. He pops the top and takes a sip. The way his lips wrap around the mouth of the bottle and the column of his throat moves with his swallow turns my mind into a playground only the most devout perverts would survive. It may be ancient history, but I know what Ford Callahan can do with that mouth.

"So," I say, blowing out a breath, leaning against a taillight of his truck. "What are we doing here?"

He sets his bottle down on the tailgate. "Birding."

I snort a laugh, untouched wine sloshing in my glass. Around the rows and rows of corn, there's a thick line of trees . . . and not a single bird in the sky.

"They didn't get the invite."

Another grin and he pulls out a shotgun, laughing when my eyes widen. "They will."

"Are we hunting? The hell kind of birding requires a gun?"

"My favorite kind. Plug your ears." Before I can set the glass of wine down, he points the gun into the air and fires once. A loud *boom!* stops my heart and makes me jump, swashing wine over the rim of my glass.

I jam my palms against my ears to try to stop the ringing.

He grins. "Here it comes."

And it does.

A chaotic chatter followed by a gentle rustle before seemingly thousands of birds lift from the trees like a mass exodus into the sky. Together, they look like a gigantic puff of dark smoke drifting in perfect harmony up into the air. There's a sudden shift—an ebb and a flow of movements that has them stretch away from one another like putty before snapping back together. They don't stop—creating fluid and swirling shapes, a huge flock making art in the sky. They fan out then suck back in, as if drawn together by magic or magnets. Thousands of little pieces moving as one. A performance for no one, yet here we are witnessing it.

It goes on for minutes—like an act in a show—and we're silent as our eyes chase them across the sky with open-mouthed smiles on our faces.

If heaven has a sky, I bet these birds fill it.

As abruptly as it starts, the descent happens; they land in trees and vanish from sight somewhere on the horizon, murmuring chatters fading before it's silent again. Like they were never even ever there at all.

I'm breathless and speechless and in complete awe.

Emotion—over fucking birds—clogs my throat.

"European starlings," Ford fills in, popping the empty shell out of the chamber and tucking the gun away down the bed of the truck. "The only bird known to do it. Murmurate it's called—up." He gestures toward the back of the truck. I don't argue, hopping onto the tailgate and scooting toward the pillows, still dumbfounded by the show we just witnessed. He does the same, grabbing his bottle of Coke along the way, settling next to me as we gaze at the now-empty sky. "They're considered invasive. Destructive little bastards." He grins. "But they put on a helluva show."

"Why do they do that?"

He takes a sip of his Coke and shrugs. "I read once for protection. One bird changing direction impacts the seven around it. I liked that. Made me think maybe—I don't know—gave me some perspective, I guess."

"How so?"

"Hm." The colors of sunset tint his pensive expression. "When you go into law enforcement, you think you're going to make all these changes—help all these people. Least I did. Some days, at the end of the day—especially the hard ones—it doesn't feel like you've done jack shit. Like more people hate you than like you.

The people holding signs about hating cops are always louder than the ones thanking us. Anyway, when I read that about the starlings, I thought, well, if one bird can impact seven and then those seven each impact seven and so on. Then . . ."

"That's a lot of sevens," I finish, something nagging at me with the words. A familiarity to them.

"It's a lot of sevens," he echoes.

I watch him drink. Think of him as a cop.

That's a lot of sevens.

"What?" he asks, nudging me with his elbow.

"I never took you for a Coca-Cola guy," I say, my wine still untouched in my hand.

"Mexican Coke," he amends with a smirk. "Made with cane sugar."

Over the side of the truck, I dump my wine and toss the glass into the grass. "Give me one." His eyebrows raise in amusement. "I'm being compliant, Ford. Give me a damn Coke before I change my mind."

He does, playing the game people play where he hands it to me just out of reach and pulls it away when I get close, making me laugh against my will.

"Tell me about being a cop. That's not what you left here to do. Why the change?"

He doesn't hesitate: "Zeb."

It shouldn't shock me; I've thought this was true since he explained to me how he didn't know Zeb was going to burglarize the house and watched his best friend get arrested. But hearing him say my brother's name makes me see him anew. Instead of ushering in the grief of what happened and let it hold him hostage—instead of leading a life of being alone and perpetually surrounded by death like I did—he's changed lives. Is *changing* lives. He left and became who he was supposed to be, and as much as I've tried to hate him for that, as much as it guts me every time I think about it, I admire it. What I feel toward him is so opposite of hate it grips hold of me and refuses to let me look away from him.

"I was a business major, not sure if you remember that," he continues. "And just . . . watching how it all happened with him changed me. All of me." He shrugs, looking away from me and up to the sky. "Tried to help others the way I couldn't help him. I blamed myself for so long." He laughs softly; his words stick into me like a sharp arrow. "Guess it was a selfish act of redemption. Lose a friend, be a cop. That make sense?"

"It does." I look at the darkening sky. Ford and I have spent all these years living our lives fueled by the same fire. Both of us holding on to the past in different ways. If he wasn't sitting here now, I never would have believed it. For so long, I thought he ran away from me. Us. I've gotten so much of him wrong. I shouldn't push it; I should let old wounds heal, but I can't keep myself from asking, "Why didn't you call me? You could have told me. Said goodbye."

He looks at me, and even in the low light, there's pain in his eyes. "I was ashamed."

I almost laugh at the absurdity. Almost scream at the top of my lungs, *What in the bird-balled universe were you ashamed of?* But then I remember: I know shame. I know regret. And I know telling him all the ways it didn't have to end the way it did ultimately won't change what happened. As much as I want to lecture him on why we could have dealt with the fallout—all of it—together, I say nothing.

Instead, I take my first sip of Mexican Coke, the sweet, fizzy bubbles popping on my tongue.

"Good, right?" Ford says, lightness returning to his voice.

I laugh around the opening of the bottle. "It's not gross." Then, "So is the date over? Birds and Coke all you got, Golden Boy?"

"Hell no." He fumbles with his phone and starts music on low, and he pulls an assortment of cheeses, meats, crackers, and little containers of olives and fruit out of the cooler. "And my mom sent an apple pie."

"Might be poisoned if she knew it was coming to me."

"She's not *that* bad," he says, opening the lid of the olives and popping one in his mouth. "And she loves you."

I give him a look, grabbing an olive of my own and biting into it.

"She always spoke in maybe-phrases." His expression is both questioning and amused as he unwraps a block of cheese and places it on a cutting board across his lap along with a container of grapes. "You know, like *maybe* she was giving a compliment, or *maybe* she was plotting my death." He chuckles, putting a grape in my mouth. "I'm serious!" I chew the grape—it's tart. "She'd say, *'Scotty, you're here'* or *'Scotty, I see Ford picked you up'* or *'Scotty, I've never seen a dress like that.'* What is that?"

"It's her," he says with a chuckle, cutting into a log of salami. "And it's better than if she would have asked *why* you were there."

I scoff, taking another sip of Coke. "That's because she *knew* why I was there."

The song switches to a new track, a bird cuts across the twilight-colored sky, and I pluck another grape from the bunch, offering it to him—he nibbles it out of my fingers, eyes smiling as his lips linger on my fingertips. I notice. He notices I notice. My vagina, that thirsty bitch, really notices.

When he pulls his mouth away, he chews and swallows slowly, then says, "I liked why you were there."

I snort a laugh, stealing a slice of cheese. "Of course you liked why I was there, you pervert."

"Oh!" He laughs, making a stack with cheese, salami and a cracker. "You have a dog eating your vibrator but I'm the pervert?" He takes a bite, crumbs sticking to his chin; I wipe them.

"You jealous of my battery-operated boyfriends?" I make a cheese-meat-cracker stack.

"Depends." He takes a swig of Coke.

"Oh?" I say around a crumbly bite. "On what?"

"On who you're thinking of when you use it."

My jaw drops; the years have done a lot to Ford, including making him more forward. I like it very, *very* much.

"Cat got your tongue, Viper?" He pops an olive in his mouth with a smirk.

"No," I say with a haughty tone, "I was just thinking how awkward you'll feel when I tell you I get off thinking about math."

He laughs, and before I can register his movements, he leans over and pecks a kiss at the corner of my mouth. He pulls back—slightly—floating his knuckles over the place his lips just were. Face inches from mine, knuckles warm on my skin. I lean into his hand; his palm opens. Cups my face. And says, "I feel like I've spent the last twenty years trying to get to the back of this truck with you, Scotty."

The words penetrate my flesh and alter my chemistry. The moment is nothing—twenty-year-old me would have called it boring—but here in the glow of string lights, it's a glimpse of who we would have been if life hadn't gone so wrong.

Same, I think. *I've been waiting and it took you too damn long*, I want to shout.

When I don't respond out of fear of having a complete come apart, he pecks one more kiss on my lips, pulls away, and makes another salami-cheese-cracker stack.

"Don't hold back, Scotty," he coos before taking his first bite. "Tell me about this math you love so much." When I laugh too hard and slap him playfully on the arm, our conversation slips into nothing important as the sun dips into the cornfield, and we sit in the back of his truck like nothing else exists. No hurts and no heartaches. No past mistakes or regrets. Just us, a string of lights, a basket of food, and Mexican Cokes.

By the time the food is gone, the sky is pitch-black and the only light around us is from the strands in the truck and the sliver of moon in the sky. "Thank you for this. It was—I don't know—different than I expected."

We scoot down the bed of the truck until we're at the tailgate.

"Better I hope," he says, hopping from the truck and positioning himself so he's standing between my knees. He takes one of my hands in his, intertwining our fingers. What comes next is familiar: He brings my thumb to his lips and dusts a kiss on the end. At once: I'm a teenager.

"You remember the first time I did that?" he asks.

"No," I lie, wanting to hear him tell the story.

He vibrates with a laugh. "Well, I do." He kisses my thumb again. "I took you out on our first date—we were out at that weird pancake house that sells hats and dolls over in Springer, remember? Puddy's?"

I fail to hide my smile; I remember. Every bit. "Maybe."

"Liar." He kisses my thumb again. "But to jog your memory, I walked you out to my truck, we were holding hands, and I said, *'I want to kiss you, Scotty.'* And you said, *'You can kiss my ass.'*"

A laugh bursts out of me; it's so on-brand for both of us. Him telling me exactly how he feels, me saying the complete opposite. Even all these years later, even with all the darts life's thrown at us, we're those two teens a couple decades removed.

"And then I said," he continues, holding our hands up between us and tapping my thumbnail with his free index finger, "*'I'll kiss whatever you'll give me. Even your thumb.'*"

He did and I loved it. At sixteen, I knew I loved him.

"You always were desperate," I tease.

He mocks offense, squeezing my hand before dropping his fingers to my wrist and toying with the rubber band on my wrist.

"Wren has one of these on," he says, giving it a slight snap.

I swallow through my guilt as he repeats the motion. "Best friend bracelets."

He makes an amused sound; I redirect his attention by sliding my hands down his arms, feeling the curves of his muscles even through his thick shirt.

"Tell me about boxing."

He rakes his hands through my hair, fingers playing with the ends. "What do you want to know?"

"All of it, I guess. How you started. What you love about it."

"I started in college." His eyes bounce all over my face. "After Zeb. I had a lot—felt a lot I didn't know what to do with, and I needed to get it out." His answer catches me off guard. I always imagined he left, moved on, and that was that. I think of Wren—her telling me she needed a way to release the pain. Him becoming a cop. Now boxing. Another piece of the puzzle slips into place. "I tried a few things, but boxing stuck. I felt better. Less . . ."

"Stabby?" I offer.

He chuckles. "Stabby works. It saved me in some ways. Shit, I don't have to explain it to you—you know how it felt."

I look away from him at this—because while I absolutely know how it felt, where he and Wren are hellbent on releasing feelings, I take the easier route of pretending I don't have any.

"Anyway," he continues. "It stuck. I've kept doing it—I love it. I'm trying to buy the gym, actually."

"Really?" A dog barks in the distance. "And do what?"

He shrugs one shoulder. "Run it. Do what I haven't been able to do in law enforcement. Help kids that need it. Kids like Wren. Zeb." He swallows, pausing for one, two, three heartbeats.

I read his hesitation and fill in the word he can't say: "Me."

He tucks a strand of hair behind my ear and nods; I want to tell him I didn't need help. That I turned out fine without some boxing gym after-school special or whatever it is he's trying to do. But there's no space for me to talk because so much adoration for him swells in me it presses against every bone in my body until my joints hurt.

"Like you." His eyes look over my face, like he's seeing all of me at once. "Anyway, I've been wor—"

I can't let him finish. Can't give him one more second of being so far away from me. Hands on his jacket, I pull him to me and press my mouth right to his. I kiss Ford Callahan like I've wanted to since the first time I laid eyes on him tonight, and he kisses me back. Both hands in my hair, he laughs against my mouth before working his tongue between my lips and exploring my mouth like he's never been there before. Teasing. Tasting.

His skin is smooth against mine, better than silk. I pull my mouth away, rubbing my cheek against his just to feel more of him. His hands travel from my hair to my hips to the tops of my thighs and grip; his mouth moves to the edge of my jaw.

"This is better than I remember," I tell him.

He laughs against my skin, bringing his hands to my face.

"My memory's still rusty." Then his mouth is fused back to mine, sucking my lip in a way that drives my hips toward his across the tailgate like a moth to a bright flame.

Ford the man kisses like sex.

I moan—from kissing—and reach for the button of his pants. I need more. Right the hell now.

He pulls away, wrapping a hand around mine. "No," he says dusting a kiss on my lips. "Not yet."

"Funny." I press my mouth to his and fight to free my hands and his belt and everything he's hiding in his pants. *Why is this buckle so complicated?*

"Scotty, I'm serious," he says. And though there's a playful quality to his voice, he pulls away from me—slightly—and squeezes my hands in his, effectively stopping me.

I look at him. He's smiling. But he's also serious.

"I want to take it slow."

What?

"Oh," I say, feeling myself flush. I pull my hand out of his grasp and bring the back of it to my forehead; it's hot. *Fuck.* He kisses me again, but I read the moment for what it is—he doesn't want me. But what is all this? The love-nest truck bed? The kissing? The sucking on my fingers? Abruptly, I'm angry. "No. You're right." My mind is reeling. I flip through my Rolodex of sexual conquests: I've never been rejected. Ever. And here, in the middle of nowhere, Ford has done just that. *Was this some kind of game?* I know what's coming and I don't fight it. The venom fills my mouth and coats my tongue. "I can't fuck the guy who killed my brother, so thanks for saving me from that mistake."

It cuts him as deep as I intend, hurt consuming his features as soon as the words are out. In an unexpected twist: I hate myself.

I slip off the tailgate, out of his grasp, and march to the passenger side of his truck, getting in with a slam of the door. I'm twenty and destroyed all over again, only this time, it's me. I did all this. *What the hell is wrong with me?* Tears fill my eyes as I stare at Ford's reflection in the rearview mirror.

Hands on the tailgate, he hinges at the waist and drops his head, defeated. Then he starts cleaning, quiet as he gathers the remnants of the perfect night I ruined. The Mexican Coke bottles clang as he drops them into a trash bag; the cooler snaps as he puts the food away. He unplugs the lights; it goes dark. A minute later, he's behind the steering wheel of his truck, silent the entire drive back.

At the A-frame, he parks, cuts the engine, and stares ahead.

It's a moment. One I've read about and seen in movies where a character has to make a choice to be vulnerable or lose everything. I hate that pile of melodramatic introspective bullshit with a passion. But sitting in this truck, I feel it. If I don't say something, I might never see Ford again, at least not this way. Twenty years ago, I went into the woods and thought he'd be sitting there when I got out. Thought he'd wait for me and chase me around forever. I learned the hard way that's not how life works. If you want something—or someone—you don't know how many chances you'll get at that.

"You remember the first time you called me Viper?" I ask, looking out my window at the lit-up house. Molly's sitting nicely on a blanket at the window, no doubt putting on a show for Ford. "You asked me out on a date, and I told you I'd rather eat shit with a spoon out of a jockstrap than go out on a date with you. And you—you did what you do, blue eyes smiling wider than your mouth—you laughed. Like you thought I was funny. Then you said, *'Well I get that you'd rather do that, but it doesn't mean you can't go out with me anyway, Viper.'* Then I said, *'I bite,'* and you said, *'I'm countin' on it.'*"

I laugh softly; he doesn't.

"I learned to cut with my words from watching my parents fight. It was their go-to. One did something the other didn't like, and they used their tongue like a knife, stabbing the other one into hurt submission." I pause, thinking of those loud nights in that little trailer. "It was always a bloodbath even without a single mark of the skin."

Ford wrings his hands around the steering wheel, no doubt wishing it was my neck he was strangling.

"I don't know how to do this—whatever this is. I haven't dated anyone since you." For the first time, he looks at me. Mouth open, eyes wide. "I've dated," I add quickly. "But it's never been serious. I did get married in Vegas once for a few hours. A Swede named Sven."

He puffs out a breath. "Of course you did."

"What do you want from me, Ford? I have absolutely nothing to offer. I'm leaving. I'm no good for anyone—for you. For Wren. I'm . . . like buying an apple tree that only grows bruised fruit."

"Good news," he says, almost amused. "My mom always says the best apple butter comes from the most bruised apples."

I drop my head on the headrest, facing him as he mirrors my position. The soft glow of lights from outside illuminate the lines of his face and I'm jealous of how close they get to be to him.

"You aren't to blame for Zeb. Or anything. And I don't blame you for not wanting to crawl into bed with me either. I was feeling a bit shunned. Believe it or not, I do not get turned down very often." Quietly, I mumble, "Or ever."

"Scotty," he says, reaching over to me and rubbing his knuckles down my cheek. "Your apology skills have come so far in such a short amount of time."

Despite myself, I laugh.

"I want to crawl in bed with you," he continues, knuckles dragging across the skin of my face. "I want to relearn every inch of you and taste your skin and hear what noises you make when I'm doing all of that. But I want to be sure that we do it better than last time."

I lean into his hand. "How?"

"We go slow. We get to know each other. We see what happens."

"We know each other," I argue. "And I'm leaving in a few months."

"I'm pretending you're not leaving," he says, with a slight tilt of his lips.

"Pretending I'm not leaving?" I scoff, annoyed, pulling away from his hand. "What the hell kind of plan is that?"

He chuckles. "The best one I could think of."

I scoff, again. "Well, it's a bad one."

"Maybe," he says, eyes smiling even in the dark. "It was either that or try to convince you to stay."

I frown. "I can't stay." *Can I stay?* I want something new. Some-*where* new. A place to be happy. Free. That's never been Ledger. Even with Ford here now, this won't last. Nothing good ever has. My parents never stayed. Zeb didn't stay. I've never stayed with any man I've dated in the last two decades. Staying feels impossible. A gamble on me nobody should take. "And even if I did *stay*, you know me."

"I don't know if anyone knows you," he says. "It gets real, and you get . . . funny, sharp, mean. You don't get real." He pauses. "And I want you to be able to say you're mine—whatever that means. Girlfriend, whatever word you want to use."

At my reaction, he laughs softly.

"You never could before. We were young, but I never really knew where I stood with you. Always wondered if I was the only one doing all the feeling." At this, I am floored. How did he not know? "I want it now. Need it. I need to know we belong to each other. That when shit gets hard the only place we can run is toward each other and not away. When I piss you off, you come find me. Yell at me then listen to what I have to say. No pushing away. No pulling back. Forced to look."

"I'm not sure I know how to do that," I admit, terrified by every single piece of it. "Any of it. The label feels like you setting an expectation I'll never meet. And the realness . . ." I blow out a breath. "I don't know how."

"You do." He tucks a strand of hair behind my ear. "Tell me something real."

I swallow, feeling myself start to implode like a dying star. I would rather jump out of a tall building than do this, but if I don't do this I might actually jump out of a tall building. Seven hundred confessions scroll through my brain, but I opt for an easy one. "I wanted to ruin your date with Anna. When I sat by you. I wanted to make her mad and leave, and I wanted to hurt you. Because I was jealous. Because I know I don't deserve the spot next to you, but I want it anyway."

"I already knew that." His eyes smile, amused. "But it's a good start."

Despite how hard it is to breathe, I laugh.

"You have to do this too, right? I can't be the only one spilling my stupid guts."

He doesn't hesitate: "My biggest regret is hurting you when I left."

I want to tell him I regret that too. That him leaving changed the entire trajectory of my life, but I don't, because he kisses me, just barely, but enough to swallow my words. I get out of the truck and close the door gently, lifting my hand in a small wave as he dips his chin. There's a weird uncertainty in the air—like neither of us know what to do. Awkward, I walk toward the house, and he drives away.

At the door, I fumble for my keys in my purse at the same time Ford's truck speeds backward down the driveway, returning to the spot he was just parked. He cuts the engine, gets out, and without bothering to close his door, jogs across the yard.

He doesn't say a word.

Not as he climbs the four steps, crosses the porch, or stops right in front of me.

Not as he presses his mouth to mine.

Stunned, I don't react, I let him. Let his mouth explore mine, let his body push against me until my back hits the front door, let his hands dig into my hips and my body arch into him. Ford Callahan kisses me like he's trying to brand himself on my tongue, and he is. I drop my purse, wrap my arms around his neck, and let him.

When he pulls away, both of his hands grab my face, and he rounds his spine so he's looking right in my eyes. "You deserve whatever the hell spot you want, Scotty."

He kisses me one more time—hard and final—then he's gone.

For as much time as I spend thinking about everything that's been wrong in my life, all I think is three and a half more months of *this* as I watch Ford's brake lights shine red then disappear into the night.

TWENTY-TWO

"Why do you seem more nervous than me?" Wren glances up from the clipboard of paperwork she's filling out, effectively stilling my knee that's been bouncing like a basketball. "I'm the one that has to go back there and spill my guts to a stranger."

I look around the waiting room, mindlessly snapping the rubber band on my wrist. What I assume is a mom and son sit in chairs across from us, the woman flipping through a magazine. Around us, motivational posters cover the walls, making me feel like a fraud—a crazy person with a kid I don't own. "I don't know. I'm worried your dad is going to kill me, I guess. Like he should be here and not me. God, I sound like such a girl and we're not even sleeping together."

She groans. "Scotty—gross!"

I wave her away as she pinches her insurance card between the paperwork and the blade of the clip before handing it to the receptionist.

"You're bringing me to therapy, not a cockfight," she says, sitting back down.

I smirk. "You said cock."

"My point," she says, with an annoyed pause, "is that he's not going to care. He'd probably be happy."

I have no way in hell of knowing if she's right.

"Wren Callahan," a woman calls, opening the door that leads to a hallway. Wren lets out a reluctant breath, stands, and pinches her sleeves in her hands.

I give her a tight smile. "Tell them everything, okay?"

She nods, then she's gone, leaving me with a ball of guilt in the waiting room for the next hour.

I snap my rubber band the entire time.

"What about this one?" Wren asks as she drops onto a couch. "It's funky."

I shake my head. "It's white—not happening. No. I want leather so when Molly does something destructive to it I can yell about the cost and say, *'Hey! That's leather!'* You know, something cliché. Or *'Do you have any idea how much that couch set me back, dog?'*"

Wren reluctantly stands, continuing our meander through the furniture store. I promised I wouldn't pry, but I can't stop thinking about therapy. What the therapist said. If I screwed the rest of her life up by bringing her there to begin with.

"How about this one?"

"You've already sat on that one three times," she says.

Right.

I can't focus.

"What happened in there?" I blurt.

"I was wondering how long you'd hold out," she says with a triumphant grin, dropping into a recliner. "Yes, I told her everything." I open my mouth; she talks over me. "And I showed her my arms. We talked about my triggers and what I can do."

Do not push. Do not push. Do not push.

"And what are they? What can we do?" I push.

"Maybe my mom in general. When I feel guilty for things she did. Basically when anything feels like my fault. Apparently we aren't supposed to take responsibility for other people's choices." She gives me a look I ignore as I sit on a recliner and kick my legs up.

"What can you do?" I ask.

"Not cut myself," she deadpans.

"Earth-shattering advice," I say flatly. "What else? What am I supposed to do? Put cameras in the bathroom or something?"

"Creepy." She looks at me like she's trying to make sure I do not go that route and drags her hand across a puffy bedspread. "Just talk to me, I guess. Keep being annoying." I blink; she smirks. "She said the rubber band was good. And she suggested exercise."

We both make a face at that, but I instantly think of Ford, telling me about boxing and the relief it gave him.

I stand and move to a sectional couch.

"Your dad boxes, maybe that? There's hitting. I know from experience how therapeutic that can be."

"No." She tilts her head as she eyes a hideous marble coffee table. "I thought maybe running."

"Running?" I ask, disgusted at the thought.

"What's wrong with running? Lots of people do it."

"Lots of people are ignorant sluts." I squeeze the cushion of an overstuffed corduroy ottoman. "I made you another appointment for next month."

She shrugs but doesn't argue. "Fine. How about this one?"

"Plaid?" I frown. "Gross!"

She chuckles, moving to the next one. "Why are you so worried about the furniture if you're just going to sell it?"

We stop at a brown leather sofa, sleek enough to look clean but pillowy enough to be comfortable. "Because I have to live with it for a couple more months, and I want to enjoy it." We sit at the same time; I grin. "Perfect."

She doesn't move off the couch when I stand. "You don't like it?"

"It's fine."

Translation: not fine.

"Well?" I demand. "What the fu—" Her eyebrows raise. "—dge shop is going on now?"

"There's this boy at school."

Every cell in my body goes into high alert. I sit on the couch. "Give me a name and I'll burn his di—" Another look. "—ll pickle."

She laughs softly. "No, Scotty. Not that kind of boy. Like, a *boy* boy." My face softens as hers goes pink. "And, I don't know. My dad is . . . great . . . but . . . I don't know if I can . . . I guess." She blows out a breath. "Can you help?"

I surprise us both by screeching.

She winces, and I pull out my phone, grinning as I assemble the troops. "You bet your ass I can."

"Which one is he?" Wanda asks between chomps of her gum from the back seat of the minivan.

"The one with the long hair."

We all stare through the windshield toward the group of kids on the other side of the fence, all wearing weird short shorts and tank tops, bouncing around like they have springs in their shoes.

"Oooh!" June says from the driver's seat. "He's a cutie. A man bun, very on-trend." She gives Wren a look in the back seat. "Bet Scotty could tell you some stories about watching your dad on the football field when she was your age."

"Pass," Wren says.

I give her a look as she watches him lift one leg to stretch his quads on the track. "Him being on cross country explains your inclination to run."

She rolls her eyes.

Wanda looks at Wren's chunky sweater. "Maybe start by showing some skin."

In unison, Wren, June, and I shout, "No!"

"Yikes, okay, just a thought. The girls always bring me what I need," Wanda says with a shimmy and arched brow. Even with the cooler fall temps, she leaves nothing to the imagination.

"What's his name?" June asks.

"Luke."

"Luke. Luuuuke. Lukey," Wanda says, trying the name on. "I like it, honey."

"Joo, Camp tell you what the schedule is? Any fundraisers or events going on at school?" June's husband, Camp, is the athletic director of the high school, making him all-knowing in times such as these.

She shrugs. "The usual. Homecoming is November, just before Thanksgiving. I could get a cross country schedule from him . . ." She twirls a red curly strand of her hair around her finger, thinking. "Oh! Oh! Orchard Fest."

I whip my head toward her. "At Ford's parents'?" Just the thought makes my stomach flip. I haven't been out to his family's orchard since high school.

June nods enthusiastically. "Event of the season, and all the sports teams have booths to raise money. Pie eating or apple bobbing. Something like that. Anyway—that's perfect. It's casual enough not to be a big deal, but there's music and a mood that makes it just a little bit romantic. Dancing." She sways side to side. "It's the first weekend in October—only a couple weeks away. That gives you time to talk to him at school."

Wren looks out the windshield to the boys, now running short sprints, then back to us. "I don't even know what to say . . ."

All at once:

"Start with hi."

"Ask him to sit by you at lunch."

"Scotty gave Camp a letter threatening to knee him in the nuts if he didn't go out with me."

Her eyes widen at our shouted advice.

I hold up a hand to silence the van. "Okay, do you have any classes with him?"

She nods. "Art."

I clap my hands. "Perfect! Tell him you want to draw his"—June clears her throat and gives me a warning look—"face," I say with a sweet smile.

Wren nods, like this isn't the worst idea.

"I'll do your makeup for the festival," Wanda declares. "You'll be the prettiest apple in the peck."

"Yeah," Wren says like she's summoning courage from the energy of the minivan. "Okay."

When we all start clapping and squealing, she rolls her eyes. "Hags are so weird."

We fall silent, Wanda, June, and I looking at one other.

And then, we laugh.

Twenty-Three

ON THE OUTSKIRTS OF Ledger, Fight Club sits in half of an old brick warehouse, the other half empty and evidently for sale based on the sign in the window partially covered in kudzu vines.

The door of the gym is propped open with a broken brick. Loud music mixes with laughter, shouts, and the smacking of gloves against bags as I slip inside. I smile at the guy behind the counter. He looks at me, eyes narrowing as he folds his tattooed arms across his beefy frame, no doubt remembering me from the one and only time I was here before. "You gonna be trouble?"

I shake my head solemnly, holding up three fingers. "Best behavior. Scout's honor."

He grunts, hands me the paper to sign and takes my credit card then nods for me to go in.

Ford doesn't know I'm coming. I didn't even know I was coming. He came to feed the birds, told me he couldn't stay because he had a class, and Wren—who had been helping me paint the back bedroom—took off to do homework. Then the idea consumed me. After he talked about it the other night, I had to come back. See what he's like in here. What the classes he takes are made of, and why he wants to buy it. As frustrated as I was when he told me he wanted to take it slow—wanted me to stay—and spend time getting to know each other, I want to know all of him. Everything I've missed about him in the last twenty years—right down to what he looks like when he works out—and I want to know it all at once and immediately. Every change, every habit, everything. If I only get Ford for a few months, I want every. Single. Bit.

And a very, *very* small part of me is curious to know what it feels like to move with the purpose of feeling different. Feeling . . . less.

I hear Ford's voice before I see him. "It's easy to be impatient," he's saying to a small group of boys. "To want to take what we feel and get right to beating the hell out of something. But the warm-up can be just as beneficial. Sometimes I think more so." Seven sets of eyes watch him as he talks. He eclipses them with his size; they're all kids. The oldest maybe twenty, the youngest somewhere around Wren's age. Their bodies are all different, lanky to portly, one kid is wearing glasses, one has braces, two have acne, but they wear the same Fight Club T-shirt as Ford.

It strikes me: Ford isn't taking a class, he's teaching it.

I slip onto a bench behind him, and he's oblivious to my presence, wholly focused on them. Watching him with them feels like I'm being let in on a secret piece of him. A gift that can't be replicated.

He takes time to look each of them in the eye. "John, eyes up, man." The lankiest of the kids looks at him reluctantly. "We approach every part of this practice like we approach our problems in life. Head on. Don't shy away from the hardest parts. You hear that little voice that screams 'run away from this and don't look back'?" Ford shakes his head, his next words underscored by a hint of laughter. "Believe me when I say, you can't outrun them. But, with time and effort, you can work through them. Feel 'em to heal 'em, so they say."

A couple of the kids chuckle, a couple roll their eyes, the rest don't react at all.

Ford passes out jump ropes to each of them. "Ten minutes. Notice what your thoughts do when you get uncomfortable."

"Then what?" one asks. "We finally get to hit something?"

The boys snigger.

"You keep jumping. Think of the hitting as the dessert. These are your veggies." He waves a stopwatch at them. "Go."

He keeps his position, a wide stance, as they start jumping. I stand and step beside him. "Coach," I say, looking up at him with a palm out. "Got an extra rope?"

He does a double take as he looks at me, taking in my yoga pants and cropped T-shirt, surprised smile overtaking his face. There's stubble on his chin and sweat on his brow. "The hell you doing here?" He looks down at the stopwatch in his hand, at the boys jumping, then back to me.

I shrug, head bobbing back and forth as I say, "Getting to know you. Give me a damn rope before I change my mind."

He does, biting back a smile as I start to jump.

The next minutes are sheer torture. It's just jumping, but it hurts and it's boring and every time the rope hits the rubber mat beneath my feet, I want to quit. Every time Ford announces how many minutes are left—with a smile and encouraging tone—I want to tie the rope around his neck and hang him from the rafters.

But I don't stop. I keep jumping and mentally telling him to *fuck the fuck off.*

When he calls time, I nearly collapse, most of the boys looking as pissed off as I feel. We gulp water, hinge at the waist, and pant. My legs feel like they've been microwaved.

"Guys, this is Scotty," Ford says standing next to me.

I give a half-assed wave.

"She your girlfriend?" one kid asks with a smart-ass smirk.

Ford and I exchange looks, his amused, mine annoyed.

"She's Zeb's sister." At the mention of my brother, my spine snaps upright. I wipe my mouth with the back of my hand, waiting for an explanation. Ford doesn't give one, yet they all look at me with a sort of recognition. There's no way they knew my brother. Most of them weren't even born until after he died.

"Guilty as charged," I admit.

"That why you're here?" one of them asks.

"Uh." *What the hell is going on?*

"She's just here to hang out," Ford answers, looking at me while holding out a pair of gloves. "She's helping me with the demos. You have to watch her, though. She's been known to go off half-cocked unprovoked. Ain't that right, Scotty?"

I look at the gloves, the boys, and then back to him before taking them from him. "That's right," I answer, turning to the boys to add, "but I only go off when provoked."

When they laugh, Ford breaks us into pairs. He kicks our asses with an easy smile on his face for the next forty-five minutes.

"So you're Zeb's sister?" the kid with braces says as we wipe down the pads after class.

"The one and only," I tell him.

"My sister did drugs. Pills mostly."

I still my rag mid-wipe and look at him. "Oh." He keeps working, not bothering to look at me. "And how is she?"

He sprays another mist of cleaner on the mat. "Dead."

I clear my throat as he wipes the surface. "That's pretty shitty."

He looks at me, surprise flittering across his young features. "Nobody ever responds like that."

"Well, most people don't understand how shitty it is," I say with a slight smile.

"Jimmy, your mom's here," someone shouts from across the gym, making him look and raise a hand in acknowledgment. I take the cleaning supplies from him as we stand.

"Does it get easier?" he asks.

I answer him the most honest way I can: "Not yet."

He nods, like he gets it, then says goodbye to Ford by way of a fist bump and jogs to his mom who's waiting at the front door.

"I'm glad you came," Ford says, standing next to me as I watch the kid leave. "You like it?"

"I won't be able to move tomorrow, but sure. What is it? Who are these kids?"

He brings his hands to his hips, glancing around the gym before answering me. "They, uh . . ." He drops his chin to his chest, sniffs, then looks at me again. "They all lost someone to addiction."

The words seep into me so deeply that the next time my heart beats it's borderline painful.

I have the sudden urge to wrap my arms around him and cry, but instead: "The jump roping was pretty awful."

He vibrates with a soft laugh. "Tell me something real right now."

"This whole thing makes you pretty fuckable."

He grabs my hand and kisses my thumb. "What else?"

"I miss Zeb," I say, the words nearly cracking me in two. "And he would love that you did this."

He makes an agreeing sound. "He'd hate the jump roping though."

Around us people laugh and gloved fists smack bags. Ford's right, Zeb would have hated the jump roping.

On the drive home, I take the long way, driving by Glory's, the overgrown cross on the side of the road, and the house in the subdivision where the shadows of three silhouettes move around a dining room table. I don't stop at any of them, but for the first time in years, I'm not mad either.

TWENTY-FOUR

"We gotta redo this whole thing, miss," the man says with a Hispanic accent. Pedro, according to the name embroidered on his shirt. "Wiring's shot. What isn't is out of code." He shrugs, like no big deal.

I blow out my breath, check my watch, and look around the disaster of a house. "The whole house? How much?"

He shrugs. "We bill after. Policy."

A text comes through from Wanda. *Body ain't gonna burn itself, honey.*

I respond with a short *on my way.*

"Fine," I snap. "How long?"

Another shrug. "Couple days. Maybe less. Maybe more."

Vince specifically said everything needed to be brought up to code for optimum resale; I don't have a choice. It doesn't stop me from imagining Pedro in a cremation box sliding into the retort with a gag in his mouth.

"Whatever." I huff. "I have to go; I'll be back this afternoon."

He shrugs. *Again.*

I hustle out of the house; Ford and Wren are in the driveway, stopping me halfway to the Bronco. "Hey," I say, rushed. Ford's in athletic pants and a T-shirt; Wren's wearing yoga pants and a long-sleeve shirt. I eye her arms; she rolls her eyes. I throw my purse into the back seat. "What are y'all doing here? In the middle of a Friday morning?"

"Wren didn't have school today and I took the day off. We wanted to see if you were free. Go for a hike."

"Another date so soon, Officer?" I bat my eyelashes.

"I'm standing right here," Wren announces.

Ford wraps an arm around her in an obnoxious hug.

"And I was just about to hump his leg." Wren gags. "But I have work . . . actually, you should come."

Their *that's weird* expressions are identical. I laugh. "Get in. It'll be fun." When they hesitate, I bark, "Now!"

It's Dondi's turn to pick the music, so naturally Bob Marley is singing "Every Little Thing Is Gonna Be Alright" over the speakers as we stand around the man in the cardboard casket. He's in a suit—one that I bought from the thrift store—and looks just as lively as everyone else Wanda works on. In his fifties, he was un-claimed in the morgue.

"His name is Leonard," I announce as we look down at him. "And we're going to tell our favorite story about him."

"I don't know this guy!" Ford says, like I'm ridiculous.

I shoot him a look. "For those of you that don't know"—I pause for emphasis—"when someone doesn't have family, we speak as though we were his family. Or friends. And tell a happy story he might have had."

"The Dondinator will start us off," Dondi says with a smile that showcases the gap in his teeth. "Leo, that one time we went snowboarding you shredded it in the snow. Totally epic." Dondi snaps his fingers as if to emphasize the epicness. "And the face-plant at the end—you were a legend in the powder, my man. Black diamonds. All. Day. Long."

Wren looks at me like she might laugh but manages to keep herself in check.

"Lenny, honey," Wanda starts. "When you showed up at Easter that one time with my sister—in front of her husband—you were the real star of the show. And you made the best collard greens and cornbread I'd ever had." She pauses, considers, then adds, "And I won $500 on that scratch-off you gave me. Changed my life."

"Len," I say, smoothing my Bob Marley T-shirt. "You had a huge di—" Wren digs her elbow into me. "—vidend portfolio," I recover with a too-sweet smile. "Which is why you could afford to bring the Rastafarian culture to the Blue Ridge Mountains. The way you blasted reggae out of the speakers of your Mercedes and spoke with the best accent—" We all look at Leonard, the whitest man alive, and know that it is highly unlikely he had this accent. "You taught us never to judge a book by its cover. Because sometimes, the most unexpected of people are, in fact, Jamaican."

Ford's eyes meet mine and they're filled with amusement. He clears his throat. "Leonard, in the time I've been back in Ledger, I never arrested you." He looks at us, like he's finished, and I give him a look that says *the hell you are*. "Right." He clears his throat again. "And also, you were always volunteering at the church, serving soup to those in need on Sundays." I nod in approval, then he adds, "And you told me Scotty Armstrong wanted to be my girlfriend."

Everyone laughs except me. "Wren."

"Uhh, well, this is awkward since my dad left out the fact you were his brother, but, Uncle Leo, you were definitely the better looking of the brothers and there's never not a day I don't wish I had your looks instead of his." Ford pokes her in the ribs in mock offense. "But in all seriousness, we'll miss you. The world was a better place with you here, and we'll all notice you're gone every single day. You had a friendly smile, and those around you noticed it. You made every room you were in feel like a party. We noticed every good thing about you." She looks up at me, like she's seeking approval, and I nod, taking her hand in mine with a squeeze.

Ford watches the whole exchange, admiration flickering across his face.

"Now," I say, "let's send him off to whatever comes next. Wanda."

Wanda pushes the button to open the retort door, rolls him inside, then presses the buttons to close the door and start the cremation. When the loud whir of the machine starts, Dondi turns up the music, beats of the islands bouncing around the sterile room, breaking up the somber reality of a life gone.

"You do this with everyone?" Ford asks, next to me as we watch Dondi show Wren some kind of dance move she laughs at.

I look at him. "I do."

He hooks a pinky around mine, leaning in close. "You're kind of amazing, Scotty Armstrong."

I look at him; he means it. It consumes me with every breath and heartbeat and swallow and blink. I move my mouth to his ear. "I'm glad you think so because I'm trying to get in your pants."

Mouth against my cheek, he chuckles. "I'll tell you something real," he says. "You don't see how good you are."

And then, with a man burning to ashes who didn't have a soul in the world to claim him as theirs, the room feels like a celebration of life as Ford wraps his arms around me and dances to the beat of Bob Marley.

TWENTY-FIVE

PEDRO IS A SHADY motherfucker. I know this because he said the electrical was done and I'm sitting in the dark. Actually, what he said was, "Should be good, miss" and sent me an astronomical bill. Which I paid.

When I texted *Why is my house darker than a shit-filled lightbulb?* he did not respond.

I tried ignoring it, thinking I could survive the darkness until tomorrow, but I cannot. Wearing only a T-shirt and a blanket around my shoulders, I wander into the shed with a janky flashlight I have to shake to keep lit in one hand and my cell phone in the other, searching for my salvation. Candles, a generator, some kind of miracle plug that brings me back to the modern world.

Instead, I find Archie's by-way-of-Wren's bag of joints.

In the spirit of embracing a blackout, I light one with the lighter that's conveniently in the tackle box.

On a stool, blanket wrapped around my shoulders, flashlight rolling across the wooden workbench, Molly whimpers next to me as I pinch it between my lips and take a sharp toke, letting it burn my throat before exhaling with a small cough. "Surprised you haven't eaten this."

She cocks her head, ears twitching as she stares at me. I snort a laugh.

I need a plan; I take another hit.

I hate asking for help, but I can't live like this. On my phone I type: *Do you know anything about electrical work? Also, wondering what my rights are if I kill someone that conned me. Can a private citizen hire you to make an arrest on their behalf? Would it be poetic justice to electrocute the electrician?* and hit Send.

Molly barks, making me wince. There are no solutions in the shed, but the unexpected joint takes the edge off just enough I'm feeling less violent. I tighten the blanket around my shoulders before walking outside. There, in the middle of the driveway, is Ford's police car, him already knocking on the front door.

"Officer," I call, Molly sprinting toward him when he turns around. "I expected a text, not a house call."

"I was on my way home when I got your messages." He strolls over to me, chuckling at the sight of the joint in my hand. "Really?"

"Archie had a stash for times such as these." I hold it up with a shrug and eye his uniform sans the outer shirt. His bulletproof vest clings to his T-shirt-clad chest, and I very much like the whole situation. "You going to arrest me, *Officer Callahan?*"

"I get you in cuffs again and I'm not taking you to jail," he says, yummy edge to his voice as his eyes linger on my bare legs sticking out from the bottom of my blanket. "I remember what happens to you when you smoke."

"Oh, really." I raise my eyebrows. "And what's that?"

"You really need me to remind you?"

He does not. Along with making me relaxed, weed makes me horny as hell. "You must, because I don't know whatever you mean."

I bat my eyelashes; he shakes his head.

When he doesn't bend me over and make me sing like a songbird, I let out a disappointed sigh and smash the joint out on the trunk of a tree, tossing it on a pile of demoed debris before we start up the steps. "So, Pedro the pissant redid the electrical work. He finished today, but the only thing working is one outlet in the kitchen." I open the door as Molly puts on an obedient show walking calmly beside me. "And he's not responding to my texts."

Ford flicks the switch off and on as I shine the flashlight around the nearly empty downstairs, the marker-covered floor making it look like an abandoned warehouse. "Where's the breaker box?" he asks.

"Utility room." I lead the way; he takes the flashlight and opens the panel. Every single switch is off except the one for the kitchen. I never checked; I'm an idiot. He flips them all, lights coming on instantly. He grins. "He must have tested the kitchen and not turned the rest on."

"I could have figured this out. Sorry to waste your time."

"Never." He pecks me on the cheek and looks around as we walk into the kitchen. "Comin' together. Walls look good."

They do. The small accent wall of wallpaper complements the deep blue paint on the other walls and the exposed beams and boards of the steep, angled roof give an unexpected texture. "Slowly. We painted the wood paneling in the back bedroom too. Plumber comes next. Then cabinets. Then the floors and bathrooms." I shrug. "Upstairs is a different story. I'm not sure what to do there yet."

He lifts his chin. "Show me."

I lead him up the narrow staircase. At the loft, I toss the blanket that's been around my shoulders on the bed and lean against the wall as he walks in, skeptical look on his face.

"It's not as bad as it looks."

He looks at me like it might be worse. I laugh.

Next to Archie's old mattress on the floor is my nightstand box and an old lamp plugged into a corner. Because I've ripped the carpeting out, a very unwelcoming subfloor lies below all of it. "I'm going for homeless chic," I explain. "The mattress I bought was on back order."

At the box next to my bed, Ford picks up an Arizona real estate magazine and haphazardly flips through the first couple of pages.

"You really doing this?" he asks, pausing on a page I dog-eared featuring a house on a couple of dusty acres dotted with saguaro cacti outside of Tucson.

"Looks like it."

He studies me, nods, then exchanges the magazine for a book from the same box, amused expression as he waves it my way. "*Eroctopus*?" he asks, biting back a smile. On the cover, a woman in a blue, clam-covered bodysuit is wrapped in a mass of octo-arms.

"I'll have you know, Octoman can give an orgasm without even touching that clam."

"Oh really?" he asks, playful look in his smiling eyes as he thumbs through it before dropping it back into the box and walking over to me. "How's he do that?"

I know Ford is trying to coax me into some kind of emotional maturity, but the way the pot is swimming in my veins and the thickness of his voice as he asks that question makes me want to push him onto Archie's floor mattress and wrap myself around him like a barnacle.

"He says the right things," I say, dropping my arms from across my chest to my sides. "Telepathically, of course."

"Of course." He stops just shy of where I'm standing, noticing for the first time the shirt I'm wearing: his. He puts his hands on my hips, turning me so I'm squarely facing him, lips twitching in an effort to not smile. I slip my fingers under the rigid material of his vest, gripping the straps where the shoulder and chest meet. "You wearing my shirt to bed again?"

"I don't usually wear a shirt to bed."

His blue eyes burn like leaves in the fall, making all kinds of delicious feelings coil in me like a too-tight spring.

"Tell me what the octoguy says that gets you all hot and bothered when you're not wearing my shirt."

I scoff as he rubs his chin against my jaw. He hasn't shaved, and it feels like a sexed-grit sheet of sandpaper, sending chills across my skin in its wake. "It doesn't work if I tell you." My voice sounds as weak as my legs feel. Mostly because of the ache that's beginning to throb between them. "And it can happen, I looked it up. A woman in Texas makes herself orgasm on her morning walks." I give him a challenging look. "I have my doubts."

"Really?" His hand slips under my shirt and rubs at the line of my hip, and his fingertips run along the top hem of my underwear like a zipper. Warmth radiates from every swirl of his fingerprints, and my pelvis tilts, willing his pants to vanish.

I look.

He's clothed.

I swear under my breath.

He rounds his back slightly and lowers his hand to my inner thigh, dragging his fingers up and stopping.

Just.

Shy.

Of.

Where.

He.

Should.

Be.

"Can't go any closer?"

My mouth waters like a creek bed.

I shake my head, tightening the grip on his vest. "Nope," I say with strained control. "Not if you know what you're doing."

He slips his finger under the elastic at my inner thigh and repeats the zipper motion. His fingers in my underwear slide up—slowly—across my hip, rounding to the peak of my ass. A lake that could rival the one outside pools in the spot I very much want him to swim in.

A smirk tugs at his lips.

"Ah." His hand retreats to my waist and my thighs pinch and rub on reflex, desperate for friction of any kind. "Too bad."

A needy whimper climbs up my throat that I swallow down.

"Well, I don't know what's in your head, Scotty, but maybe I'll tell you what's in mine." His voice is low as his lips hover over mine; he could kiss me, but he doesn't. I reach my mouth toward him, he pulls away.

Damn him.

"At night, I think you forget that you have a house made of windows and walk around in only your panties. Black. Lace. Tiny."

I swallow thickly. "Really? You spy on me, Officer?" I lick my lips. "What else do you see?"

"You calling me," he continues, gripping my hips tighter as if to remind me he's in control. "And telling me you need help with something, even though you don't. Because you just want me to see you. When I show up, you've put on a shirt. Mine."

I force myself to breathe, every muscle below my belly button clenching with fury. Like if they aren't contracting my body will completely disassemble.

"Then I kiss you, pressing you against the windows so everyone can see that you're mine. That you've chosen me. And—"

"You're an exhibitionist now?"

He chuckles against my skin. "Well, you're begging me; what else can I do?"

I chase him with my hips; he holds them still.

"A gentleman?"

"Hardly." He pushes himself against me and makes one thrust of his hips—even with the duty belt and vest, I don't miss that he's as turned on as I am. And there it is: my first whimper. He pulls away; my whimper turns to a whine. "Stop interrupting me. Where was I? Right, peeling the little panties down your legs. I taste you first. I want to be gentle with you—just a kiss. But that flavor of you on my tongue?" A growl rumbles somewhere deep in him, and I writhe between his hands, gripping his vest so tightly he staggers toward me a step. "I can't be gentle—I've been hungry for the very thing you have for years. I'm starving; you let me eat. I use my teeth; you like it. Love it, because you scream." His hands travel from my hips to my waist until they wrap around my ribs; his thumbs rub across the bottom curves of my breasts until my nipples get so hard it feels like my skin is cracking open.

With one hand firmly gripping my hips, he uses the other to lift my shirt up, high enough on my chest it renders me fully exposed.

He moves so slowly that the anticipation physically hurts. Whatever he's about to do, yes, please. And then some.

He rounds his spine.

Lifts his chin to give me a wolfish grin.

Stills.

And breathes—gently—across the peaks and valleys of my breasts.

I need his mouth. His hands. Anything more than the air between us.

"How'm I doin', Scotty?" he asks, low. I fight his grasp to get closer; I get nowhere. He releases my shirt and pins me in place with both hands. "I don't know what that means."

"You know what it means," I grit out, struggling to keep looking at him or stand upright.

"Say it, Scotty," he says, breath hot on my earlobe. "Tell me right now how you like what I'm saying. How you wish I'd peel those pretty little panties down your legs."

Oh, God.

He takes a small step back, his hands pulling away. I need him touching me like I need oxygen.

"Fine," I confess out of sheer desperation. "I like it." My fingers claw at his vest as my hips struggle to rock in his grip. I look him dead in the eyes. "And you damn well know it."

He smirks. "Good."

One word and my body is set ablaze.

"Tell me you think of me when I'm not here." The words sound like they've been dragged across gravel. "Tell me it's me when you're alone in bed with your hand between your legs."

Through clenched teeth: "Yes."

My mouth opens. He notices.

In my mind: Kiss me, kill me, or make me come; something's gotta give.

He pauses.

Moves his mouth to my neck.

Breathes

a

single

hot

breath.

And *licks.*

My moan is instant, guttural, and does absolutely nothing to feed the angry bitch between my legs. And with the build of pending pleasure, there's an instant shot of panic. A trapping. In a frantic motion, I release his vest, fight against the strength of his hold on me, and spin away from him to face the wall. He doesn't seem to care because he adjusts his grip and presses into me, pushing me flat against the wall. My head turns so my cheek is flush with the cool wall, the front of him against my back. Despite every distracting accessory on his belt, against my ass, he's hard as a steel pipe.

In my ear: "And when I finally slide into you from behind—so slowly you beg me to go faster—your body shakes." His voice is so low and deep it's like he's penetrating me with a phantom appendage.

Oh, God.

"And that's when I know it's happening."

His fingers find the hem of my underwear, once again sliding his fingers along the line so gently yet so achingly far from where I want them. I slam my palms against the wall with a grunt, fingers uselessly clawing at the smooth surface.

My muscles tighten.

"That you're about to feel as good as you're making me feel. And when every slam of me into you is harder than the last—"

My breathing stops.

"You chant my name, loving every single—"

My thighs clench.

"Second."

Rub once. Twice. Three times . . .

"Then you beg—"

My cry cuts him off as an orgasm rips through me and makes me peak with a scream, smashing my forehead against the wall.

A wave of pleasure starts somewhere deep before washing over every square inch of my body like a filthy baptism. I press my palms into the wall, but they get me nowhere, the leverage only slamming me against Ford's chest and makes me want more of what he's refusing to give me.

Finally, I feel his mouth on the nape of my neck, line of kisses trailing up toward my ear.

I spin around in his arms, panting as I face him. He smirks a wicked shape; it's as devious as it is pleased. "Jesus," I say with a breathy laugh. "Are *you* Octoman?"

He chuckles into my hair and rubs his chin against my cheek. "I've been meaning to tell you that."

For the first time all night, he kisses me. He wraps his arms around my waist—tight and like he's holding me together. When his tongue dips into my mouth, my fingers trace the line of his jaw, slip into his hair, and interlace behind his neck. He tastes like Coke from Mexico, and I suck his tongue like I'm trying to suck the flavor off him, my body still buzzing from the euphoric high he sent rattling through me.

"You turned away from me," he says in a murmured voice between kisses. "Why?"

I did not expect him to notice.

"Sexual instinct," I lie, kissing him back. "I thought you'd feel good behind me. I was right."

"Hm." Another kiss.

"I sleep in your shirt every night," I confess. He hums in approval, not taking his mouth off my skin. "And I'm wondering if you can define what take things slow means because my body is a bit"—I whimper as he bites my ear—"eager."

"Just waiting on you to say those four easy words of 'I'll be your girlfriend.'" He teases with a sing-song voice, making me roll my eyes as he pulls away to check his watch. "But Wren should be home from her friend's. I at least need to text her."

I shake my head, kissing him lightly. "No, go."

"You sure?" Another kiss.

I nod, scratching my fingers in his scruff. "No." Another kiss. "But I have light." Kiss. "I don't like her being alone. Go."

His eyebrows pinch just slightly. "She say something to have you worried?"

Any remnants of pleasure completely dissolve, replaced only by guilt. I shake my head and force a small smile, tracing his face with my fingers. "No. Fine. Just, you know, I think she likes being around you for some reason."

He laughs with an exhale as he releases my waist and adjusts his pants with a grin. "Walk me out?"

At his patrol car, our kiss is long, the way teenagers kiss squeezing the last minutes out of curfew: tongues too deep to be sensical, hands too busy to latch on to anything.

"I guess I have no use for you now that I know I don't need a dick to feel that good," I tell him as he gets into his patrol car.

"Ah, I see how it is." He starts the ignition as I lean into the space of his open window. "Give me something real. Anything."

"I like what just happened." It's too obvious to be enough. Wiggling my toes into the gravel driveway, I add, "And I miss you when you aren't here."

I brave a look at him, and he smiles, and it's so kind and so gentle I wish I had a camera to take a picture of it. "Well, Scotty," he says, "I've missed you for twenty years."

Same.

Scotty

Remember that no-touch orgasm I told you about?

June

With the octopus guy in your weird books?

Octoman.

Whatever.

Ford came over last night . . .

Stop.

And he got me to scream his name without even touching the devil's doorbell.

STOP!

He's filthier than I remember . . .

TMI. We have to name it!

Octogasm

Too fishy.

MONSTERGASM!

Tell Campy to whisper dirty words in your ear then breathe on your nipples. Monstergasms are better than showergasms.

Wow.

But I did good on that name, right?

Almost as good as Ford did with the execution.

Gag.

TWENTY-SIX

"WHAT'S GOING ON?" WREN drops her bike and eyes my athletic clothes as I stand on the porch. Between the loud buzz of power tools, a crew of men shout instructions as they carry kitchen cabinets into the house. "Why do you look like that?"

"We're getting fit." I thrust the bag I'm holding toward her. "There's nothing to do inside, this dog hates me, and I read exercise might help. Your shrink told you the same thing. Go figure."

She frowns. "Do I have a choice?"

"Sure," I say, crossing my arms over my chest. "Do you want to tell your dad about your little love marks or should I?"

She rolls her eyes—much more pronounced now that they aren't surrounded by black. "You're the worst."

"I know I'm not." I smile with all my teeth. "Go get changed."

When she emerges, she's unexpectedly beautiful. Her hair is pulled up in a ponytail, showcasing the soft features of her face and a kidney bean–shaped birthmark below her left ear I've never seen. The navy-blue long-sleeve shirt makes her big blue eyes pop, and she's significantly more approachable in tennis shoes versus her usual combat boots. Molly on a leash, we take off at a jog.

Less than a quarter of a mile later, we're both doubled over and panting.

"This sucks," she gasps. "I don't know why Luke does this willingly."

"I was thinking the same thing." My words are stuttered by shallow breaths. "With another word thrown in."

Molly, being the demon she is, barks next to us, unaffected.

Wren and I don't need to say a word: Instead of going any farther, we turn around, walking toward home.

"Are you and my dad dating?" she asks.

"Uh." I squint, considering the fact that he's become a constant intrusive thought and knows how to fuck like a fictional monster. "Not per se."

"Well do you like him?"

I scrunch my nose. "Maybe."

"So what's the problem?"

I look at her. Thinking about all the ways I've pushed her that she most certainly has not wanted to be pushed. All the cuts on her arms and displaced pain she carries and feeling the teeniest bit guilty at the double standard I've set. "I've never really dated."

"Ha. Ha. Very funny." When she sees I'm not joking, her eyes widen. "Wait—for real?"

"I've dated," I explain. "Just not really what you're thinking. Seriously. Exclusively. Longer than two months."

I meet someone, enjoy the newness, and then end it based on real or fabricated problems to avoid the ultimate end looming around the corner: Nobody will show up or stay forever. A point repeatedly driven home throughout my life.

"Why?" she asks, stunned. "You're, like, gorgeous. And funny. And, I don't know, perfect except for all the swear words and the way you kind of bully me into doing things."

I grin victoriously. "I knew you thought I was funny."

"I'm serious, Scotty." Her eyes look over me. "Is this the astronaut thing?"

My eyes narrow.

"On the first day we met, you told me you didn't have kids because you didn't have good parents. And I said, so because you have bad parents you can't be one. And then you said, would you go to space without going to astronaut school."

"That sounds like something I'd say." She gives me a deadpan look. "Fine. Yes. Maybe." I throw a hand in the air. "I don't know."

We stop for Molly to sniff a tree.

"If your theory is right," she says, "people should never try anything new. My dad's parents weren't cops, he went to the academy to learn. And your parents were awful but look at you"—she gestures the length of my torso—"you're all this." I study the yellow leaves of a tree. "And if you're right—" Her voice lowers, and we stop in the middle of the street. "Then I should never be a mom either. Or a wife. I shouldn't even bother to talk to Luke because I'm never going to be anything anyway."

I don't know if I want to slap her or hug her and never let go. I opt for scolding. "Don't you ever say that. You hear me? You deserve everything you want and then some. You deserve to be happy and be loved and give love. If you ever say that shit again, I'll—I don't know what I'll do—tie you to a tree and tell Molly to gnaw your legs off then piss in the wounds. Got it?"

"Huh," she says as we start to walk again. "So the rules of misery don't apply to everyone, just you?"

I look at her, and she smiles. The little shit is playing me. As annoyed as I am, she has a point.

We're quiet the rest of the walk until we turn into the driveway. There, Ford is waiting in jeans and a flannel next to his truck, exposed forearms I'd like to lick and amused look on his face as we trudge toward him.

"What's this?" he asks, smiling as he takes in our outfits.

"Your *girlfriend* is the devil and made me run for five whole minutes," Wren says giving him a hug. I don't miss her emphasis nor slight glint in her eye.

"Surprise. I sleep in the retort," I deflect.

"Explains so much." Ford says to me. Then to Wren: "You sticking around?"

She shakes her head walking over to her bike and scooping it up. "I have homework." She smiles sweetly. "And Scotty said she wanted to talk to you alone anyway."

By my side and out of Ford's sight, I flip her off.

She grins, pushes her bike a few steps then calls over her shoulder, "Don't be late for dinner, Dad."

His whole face smiles as he watches her ride away. "She's in a good mood."

"She's something all right."

The man installing the cabinets waves me over from the porch. "All done," he says as the two crew members load tools into their truck. "Check her out."

Inside, despite the grafittied floors and bare walls, it's degrees cozier. The cabinets have a bright finish with gold hardware on the bottom; instead of cabinets up top, it's simple open shelving.

I run a hand over one of the doors and open it, not bothering to hide my smile as I imagine stacks of colorful dishes and mismatched mugs. "I love them."

The man grins, handing me a clipboard. "Always good to hear. Sign here and here," he says. "We'll email the bill."

There's no lingering small talk or handshaking. He takes the clipboard, picks up a tape measure, and he's out the door.

"Looks good," Ford says, leaning against the edge.

I open a drawer, empty for me to fill with temporary silverware.

"It does." I lean into him; he wraps an arm around my shoulders.

It's hard to believe this bright space filled with colors and modern furniture and prints was ever the place it started out as. Though the walls are bare and the bookshelves only house Zeb's old records, it breathes with life.

"Have time for the birds?" I ask.

He clutches his chest in exaggerated gusto. "I thought you'd never ask."

Hand in hand, we walk to the porch, sitting so our legs dangle over the edge and our knees touch.

"That one," Ford says, pointing to the large blue bird on the feeder.

"Blue jay," I say with a know-it-all tone.

"That?"

I scoff. "Nuthatch."

He grins, bumping my shoulder with his. "You trying to seduce me, Scotty Armstrong?"

"Is it working?"

"I don't know," he coos with a handsome face and ridiculous tone to his voice. "You ready to say you're mine?"

Like a switch flipped, I'm irate. He's putting me in an impossible position. It's not just about the ridiculous title he seems so hellbent on, it's about me finally getting out of here. Saying yes to him means saying no to everything I've been working toward. My out. My sanity.

"Why?" I demand. "I'm leaving. Why can't we just be whatever we are without all of this?"

He shrugs. "Because I want it." Then: "And I don't want you to leave. I'm pretending you're not, remember?"

I make an annoyed sound. I have to leave. That's the whole stupid point of this whole stupid thing.

"Because you're delusional and playing make-believe I'm supposed to feed into your teenage insecurities?" I demand.

He snorts. "Sure. I like that."

While I want to maim him, this featherhead is smiling. He doesn't see that even if I wasn't leaving, this wouldn't work. *I* wouldn't work.

Game on.

"I slept with Ben," I admit, causing his brows to pinch and smile to falter. "The bartender at Liberty Tap."

"Okay. Well—"

"And a few of the cops you work with."

"Okay," he repeats, this time dragging the word out. "Not exactly what I was hoping you'd say but—"

"Well, you need to hear it," I snap. "You keep coming over here like a dog waiting for a bone, but you're ignoring the fact the bone's been chewed. Repeatedly. By people you know."

He looks at me, expression neutral. As if he knows I have more to say. Which I do.

"And I've never been in a real relationship, so, you know, there's that. I flirt, I fuck, I flee, that's what I do. What I've always done." I laugh a kind of psychotic sound. "And I'm fine with that. It's *my* idea. And nobody gets hurt."

"You don't feel hurt?"

"No."

"You don't lie in bed some nights and wish someone was there with you?"

"No."

"You done?"

I huff. "For the moment."

"I'm flattered."

I glare at him.

"We've been apart a long time, but I know enough of you to still know this: You're the biggest viper when you feel something." He pecks my cheek. "You think that you'll tell me all this and scare me off but I think you're scared because you want all this. And—"

"No—"

"And," he repeats over me. "Maybe if you let yourself have this you might have to accept you've been wrong about how people look at you and you look at them. Like maybe where you came from doesn't matter to anyone at all. Like what happened all those years ago doesn't have to mean you can't be happy."

"But—"

"Here's the last thing I'm saying about it," he continues. "I'm not gunning for a title—it's not about you telling someone you're my girlfriend or wife." At the word wife, my eyes bug out of my head, and he chuckles. "I'm not forcing you into anything, Scotty, I'm being honest with what I need. Us being casual and you being able to push away whenever you want isn't going to work for me. Not now. Not with Wren. You act like you do, I'm going to keep showing up. Proving you wrong. Proving this can work better than before. Trying to convince you not to run off to the damn desert." My jaw drops; he grabs my hand and kisses my thumb. "I need to know you can handle that. And I think you want to say yes, you're just scared."

I scoff. "I think you have mommy issues."

He vibrates with a laugh, rubbing his nose on my cheek. "If you say so."

I lean against him, the prickly feeling of unshaved skin rubbing against my face and sending chills down my neck. "I say so."

He grabs my chin, gently guiding my eyes to meet his. "Want me to tell you all the women I've slept with?"

I nearly gag, instantly jealous of a line of faceless vaginas. "No."

"That's a shame. So many good stories I could share."

I level him with a look. "I hate you."

He kisses me on the cheek and stands. "I don't hate you even a little bit, but I have to go."

As he strolls toward his truck, I memorize his angles and lines. The easy way his broad shoulders sit back and long arms swing. The lines around his eyes as he smiles and waves from his truck. The casual drop of his arm out the open window, letting it hang as he drives away.

Ford wants to show up, and I believe him. Believe he wants to, and he will. More than that, I want him to. Over and over. Just like I did when we were kids.

Even though I'm scared.

Even though I'm leaving.

Even though I have no clue how to be what he and Wren deserve.

Damn him.

Twenty-Seven

"I don't like those frozen cubes of shit you buy." Glory's judgmental tone is in full force as I refill her empty freezer with said *cubes of shit*.

"Buy your own then," I tell her, closing the freezer door. "If you ate like an actual adult, I would just buy you ingredients and you could cook."

Glory takes a drag of her cigarette, glaring at me from where she leans against the kitchen counter. "Don't belittle my diet. I have allergies."

I snort. "Since when?"

Her eyebrows raise, annoyed I would ask such a ridiculous thing. She taps her ashes into the sink, watching me as I restock her fridge then pull cleaning supplies out of the cabinet.

She's out of her usual cutoff uniform and wearing a white dress with blue flowers; her normally stringy hair is combed and pulled back into a tidy bun. The dress swallows her slight frame, hanging lower than it should at most places, but she looks nice, especially for her.

"What?" she snaps.

I roll my eyes, squeezing beside her to fill a bucket at her ashtray of a sink with hot water. "You look nice. You going somewhere?"

Suds fill the bucket.

"No thanks to you."

I would thoroughly enjoy dunking her head into the water and holding it there. Instead, I smile tightly, remind myself I'm all she has, then play the game she loves so much of making me drag information out of her. "Okay," I drawl. "Where are you going?"

"Not that it's any of your business." She cocks her head, exhaling smoke. "But I have a date."

I lift the bucket from the sink and set it on the floor, poking the mop head into it before dragging it across the linoleum floor. "With who?"

"Dan Glibbs. I met him at the VFW playing Bingo."

I push the mop back into the bucket, swirling it around with the soap before lifting it out again. "I didn't know you went to the VFW."

"I work there."

My chin jerks back and the mop stills. "Since when?"

"Since forever. If you'd bother to come around, you'd know these things, Scotty Ann. I can't just sit here forever. My husband died. My son didn't care enough to live. My daughter doesn't care about me." She gives me a hurt look; I do not remind her I just bought her groceries and am mopping her floor. "Hell, nobody cares if I'm dead or alive. I bet you wish I was in that truck with your daddy—" *Some days . . .* "God rest his black soul. You know, this is just how my life is. I'm like one of those soldiers nobody knows the name of, dead on a battlefield just the same. Nobody has time for little old Glory Joplin."

I roll my eyes; her use of her maiden name is a direct indication of how big of a pain in the ass she plans on being.

"What does that have to do with working at the VFW?"

She stubs her cigarette in the sink and leaves it then bats a hand through the air. "I started last month."

I resume mopping.

"I can see how a month of working would feel like forever to you." We exchange glares. "A job is good for you. Get you out of the house, get you around new people. Maybe you'll like this Dan guy. Maybe he'll even tolerate your cheery-as-a-rotted-corpse personality."

"There it is," she says, tossing her hands in the air and walking out of the kitchen but continuing her tirade from whatever she shuffles around to do in the living room. "You can't just let me be happy. Always have to cut me down and tell me about this and that. You ever think I am the way I am because of you. Hm? Hm?"

I bark out a laugh, which draws her back into the kitchen. I pluck her cigarette butt out of the sink, toss it in the trash, and start to rinse the mop. "That's like blaming stink for shit, Glory."

"Stink for shit." She scoffs. "I'm out there doin' some-thin'—what do you do? You and your fancy clothes and your business and people sayin' all this and that about how good you are and givin' you a house. While you're out there trying to be a trailer-park hero, you ever think about how ridiculous that is?"

Do not engage; three more months. Do not engage; three more months.

I swallow, very slowly, returning the mop to the bucket as she rattles on, something about me being alone because the blazer I'm wearing makes me look like a man. I'm ready to shove the mop right up her ass.

Do not engage. Do not engage. Do not engage.

"Well, Glory," I say through clenched teeth and a death grip on the mop handle. "I'll make it easy on you: I'm leaving in three months."

She stills.

"To go where?"

I shrug, resume mopping, needing something to focus on other than the rage coursing through me. "Don't know yet. Out west, I think."

She's quiet, scowling the entire time I mop the kitchen and then start scrubbing a dirty pan from the stovetop in the sink.

Three more months, I mentally chant. *Threemoremonthsthreemoremonthsthreemoremonths.*

"You runnin' from the Callahan boy?"

I drop the pan with a clatter, not bothering to shut the water off. "What the hell does he have to do with anything?"

She chews her lip, hazel eyes narrowing as she looks me over before the angle of her lips curve from sheer amusement. "Shit, Scotty Ann." She cackles like I've told the funniest joke of all time, only stopping to take a deep breath and wipe a line of amused tears from her eyes. "You're *seeing* him."

It's not a question; she knows. *Do not engage.*

"You love him?"

Do. Not. Fucking. Engage.

She laughs again; there's a cruel edge I'd recognize anywhere. Her verbal call to arms.

"He tell you he helped buy that car for me and got me the job at the VFW?"

He what?

I glare at the sink, gripping the edge of the counter until my knuckles go white. A fresh shot of rage pumps through me. He couldn't have. He wouldn't . . .

She makes an amused sound. "Figures. You two and your secrets." Her smile is sharp enough to cut stone. "Told me he's carried all kinds of guilt with him. Making amends. Felt bad he tore out of here after Zeb couldn't keep his nose clean. Now—" She shrugs; it turns the cheap floor beneath my feet to quicksand. She's not lying; he's told me as much. *Making amends.* The boys at the boxing gym. Helping me. I want to vomit. She shakes her head, mouth in a mock pout. "He helped me out. Now he's helping you out. He's not *seeing you*, dummy, he's using you to make himself feel better about Zeb and your daddy dying. Sees you all alone trying to be someone else . . ." Her voice trails off with her implied *he feels sorry for you.*

All I can say is a weak, "No."

Even though I'm leaving, even though deep down I knew this thing with Ford would end poorly, I can barely breathe. Can barely see straight.

She keeps talking, but it's all the same bullshit. She calls me a fool. Tells me I'll get what I deserve for turning my back on her. Laughs because I'm living in a hand-me-down lake house.

My ears start to ring; the small house gets smaller. I need to get the hell out of here.

I slam the faucet of the sink off and push past her to grab my purse. My chest squeezes. *Is this a heart attack?* I press a hand to my sternum, heart pounding. I refuse to die standing in this shitty trailer trying to help a woman who never bothered to help me.

"Guessing Ford don't know about your dirty little secret either?" she asks, thin eyebrows high on her forehead as the wind gets knocked right out of me. I fumble for my keys; she's either oblivious or fueled by the come apart I'm having right in front of her. "I thought of telling him but"—another casual shrug—"no need for me to go poking around in other people's business. He'll figure it out soon enough, I'm sure." I brave a look at her; she gives me a pout. "I ain't perfect, but at least I didn't throw you away."

Tears fill my eyes and fall down my face. I don't bother to wipe them. This is what I get for showing up for a woman who has never once shown up for me. I let Glory Armstrong see my weakness, and she did what she does: stabbed me with it until I bled. I don't fight her, there's no use. She'll win. She always wins. Heart shattered and in a furious haze, I leave without a word. In the Bronco, I can barely get the key in the ignition through the tremble in my hands.

"Hey!" Glory hollers from the porch. "You left the bucket of dirty mop water. What the hell am I supposed to do with that?"

I don't respond; I drive. Fast. If what she says is true, as mad as I am at her, I'm furious with Ford. The only thing keeping me upright: In three more months, I'll never see either of them again.

TWENTY-EIGHT

My heels click at a quick staccato as I storm into the police station like a general out for blood on the battlefield. Familiar officers wave, a few call out greetings; I ignore them.

Scan the room.

Stop in the middle with hands cupped around my mouth.

"Hey!" I shout, silencing the few people talking. "Where's Ford?"

"Ohh, someone's in trouble," a young officer sings with a laugh. At my snarl, his laugh dies. He clears his throat. "I think he's in the back. Second door."

I don't knock, I swing it open. He's in his uniform, drinking coffee out of a paper cup, flipping through a file. "Scotty." He looks over my shoulder like he's expecting a horde of people behind me as I march toward him. "Everything okay?"

I don't hesitate, I slap him across the face.

Eyes wide, he brings a hand to his cheek.

"Tell me," I say, not fighting the angry tears in my eyes. "Right the fuck now, Ford. You buy that car for Glory?"

His face falls and I have my answer: He did. He doesn't need to say it, it's written all over him. I turn to leave.

"Wait." He wraps his hand around my bicep, stopping me, his eyes pleading. "I should have told you."

I laugh, loud and furious. "Should have told me?" I cry. "Is that what this all is? You repainting yourself as a hero for dropping a friend off at a house twenty years ago? I'm some kind of—of atonement? Get the lonely girl to forgive you for leaving and then fuck the guilt out of your system? Saving me the way you couldn't save him? Show up until you've done your time?"

"Scotty, no. *No.*" His eyes are desperate, like he believes his own lies. "I'm in love with you. I don't think I ever stopped. I fell in love with you when we were kids, and I knew—"

"Tell me this is a joke," I cut him off, snatching my arm out of his grasp, blood boiling. I almost didn't bother coming. I sat in the parking lot for ten minutes staring at the station. Torn between needing to hear him say the words and never wanting to hear him say another damn word for the rest of my life. Now, with the truth out and my whole body feeling shredded, I wish I would have driven away. "You don't get to say that to me. After you get Glory—the woman who couldn't get around to picking me up from school, never called me to tell me about my brother dying—a car. And a job. On Ford's Retribution Tour." I pause, a new hole digging inside of me. "The house?"

He blinks.

"Dammit, Ford." I'm seething and shouting, my body trembling with every word. "Did Archie give me the house on his own, or did you have something to do with it? Your families were friends."

"No." He shakes his head. "He asked me if I thought you'd take it, and I said I didn't know. Actually, I said I don't think anyone can predict what Scotty does." He almost laughs and I glare. "It's not like you think. Scotty, Archie was—"

"Stop." I don't care what he has to say, I'm done here. I glare at him, shake my head, and turn to leave. I knew this would happen. Knew this wouldn't last. Couldn't last.

He grabs my arm again, stopping me. "Wait."

We stand that way, his hand around my arm, staring at each other. Tears burn my eyes that I have no way to stop from dripping down my face; it's foolish to not want to believe the truth that so clearly seems to be real. Ford is with me to make himself feel better.

"I have something for you—that you need to see. Will you wait if I go get it?" His eyes search mine and I look away, not answering.

He reads my silence as a yes because he disappears down the hall and returns with an envelope, my name scribbled on the front. I look at him. He's not smiley; he's serious. Maybe even scared.

"This explains everything." He holds the envelope out to me, and I take it, staring at it like it contains a live bomb. "Every part of why I left. Why I'm back. Why I helped Glory. Take this, go through it. And"—he shakes his head—"just take it." He kisses me, hard and like he's saying goodbye.

"Callahan," someone shouts from down the hall. "We have a call."

He looks at me, I say nothing, and then he's gone, leaving me alone with an envelope and gut filled with dread.

TWENTY-NINE

ZEB USED TO GO to a scenic overlook on the outskirts of town with his guitar to write music. *"Lyrics just live out in this mountain air,"* he'd say. Sometimes I'd go with him, sitting on a rock and reading a book while he strummed chords and wrote lyrics in a notebook.

The Bronco must drive itself, because I don't remember anything between the police station and cutting the engine in the parking lot. Memory told me it was a grand vista with valleys as deep as the mountains were high, but the harsh lens of reality reveals that image to be a lie. It's nothing more than a slab of asphalt and a glorified ditch.

A motorcycle rumbles up beside me and parks; a man takes off his helmet, flicks me a wave and wanders to the tree line where he takes a piss before getting back on his bike and riding away.

With a shaky breath, I open the folder, my hands trembling as I dump the contents—a file folder and two cassette tapes—onto the passenger seat.

I pick up the cassette with *875 Valley Drive* scribbled on the lines in the front into the tape deck and voices start instantly.

Dispatcher: *9-1-1 What is your emergency?*

Caller: *It's my friend, he's breaking into a house. 875 Valley Drive in Ledger.*

I suck in a sharp breath, recognizing a young Ford's voice instantly.

Dispatcher: *Is he armed?*

Ford: *I don't know. I don't know! I tried to talk him out of it, I told him not to.*

Dispatcher: *Is there anyone else in the house?*

Ford: *I don't know—I don't think so. [voice cracks] Dammit. I don't want him to go to jail. Can someone come and help him? An officer? Talk to him. I don't want him to go to jail.*

Dispatcher: *Sir, please stay calm, I've notified the police.*

Ford: *[sniffs] I think he's high. I don't know—I don't know!*

Dispatcher: *Sir, can you tell me where you are? And your name.*

Ford: *Ford. Callahan. I'm in the truck. He's my best friend. His sister . . . I just want to help him.*

Dispatcher: *Sir, is his sister in the house?*

Ford: *No. She's on a trip in the mountains. I—I love her. He can't go to jail.*

Dispatcher: *I understand, sir, help is on the way.*

The tape clicks to a stop, and a loud silence fills the air as a brand-new truth crushes down on me: Ford called the cops on Zeb. He set every single thing that came next in motion.

I pick up the file, terrified of what's inside but opening it anyway.

The first page contains a mugshot. Zeb's. Despite the sudden oppressiveness of gravity pulling down on my shoulders, I smile slightly, dragging my thumb across his features. Same dark hair as mine, but instead of the hazel eyes I got from Glory, he had our dad's brown. Maybe it's the ink or the lighting used when they take a mugshot, but they're lifeless. Maybe that's the way they were in those last years, and I just never noticed. Never wanted to notice.

He has a faded scar under his right eye, a cluster of four freckles under his left. His lips are as flat as his eyes. He looks like Zeb's ghost. He was.

I scan the rest of the page, stopping at the bottom line: *Bail posted by Archie Watkins.*

No matter how many times I read it, the words don't make sense. I always wondered who bailed my brother out—who had the money or cared enough or both—but Archie? In all his years of morning visits, he never told me. Never brought my brother up once.

I flip the page. Zeb's death report. Cause of death: *heroin over-dose.* I knew as much. I called the police station after, but the details were vague. The officer was short with me. I always assumed it was because Zeb was just another addict, and I was just another family member he didn't want to deal with. *Neighbor or something found him*, the officer had said, not bothering to get the police report. *Dead when we arrived.*

I continue reading.

> *Zeb Armstrong, age 21, deceased upon officer arrival on April 17, found in his home by friend Ford Callahan.*

What? I reread it, nauseated, my stomach twisting as my eyes move faster than I can keep up with.

> *Callahan returned from college, concerned when he couldn't reach Armstrong after calling repeatedly and unable to reach immediate family. He called 9-1-1 after finding deceased nonresponsive with a needle in his arm, administered CPR until paramedics arrived.*

The rest of the words on the page are a blur. Ford found Zeb. Dead. He pressed into his lifeless chest and breathed into his breathless mouth trying to save him. Emotion clogs my throat. The other tape, scribbled with Zeb's apartment address, must be the recording of Ford calling 9-1-1 when he found Zeb dead. I can't listen to it.

For twenty years, I hated Ford for leaving without a reason. Without caring he left me drowning in sadness . . . alone. Turns out, he cared more than I ever knew. Carried more than I ever knew. The same way I made choices like I was standing in a burning building, so did he.

Tears fill my eyes. I should have chased him. I should have made June drive me straight to his parents' house or his apartment at college the second I didn't see him standing at a trailhead waiting for me.

Reading the whole thing again, my life becomes a heaping pile of shoulds. Even if what Glory said about him feeling guilty is right, he's lugged all this with him for all these years. I've always thought I should have done more; Ford called the cops in an attempt to do just that. Zeb died anyway.

I move to the next paper—a printed article with a young woman's face in a photo. She's pretty, young. Blonde with a smattering of freckles on her cheeks. The headline: "Local College Student Killed by Drunk Driver." The article names Riley Vander as the driver—Wren's mom. None of the other names are familiar, but there's an inkling like I know them as I read.

Michelle Hill was survived by her mom, Emmeline, and brother, Michael, in their hometown of Ledger, North Carolina.

I suck in a sharp breath: *Riley killed someone from Ledger?*

The names mean nothing to me, but knowing the small town, I've probably at least seen them. Ford too.

Finally, the last item, a small envelope, my name written on the outside. I peel it open; it's dated from April.

Scotty,

I'm writing this with a sore jaw thanks to you. Our first meeting in twenty years and you didn't blink at the opportunity to take a swing at me. If I didn't know it was a direct reflection of how badly I hurt you, I'd laugh. But I deserved it. I know that.

Despite my tears, I laugh—the first day we ran into each other at Fight Club.

I left Ledger a scared boy, thinking if I got away, I'd be able to sort out what happened. Maybe escape it. I was so sure you'd never forgive me for what I believed at the time was my fault. I've learned a lot, and I've accepted it all for what it is—I tried to save Zeb and failed. I couldn't have known what would come next. What events me calling the cops would set in motion. My only solace all these years later is that I did try. Sometimes, that has to be enough. Trying even when the results are failure.

I have a kid who reminds me of you a little bit—a spitfire through and through who hates me as much as loves me some days. I only dated her mom briefly, but she was an addict. I thought I could save her the way I couldn't save Zeb. The way I've tried to save every addict I can't. I had a partner call it a savior complex—he probably wasn't wrong. Either way, I failed again. She killed a girl driving drunk and high and went to prison. The girl she killed was from, of all places, Ledger.

So, I'm here now, probably twenty years too late. I have no idea how I'll ever give you this after seeing you today, but I'm hoping I do and you'll read it. Hope you know I've missed you. Hope you'll forgive me.

I'm going to try to do right by Zeb. I stopped by to see Glory and she's as ornery as ever. In some small way, hearing her spin her tales and gripe about things the way she always has while she sucks down her Lucky made me feel like a kid again. Like I was just sitting on your living room sofa waiting for you or Zeb to finish getting ready so we could go to the lake.

*If you're reading this, I hope you forgive me. Even if we
aren't destined for anything more than what we were,
I have no doubt, even now, I still love you. I probably
will forever.*

Ford

I read it—over and over—as if I'm trying to rewrite every memory of the last twenty years. I read it until my ringing phone pulls my eyes away from it. *June.* I send it to voicemail.

She calls back immediately; I answer with a sniffle.

"Joo, listen, I just found—"

"Scotty," she says, frantic. "There's been a shooting at the Fast Fuel. The one on Route 17."

"Okay," I say, confused. "Wha—"

"It's Ford," she fills in. "He's been shot."

THIRTY

I CAN COUNT THE number of times I've been to the Ledger hospital in the last twenty years on one hand. I hate it here. The smell. The lighting. The constant sound of a lung being hacked up in the background. It reeks of hopelessness and disinfectant.

June got the information on where Ford was through her network of Ledger know-it-alls and texted it to me on the drive. Outside of the exam room she sent me, I hear his voice through the cracked open door and relief floods through me. He's alive enough to talk.

"Hurts like hell," he says with a hint of amusement.

"And here? How's this feel?" a male voice asks—my guess, a doctor.

Ford coughs, and it's punctuated with pain. "Like a massage."

I chuckle—so does the doctor—and push the door open.

A man in a white coat with a stethoscope around his neck glances my way then looks back to Ford who's sitting at the foot of the hospital bed, shirtless. My eyes roam all over him—looking for blood and bandages—but there's only a bruise on his ribs below his left pec.

Again: relief.

"You know the drill, Officer. Vest took the brunt of it, but you'll be sore. Take it easy. Call us if you need anything."

"Thanks, Doc."

The doctor closes out an image of an X-ray on a computer screen, tucks a file under his arm, and gives me a tight-lipped smile as he leaves, closing the door behind him with a soft *click*.

I look at Ford again, shot but okay; the contents of the folder feel like an irrelevant meteor in a distant galaxy.

I step between his knees, gently tracing the perimeter of the bruise. "You get shot on purpose to make me forgive you?"

A slight smirk tugs at his lips and he lifts a hand to my face, grazing his knuckles against my jaw. "Did it work?"

"Depends." I laugh softly, swirling circles around the mark with my fingertip. "You get the bad guy?"

"We did." His fingers wrap around my wrist and bring my hand to his mouth, kissing my thumb. In a soft voice: "Hi."

"Hi," I echo, voice cracking slightly as I meet his eyes.

"I should have told you about Glory." The bed shifts under his weight. "I know it's complicated between you two. I helped her with a down payment on the car and set her up with the job so she could afford it. She told me you buy her groceries . . . I was just trying to help. Fill in for Zeb in some way."

His hand moves back to my cheek, and I lean into his palm. A smile tugs at my lips. "So, we're, like, siblings now? Kinky."

The pad of his thumb rubs my cheek as he chuckles. "Not even close." He kisses my forehead. "I didn't mean to lie. I don't want to. It all hurts. Saying the hard parts out loud makes them real—I just wanted it to not be. Just for a little while."

These words could be a slogan for my life.

"I don't know if you know this about me, Ford, but staying quiet about the hard stuff is my specialty."

He plants a soft kiss on my mouth. "You?" He chuckles. "Never."

"I get why you left now." His eyes search mine. "I wish I would have known. I wish . . ." I swallow every confession I'm not ready to make. "Things happened after you left, Ford. Big things that I don't know how to explain. Yet."

He nods, tucks a strand of hair behind my ear then rubs his palms down my arms. "Okay."

"When you left"—I sniff—"it was like you vanished." He opens his mouth; I shake my head. "But I didn't call either. And I should have. I should have hunted you down and caused a scene like we all know I'm capable of."

"Life happens the way it's supposed to, you know?" he says, our fingers gentle on one another. Down arms, across noses, through hair. We touch each other like we're freshly glued pieces of broken glass on the cusp of a reshatter.

I stare at the blooming bruise. Ford could have died today—he could have been taken from me before we ever got the second shot at whatever this is. I never would have survived it; I would have hated myself for the rest of my life for pushing him away. For running away. For the last words between us being him telling me he loves me and me slapping him across the face.

"I don't know if I can be what you want," I tell him. "Don't know how to be good enough for you. For Wren. How to dilute myself to be a more palatable flavor."

His smile is so gentle it nearly hijacks the tears right out of my eyes.

"You're my favorite flavor—always have been, always will be." He wraps his hands around my hips and squeezes gently as a smirk plays at his lips. "Even if it burns going down."

I snort a laugh; he dusts a kiss on my lips.

"And you're good for Wren. Great for her."

I want so badly to believe that's true. To be what he thinks I am.

"I'm yours." The words pop out of my mouth like a spring in a too-small box. They're all I thought of the whole drive over. If he would have died—he'd never have known. If he would have died—the regret of that alone would have ended me. "Whatever you need to call that." I swallow around the fist-sized lump in my throat. "I always have been. Me thinking you were dead made me realize I should probably tell you." Then, "Because I've clearly ruined you for other women."

His lips twitch; he drops his forehead to mine.

"Scotty Armstrong, you asking me to be your boyfriend?"

"I'm asking," I say, biting back a smile, "for you to be my sure thing, Ford Callahan."

He looks at me, whole face as bright as his eyes as he sits upright. "Guess that means we'll have to make the announcement at Orchard Fest."

I groan; he laughs, grimacing slightly and clutching his ribs. "And the desert?"

As much as I knew this would come up, every fiber of every muscle within me goes wooden.

Less than three months away from escaping Ledger and everything that's ever been wrong and ugly, and yet looking at him, it's like there's not a place far enough away to escape whatever this is between us. It will follow me. It will stick to me like a shadow like it has for the last twenty years.

He wants me to stay; it's underscored by every word he does and doesn't say. All over his face. His scruff-covered, salty-haired, smiling-eyed face. This perfect man wants me to stay.

For the first time since all of this started: I want to.

His eyebrows lift. "Scotty?"

I want to stay.

I rub my palm against my chest; it aches.

I can't breathe.

I can't think.

Ford goes blurry.

Stay.

Stay.

Stay.

"Um." I blow out a shaky breath as my brain screams at me.

Stay with Ford, leave Glory.

Stay with Ford, leave the ghosts.

Stay with Ford, leave the trailer park.

Stay, leave.

Stay, leave.

Stay leave.

"I don't—"

The door flies open and Wren bursts into the room with a shouted "Dad?!"

She looks at me, wide-eyed as she rushes across the room. At Ford, she does the same frantic search for wounds I did. "You got shot?" she asks, horrified. "Are you okay? Are you-you-you bleeding?"

He laughs as I step aside, giving him space to hug her and let the rhythms of my body return to normal.

"I'm fine, kiddo," he tells her. "Sore. No broken ribs, just some bruising. Grandma bring you?"

When she nods, my stomach drops straight to the floor. *Charlene.* I need to get out of here. Since Ford left, I've seen her once, five months after Zeb died, standing in the bread aisle at the grocery store. She looked at me and knew everything I didn't say; there was no hiding it. When enough time passed and I never heard from Ford, I always wondered if she knew telling him would drag him back here and ruin his life.

"I should go," I whisper to Ford, throat pinched and panic crawling under my skin like seven million tiny spiders.

"No. Stay," he says, reaching for his shirt behind him on the bed.

"Really, I—"

"Ford?" I don't have to see her to recognize the voice. Charlene Callahan is in the room, shrinking its size to a small cage.

I look at her, force a smile. Her eyes meet mine—briefly—but they move to Ford, doing the same once-over both Wren and I already gave him, worried look on her timeless face. She's beautiful in a classy way. Chock-full of southern charm, she's always stood out—shining slightly brighter than everyone else in her cashmere sweaters and chino pants.

"Mama," Ford says slipping his shirt over his head and dragging it down his torso, wincing as he stands from the bed. "I'm fine. You have that look in your eyes."

She scoffs, her dark hair—now laced with more strands of silver than not—swaying as she gives a disbelieving head shake. Even during an emergency, she has great skin and style. "My son got shot, Ford, did you want me to come in with a party hat?" She steps next to him, giving him a hug and looking him over again as I take a silent step back.

She notices. "Scotty," she says. Her voice properly southern, her smile genuinely forced. "You're here."

I give her a tight smile and cut my eyes to Ford. He stifles a laugh, draping an arm around Wren and clutching a palm over his chest.

"Hi, Mrs. Callahan." I barely recognize my high-pitched voice. "I'm here. Surprise. Twenty years later and Ford's shot." *What?* I clear my throat and lift my arms as if I'm going to hug her. When she stares at them and pulls her chin back, I drop them by my side. "Right."

This woman turns me into a fucking moron.

Her Callahan-patented blue eyes travel over the length of me, taking in my usual attire of fitted pants, heels, and a blazer, lingering on the Weird Al Yankovic shirt with a skeptical look.

"You haven't changed," she says with raised eyebrows and a tilt of her head and lips I can't decode.

"Crematorium air," I say with a grin and a fist pump through the air I don't think I've ever made before. "Keeps me preserved."

Wren's eyes narrow, Ford stifles another laugh, and Charlene crosses her arms over her perfectly pink sweater, staring at me before letting out an exasperated sigh and turning back to Ford.

She starts talking to him about job safety, and I have the sudden urge to flee like a criminal. *I'm going to go,* I mouth to Ford over her shoulder.

Charlene says something to Wren, prompting her to start rattling off the series of events that led them to finding out he was shot and Ford nods as he listens to them. To me he mouths, *Okay, girlfriend.*

I flip him off so only he can see.

Then I replay his words the whole drive home.

THIRTY-ONE

"People who run for fun," I pant, hinging at the waist, "are fucking lunatics."

"Swearing," Wren gasps, hands squeezing her hips as she walks a circle on the pavement trying to catch her breath. "But we made it a whole mile today."

I shake my head, convinced my lungs are too collapsed to talk, and start walking toward the house, Wren following suit. Molly trots beside us like she could go for eight more miles. I can't complain too much. I don't know if it's the running or the fact I've run out of things for her to eat, the dog has been significantly less feral.

"How's school? And Luke?" I ask with deepening breaths.

"I've been talking to him in art. I drew his face." She smiles shyly. "He asked if I was going to be at Orchard Fest this weekend."

"Attagirl." I nudge her with my elbow, but she doesn't react. "What's wrong?"

"There's this girl—Becca—she's popular and maybe they dated or something." She pinches the sleeves of her shirt with her fingers. "I think she knows I like him. The way she looks at me . . ."

"She a bitch?"

Wren laughs softly. "Something like that. I think her mom went to high school with Dad. Letts is her last name."

I scoff. "Jessica Letts? Adam her dad?"

She nods; my face puckers. The name alone could make milk curdle in an udder.

"We went to school with them. Rotten apples don't fall far." Jessicunt, as I liked to call her, took every opportunity to remind me that I lived in a trailer park when Ford turned her down. My junior year, she wanted him, he wanted me, and she retaliated by making copies of a picture of the trailer I lived in with the words Ledger Dump typed across it and then plastered them in the halls. I wanted to punch her face; instead, I got naked with Ford on the hood of her car one night while she was at a late cheerleading practice. Even though I never told her, our satisfying tryst made her significantly more tolerable. "Ignore her. She probably inherited her mom's saggy snatch."

"Scotty!" she groans. "Gross!"

I cock an eyebrow; her groan turns to a laugh. "I'm serious. All the rotten ones do."

"Maybe," she says as she kicks a pinecone.

"How was therapy yesterday? You were quiet on the drive back."

"Fine." She kicks another pinecone.

"You shook up about your dad being shot?"

She looks at me, eyebrows pinched and as if that was a ridiculous notion.

"She asked if I ever think about visiting my mom."

"And?"

Another shrug, another kicked pinecone. "And . . . sometimes. Seems messed up that the only way I'd get to see her is if she's trapped without a choice, though."

"When was the last time?"

"A couple months before she got arrested. She picked me up and we were supposed to go to lunch. We ended up outside of some apartment complex where she went inside for a 'few minutes' and didn't come out for an hour and a half. She dropped me off at home with a bag of McDonald's. When I told my dad, I thought he was going to kill her."

I would have supported this. And burned the body.

Her shoulders slump, pulling my heart with it.

"She probably got sucked into a game of Monopoly. Those games never end, you know?" She looks at me. "That's why I steal everyone's money when they aren't looking. Speed the damn thing up."

"You play Monopoly?"

"No."

She smiles, just slightly. "I know what she was doing."

"I know you do." The pavement turns to gravel as we turn into the driveway. "But it's her loss, you know?" She looks at me like she doesn't believe me as I take Molly off of her leash. "You've mastered the art of eye-rolling. And"—I shrug—"it's too bad for her if she's spending her life not being at the ass-end of that." She snorts a laugh. "Plus, from someone who sees their shitty mom on a regular basis, you're not missing much."

"Why do it?" Wren asks as a crisp breeze stirs fallen leaves and the dog takes off after a squirrel. "Why go see her at all?"

How many times has June asked me this? How many times have I asked myself this? Every visit leaves me more frustrated than not, and yet, once a month, despite the hurt and heartache it causes, I go. I buy her groceries. I do a few chores in hopes of making her feel less alone. I try like hell to remember she lost the same people I did.

"Because nobody else does," I admit. "And because she's my only family."

Wren says nothing; a cardinal lands at the feeder. I wonder if it's Zeb.

"Miss!" A man's voice cuts across the lawn. "Floors are in!"

Molly somehow has the energy to sprint, and we follow behind, the sight in the house taking my breath away the moment I reach the doorway.

It's just boards of reclaimed hickory, hammered and stained then laid down right next to each other, but it's morphed the house from construction zone to home. The strong angled walls have gone from being awkward to feeling like the arms of a mother welcoming her family home.

"Are you going to cry?" Wren asks with disbelief.

"No." I knuckle the *not* tears from beneath my eyes. "I'm allergic to the glue they used." She gives me a skeptical look; I turn to the man who installed the floors. "They're beautiful."

He lifts his hat by the rim then does a swirly motion through the air, gesturing to the rest of the crew to pack it up. I sign the clipboard, he hands me a paper with his name, Floored by Fred, and with a gruff voice says, "Leave five stars and tell your friends."

Bet he's a snuggler.

"Looks good, right?" I say, looking around again, seeing it all together, every detail fitting perfectly with the next.

"It does. You still selling?"

I do not want to talk about this.

"Why wouldn't I?"

"Gee, Scotty, I don't know."

We exchange annoyed looks then she walks outside, rummages through her bag, and returns with a thin square wrapped in a brown bag. She shoves it toward me.

I blink.

"It's a gift, dummy."

"A gift?" I take it gingerly, looking from the brown square to her. "Why the hell would you get me a gift?"

"Just open it and don't be weird."

I do as she says; it's a record. I chuckle softly, reading Miranda Lambert, *Postcards from Texas.* I flip it over and read the track list, swallowing around the tickle of emotions.

I look at her. "You got me a record."

She frowns. "You have a weird face."

"I don't."

"You do," she punctuates. "It's dopey."

"I don't do dopey."

Her expression says otherwise.

I gesture with the record. "Fine. In a non-dopey way, thank you for this. I've never actually had a record that belonged to me first." It's true. It's just a record, but in my hand, it's something precious. Like a long-lost artifact people spend forty years wandering through the desert to find. Something travels between us when we look at each other. Something endearing. A little like love. "I can't wait to play it and dress like a sexy cowgirl when your dad comes over."

She groans. "You ruin everything."

I grin.

"Let's listen."

I take the plastic wrap off and slip the record out, putting it on the player and dropping the needle. When the first lyrics start in a song about an armadillo, I shake my hips to the beat, laughing at her annoyed expression as I circle around her.

"You can't fight the Miranda effect, Wren. Don't bother," I tell her, poking her in the ribs. "Three songs and you'll want to buy pink sunglasses and ride a horse out of town."

She grunt-laughs. "You're weird."

"No," I say, grinning as the beat changes from slow to fast. "I'm dopey."

She rolls her eyes, but she doesn't fight me when I drop an arm around her shoulder. In fact, she sways right along with me for the entire next song.

THIRTY-TWO

"Aren't you sweet as a bootlegged jar of apple pie moonshine?"

Wren tugs at the square neckline of her dress, the deep-red fabric beautiful against her fair skin as she climbs in the Bronco. "These shoes suck."

I glance at the leather ankle boots, a far cry from her ridiculous combat boots she usually wears, and back out of the driveway as she tosses a duffle in the back seat.

"Let me know if Luke agrees." I shift into drive. "What's in the bag?"

"I'm staying with my grandparents tonight."

Ford's already at their farm, home of Cider Hills Orchard, a symbol of all things fall in Ledger. Though I haven't driven out there in years, the way is still second nature. Ford picked up Zeb and I so many times and drove us out to his parents' property I could find it drunk and blindfolded. Not that I would recommend either.

With the windows down and the cool October air blowing through the cab, I crank the music, Wren smiling as her favorite violin sounds fill the cab and dissipate into the mountains around us. In the late-afternoon sun, the trees are a palette of autumn. Like tubes of yellow, orange, and red paint exploded from the sky and landed on leaves.

I park at the property and a wave of nostalgia washes over me. Hours spent picking apples, riding four-wheelers, and dreaming Ford's life was mine. Even all these years later, standing at his family farm feels a bit like the moment in *The Wizard of Oz* where Dorothy's life goes from being a dusty sepia-toned scene in Kansas to the technicolor dreamland of Oz.

The fields of grass are already covered with cars and ATVs, and bluegrass music floats toward us from a large white canvas tent. Kids run by with a shriek.

"You nervous?" I ask, glancing at Wren.

She eyes my outfit, a burnt-orange sweaterdress that slips off one shoulder and hugs my body like a glove stopping shy of cowboy boots that hit just below my knee. Compared to the sea of denim and flannel that surrounds us, we look lost. "Are you?"

I lift my eyebrows. "I'm at your perfect grandparents' farm dressed like a forty-one-year-old slutty pumpkin with the first boyfriend of my life, what could I possibly have to be nervous about?"

She snorts. "Good luck with that." Looking back to the crowd, she swallows slowly, lifting her chin. "I'm going to find my friends."

Alone, I'm nervous as a bird with its wings tacked down. I'm fully prepared for Ford to take one look at me and tell me he's changed his mind. But when I spot him through the crowd, carrying a stack of pies and laughing with someone who stops him to talk, my heart flip-flops. His eyes meet mine before dragging down my body, and his expression is full-blown approval. Every ounce of worry dissolves. Because: *mine*.

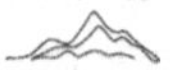

"That something I should know about?" Ford asks as he hands me a cider, tilting his head toward Wren standing across from us under the large tent. She shyly tucks her hair behind her ears as she talks to Luke. He's a cute kid. Instead of the man bun he had on the track, his hair is down, brushing against the collar of his flannel. Hands stuffed in his jeans, he's just as nervous as her.

"Luke. He's on the cross country team," I explain as they laugh. "She has a crush."

"Don't like it," he says as he takes a sip of his cider and keeps his eyes on them.

"Don't worry." I bump my shoulder into his. "I gave her rubbers."

He frowns; I laugh.

On a small stage, the band's upbeat fiddle-laden song shifts to something slower, couples instantly pulled to the hay-covered dance floor. Around us, under this tent and beyond, tables of pies, ciders, and other fall treats are for sale as well as other fundraising efforts—apple bobbing for the basketball team, pie eating for the football team, even a dunking booth for the swim team. Kids of all ages stand in line to participate, laughing and whispering to one another. Bales of hay and upturned wooden barrels double as tables and chairs. Strings of lights float over us like a million stars in the sky.

"You're beautiful," Ford says, rubbing a thumb on my bare shoulder.

I set my cider on a barrel and slide my fingers under his flannel. "You're not so bad."

"Not so bad?" he teases, setting his drink down and slipping his hands around my waist, tugging my hips toward him. "Still so one-sided."

"Fine." I feign consideration. "I'd let you cop a feel."

He laughs, pecks me on the cheek, and in my ear whispers, "I'm counting on it."

Despite the wholesome crowd around us, my body purrs like a dirty kitten.

"We have to dance, you know," Ford says.

"Oh really?" I look at him. "Says who?"

"Says everyone." His hands grab mine, and his lips lift as he spins me in a slow twirl. "It's how it works when you go steady. You have to declare your couplehood to the town."

"Go steady?" I say through another laugh. "Do people even say that?"

"Sure," he says, pecking another kiss on my lips, pressing me flush against him with one hand splayed across the small of my back and the other holding my hand. "All the cool kids."

"Hm." I nuzzle my nose against his cheek. "I thought you knew I told the cool kids to go fuck themselves."

At this, he laughs. "I can't wait to get your dirty mouth on my—"

"Ford, there you are!"

Charlene.

Ford and I step away from each other, giving her our full attention. While most people associate an orchard owner with wearing flannel and denim, unlike everyone else, she's in sleek pants and a chic red sweater. His dad, Earl, handsome as ever with a new softness to his face and grey hair on his head, is a sight for sore eyes covered completely in denim.

"Scotty Armstrong," he says with a grin, pulling me into an unexpected hug, which smells like whiskey and cinnamon. "I heard you would be here. It's been too long!"

While Charlene turns me into some kind of bumbling buffoon, Earl has always been a comfortable space. "Earl, you haven't aged."

He chuckles and slaps his belly—a bit rounder than it used to be. "Charlene disagrees."

Charlene waves a weak dismissive hand through the air with an amused eye roll then averts her attention to me, taking in my dress, eyes lingering on my exposed shoulder as Earl and I make small talk about the crematorium and the orchard.

"That's quite a dress, Scotty," Charlene says, tone unreadable. "Some things never change."

"But some do," I blurt against my will. "I have a job. And a house. And a dog." Stop. Talking. Scotty. "And my checks don't bounce like my mom's did at the FoodMart."

Earl looks at me with an amused expression while Ford clears his throat, a piss-poor attempt at hiding his laugh.

Charlene nods, same unreadable smile on her face. "Well, isn't that all just great news for you."

"Yes, ma'am. Miss. Missus . . ." I quit.

She looks away briefly at the sound of her name, waving across the tent before looking back to me.

"Well, Ford's a big boy. He knows what he wants."

She hates me.

"Especially that time Earl caught us in the barn," I joke.

Earl chuckles at the reference of teenage Ford and I half naked between bales of hay, while Charlene remains neutrally frigid. Finally, Ford steps in. "Mama, you need help with something?"

Her eyes linger on me a few more seconds then turn to him, smile changing to a warmer shape. "Oh yes. We need to move the cider. Come. Earl, help Ford."

Earl and I exchange a look that roughly translates to *some things never change,* and he and Ford follow on her lead through the crowd, Ford winking at me as they go.

I beeline to the hard cider booth and order the largest cup they have, downing it in gulps.

An upbeat song plays, couples twirl around, then another slow song, this one pulling Wren and Luke onto the dance floor.

Her eyes meet mine, and I put my index fingers together in a kissy motion that she glares at. They're far enough apart it's both cute and awkward, dancing in a motion like a teetering seesaw. She looks at him with hearts in her eyes.

"Can you believe them?" a blonde teenage girl says with a scoff to a brunette in front of me. "I heard her mom was in prison."

My ears perk and hackles raise. *Who the hell is this pint-sized bitch?*

The brunette makes an agreeing sound. "And those weird boots she usually wears?"

Their giggles hit my eardrums like nails on a chalkboard.

"My mom said her dad used to be something around here but got himself involved in some kind of trouble. Had to tuck tail. Can you imagine? Owning all this and not being able to keep it?" She clicks her tongue. "Heard he got on drugs and ran away or something."

"Good ones never know what's good for them."

They giggle; it encourages my step toward them.

"Apples don't fall far," the blonde one says as I step directly behind them. "I don't know what Luke even sees in her. She's so—"

"Sweetheart," I say, making them both turn to look at me, confused. The blonde one I recognize instantly; she has the same face as her swine of a mother. Poor thing. "You're Jessica Letts's girl, aren't you?"

"The one and only," she says with a tone that makes me wish she was in an urn.

"Jessicunt was what I liked to call her." I pause and smile sweetly to let that sink in. When her expression falters, I know it has. "She ever tell you she ate nearly every dick on the football team when we were in high school?"

The brunette laughs, earning a glare from Minicunt that makes her fall silent.

"Figured as much. Not Ford's though—that's Wren's dad, who—how'd you word it? Right, *used to be something*." I shrug. "Either way, probably why your dad married her to begin with. Bet you started there, actually. Swallowed into conception—wonder if that's a thing." I tap my chin. "Heard they got divorced though. Shame. A willing throat is so hard to find these days."

She scoffs, but her brown eyes reek of scared shitlessness. My favorite.

Her eyes roam from my boots to my bare shoulder. "And—and who are you?"

"I'm the one that will ruin your pitiful little lives if you ever say anything about Wren Callahan, her combat boots, or any boy she chooses to look at. If she shits in the middle of the hall at school, you will tell her it smells delicious, scoop it up with your fingers, and swallow it down your rotten throats. Got it?"

Two teenage mouths gape at me and my smile widens. "I'm sorry—what was that?"

"G-g-got it," the brunette says.

"Good girls. Now run along and get some cider. Oh! And do tell your mom I say hello." I shouldn't, but: "And Ford's still mine."

Without hesitating, they scurry like scrawny mice from a hungry cat. Through the crowd, they stop next to dear Jessicunt. She scowls at me when I wave, too-big smile on my face.

"Well, well," a female voice says from next to me. *Charlene.* "You always have had quite the way with words. You could have been a poet, Scotty."

Fuckity-fuck-fuck.

The damage is done, so I simply shrug my bare shoulder, resigned to the fact this woman will hate me forever. "You called it, some things never change, Mrs. Callahan."

"Charlene," she corrects.

My eyes widen, but I repeat, "Charlene."

Her lips twitch as she looks to the Letts girl then back to me, something on her timeless face like amusement. I brace for the impact of whatever she's about to say, but it in no way prepares me. "I always admired you."

My head snaps toward her so fast I nearly give myself whiplash.

She chuckles. "I know, I know. Compared to your mother you probably think I'm the most uptight woman in the world. I was raised by Southern Baptists," she says, adjusting the cuff of her sweater. "Can't blame me for turning out so good."

A joke?

I'm slack-jawed, stunned to silence, and she's . . . *smiling?*

"Anyway, you just said things that needed to be said, no matter what they were. Just barfed it all out." She makes a puking gesture with her hands that makes my eyes double in size. "Consequences be damned."

"Yes," I finally croak out. "That does seem to be my strong suit."

She chuckles softly again, and there's an undeniable warmth in her eyes as she rubs a palm on my back.

"You would have made quite a mother, Scotty."

The world stops with a scratch of a record, and we stand there, sharing a million words without saying a single one in the middle of the fall-themed chaos. I've always assumed she knew, but now I know she did.

Ford and Earl carry a stack of pies across the tent from us.

"You never told him," I say.

"Wasn't my place. He left for the same reason you stayed. I figured you had your reasons. Everything that happened with your brother—" She pauses, look in her eyes like she's somewhere twenty years ago, but a rawness in her voice like it all happened yesterday. "It was hard for Ford. Calling the cops. Finding him the way he did." She flicks a smile and wave to someone who passes by. We both look at Ford, now laughing with jugs of cider in his hands. "But he had to leave so he could come back."

I let her words sink in; they aren't new, but coming from her, they hit different. Harder.

A woman calls her name, and she holds up a finger to buy another minute.

"I never left," I say, more to myself than her. "He left and came back good, and I . . ."

She squeezes my arm, the unexpected contact making me flinch. "Scotty," she says, her tone firm yet warm, "there are a million ways to be good."

I nearly collapse.

"Mama," Ford says, stepping next to us and slipping his hands around my waist. "Stop trying to scare off my date."

Charlene lifts her chin, but her eyes stayed locked on mine. "Wouldn't dream of it, darling."

With a squeeze of his bicep, she disappears into the crowd, leaving me shell-shocked and stripped bare.

Ford spins me to face him, handsome smile on his face as the strings of lights make his eyes shine like two balls of blue fire. "I've been a bad boyfriend."

"The worst one I've ever had," I say, wrapping my arms around his neck. "I was starting to have second thoughts about this whole thing."

"Not allowed." He kisses my bare shoulder then looks at me, expression turning more serious. "What's wrong?"

Your mother just punched me in the throat with her words.

Through the crowd, I spot Charlene standing with a small group of women. Her eyes meet mine before she laughs at something they say and looks back to them.

"Nothing," I tell him. "Being around so many live bodies is a shock to my nervous system."

His lips twitch. "You're nervous."

"No," I argue.

"Yes."

"Fine," I relent with a sigh, his palms moving across my back. "A little."

He chuckles, tilting my chin to look at him. "It's me, Scotty. It's us. We're old news, really. Half the people in this tent have already seen us make out."

At this, I laugh. He's not wrong.

Without warning, he pulls me onto the hay-covered dance floor. The music is fast, but Ford moves us slow, dropping his forehead to mine. With one of his hands on my back and mine around his neck, our connected hands tuck between us.

I tense; he grips me tighter.

"Don't get skittish on me, Viper."

I glance from him to everyone around us, including Wren and Luke who are laughing as they dance. It's hard to breathe. I'm split between existing in this moment and knowing I don't fit here at all. It's a cheesy scene in a movie that would make me audibly gag, but as much as I want to drop a match to the bales of hay and run, I want it to stretch on and on and on.

I need air.

I push back from Ford but he reads my panic, holding me tight and kissing me hard. I freeze. His thumb pressed against my chin, he opens my mouth, and though it's just barely, swipes his tongue along my lips. The taste of cider on him holding me captive in the now. He slips both hands into my hair and grips his fingers into my scalp, claiming my mouth as his in front of everyone in Ledger.

When someone lets out a loud *whoop!* from next to us, reminding us we are far from alone, we laugh into each other's mouths, pulling apart. I tuck my chin to my shoulder, a rare feeling of shyness washing over me.

Ford's chest rumbles with a laugh. "All I need to do is bring you out to a dance floor to quiet that tongue?"

I press my face against his shoulder to stifle my laugh. "You're turning me soft, Golden Boy," I say. "Too much wholesome behavior and baked goods."

He pecks me on the cheek as the song ends, the lead singer leaning away from the mic and calling Ford's name.

"Duty calls." He picks up his cup of cider from a barrel-turned-table and steps onto the stage, positioning himself behind the microphone.

"Hey, everybody," he starts, making the crowd fall silent. "On behalf of my family and I, we want to thank y'all for coming out to this year's Orchard Fest to support the farm and the community." He pauses for a soft applause. "Mama, how long have y'all been doing this out here?" Across the tent, Charlene calls a number to him while holding up her fingers. "Thirty-six years," Ford says with a grin, causing another round of claps and yells to break out. "We appreciate y'all. Thanks for that. I know the high school athletics department really appreciates you spending all your money." He gestures toward the athletes with his cup, and they give obnoxious yells, making everyone chuckle. "Enjoy the night. Thank y'all again." He lifts a hand in a wave, moves away from the mic, but seems to decide he's not finished because he stops, cranes his neck so his mouth is behind the mic again, and gives me a devious grin. "And, one important announcement I forgot to make"—I glare at him—"Scotty Armstrong is my girlfriend."

The tent erupts with laughs and claps, and I mouth, *I hate you* to him. He grins, wide, and raises a cup of cider to the crowd, finishing it off with, "Thank y'all for coming out tonight. Have fun." Then he steps off the stage, sets his cider down and pulls me to the center of the dance floor.

"You're a damn asshole."

He twirls me and pulls me back to him, our boots shuffling in the hay. "There's the viper," he says, his hand splayed across my back as we dance. "You know everyone here's jealous of me, right?"

More people join the dance floor; I pinch my lips to hide my smile. "Liar."

"I'm telling you." He twirls me again, gripping me tight when he pulls me back in. "Every man wants to know what you're hiding under this dress, and every woman wishes she looked half as good as you."

I lift my chin to meet his eyes. "And what are you thinking?"

"I'm thinking you just made out with me in front of half the town and I'm going to be the one to peel that dress off as soon as we can convince everyone to eat all this damn pie."

I laugh and it's genuine. As unexpected as this whole night has been, I can't wait for it to be just him and me, nothing in between.

At the end of the song, Wren's next to Luke, holding hands. My heart bursts.

"She's happy," Ford says.

"She is."

"Because of you," he adds.

I scoff. "Hardly."

He gives me a knowing look over the rim of his cup.

"Ford Callahan," a woman's voice shouts. "Didn't even get my blessing." June pounces toward us in a calf-length denim dress and boots, curly red hair down and framing her smiling face. "I've been looking for you!" She wraps me in a hug.

"Ford and I were just talking about how we should fuck in an apple tree," I say with a grin.

She hugs Ford. "I'm sure Charlene would love that."

She might.

Camp walks up, easy smile on his face, and hugs me.

"Scotty," he says with a drawl, turning to shake Ford's hand. "Makes sense it took the cops to drag you out to one of these things."

"Oh, Campy," I say with a grin. "You know me so well."

When the next song starts to play—fast and filled with fiddles—it's June pulling me onto the dance floor.

Hand in hand we dance, laughing and singing. "You're happy," she shouts over the music, bouncing to the beat like the mom she is. "And you have a boyfriend."

I snort a laugh, putting my hands on her shoulders so we dance like middle schoolers. "And?"

She laughs as we sway. "And you're about to have great sex I want to hear all about."

"Maybe I'll record it."

Her face twists. "Boundaries."

Wren appears next to us, and we take her hands in ours. The three of us twirl like our only purpose in life is this very moment. And when my eyes meet with Ford's, he smiles, looking at me like I'm worth it.

For the first time in my life, with my best friend at one hand, a kid that doesn't belong to me in the other, and a man looking at me like he thinks I'm the best thing he's ever laid eyes on, I don't want a single thing to change. Not even the past.

THIRTY-THREE

"I don't know why we're at your house," I murmur into Ford's mouth. He fumbles to get a key in the door with one hand, refusing to take the other off me.

"I can't do what I want to do to you on Archie's floor mattress," he says, swinging the door open, our lips fused as we tumble into the darkness.

My body curves into his, and just his fingers gripping into the fabric of my dress makes my hips go soft. The fact I'm still clothed is mostly unbelievable since his hand on my thigh the entire drive home had me burning like a kerosene-soaked bed of charcoal. When he started sucking on my shoulder, I swerved off the road.

A lamp topples to the floor when we bump into a table, and it pulls us apart with a breathless laugh. Ford flicks on a light; I pick up the lamp.

As excited as I am to see what grown-up Ford can do with that body of his, being in his house is just as intriguing. I've dropped

Wren off, but I've never had a reason to come in. Never let myself get close enough to be invited. And now here I am, ground zero of where Ford and Wren are a family.

It's a modest ranch house, nothing fancy on the outside, but inside it's completely updated. Cozy and lived in. I step out of his grip and start to wander around the living room. I run my fingers across the back of a sectional couch and wooden coffee table, pausing at every picture covering the walls and bookshelves. Ford and Wren at all phases of life. Halloween costumes. Christmas mornings. Wren holding signs of first days of school, Ford receiving awards in different uniforms. A life so different than the one I've had. There are several of him as a kid; one of me, Zeb, and him. At that one we exchange a look, but the thickness in my throat warns me not to dwell on it. I pick each of them up and set them down, and he walks behind me, filling in a few times at what I'm looking at. At one of a little Wren and a woman I don't recognize, he says, "Riley. Her mom."

I think of the article and the woman she killed. He got shot and we never talked about it. Now isn't the time either.

I simply nod, setting it back down. "I have to tell you something," I say, looking at him. "I've been taking Wren to a therapist."

He smiles gently. "I know. Insurance contacted me about a form filled out wrong. I put the pieces together. She listed me on the paperwork, so they could at least tell me she was going. Figured you'd tell me when I needed to know."

Relief is instantaneous.

"I can't tell you why. I promised her."

He tucks a strand of hair behind my ear. "Okay."

I blow out a breath, lips making a raspberry sound, feeling lighter as I look to the bookshelf we've stopped at. "I don't know why you trust me with her. I feel like everything I tell her is most definitely the opposite of what I should be saying. I'm no parent, Ford. There's a good chance I'm ruining her for life."

He chuckles, taking a step as I do. "Scotty, there are a million parenting handbooks out there with a million pieces of advice. The truth is, nobody knows how to do it. Every kid is different. Every damn one. And guess where the book is that teaches you how to deal with a teenager whose mom was an addict and killed a girl?"

I look at him.

"Exactly. None of us know what we're doing. You're helping, whether you see it or not, you are."

"Maybe." A notebook with birds on the cover grabs my attention. I pick it up and thumb through it. A list, some of the boxes checked. I look at him.

He smiles, almost sheepish. "Birds of the southeast. I'm trying to see them all."

I laugh softly, setting it back down next to a bird guidebook and a pair of binoculars. "What a strange feeling it is to be jealous of birds," I tease, rounding the room to stop at a small space of wall. "And I like your house."

"Mmm." He rubs his nose against my cheek. "I like you in my house."

"Really?" The touch of his hands as my back hits the wall nearly makes me melt. "What else do you like?"

Against my bare shoulder he works lips and tongue across my skin, barely stopping to say, "I like how your nipples look in my shirt you wear to bed."

Ladies and gentlemen, we are off to the races.

"Silenced again, Viper?" He slides my dress up my hip, leading to me hooking one leg around him.

"No." My voice is raspy as his mouth moves from my shoulder to jaw. "I'm trying to figure out the virtuous way to tell you that I'm hot and bothered and you're taking too damn long."

He growls—a very sexy noise I want to record for every lonely night I ever have—and lifts me up, my dress bunching around my waist as he presses his lips to mine. He carries me down the hall, stopping to kick open a door.

When we cross the threshold of his bedroom, it's as if it has been charged with pure sex. Like pheromones in the air turn us into animals making us move in a fuck-driven fury.

His shoes, my boots.

His shirt, my dress.

Mouths connected, I unbuckle his belt. He pulls his jeans down. Steps back, just slightly, looking at me like he's studying me. Like he wants to be able to recall the black lace of my bra or the thin strips of my panties. Learn the freckles on my skin the way some people know constellations in the sky. He puts his index finger on my sternum, dragging it down between the swell of my breasts to my belly button. Lower. With just his index finger over the black satin of my panties, he *just* touches me—near but not on—and he watches me. Every movement of my muscles. Every rise of my chest.

I reach my hands in the top of his boxers and he stops me.

"I've waited too long to rush this, Scotty."

The slowness he moves thickens the want in the air until it's so severe, it's hard to breathe. Hard to think through the anticipation. The aches. The hunger my entire body is experiencing.

Fingers working, he presses into me but not hard enough. I need to feel him. Taste him. *Something.*

Too fast for him to stop me, I grab the band of his boxers and drag them straight down his legs, dropping to my knees.

"Sco—" Him in my mouth, the rest of my name turns to a moan on his lips. And though he's not touching me, his fingers in my hair and him filling my mouth to the point of watering my eyes makes me wonder if I'm going to get off, just like this.

It would be a first, and with him, I'm here for it.

When his hips chase my mouth with more urgency, my lips are on his thighs, his hips. I pause at the bruise on his ribs, touching it gently, licking it then kissing before moving across his chest until I'm standing again, sucking his neck.

His hand slides down.

Low.

Lower.

In.

Pumping.

Hard.

My hips grind his hand.

"This is new," I say with a gasp.

"And?" He doesn't stop, just pulls back enough so he can see me while he works. It's sexy, him watching me as I relearn every move, taste, and sound of him.

Pump. Pump. *Pump.*

"And," I grit out, grinding against his hand more uncontrolled and desperate for more friction, "I approve."

His mouth is back on mine. One hand works, and the other fumbles with my bra.

It's off; his free hand finds a breast, pinches until I moan. *Again.* His hardness presses right into my belly and hits my skin like a branding iron, heating me straight to the core.

"I need to taste you."

Yes, please.

I don't need to respond; he's sliding my panties down my legs—fast—directing me to the bed. I comply. He's on his knees, draping my legs over his shoulders and turning my whimpers into cries when I feel his tongue on my flesh. I am about three breaths away from detonation.

"Holy shit," I say through gritted teeth as my back arches off the bed and he becomes a sorcerer of eatery with every swipe of his tongue and nip of his teeth.

Then he's up, kneeling above me, hard and hot. "Are we supposed to use a condom?" he asks, fumbling with a drawer at his nightstand. "I don't know if I have one. I haven't been—you know—but . . ." He looks at me, almost panicked.

I laugh; it's breathy. I kiss him. "I can't get pregnant." He stills for a split second before I add, "And you could be covered with syphilis and you'd still be given access."

He responds by way of pressing all of him against all of me. And while everything has been frantic and urgent, everything now is like we're moving through honey. Every touch slow, every move on purpose. Our flavors on our lips come together to make a taste that is so very distinctly us.

"You ready?" he asks, so sincere—so consuming—once again it's hard to breathe.

I nod from beneath him, tilt my hips at the same time there's a hitch of his, and he's in. Stretching. Making my fingernails dig into his back.

"God, Scotty," he groans as he moves between kisses. "You feel so damn good."

I pull my mouth from his to watch where we connect, falling into an erotic trance of him. Us. The tension working the muscles of his arms and neck as he hovers over me. The movement of his chest and stomach as his spine undulates all of him in and out of me. The light from the window as it paints his silhouette.

It's perfection. He is. Every damn inch of him.

Then there's a shift; he's close. His movements are less controlled with every thrust, and his jaw is in a permanent clench. Breaths shaky. His lids go heavy, dark in the dim light. And with the swelling pleasure building, there's a familiar pang of desperate panic shooting through me I can't ignore. I smash my mouth against his then push my palms into his chest. He pulls back but follows my lead, repositioning himself behind me when I get on my hands and knees.

He stills, tracing his fingers down the length of my spine.

He sees.

Not now.

I look over my shoulder, and his eyes meet mine.

"No," I demand. "Don't stop."

Hands at the crease of my hips, he nods and does what I need him to: holds me tight and fucks me hard. He slams me to the hilt, one, two, three more times, drawing all my attention inward to that glorious spot he's hitting until I shatter with a cry, wave after pleasurable wave rolling through me.

He doesn't stop. On the contrary, me hitting a peak prompts him forward with a new sense of urgency, amplifying every sensation as he drives into me. His fingers dig deeper into my skin and every thrust hits harder than the last until he finishes with a slew of sworn words that come off his tongue like a prayer. He empties, holding on to me the whole time, and we crash to the bed to the soundtrack of strangled breaths and soft laughs, two puddles of satiated bliss.

Grown man Ford Callahan absolutely lived up to every battery-operated fantasy I've conjured up about him.

On my belly with a sheet over my legs, I fold my arms under my cheek and face him. He's on his back, one arm bent behind his head, the other resting across his chest, rising and falling with the cadence of his breath.

He looks at me, sexy smile on his talented mouth. "You're louder than I remember," he says.

"Really?" I hum, satisfied drawl in my voice. "You didn't seem to mind."

He rolls on his side, sheet draped across his beautiful body as he runs a finger up and down the music notes of my spine. The same as Zeb's. The same as his. "You didn't tell me about these."

"Girl needs some secrets." He makes an agreeable sound but says nothing, continuing the hypnotizing movement. "He ever tell you why he got them on his back?" I ask. He shakes his head. "He said, *'Keep the things you love at your back and they'll never break your heart.'*"

He laughs softly. "That's either incredibly insightful or terribly tragic."

"That was him, right?" I say with a laugh of my own. "He probably just got a drunk tattoo and made that up later."

He puffs a soft laugh, moving his fingers from my spine to my shoulder. "How long have you known you couldn't get pregnant?"

"Umm." I turn my head away from him, propping my chin on my folded arms, looking at the wood grain lines of his headboard. "I actually got pregnant once. A careless thing." I clear my throat. "I got an infection and scar tissue kind of took over after that."

His hand stills. "God, Scotty. I'm sorry."

I force myself to look at him and speak around the boulder in my throat. "It's fine. I wouldn't have made any kind of mom, anyway."

His mouth moves like he wants to speak, so I silence him by propping myself up and kissing him. When I start to pull away, he pulls me back, making it last longer. A sweet tangling of our lips and rubbing of our tongues.

"You're more beautiful now than you were twenty years ago," he says when we finally pull apart, his hands going to my hair.

I grin. "Liar."

"Maybe," he says, slight smile on his lips. "A liar in love sees what he wants, I guess."

My head jerks back. Between the sincere look in his eyes and what he's just said, a five-alarm siren blares through me, and my throat pinches so tightly I wonder if I'll black out.

He loves me.

I peck one quick kiss on his lips and pull out of his arms, swinging my legs out of bed and working to find my clothes strewn about the floor and tangled in the sheets.

"What are you doing?" he asks, brow furrowed.

"Um." I focus on sliding my panties up my legs, ignoring the fact my thighs are still slick with him. "I, uh, have to get going."

"Going?" He sits up fully, watching me pull my dress overhead. "Why?"

Because you just said that and I'm freaking out.

"Molly, for one," I say, tugging a boot on.

"The dog that essentially takes care of herself?" he asks, not hiding his irritation.

"The one and only." I force a smile, shoving my foot into my other boot and sitting on the edge of the bed next to him. "But, I liked this. Tonight. This. You. A lot, really. Even better than without touching."

When I grin, he doesn't.

"You're leaving and aren't coming back?"

"Uh." I look away from him. "Not tonight, no. Tomorrow I have an LL thing. But after?"

He nods slightly, as if still processing, and looks away from me. When he says, "Maybe," I know I've hurt him, and I hate myself. But I can't change that here, not now. Not with the way he's looking at me and making me feel.

I lean in and kiss him lightly. He doesn't move to make it last or follow me out when I stand. I'm in the doorway when he says, "Give me something real right now."

I take in how beautiful he is in his bed and wish so badly I was lying naked next to him. "I wish I didn't have to go."

Before he can say anything or try to convince me otherwise, I go, stopping only in the living room to thumb through one of the books and snap a picture.

Alone in a lumpy bed on the floor, I spend the entire night wishing I knew how to stay.

THIRTY-FOUR

"Hi. I'm Blair, and I'm addicted to exercise." Blair laughs softly, looking around the room like she'd rather be doing anything but. She's beautiful—in perfect shape and wearing jeans and a sweater that complement her athletic physique. "And I feel stupid talking about it. Like, who can't stop running?" She makes a face, almost making fun of herself. A few people chuckle. "Anyway, I've sat here, month after month and just thought, what the heck, Blair, why not share. So, here we are.

"I don't have a big success story. I'm not *clean*. Every day I struggle to stop running. To get off the Peloton. To not do another set with the weights. But I have been stopping more. Most of the time. Just one day at a time, that's what's worked for me. I just say, Blair, you run two miles today, and then maybe tomorrow you can run three. Or whatever it is.

"I wasn't healthy as a kid, and my parents weren't healthy. I got made fun of a lot for being fat . . . In my twenties, that changed. I got healthy and lost the weight. And I married a man that's—" A breath whooshes out of her and her eyes go glassy, voice cracking with her next words. "He's dang perfect. And I don't just mean handsome, I mean, the man just worships me. And we had babies. Three. Perfect babies just like him. And gosh, the number they did on my body." She shakes her head with a slight laugh and wipes under her eyes.

"I started working out to get the baby weight off, and I just forgot to stop, I guess. And now, I think, I don't want him to see me in case I don't live up to his standards. I've lost the weight but still have the stretch marks. Look good in jeans but not a bathing suit. All the stories we tell ourselves. And I think of my parents—so stinking unhealthy—and it just makes me go and go and go. Like, what if one day, he looks at me and sees the fat girl and her parents then decides to get the heck out of town. Like he got conned."

She sniffs and toys with the hem of her sweater. "So that's my sob story." She laughs, but it's empty. "One day at a time."

Mel gives her a sincere smile.

"What do you do when your husband looks at you?" I ask, not missing the shocked look on Mel's face at my gentle tone. "Or compliments you?" Everyone turns toward me, blinking. "Or when that voice you mentioned gets too loud?"

"I used to deflect. Convince myself he's lying. Just being nice. Heck, I'd try to convince him he didn't know what he was looking at by pointing out all my flaws. Like I was trying to scare him off before he figured it all out on his own." Even I can't ignore how familiar this sounds. "I'd hide myself all the time. But one night we were watching that movie *Shrek*—the one about the ogre. My kids were laughing about how Fiona looked—that's the lady ogre—and he said, *'I'd love your mother if she was an ogre. I'd love her without hair and without legs. And if she had hairy warts, I'd kiss them.'* And I looked at him, and he meant it. And that night I let him see me naked—" She looks at Mel. "Sorry if that's too much information." Mel smiles and mouths, *it's fine.* "Anyway, I just let him look at me. And it was hard that first time—it had been a while. And I cried like a baby. But then I just kept letting him. Even when it was hard. Even when I'm scared he's going to see something he doesn't like and take off like a jackrabbit. And that voice?" She shrugs. "I've just learned I can't control it. We all know a loudmouth, right?" Mel looks at me with raised eyebrows. "But, I keep telling myself, just because it's loud, don't mean it's right." She laughs like she doesn't believe it, but a smile also lingers like she wants to.

"Thank you, Blair," Mel says from the podium. "Who wants to go next?"

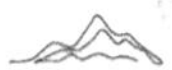

"That was very un-rabid of you today," Mel says with a drag of her cigarette. "You sick?"

I laugh softly, shrugging my shoulders as I look out at the mountainous horizon line and watch Gary trudge across the parking lot.

Ford rolls by in his truck, waving at Mel who waves back. He lifts his chin at me, and it sets a hive of bees loose in my belly as I force a smile.

Mel lets out a smoky exhale. "The world is smaller than we give it credit. You know Ford helped me get in touch with the right people to start these meetings?"

"I didn't know that." Out of the corner of my eye, I notice June, waving with two cups of coffee by her minivan. "Doesn't surprise me though. He's that kind."

Mel's brows lift. "That kind?"

"The kind that makes everything better by simply existing."

She regards me a bit.

"You love him." Just like when Glory said it, it's not a question. "Makes sense. He's about the only person I know who could tolerate you."

I chuckle softly.

"I'm not sure I know how to love."

She blows out a final smoky breath and stubs out her cigarette. "Of course you do, Scotty. One day at a time, just like Blair said. We don't talk about it enough. We look at big victories, always comparing our beginnings to someone else's end. Hell, every book on the shelf started with a single word, but we don't think of it that way. We see the collective. You want to love that man?" She points the stubbed-out nub of a cigarette at me. "You start from there and do it like Blair did. Slow, scared, but without looking back."

I let the words replay themselves. "Maybe."

She picks up the LL sign with a huff. "You're annoying when you're nice."

"You're annoying when you're a sober savant, I guess we're even."

We exchange a look of teasing contempt before I jog across the parking lot to June and take the coffee she offers with greedy hands and a *gimme*.

"You were good in there today," she says, taking a nonchalant sip from her cup.

I snap my eyes to her. "You listen?"

She scoffs. "You're going to LL meetings, of course I listen."

"That's fucking rude, Joo!"

She barks out a laugh. "Says the woman who eavesdropped on my therapy sessions with dead bodies for years."

"Where do you listen from?" I ask, incredulous. Feeling violated as I look at the church.

"The hall." She shrugs. "The door is cracked, so I just stand out there and can hear. Your loud mouth makes it easy."

We settle on the bumper of her minivan.

"Wanna tell me what happened with Ford last night?" she asks.

"Hmm." She frowns at the word, and I grin before taking a sip of my coffee. "He said he was in love with me and asked me to stay the night."

She drops her head onto my shoulder as we look at the mountains. "You tell him?"

I shake my head, taking another sip.

"You need to, Scott. All of it."

The idea opens a deep abyss inside of me.

"I don't know how."

"Just . . . I don't know . . . start with something. Anything. It's Ford, you know? For a cop, he's, like, the least scary person there is."

We both laugh at this then fall quiet, drinking our coffee as we watch cars drive by, and the sun paints the burnt orange and yellow slopes of the mountains around us.

June fidgets next to me, opening and closing her mouth several times without saying anything.

"Alright," I say, knowing damn well she's dying inside. "Let's hear it. Which vice are we starting with?"

"Thank God!" The words gush out so fast and loud it's like they've been trapped in her mouth for months. "I'd like to start with the nude maids, please and thank you."

I laugh, hard, and then we do what we do: We drink our coffee and talk until we run out of words. As confused as I am about Ford, the house, my whole life in general, I've forgotten how my best friend always feels like home. How without her friendship, I might not have survived all my hardest days.

"You know," June says, opening her driver's door as we pack up to leave. "You move to the desert, we don't get this."

I lean a hip against my Bronco. "You're using me for my connection with the addicts?"

She grins. "It's your only redeeming quality."

Outside the two-story house in the cookie-cutter neighborhood, I cut the engine and park along the street. The familiar woman walks to the mailbox and sees me, smiling as she crosses the street to where I'm parked.

She has long dark hair, a curvy build, and the same friendly face she had twenty years ago when I met her. She was young; I was younger.

"Scotty." She swats me lightly with a stack of mail, smile webbing lines out from around her eyes. "Will you just knock on the door one of these days already? How many times do I have to invite you?"

"Hey, Merritt. I don't want to intrude." I look around the neighborhood. "Just creep the neighbors out."

"Yeah, well." She chuckles and pushes her bangs out of her eyes. "HOA president lives across the street; it would be good for him to be creeped out."

"Everyone good?"

She nods. "Everyone's good. He's not here right now—basketball or something—but school is going good. Good grades and not partying too much."

"The gene must have skipped a generation," I joke.

She grins, looking at the house. "I got supper on, so I have to get back inside, but I mean it, Scotty, anytime. Too many Sundays of you coming by not to say hello. For him not to know you."

A knot forms in my throat, and I start the engine. "Maybe."

Merritt taps the door with her mail. "Hopefully."

THIRTY-FIVE

"We have Wyatt Duncan today," Wanda says with a smack of her gum as she wheels him across her workshop. "Already got the music playing too. Hear that?" She pauses with a smile, tilting her head. "Old guy liked Frankie Sinatra."

Dondi emerges from the body cooler, face lighting up when he sees me. "The Ash Queen is in the house of flames."

"Dondi," I say, barely glancing at him from the paperwork I'm flipping through. "How's it going?"

"Wanda has revealed new colors in the rainbow," he says wistfully. When I look at him again, he and Wanda are giving each other goo-goo eyes.

"Okay."

"And Mr. Selleck said he's noticed you haven't been in as much lately and wanted to know if it meant you were thinking about selling."

"Sure," I say, only half joking. "Tell him to meet me in the retort to iron out the details."

He laughs. "Funny as ever." Then he gives Wanda a kiss that makes her giggle and takes a dramatic bow my way. "The Dondinator is off to transport those who can no longer transport themselves."

When he's gone, I look at Wanda. "Are you two . . . for real?"

She smacks her gum. "Real as Reba's red hair, honey."

I do not know if Reba's red hair is real.

I place the stainless-steel ID tag in the casket next to Wyatt as Wanda hums along with "Fly Me to the Moon," breaking up her song with a pop of a bubble.

"Did you try to kill your ex-husband?"

She's stunned for exactly a split second before a mischievous smile curls her lips. "Between you and me"—her eyes dart around the room as if making sure we're alone—"yes."

At my bulging eyes she swats a hand through the air with a chuckle. "You already knew the truth, honey. I could tell."

I bat my tongue around my mouth as I let this sink in. "Should I be worried about Dondi?"

A laugh pops the bubble she's blowing. "I'm sorry." She puts a hand over her mouth trying to stop the laugher but only making it louder, tears dripping down her face. "No, honey."

She composes herself, dabbing her eyes with her index fingers, mascara smudging the tips of each. Hands on her hips, she looks at me. "Cal—my ex-husband—beat the shit out of me."

"What?!" I am floored.

"Shocked it didn't make it into the papers?" She lifts a brow. "Means he did it right. That's how it works—they get good at it. Hitting you where it can hide. Making you think it's your fault. Making you think it won't happen again and again and again. I said to him one day, *'Cal, I make you mad enough, why don't I just leave and we'll both be happier?'*" She shakes her head with a sad smile. "No way in hell he was letting me leave. But I wasn't spending my life like that, either. Covered up because he didn't like the way I dressed or because I was marred with bruises." She pops a shoulder. "I grinned, took it, and started putting antifreeze in his shakes. I didn't know what I was doing, that's how I got caught. But that's also why the charges got dropped. I wised up those last few months, started taking pictures of every mark he put on me. My lawyer said drop the charges and we won't show these. And voilà," she says with a smile and wiggle of her fingers. "You got Wanda."

And just like that, Wanda the Wicked becomes my new hero.

"Aren't you worried about repeating the past? That Dondi might—I don't know—be the same or care or . . . something?"

She laughs loudly at this. "You know what Dondi does when he and I go out?"

"I can only imagine."

"He lets me shine, honey. My clothes and my makeup, he loves me for it. Other men look, he doesn't care. I think he kinda likes the attention." She gives me a look that says *what a mythical creature.* "And he's a vegetarian. If he won't eat a chicken nugget, Dondi's never laying a finger on me. If he did"—she shrugs—"I know better now. It happens once and I'll fight back."

"So you're just going to be with him? Just like that? Regardless of everything?"

She grins. "Just like that, honey. That's how life works. We die a million times to get to who we're supposed to be. I'm not who I was—that woman is long gone. She picked a bad man and chose a bad way to get out. She was desperate. And I told Dondi everything. I'm never going to shrink down for someone else again—the good or bad parts. Hide them or pretend they aren't there, even if they make me feel ugly." She looks at me, emotion filling her eyes as her voice cracks. "You know what he says when he introduces me to his friends? He says, *'This is my girlfriend Wanda, she's the bravest woman I've ever known.'*" Tears line her spider-legged lashes.

I see her anew. Dondi too. These two mismatched people separated by decades have seemingly found what they need in one another. Despite complicated histories and quirks, they're . . . happy. It's as simple and weird as that. Dondi and Wanda make each other happy.

"Are you worried he'll change his mind?"

Her lips pinch like this has never once occurred to her. "I've never thought about it, but the convincing him otherwise sounds fun." She shimmies her shoulders, and her chest jiggles.

I can't help it, I smile. "You're kind of a badass, Wanda."

"Well thank you, honey," she says with a knowing shake of her head.

Wanda lines the casket up with the retort, and I think of Blair—baring her body to her husband and literally running herself crazy to keep him, even though she doesn't need to. I think of my parents. Zeb. The hamster wheel of shit that seems impossible to jump from, yet Wanda did. Without running away. Without even changing who she was. If anything, it seems to have made her *more* of herself.

I clear my throat. "Would you want to run the send-off today?"

She stills, mid-blowing of a bubble, and stares at me. When she sees I'm serious, she sucks the gum in her mouth and looks down at her outfit, smoothing her hands down her bold, striped, too-fitted shirt before looking at me. "Like this?"

I smirk. "You think I'm going to be the one to try and hide Wanda the Wicked?"

Her face fills with a mixture of flattery and downright disbelief. "Well, okay then, honey."

"Okay then."

When the family arrives—Wyatt's wife and two grown sons—I watch from my office. Wanda's louder than I am, more affectionate with them as she hugs each of them and cries right beside them, but she cares and it's evident. Not for the same reasons as me, but she cares just the same. She could run the place. I see it—she's proven it the last couple months of me being gone—and I know if someone like Zeb ever got dropped off, he wouldn't be alone or in a sheet. She would sit with him and see him until the very end.

And though it's been part of my plan for getting out of here since Lydia gave me the house, I've yet to put much serious thought into what it looks like if I'm not here. Not just what would happen without me here, what I would do without being here. For the first time in twenty years, I wonder what life might be like if it wasn't consumed with death and ashes.

Thirty-Six

"Is that a mile?" Wren asks, barely out of breath as she jogs next to me.

I nod.

"Ha," she huffs out, slowing to a walk. "We're getting better."

I slow to match her pace, Molly doing the same. "I'm definitely feeling less pissed about the situation."

"What happened to you this weekend?" she asks as we turn back toward the house. "After my dad's declaration I thought you'd, like, live at my house or something."

"Just because your dad went all '90s rom-com with a microphone doesn't mean I don't have a life."

She rolls her eyes with a light shake of her head. "Okay."

"What about you and Luke?" I ask in a sing-songy voice. "You make out behind a barrel of cider?" She makes a face but her cheeks flush. "You did!" I shout, bumping my shoulder against hers. "And?"

"And what?" she asks, unable to hide a smile.

"And, I don't know, are you a thing or like, you know, taking blood oaths and eloping?"

"No." She snorts a laugh before her expression turns serious. "I've been thinking about my arms. My scars, I mean—no." She reads the look on my face, answering my unspoken question. "I haven't done it. Just, I don't know, at some point I might need to explain it. If I'm wearing less clothes."

I suck in a sharp breath. "Sex?!"

"Scotty! I'm fifteen." She says it like I'm preposterous.

"Right. I was sixteen when your dad got the goods from me." She groans. "I'm just saying there's time."

"Anyway. Do I just tell him? Or hide it? Or lie? Or . . . ?"

We stop walking and I look at her. She looks young—so young—and scared. And, as different as our problems are, I get it. "I think, when you decide he's worth seeing more of your skin, you know he's worthy of knowing. If you own your choices, they can't own you." Wanda and Blair flash through my mind. "And if he can't handle it, that's a him problem, not a you problem."

Some of the worry leaves her face. "Okay."

We walk until Molly stops to sniff a tree.

"Remember that girl I was telling you about that I thought liked Luke?"

I scoff. "The Letts girl?"

"Yeah, Becca. Well, so weird, since the festival she's been nice. Really nice. I guess I read her wrong. We're hanging out after school this week."

I stop dead in my tracks in the middle of the road. "Why in a shit-swirled milkshake would you want to do that?"

"Uh, because she's being nice," she says, using a tone that makes my middle finger twitch. My eyes narrow as I recall just how *nice* the Letts girl was before I squashed her like a cockroach. "And my only friend can't be a forty-one-year-old loner."

"Okay," I drawl, walking again as I grip Molly's leash so tight it burns my skin. "Do you think it's smart? I knew her mom and, I can tell you—"

"Everyone isn't their mother," she snaps.

And there it is. All roads lead to us not being our mothers.

I wonder if she wants to slap me as badly as I want to slap her. We say nothing as we walk. I debate telling her about the festival and what the girls said, but it will crush her. All the progress she's made will be erased.

"Right," I finally say, taking the route less violent. "All I'm saying is be careful."

She rolls her eyes. "Let's run the rest of the way."

Before I can object, she takes off ahead of me, leaving me in her dust.

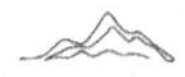

Wren stays long enough to greet Ford with a quick hug and grab her bike.

As she rides away, I decide teenagers are assholes.

Ford, however, standing in his uniform with arms folded over his chest and leaning against his patrol car looks like a delicious snack I'd like to devour. It's only been a couple days since the festival—since I left him in the middle of the night—but I've kept my distance. I texted him a few times, but other than the LL meeting, I haven't seen him. And I've missed him. I wrap my arms around his waist and lean my cheek against his chest.

"You know," he says, the deep timbre of his voice vibrating my face, "I think girlfriend status means I'm supposed to see you more, not less."

"Told you labels were stupid."

He laughs, wrapping his arms around me. I prop my chin on his chest to look up at him; he plants a kiss on my lips. "You want to talk about what happened the other night?"

"Not yet."

He kisses me again. "I can handle that." Another kiss. "How was Wren today?"

"Fine." I push off his chest with a sigh. "She's hanging out with the Letts girl."

He chuckles. "Let me guess, you told her all about how you felt about her mom."

I give him a flat look. "I told her I didn't think it was a good idea and then she got, I don't know, pissed. Short. Like a different personality came out to play that made me . . . murdery."

"She's a teenager. Murdery is the name of the game." He takes my hand in his and kisses my thumb as we walk toward the house;

I consider his explanation and decide I hate it but bite my tongue. "What's that one?" he asks.

I follow his gaze to the bird feeder and grin. "Carolina chickadee."

"You trying to seduce me again?"

I laugh, climbing the steps and push the front door open. "Only if it's working."

"You saying the alphabet would seduce me."

"Bet you really enjoyed preschool with Ms. Mitchell."

He drops my hand and swats my ass, grin on his face as we step inside the house. "Damn, Scotty. Looks good in here."

I pinch my lips between my teeth, a futile attempt to hide my smile. Because he's right. It looks good. Damn good. The tan leather sofa is complemented by the dark wood floors; the natural light from the windows paints the whole house so perfectly it could be in a magazine or on one of the many blogs I scoured to pull it together. Canisters of flour and sugar, a coffee maker, and a toaster sit on the kitchen counter under shelves of mismatched mugs and glasses Wren helped me pick out from a local thrift shop. Zeb's record player with a box of records sits in a corner opposite a tall cactus in a large terra-cotta pot. The walls are bare, open for whomever comes next to fill them.

Ford runs a hand over the white marble countertops in the kitchen, tracing a subtle gold swirl. "What's next?"

"Well," I sigh, toeing off my tennis shoes. "Wren picked out a chair—some purple monstrosity—and I got a coffee table made by a guy who makes custom pieces from Rocky Ridge. That comes next week." I go over the list in my head, having just sent an update to Vince this morning. "They've been working on the bathrooms, which are still a demolished disaster. I have to pick tile for the backsplash, which, it needs to be the right color, you know?" I look around, shrug. "I guess that's it. Host Thanksgiving for June next month and get it listed." I pause, rework the list out in my head, then add, "Oh! And I got a huge-ass bed coming in a couple days."

I grin, proud of how far it's come.

Ford works his teeth over his bottom lip.

"You let Wren pick an ugly chair?"

"Yeah . . ."

"And you picked out a huge bed, custom table, and can't find the right color tile?"

My eyes narrow. "So?"

His eyebrows lift. "Doesn't sound like you want to sell."

I scoff. "I do."

"You say so." His lips twitch, making a look like he doesn't believe me as Molly trots over to him. "Sit," he commands. That bitch does.

"That dog is an asshole."

He chuckles as he scrubs her head. "How was work today?"

"Fine. Wanda tried to kill her husband. I guess I knew that." Ford's eyes widen so dramatically I laugh. "But . . ." I sit on the couch, he follows suit.

"But?"

I drop my head onto his lap and stretch my legs out; he runs his fingers through my hair. It strikes me how easy this feels. How comfortable and safe.

"But for the first time I imagined not being there. Doing something else."

"Like what?"

I stare at the apex of the ceiling.

"I don't know. Some days it feels like the reasons I started doing it don't match who I am today. Or who I want to be tomorrow." I make an exasperated noise and rub my hands on my face. "I don't know. It was a weird day, I guess. And I've known if I move I would sell it and do something else, but today I really pictured it. Me not there."

His hands are still in my hair, and he drops his chin to his chest to look at me. "*If* you move?"

I stare at the ceiling; I'm not talking about this. I don't know what I'm doing so my only plan is to vocalize none of it.

"Ah," he says, amused. "We're doing that thing where we pretend you didn't say something real." I sit upright and elbow him in the ribs without looking at him; he grunts through a laugh. "But," he says with an exaggerated pause, "I get that better than anyone. You want to do something different, do something different."

Those words hang between us as I try to picture it.

"I can think of a few things I'd like to do differently," I say, biting my lip and leaning into him.

He rumbles with a laugh. "Not in Archie's bed you don't."

"Prude."

"That's not what you said Saturday," he says in my ear, kissing the lobe and making a delicious warmth trickle over me. "But I have to go. Wren has something at the school I need to drive her to."

I groan again. "First the Letts girl then my good time, kids are the worst."

He laughs, stands, and tugs my hands so I do the same. "Only sometimes."

Scotty

How do you tell a teenager they have shitty taste in friends?

You there?

June

Sorry, I couldn't respond because I was laughing so hard over you thinking this is an actual option.

You're worthless.

Still laughing.

What kind of job should I have after I sell Happy Endings?

<incoming call from June>

THIRTY-SEVEN

"I'D LIKE THIS BLINDFOLD a lot more if you were naked and on top of me," Ford says, staggering through the grass, arms waving blindly in front of him.

I adjust the bag over my shoulder and guide him with my hands on his waist to the edge of an overgrown field surrounded by trees. "Sadly, I think you'll like this more."

He blinks to adjust his eyes as I remove the handkerchief from his head.

"A field?" he asks, confused.

"A field at over three thousand feet elevation," I correct.

"Okay." His obvious confusion makes this so much better. "And that's significant because . . . ?"

"Because the owner—who I found online in a bird forum—has been seeing golden-winged warblers migrating through on their way to South America." I grin. "According to your list you haven't seen one." I knew when he showed me his notebook at his house, I had to do something to be part of it. Give him one. Even running out of there like the house was on fire, I stopped to snap a picture. I pull two pairs of binoculars out of my bag. "He gave me permission to bring you."

His smile is like watching a star being born. "A golden-winged warbler?"

"Don't come on yourself, Golden Boy. Take the damn binoculars."

He laughs—giddy—and kisses me before taking them. I pull out my phone and follow the directions the owner sent me, walking along the rickety fence line until Ford stops me with a palm to my chest, cocking his head to the side to listen.

Binoculars at his face, he gestures for me to do the same. And there it is, a bird in a bush: grey, black, bright yellow, and white. *That's it,* he mouths, eyes wide and bright, looking back through his binoculars until it flies away.

I laugh at the sight. Ford is a complete nerd but makes bird-watching hot.

"Do you know how rare that is?" he asks, shaking his head in disbelief as we stand at the edge of the field. The passion in his voice would be hilarious if it didn't make him so much more appealing. Interesting. Seeing Ford Callahan look at a rare bird is like witnessing a once-in-a-lifetime cosmic event. The more he talks, the more an anxious pressure builds in me. "Their numbers are declining—severely—some people say it's because of the—"

"I've never stayed the night with a man," I blurt, effectively silencing his birding monologue. I fill my cheeks up with air and let them deflate, looking at the overgrown field instead of him and drawing courage from Wanda and Blair to keep me talking. "Since you, I've never slept in bed with anyone except June. Never had a sleepover with anyone else. I-I-I don't let anyone see me when I orgasm. That's why I turn away. After you . . ." I blow out a breath. "Just, after you it changed. I got scared that all my bad parts are all that will show. Every mistake. Every flaw. And I don't know how to handle watching someone feel so good. Like—" I scoff. "How can Scotty Armstrong ever make someone feel all that? So, I just don't look or let anyone else look. Ever. I turn away, so I can pretend I'm someone else and they can too. I read monster books because they don't make me feel bad about my life. They're ridiculous—though the sex is fascinating—" I shoot him a look that he smirks at. "But, I just . . . it's stupid, but some days I think, if a man can love a snake, maybe there's hope for me yet."

He's quiet, looking at me as I aimlessly move the dial on my binoculars.

"Well, say something already. I'm being vulnerable and sharing. Aren't you supposed to tell me good job or give me a damn gold star."

I brave a look at him, and he puts his binoculars in the bag before taking my face in his hands. "Good job." Then he kisses me, consuming me like he does with all his flavors and textures. Teeth, lips, and tongue. He pulls back, looking me square in the eyes, and says, "There's no rush—on any of this—but you need to know, I don't need to be inside you making you scream my name to feel good. You can turn away as much as you want. I still see you." Another kiss. "I'll follow your lead." With a smile he adds, "Not that I have a choice in the matter."

I nearly cry at the enormity of his words. *What is happening to me?* "I don't deserve you."

"You do." He slings an arm around my shoulder and cuts sinful eyes to me. "But I can find ways for you to make it up to me if you really need me to."

I laugh, kissing him one more time as I pick up the bag. "Well before you imagine me on my knees, you should know we're having turkey for dinner."

This earns a chuckle from him as we fall into step toward the Bronco. "A little early, but okay."

"I've never made one before and Thanksgiving is serious business for June," I explain. "I bought some for practice."

He slides his phone out of his back pocket and fires off a text before putting it away. "Sounds like the best date ever." At the Bronco, he looks at me, lips twitching as we open our doors. "How does a snake have sex with a person?"

In the driveway of the A-frame, I'm significantly lighter. It wasn't just being with Ford and seeing the ridiculous bird, it was telling him something more real than I have before. It's pulling him toward me instead of pushing him away. And though it's not everything, it was like a ton of bricks lifted off my chest in the instant the words were out.

At the house, Wren is sitting on the porch next to Molly. I look at Ford, confused. He gives nothing away.

"Hey," I say to her as I climb the steps. "What are you doing here?"

Wren points to a pile by the door: two sleeping bags and a duffle. "Dad texted."

I look at Ford.

He clears his throat. "I figured a turkey required at least three people. And maybe a movie." He pauses, rocking slightly on his heels. *Nervous?* "And Wren and I could sleep downstairs if it gets too late."

I bite my lip as a warm realization ripples through me. "A sleep-over?"

He shrugs, eyes smiling. "A sleepover." Then, "If that's okay."

"Yeah." I swallow. "That's okay."

"I'm starving," Wren says, oblivious to what's happening. To the fact she's watching me fall so deep in love with her dad I'll never be able to come back from it. It's not like it was when we were teenagers; it's more. Like I've unknowingly carried all those feelings with me for all these years and now it's morphed into something so gigantic it can't fit into any one place. I don't know what to do with it—don't know how to tell him or show him or be any sort of lover he deserves. I might never be able to say it, but the way he looks at me, it's as if he knows this is it. He's it. The thing that I can never untangle myself from. Whether I'm in a desert or he's in another city—we're it. And more: I don't want to leave him ... or her. I want them both—this feeling of us—for as long as I'm allowed to have it.

Then: What if I didn't leave at all? What if I stayed and this was just my life? Me, Ford, and Wren in an A-frame on Lake Ledger. Could it be this easy?

Instead of saying any of this, I take the turkey out of the fridge and pull a recipe up on my phone, reading through the steps.

"Four hours!" I shout, stunned, internally swearing at June for making me do this. "What the hell kind of food is this?!"

Wren and Ford laugh behind my back. As I preheat the oven, Ford orders a pizza. It arrives at the same time I put the turkey in.

We sit on the floor and play cards, laughing as Ford retells the story of seeing his beloved warbler, and eat pizza while we watch a movie. Wren rolls her eyes every time Ford kisses me.

For dessert, we have turkey. It doesn't taste half bad for sitting in an oven for hours and hours.

The night, in short, is a domestically boring experience and exactly like the kind of magic I've never believed I'd be privy to. Never believed could exist for me.

And when it's late—so late Wren has already fallen asleep on the couch—Ford kisses me good night and crawls into a sleeping bag on the floor as I go upstairs. I last five whole minutes in Archie's bed before the short distance between us starts to feel like a million miles. I scoop up all my blankets and drag them down the steps, making a bed on the floor next to Ford. His fingers interlace with mine as we stare at each other in the darkness, a moment more intimate than anything I've ever felt naked.

"Ford," I whisper when it looks like he's fallen asleep.

"Hm?" he says, not opening his eyes.

"How freaked out would Wren be if she woke up and I was in your sleeping bag."

A sleepy laugh rumbles in his chest.

"Ford," I repeat.

"Hm?"

"Thank you."

He squeezes my hand. And then, we fall asleep.

Together.

Thirty-Eight

"How did it go?" I ask Wren as she gets in the passenger seat and buckles her seatbelt.

"Fine."

"*Fine*," I mock as I back out of the space in front of the therapist's office. "You wanna talk about it?"

She shrugs.

"You tell her you took up hard drugs and started hanging out with the demon spawn of Jessica Letts?"

"Can you not?"

"Can you not?" I echo in a namby-pamby voice.

We're quiet for a full angry violin song, her snapping the rubber band on her wrist the entire time.

Finally: "We talked about what my mom did. So that was fun."

I turn the blinker to change lanes. "Moms are a barrel of laughs, aren't they?"

Out of the corner of my eye I see her pinch the sleeves of her sweater.

"It's like I feel guilty for her," she continues. "She killed someone. Sometimes when I think about her it's all I think about her. Like the bad thing is all she is. And—" Her gaze swings out the passenger window and she lets out a sigh. "Sometimes I wonder if I could have done something to stop it. Stop her."

I slam on the brakes right in the middle of the road, cars honking as they swerve around us.

"No." My voice comes out angrier than I expect. "This is not on you, Wren. Ever." She says nothing. "Your mom made her own choices. She's her own person. What she did or didn't do is not ever *ever* on you. Got it?"

"You blame yourself for your brother and dad." Her gaze shifts back to me as cars continue to swerve around us. "It's not that different, right?"

Her words hover in the Bronco, violins ripping through the speakers as my pulse rams at the back of my throat. I do blame myself, but it's different. It has to be. *Right?* At once I'm twenty and begging Zeb to get help, him telling me I'm overreacting. He never once listened to a word I said about him using. Never once tried to get help.

"And," she continues, blowing out a breath, "I think about the girl that died and her family. I wonder if they hate me."

Through my spinning thoughts, my mind goes to the article in Ford's folder, which has been totally off my radar. Ford knows the family, he has to. Emmeline Hill, I remember the name but absolutely can't place it.

"My dad knows the mom—he told me. She works in a nursery."

A nursery.

Emmeline Hill.

That's a lot of sevens.

How the hell did I miss that?

I floor the gas, jerk the wheel, and make an illegal U-turn, causing a minivan to stop in the middle of the road.

"I thought we were going to pick out tile for the backsplash," Wren mumbles.

"Change of plans."

At Blue Ridge Blooms, she looks at me when I turn off the Bronco. "Plants?"

"Humor me."

She rolls her eyes but does what I say.

The late October air is cool, borderline cold when the wind blows, and even in my thickest blazer, it chills me to my bones. There are only two other vehicles in the parking lot, one I recognize. We wander through a storefront filled with bags of soil, seeds, bird feeders, and birdseed to a greenhouse that's unseasonably warm.

Across the rows of potted plants I spot Mel, watering some ferns with a hose.

She sees me, shocked expression flittering across her face before she waves.

"I must have pissed someone off in my last life to require me to see you more than once in a month," Mel says with a wry grin as she tugs her gardening gloves off and tucks them into a green apron tied around her waist. She looks at Wren. "And I see you've started taking hostages."

"If it wouldn't drive you to drink, Mel, I'd tell you to fuck off."

She chuckles and eyes Wren again.

"This is Wren," I tell her. Wren's mouth curves into a small smile but she stays quiet. "Callahan," I tack on.

Mel looks at me, then does a double take. "I see."

"Wren," I say, looking at her and feeling my own heart ache with what I'm about to hit her with. "Your mom killed Mel's daughter."

Wren blanches before her face fills with emotion. But it's not me she's looking at, it's Mel. They stare at each other, saying nothing, no doubt trying to digest what those words mean to each of them.

Wren straightens and lifts her chin as if fortifying herself to speak. When she opens her mouth, instead of words, it's a loud sob that escapes her.

"I'm so sorry," she cries, tears streaming down her face, every single one of them hammering a dent in my heart. She jams her palms in her eyes, another apology coming out barely discernable.

Mel, without missing a beat, wraps her arms around her and takes her into her chest, acting every bit of the mother she is as tears form in her own eyes. "Sweetheart, you have nothing to apologize for." She rubs a palm across Wren's back. "Nothing in the world."

They seem to stand like this for a year, a tangled-up mess of cried apologies and arms. When they pull apart, they both wipe their eyes.

I realize I'm intruding.

"I'm going to go look at bird feeders so you two can talk for a bit. Gotta stay on your dad's good side so I can get in his pants, you know?"

They grimace and I grin, leaving them as they sit on a metal bench between rows of plants.

Thirty minutes later, Wren gets in the Bronco with a bird feeder that holds jelly and orange wedges as Mel and I stand on the sidewalk.

"Never took you for an Emmeline," I tell her with a sideways look.

Mel chuckles softly. "Your delivery could've used some work," she says. "But she's got a heart like Ford. Thank you for this. Ghosts come in all forms but haunt us just the same."

"I knew you had a weakness for good girls raised by bad women." I give her a cheeky grin before turning my attention to Wren through the windshield. "She's carrying a lot of hurts—a lot of guilt that shouldn't even be hers to begin with—I thought seeing you would help. Make her realize that she doesn't have to be what her mom did. That her rocky start doesn't mean a rocky future."

She makes an agreeable grunt.

"Scotty," she calls as I walk to the driver's side of the Bronco; I glance at her. "You and she aren't so different. You should take your own advice. Might do you some good."

THIRTY-NINE

"You're looking . . ." I assess Wanda's clothes clinging to her body like neon plastic wrap, leaving nothing to the imagination as she wheels a casket into the cremation room. "Bold."

She fluffs her hair, smiling wide. "Bold and the beautiful, just like my favorite soaps."

I laugh under my breath and turn my attention to the woman in the casket. Alida Boudreaux is Black and in her early sixties with perfect skin that glows against the shine of the gold dress she's in. Even though I know she's dead, it's as though her full lips are smiling.

"Wanda." She looks at me. "You ever confront your ex-husband?"

"Psh!" She cuts her hand through the air. "Got me nothing but a black eye when we were married if that's what you mean. After though . . ." Her voice trails off as she chews the inside of her lip. "After, we were in a room and the lawyers stepped out. For whatever reason, they left us alone. He looked at me, just like I'm looking at you right here, and he said, *'I loved you the only way I knew how, Wanda.'*" Her eyebrows hitch high on her head. "I rolled my eyes at the time, but now"—she shrugs one shoulder—"now I think maybe I get it. Not that it excuses it. Don't change how I feel about the situation or him, but . . . broken people break people if they don't get their shit fixed." She blows a bubble. "Even though I tried to kill him, part of me hopes he figures it out. Hunts his demons down and destroys 'em so he can move forward." She pauses as if replaying her words for accuracy. "Of course, the rest of me hopes someone ties him to the train tracks like a penny, and he gets flattened right out of existence." She giggles.

Despite how morbid it is, I chuckle as I adjust the volume of the music—a Zydeco band whose rich sounds of saxophones shift the atmosphere of the whole building to that of a bar during Mardi Gras.

"Looks like the family's arriving, honey." Wanda nods toward the window looking into the witnessing room where people have started to file through the front door—a shocking amount—all dressed in bright colors and large hats, same dark skin as Alida's.

"Let's send her off, then," I say as I hang the clipboard on the hook.

The door to the witnessing room bumps against someone as I open it, forcing me to wedge my body between a sliver of opening. The room is packed with people. Some crying, some laughing, emotions amplifying when they see my outfit, a cartoon fleur-de-lis playing an accordion on a T-shirt under a bright purple blazer.

When Alida's favorite song "Tee Nah Nah" starts to play through the speakers, their shouts and cries reach a crescendo.

"Would y'all like to see her before we start?" I ask.

It's always a crapshoot of what people prefer. Some want to say goodbye, others opt to stay in the witnessing room and simply watch. In almost perfect unison, their yeses come as a collective holler. I barely get the door fully open before they push their way by me to where her body rests in the simple cardboard casket. There have never been so many people in the room.

Alida's daughter stops beside me as we watch the horde of people surround her mother. "Who are all these people?" I whisper, several of the women dabbing their eyes with hankies.

Her daughter, Flavie, probably mid-twenties, smiles. "A sister. Brother. Friends from church. That's my brother and his wife." She points to a younger couple holding a baby. "That guy over there is our mailman, and I'm pretty sure more than the mailman." She laughs, but it's watery. "We moved here from New Orleans when I was a baby. Whole family did. Just up and left the swamp for the mountains."

She and I stand quietly at the perimeter as the rest of them form a horseshoe shape around Alida, hands connecting.

"She must have been a hell of a woman," I say.

"Get over here, Flavie," a woman calls over her shoulder, contagious smile on her face.

Flavie raises a finger to them, looking at me. "In some ways yes. But"—she shrugs—"we're human. She was a pain in the ass.

Drank too much liquor. Lost her temper too easily. A straight shooter 'til we bled." She laughs softly.

"How so?"

"She told us hard truths. Constantly. Sometimes it was harsh." She cocks a brow. "Dress too short to church for her liking?" She scoffs. "She'd tell us in front of God and everyone that Jesus wouldn't be impressed by a leggy whore with no shame." She chuckles. "But she never lied. Never held back. Told us when she messed up as much as she told us when we did. We did something to piss her off?" She smirks. "She let us know on the spot, no matter where we were. And then it was over. Never threw it in our face or played games. She showed her cards, for better or worse. That's how she loved us—hard and with honesty. Wasn't always pretty, but it was true."

One of the women starts to hum, the rest following until the smooth sound becomes louder than the speakers.

"She spanked us but made us biscuits." She shrugs. "Did a lot wrong but did a lot right too. In the end, the light finds a way to outshine the dark."

Flavie squeezes between two people and locks her hands with theirs and the first lyrics, sung in unison, follow.

Amazing grace . . . how sweet the sound.

They continue on, every lyric of the familiar hymn sung with the execution of a well-trained choir in front of a machine made to turn bodies to ash. The strength of their voices never wavers despite the emotion that fills their faces.

. . . that saved . . . a wretch . . . like me.

They continue through the whole song, and it's as deafening as it is beautiful. Impossible to look away from. Singing every word like it matters. Like Alida can hear them wherever she's gone off to.

The earth shall soon . . . dissolve like snow . . .

Wanda and Dondi, who usually stay in the back until it's time to roll the body in, peek their heads around the corner. Wanda's eyes meet mine: They're wet. When I bring a hand to my face, mine are too.

The song ends, but an echo of the words stay. Like the lyrics merge with the air and imbed themselves into the walls. Wanda works the machine, rolling the box holding Alida in to be cremated. I sniff, looking at all of her friends and family. Imperfect people loving imperfect people.

"Would one of y'all like to push the button or would you like us to do it?" I ask.

Flavie puts her hand on the red button and looks at the rest of them, rivers of tears covering her cheeks. Like a secret language, they move toward her, hands piling on top of one another like a team in a football huddle.

"Bye, Mama," she says, a wet smile on her face. "We'll miss your mouth and your wisdom."

Together, they push, and the loud hum of the machine fills the air.

For the first time in my two decades of working in this building, I'm jealous of the woman burning to ashes in a box.

FORTY

I've been quiet most of the afternoon. I'm a lot of things, but blind isn't one of them. I know what this is: Alida's send-off shone a light on some corner of me that I've kept dark. The desire, despite how uncomfortable it feels, to have people around me. People who would miss me if I were gone. People who I let get so close to me—despite my flaws—and would want to say goodbye. For so long I've pretended not to want it, now there's no denying that I do.

Hours later, climbing the steps of my porch, there's an ache in my chest.

Molly must sense it because when I walk inside, instead of barking and pouncing on me with something valuable half chewed in her mouth, she nuzzles her nose against my leg until I pet her. At my quiet *sit*, she obeys.

The apocalypse is upon us.

I drop my purse at the door, the Miranda Lambert record on the player, and my body onto the couch. Molly rests her head on my lap.

Despite my best efforts not to love the house, I do. Even without a picture on the wall. Every little detail makes it beautiful. Every single piece tells a story.

I feel the poems under my toes and hear their words in the silence.

A single industrial bulb drips from the ceiling overhead—which I hired Pedro to install after I realized he wasn't a hustler—and I hate it will light the way for someone else.

Along with the three woven barstools at the kitchen counter I found on the side of the road.

And the ridiculous purple, velvet, wingbacked chair Wren loves but is constantly moving around.

And the coffee table of natural wood with the raw edge exposed from the furniture craftsman in Rocky Ridge.

Molly stretches with a growly groan, her black-and-white pattern popping against the bright green fabric of the rug that spreads across the living room floor.

Through the windows, Ford's truck appears. He gets out, the shirt of his uniform unbuttoned and untucked revealing his vest. He makes his way to the house, but there's a slow slump in his step. He looks how I feel.

"Scotty," he says, smiling slightly when he opens the door and sees me.

"Hey," I say, not moving from the couch.

He pecks me on the lips and sits next to me with a heavy sigh. "Hey."

I curl into him, tracing his face and neck with my fingers. "Where's Wren?"

He drops his head back and looks at the ceiling. "At Becca's studying."

I snap upright. "The pint-sized Letts bitch? Why?"

"Because she asked." He turns his head to face me without lifting it from the back of the couch.

"Listen, I know she's not my kid, but I heard that little shit—"

He shakes his head. "Not now." Then his eyes close and I can see the exhaustion all over him. His normally crisp uniform is stained with streaks of clay-colored mud, nearly hidden by the dark color of the fabric.

"Okay." I swallow my argument and take his hand in mine. "Something happen?"

He opens his eyes, rolling his head on the back of the couch until his face is angled toward the ceiling. "There was an accident out on Highway 68. Seven-year-old kid was crushed in the back seat. I had to pull him out. They don't think he's going to make it."

My eyes do a full-body scan looking for injuries, landing back on his uniform. The mud is blood. The boy's. Ford is smeared in mortality and pain. I frame his tired face with my palms, desperately wishing I could absorb all the hurt from him and carry it as my own.

Around us, Miranda Lambert's smooth, twangy voice sings about loss like a well-placed song in a sad movie.

Pull, don't push.

I stand, tugging his hands in mine until he stands.

"Let's get cleaned up."

He doesn't say anything, just follows me up the spiral staircase into the mid-renovation bathroom. The bathtub is the crown jewel: an oversized modern claw-foot, the biggest one I could buy.

"How are we going to get clean in here?" Ford asks with a slight smile from the doorway.

I chuckle as I toe my heels off, the new white octagonal tile a cool relief against my bare feet. "No shower. No sink. No working lights." I wave a lighter through the air then light three pillar candles. The soft flicker of the flames dance against the aqua subway tiles on the wall. "But the tub works. And it's gigantic." I cut my eyes to him. "Big enough for Octoman."

He makes an amused sound as he eyes the exposed pipe of the showerhead and the sinkless vanity, but he doesn't argue, slipping off his uniform shirt and toeing his shoes off as I start the water and check the temperature with my fingers; it's near scalding. I add a large pour of bubble bath, the scent of vanilla filling the air.

Ford takes his belt off—filled with all his cop paraphernalia—hanging it over the vanity before moving on to his pants. I cross the room and wrap my hands around his, stopping him. "Let me."

He kisses me lightly, tilting his head in compliance.

The music downstairs shifts to another track—sexy and about wild mustangs—as I undo the Velcro straps of his bulletproof vest, working it off him and dropping it on the floor before moving to his pants, dragging them down his legs along with his briefs.

When I stand, I lift the bottom hem of his T-shirt, and he raises his arms as I pull it over his head. My hands go to his gunshot bruise, hardly faded at all, tracing it gently. A reminder of how life can change at the speed of a bullet. Then he's there, naked and tattered as I stand completely clothed. It would be filthy if it wasn't so tender. If looking at him didn't feel so raw.

He kisses me, soft. "My turn."

I shake my head, rubbing my cheek against his. "You get in."

He looks like he wants to argue, but the lull of steamy water pouring into the bubble-filled bathtub wins. He steps in, making a face at the temperature that I laugh at while he slinks down into it.

"I like it hot," I say with a grin as I shimmy out of my pants.

When I'm naked, I walk freely, knowing he's watching, and go to his belt, fumbling to release the item I need.

"Handcuffs?" he laughs as he drops his head back to the edge of the tub and looks at me with one eye. "Should I be scared?"

"Probably," I say as I step into the tub, turning the faucet off as I sink into the water with a long *ahh!* On a stool next to us, there's a stack of towels and washcloths. I exchange the cuffs for a washcloth and position myself between Ford's long, outstretched legs, dunking it under before dragging it along the side of his neck and down one arm he has draped along the edge.

He makes a small moan, and his eyelids go heavy as I repeat the motion on the opposite side. "I'm sorry about the kid," I say, straddling him so I can squeeze water over his head. "That's hard."

He opens his eyes. "You see death every day."

"I don't see it happen." I dunk the cloth underwater again and reach my arms around him to scrub the slopes of his shoulders. "I don't have hope when I'm dealing with bodies—you do. There's a difference. Hope's the MVP of cocksuckers."

He chuckles softly, running his bubble-covered fingers through my hair. "Not always though. Hope sometimes gives you a reason to keep trying. Keep showing up." He smiles and leans forward, dusting a kiss on my lips before relaxing back. Beneath the water, his hands find my hips and drag me toward him. "Without hope I wouldn't be in this ridiculously big bathtub with you."

The look in his eyes is genuine, and it sparks a nascent flame of panic in me. At the intimacy of the moment. How good it feels. How much I want him. How much I want him to want me. The tug of what I want against everything I'm so sure I don't deserve to have.

I grab the handcuffs—the abruptness of my movements a stark contrast to the slowness of the music drifting from downstairs and the tenderness on Ford's face. He watches but doesn't react. Not as I fumble to get them open. Not as I wrap one around my right wrist and the other one around his left, tethering me to him.

He holds his hand up, elbow still submerged, amused expression on his face. "Not what I expected."

"I want to love you," I blurt. "Without looking away. But I'm not sure how, so"—I tug at my wrist chained to his—"I'm forcing myself. To look. This was plan B."

He chuckles and spins our hands so our palms face one another and fingers interlace. "And plan A?"

"A choke collar and cage."

A loud laugh bubbles out of him and then his mouth is on mine. With the hand not chained to mine, he pulls me onto his lap where I feel all of him. He's hard—the way he's been since I stripped his pants down his legs. My heart beats fast; his mouth moves slow. It's terrifying. Far from a virgin, it's exactly how I feel.

I position myself on top of him, straddling him so I can take him inside of me. I lower; my body willingly yielding to him where we meet. I'm greedy for more—he stops me, serious look on his face. "You sure?"

I nod.

His eyes flare, breath quickens. Then he grips my hip and slams me hard, sending soapy water sloshing over the lip of the tub as I cry out from the sensational severity of it.

And as much as I crave movement, I still, zeroing in on his gaze and letting it consume me.

It's nothing—just eyes pointing toward each other—but the intensity of it nearly swallows me whole.

"What do you need?" he whispers.

My simple response: "You."

With the cuffed hand, he cups my face, and I drop my forehead to his as my hips find a rhythm grinding against him. All I need him to do is be there and let me work, and that's exactly what he does. Through every rock of my body and cry from my lips, he stays there, eyes locked with mine as water leaves the tub in buckets over the edge and splashes onto the floor.

Rock after rock after rock of my hips.

"Scotty," he grunts, eyes not moving off mine as I grind. "I'm close, baby."

I whimper but can't speak. Can barely keep myself moving. He feels the shift and picks up my slack, guiding me with his free hand, water sloshing.

I stare at him through every emotion each thrust brings. The grip of panic. The fear he'll hate what he sees. The sting of tears from the magnitude of the moment.

Through it all, I look. Even as the orgasm slams into me as fast and hard as a freight train.

My head fights to jerk away; Ford holds it firm.

My eyes start to close; "Look at me, Scotty."

And I do. Fully. While pleasure sends me floating away before bringing me back to the now-cold water of the bathtub and the depth of the moment. All the while, he keeps moving, rocking our hips for as long as it takes for him to feel exactly what I do.

Then Ford shatters, and I watch every single piece of him. The slight way his blue eyes roll back. The way his jaw locks then goes slack. The jagged breaths followed by a period of no breath at all. The coarse way he shudders, the softness of how he chants my name. The whole-body tension followed by full-blown come apart.

The air is cold, water is everywhere except in the tub. We're a tangled mass of wet legs and cuffed wrists, but I don't want to go anywhere. I want to live in this bathtub with goose bumps on my skin attached to Ford Callahan for the rest of my life. "You did good," he says, rubbing his nose against mine. "You okay?"

I look at him, open my mouth to say something clever, but instead, I cry. Tears stream down my face and mix with bathwater as I look at him, and he wraps his free arm, still slick with water and dappled with bubbles, right around me, tucking the cuffed one between us, our fingers intertwined.

I shift off him and curl into the space between his legs sideways, angling my head so I'm looking at him. "I'm sorry," I say with a laugh. "I don't know why I'm crying. That was good. You were—" I sniff, trying to find the right word, feeling lame when all I can say is, "Beautiful."

He smiles in that true way he does. "So were you." He kisses my thumb. "Can I tell you I love you?"

I look at him, biting my lip. "Will you know I feel the same way even if I don't say it?"

He presses his lips to mine, saying against my mouth, "I'm in love with you, Scotty Armstrong."

Sitting in a bathtub naked and handcuffed, those seven words forever change the rhythm my heart beats in my chest. Swift as a starling shifts direction midair.

"Hm." I pull back, biting my bottom lip. "I'll need more evidence, Officer."

He growls—it's sexy—and pulls me to stand at our cuffed connection. He scoops me up, naked and slippery, and I shriek through a giggle as he carries me to the bedroom. Ford drops us onto the new mattress and touches me like I've never been touched before. He makes love to me. And when soft swears and whimpers of his name come from my lips, he doesn't look away.

Neither do I.

Scotty
I might be in love with Ford.
June
Are you still moving to the desert?
I hate you.
I know you don't.

FORTY-ONE

"Are you sure this is right?" Wren looks skeptically from the bright-green backsplash tile of the kitchen to me.

I purse my lips and tilt my head, trying to find an angle that makes them look straight. All signs point to drunk kindergarteners doing the install. "No."

"So what do we do? Pull it off and redo it?" She's annoyed.

I shake my head and drag a sponge across the tile to wipe the last remnants of excess grout, wishing and failing for it to make the tile less crooked. I frown when it doesn't. "We'll just leave it. If you kind of close your eyes"—I take a step back and squint—"maybe no one will notice."

She looks at the botched tile job, peeling her gloves off with a disbelieving snort. "They'll notice."

When she turns away, I flip her off.

"Now what?"

With the backsplash done, there are no more projects. It dawns on me that maybe Wren might stop visiting. Of course, if I sell it in a few weeks, I guess I wouldn't be here for her to visit anyway. Even I can't deny that I'll miss her.

"Well, I guess our work's done," I say as I mentally try to make up projects we could do. "We could do outside stuff? Landscape?"

"Now?" she asks, skeptical. "It's almost winter."

Right.

She sits on one of the stools at the counter, Molly propping her chin on her knee.

The oven dings. Wren looks at me.

"Test turkey's ready." I grin. "I tried a brine. And something called a spatchcock."

Her face twists. "How many turkeys did you buy?"

"Five."

"Five turkeys?!" she asks, incredulous. "Who's going to eat all that?"

I grab potholders out of a drawer and open the oven, pulling the turkey out with a grunt. "So far? Mostly Molly." I set the turkey on the stove, peeking under the foil to see the golden-brown skin. Looks done. "If I ruin this turkey, June will never let me live it down. I have two weeks to get this shit right."

"Judging by the backsplash . . ."

"Ha. Ha." I lean on the counter. "So what's new?"

She shrugs. "Luke asked me to Homecoming."

Do not react. Do not react. Do not react.

I shriek and clap; she groans. "I knew you'd do that."

"No you didn't. What are you going to wear?"

Her eyes drop down, fingers pinch the sleeves of her sweater, and she shrugs. My heart wobbles.

I lift my chin. "Let me see."

Reluctantly, she pulls her sleeves up. No new marks, only fading white lines going up her forearms. If I didn't know, I wouldn't notice, but she'll never believe that. "Wanda has some makeup that might cover it up," I offer.

Her *hell no* look tells me that won't work.

"What about a long-sleeved dress? I'll take you shopping if you want."

She perks up slightly. "Yeah?"

"Of course," I say. "It's one of my five skills."

"You have other skills?"

I look at her with a cocked eyebrow. "Ask your dad."

She groans, and I grin, dropping the oven mitts on the counter.

"You still hanging out with the Letts girl?"

A familiar eyeroll. "She's not bad, Scotty. She's nice. I told her about my mom, and she like, listened. Like, asked me questions about her. Cared."

"You what?!" I viscerally hate this news.

"What? You act like you don't want me to have any other friends."

I scoff. "Of course I want you to have other friends, Wren. Just not her."

"Good thing it's not up to you," she mutters, a coldness filling her eyes as we glare at each other. If I didn't like her so much, I'd hate her. *Fucking kids*. I jerk open a drawer and drop two knives on the counter. She blinks.

"Let's carve pumpkins. I bought some for decorations and they need faces."

She frowns.

"Halloween was weeks ago."

"And?"

She stands, going to the door and waiting for me with a flat look I match. Inside I'm throwing a celebratory parade as I swipe the knives and go to the porch.

We do not talk as we stab the pumpkins. I haven't done this in years—maybe ever—so when I look inside and see the amount of slimy seeds, I gag.

"The hell? Why do people do this?"

Her nostrils flare. "Your idea."

"It was a bad one," I say, stabbing my knife straight into the stupid gourd and letting it stay.

She fights a smile, following my lead and stabbing her own knife into her pumpkin. Legs dangling off the porch, we look at the water. The trees that were exploding with color just weeks ago now form a sea of sticks. When the wind blows, it's bone chilling. The lake is empty, the sky is grey. One lone bird flies across the sky.

"Will you take a picture of us?"

I look at her. "Like a selfie?"

She rolls her eyes. "Yes. *Like a selfie.*"

"Okay." I take my phone out and hand it to her, confused.

She tucks her hair behind her ears, leaning into me as she holds the phone out, pressing the button about six hundred times as we make an assortment of faces. She selects a few and emails them to herself then hands the phone back to me.

"What was that for?"

"They play a slideshow at the homecoming dance of all the students and asked us to submit pictures with friends and family."

I nod—slowly—swallowing around the instant thickness in my throat. "You're using a picture with me?"

She looks at me like I'm an idiot. "You've blackmailed yourself into being my best friend, Scotty. Of course, I am."

I blink away, unshed tears burning my eyes.

"Well make sure you use one where I look hot."

She snorts as Molly circles around our pumpkins with a disinterested sniff.

"You still want to come over and run in the afternoons?" I ask.

She's quiet a beat, and I take that as my answer. My disappointment at this realization is foreign.

A female cardinal lands on one of the feeders—it pecks at seeds and flies away.

"I think women your age are at an increased risk for falling," Wren finally says without looking at me, kicking her dangling legs over the edge of the porch. "Pretty sure it's my duty as a citizen to not let you run alone."

I don't even bother hiding my smile. *Little shit.*

Forty-Two

"How do I look?"

Ford and I still as Wren walks into the kitchen of the A-frame. She twirls, her midnight-blue dress covered in sequins catching the light. Her makeup is subtle, her hair is down, her smile is bright. Simply put, she's stunning. Even though she isn't my kid, the pride in me replicates what I imagine a mother would feel.

Ford clears his throat multiple times, taking in how pretty she looks. How grown up. Though the dress has long sleeves, his eyes linger on the hemline that hits mid-thigh and the pair of silver strappy heels. "Why can I see so much of your legs?"

I slap his chest and he grunts. "Ignore him, Wren, you look perfect." Then for good measure: "I'd do ya."

Ford grunts; Wren's face twists. He wraps an arm around her shoulders, pulling her into a half hug. "You do look perfect." He kisses her on the head. "But I still don't like all those legs."

She gives a token smiley eye roll.

A knock at the door pulls a nervous breath out of her. She looks at me, and I give her an excited smile. "Ford, answer the door for dramatic effect," I instruct. "You know, scary cop dad threatening to clip his balls off."

They both look at me.

"Do you not watch TV?" I huff. "I'll do it."

I open the door to find Luke standing on the porch, dressed up and nervous. His long hair is down, brushing the collar of his black shirt. He smiles, his mouth slightly too big for his still teenage-sized head.

"Hello, Luke," I say with a grin and completely calm voice. "I'm Scotty and I burn dicks for a living. Hurt Wren and you're toast." The color drains from his face. When I look over my shoulder, Ford is biting back a smile while Wren looks mortified. I step aside, opening the door fully. "Please come in."

"Uh." He looks at Wren, who offers him a weak smile from inside. "Okay."

Ford, the big wuss, steps in and saves him. "Luke. Ford. Wren's dad." He extends a hand that Luke takes and shakes. Luke's introduction is a nervous squeak. His face is so pale I wonder if he might faint. Poor kid is terrified.

We stand, looking at each other in the middle of the living room, nobody saying anything. I do it to make things uncomfortable, Wren and Luke because they don't know what to say, and Ford, I suspect, is mentally cursing this boy for ever being born.

"Well," Wren finally says breaking the silence. "We should go, right, Luke?"

He nods, and Wren teeters toward the door in her heels, adorably awkward as they start to leave.

"Be home by eleven," Ford calls from the doorway as I tuck myself into his side.

"And don't do anything I wouldn't do," I shout for good measure.

Wren lifts a hand in the air but doesn't look back as Luke opens the passenger door for her. I don't have to see her face to know she's fighting a smile and rolling her eyes.

We watch them until the car pulls out of the driveway and the lights disappear down the road.

Ford blows out a heavy breath. "God, Scotty. It's so much harder than you think," he says, looking down at me and tightening his hold. "Watching a kid that's yours go live a life without you . . ." He shakes his head. "That alone feels like punishment for all the shit we pulled as kids." He chuckles softly. "Doesn't even take into account whatever it is they go to do."

His words aren't made to hurt me, but unknowingly, they do. They send a million cuts lashing across my heart and into my soul. Because I do know what it's like. More than he knows.

As I look up at him, June's annoying voice blares in my ears, *"You have to tell him."*

"Ford . . ." He looks at me, blue eyes familiar and bright.

The oven dings.

Ford pecks a kiss on my mouth.

I lose my nerve.

"Turkey time," he says with an amused tone, taking my hand to pull me inside. "And then we have this house to ourselves."

Say it. Say it. Say it.

Instead: "I've been meaning to see what else we can do with those cuffs of yours."

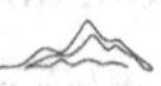

The front door swings open an hour before curfew and Wren barrels in, makeup running down her face.

She's disheveled and crying; Ford and I leap from the couch.

"What the hell happened?" Ford demands as I look her over for wounds. "Where's Luke?"

She shakes her head, sniffs, and wipes her nose with the back of her hand. "The-the-the-the slideshow," she stutters, fresh wave of tears filling her eyes. "B-B-Becca changed my pictures."

My hackles raise. I put my hands on her arms, rounding my spine until my eyes are level with hers. "Wren, what happened?"

She looks at me, sniffs, and says, "She put my mom's mugshot in the slideshow." Another loud sob bubbles out of her.

I pull back, and Ford and I exchange a look. A play right from her mother's handbook. *That rat-faced little bitch.*

"Wren, it's going to be okay," Ford says softly, wrapping his arms around her. "It was bound to get out. Kids are just mean."

At this, I guffaw. "Mean?!" I ask incredulously. "That girl's a damn snake in the grass, Ford. I told you this would happen!"

"Scotty," he snaps, tucking Wren's face against his chest. "Not now."

"Not now?" My eyes narrow, hands gesticulating wildly as I talk. "When the hell do you want to talk about it? Because now that she's pulled this little stunt—which reeks of familiarity in case you haven't noticed—seems like the perfect time. I knew when I talked to her at Orchard Fest that—"

Wren jerks away from Ford's chest and looks at me. "You *talked* to her?"

She and Ford stare at me.

"Yes. I *talked to her*," I snip, annoyed these deaf dodos won't listen. "Put her in her place was more like it. She was saying—"

"Why would you do that?" Wren demands, voice glacial.

"The dog listens better than you!" I cry. "I've tried to tell you." I cut my eyes to Ford. "Both of you."

"I don't need you to talk to her, Scotty," Wren seethes, swiping the tears from her face.

"Wren." Ford manages to stay calm. "Just relax."

"You don't need me to talk to her?" I scoff, voice turning to a shout. "Apparently it doesn't matter because you still tried to be her friend."

Ford grabs my arm; I jerk it away.

Wren swipes at her eyes with angry hands. "You're just mad because I have a life and you don't."

"The Letts girl is a *life*?" I laugh—it's maniacal. "Okay, Wren. *Sure.*"

"Wren," Ford says, voice low as he steps closer to her. "Maybe—"

"No, Ford." I hold up my hand. The Miranda Lambert record that's been playing ends, a clicking silence filling the air, ramping up the tension. "Let her talk. Because I'd really love to hear this. Really love to know why I shouldn't have defended her to that little she-devil, because I promise I'll never do it agoddamngain."

Wren steps away from Ford, squaring up to me, looking much more woman than girl in this moment, her gaze so cold it could freeze fire.

"I don't need you to *defend* me," she spits out, fuming. Each word makes my stomach drop closer to the floor. "You aren't my mom, Scotty—thank God. Because you ruin everything."

When I think she's done: "You're so fucked up you ruin everyone."

It stings like a bitch-slap to my face and heart. I can't see straight. Can't breathe.

"Wren," Ford barks. "Enough. Go to the truck. Now."

I'm trembling; her chest is heaving. Tears are running down both our faces for very different reasons.

When her eyes meet mine again, they're full of fight. "You couldn't save your brother, stop trying to save me."

"Wren!" Ford shouts. "Now!"

She storms out.

Nail to the heart.

Slams the door.

Nail to the heart.

Leaves the house quietly loud.

Nail to the heart.

"She didn't mean it," Ford offers. "She's ju—"

"Go," I demand, jerking the door open with a shaky hand.

"Scotty, she didn't mean it," he repeats, reaching for me. "She's just upset."

I jerk his hand away and shove him onto the porch with both palms to his chest. "Stop, Ford." His name is a soggy shout on my lips. "I know what I am. She's right. This was a mistake. You need to go." He opens his mouth. "Now!"

His expression is pure defeat. Because of me.

He might think he wants this, me, but he can't. Not after this. I won't let him.

"Scotty, she's a teenager," he pleads. "She didn't mean it. I'll talk to her. This will be fine in the morning, she's just—"

"Stop!" I demand, looking at him, feeling so desperately empty all I can think of doing is lying on the floor and letting myself die. Wren is right—I'm too fucked up for any of this. His face . . . his beautiful face and familiar blue eyes shatter the final fragments of my heart. I'm twenty years old all over again, standing at a trailhead expecting to see him but instead finding the life I imagined completely obliterated. I should have never ever agreed to any of this.

"I love you," I say, voice sounding far away.

"I lo—"

"I love you, and Wren's been cutting herself," I say over him, making him go deathly silent under the porch light. "And I never want to see you again. Either of you."

"Sco—"

I slam the door in his face, and then I drop to the floor and cry.

<outgoing call to June>

FORTY-THREE

I BLINK AT THE field, trying to remember how I got here.

After I called June, I hibernated into a cave of blankets and stayed in bed like a wounded bear. The house I had come to love like a cozy nest betrayed me by morphing into a depressing museum without permission. Every item was a memory belonging to Wren or Ford. When I contemplated burning the damn place down, I poured a drink.

Ford texted and called too many times to count; I smashed my phone.

Molly whimpered in the kitchen; I threw a turkey leg against the crooked tiled backsplash.

I went for a run; I cried.

I played some of Zeb's records; I snapped four of them in half.

Finally, I climbed into the Bronco and just drove, without music or direction and with the windows down despite how cold it is.

Muscle memory got me here because I don't remember making a single turn.

The field is the one where Ford brought me on our date. The one I ruined like I ruin everything. Like the universe has preordained to be ruined because it's me. Like no matter what I do or how I try to help, heartache is all I will ever have. Ever cause.

Where the landscape was filled with yellowing cornstalks and still mostly green leafed trees when I was here before, the corn's been harvested and the trees are bare. *Dead like me.*

Unable to contain it, my mouth opens: I scream. I drop my head back and don't stop until my throat feels like it's bleeding. Until I can barely breathe.

As abrupt as I start, I stop. Breathless and panting as I look out at the field of death.

And then it happens.

The murmured chatter.

The soft flutter that turns loud.

The thousands of birds that act as one.

The starlings lift from the branches of the bare trees, raising into the air like a big cloud, stretching apart before snapping back together. I watch them put on a performance more beautiful than I deserve. One bird changing the direction of the seven around it. Just like Ford.

When they stop and the sky goes quiet, I realize I'm crying. Maybe I never stopped.

"Hey," Ben says, leaning over the bar with a low voice. "You sure you need a drink, Scotty?"

"You turning me down, Ben?" I ask with a too-long wink.

He's probably not wrong. Between the field of lost dreams and Liberty Tap, I stopped at a liquor store, bought a bottle of whiskey, and slammed half of it in the parking lot before I walked in here.

He hesitates, eyes pinging down the bar. "I'm serious. You okay?"

I wave my hand through the air. "I'm fine. A bad day." I pause, shake my head and chuckle. "No, that's not right. A bad life," I correct. "A bad life. Just one teensy drink and I'll leave. Cross my heart." I use my fingers and put an X across my chest to prove my honesty.

He sighs but reluctantly pours me a glass, much less than usual, which makes me snarl. I barely taste the first sip. It barely even burns.

The bar is almost empty. A few people dining at tables. One other couple at the bar. I don't know what time it is. Maybe everyone's already home. Maybe it's breakfast. *Maybe I don't give a flying fuck about time.*

Ben cuts lemons behind the bar, and I turn my attention to the couple. The woman's back is to me, but I can see the man's face, animated as he speaks to her. He leans in close, probably giving a stupid line. He's okay-enough looking. Three more whiskeys and he'd look good enough to fuck, I suppose. He laughs a loud abrasive sound, and I wince.

Four more whiskeys.

Ford and I never had a proper date here, and that makes me want to impale myself with the knife Ben is using to cut lemons.

"You're so nice, Ben. I shouldn't have slept with you."

He looks at me, mouth open as he hovers the knife midair.

"Because I'm so mean," I clarify.

He laughs softly, resuming his work with the lemons. "Maybe don't tell my new girlfriend."

"You have a girlfriend," I echo, dropping my chin to the back of my hand on the bar as I watch him work. "You ever lose someone?" I ask.

He glances at me with a slight smile. "Haven't we all?"

"Who?"

"My brother a few years back. Motorcycle accident."

"I'm sorry," I say, my voice wobbling. "I had no idea."

He pulls a towel from over his shoulder and wipes his hands, squaring up to where I'm slumped, shrugging slightly. "Name of the game, you know?"

"How so?"

"C'mon, Scotty. You're around death every day, you know more than anyone the trade-off of living is dying same as loving is losing."

I sit up with a start, feeling like in fact I did *not* know this.

"How are you so blasé about it?"

"Blasé?" He chuckles and scrubs a hand across his bald head. "Far from. My brother and I were out riding bikes the day he died.

We stopped for lunch at a little burger place and bickered about the route. I wanted to go through the hills; he wanted to ride by the river. I won." He smiles but it's hollow. "We went to the hills . . . truck hit that sonofabitch on a left-hand turn. Killed him instantly."

The story sits between us, horrendously heavy.

"You blame yourself?" I finally ask.

"Hm." He sighs. "I did for a long time. Always thought I should have just agreed to go to the river. Should have kept my mouth shut. Should've, should've, you know?"

My throat feels like it's been filled with sawdust. I absolutely know.

"Now?"

He shrugs.

"Now I know I was giving myself too much credit for how much I can control. I'm not God; life's a gamble. Shit happens. Some of it really sucks." He smiles—really smiles. "If that day was bound to be his last, I'm glad we had it together. And I see him every time I take a ride."

It's as sad as it is beautiful; I'm envious of this viewpoint. Of his ability to stand and smile and speak without jaded animosity. Wren's shouted words blast through me.

"I was told I'm fucked up and obsessed with Zeb's memory."

He considers this. "What do you think?"

I drop my forehead to the bar. I think of Ford. Of Glory. Of Zeb. Of me coming out of the woods twenty years ago and never being the same. Of never letting myself see the world the same. All was lost—every single person—because I didn't do enough to keep it from happening. Then, I think of the baby who was never destined to be mine—in my arms then gone.

A life defined by loss, fighting anyone that tried to test that theory.

Fighting Ford.

Fighting June.

Going to LL meetings and fighting the whole room.

I wish so badly I could see things the way Ben does. The *shit happens* mentality he was so blessed with. I don't know how to let it go. If I *deserve* to let it go.

"I think I should move," I blurt, making Ben's brow furrow. "To Tucson." I don't know if that's directed to him or myself. "Somewhere far away. I wasn't going to. I was going to stay. But …" My voice trails off as my eyes start to burn. "I don't know how to see it like you."

When I saw Wren sitting on my porch with sleeping bags, something flipped like a switch inside of me; I never wanted to leave them. They wanted me to be part of their lives, and as much as I fought it, I wanted that too. Desperately. But now I see I'd gotten it all wrong. We were good while we lasted, and that's all this was. A few good months before the crash and burn I pretended I could avoid for once. I can't subject people to this. Can't be with Ford the way he deserves. Wren was right. I ruin everything and everyone.

I stand up, slam the rest of my drink, and sway slightly as I put my coat on.

"I'm not like you," I slur. "I can't-can't-can't love knowing loss comes. I am loss. That's my superpower. Losser. Loser. I lose." I might be crying. "And I take happiness. I'm the dementor. Ford knows. He's good like you. He's great. The best. Ford is the best person I know." Ben stares at me as I ramble on. "Nobody will even sing at my cremation."

I openly weep at the image of me burning to ashes with nobody there to press the button.

"You sure you should drive, Scotty?" Ben asks in a low voice, concern etched on every feature. He looks so sincere. He's so nice to me.

"I'm—"

"Hey!" the abrasive laugher calls over his date's shoulder. "Hey, I know you. You own the crematorium, right?"

I force a weak smile as I push my barstool in. "Guilty."

"My ex-wife works there. Wanda."

This news makes me stone-cold sober and rabid as a rottweiler.

"Cal?" I ask, seeing the man in a new, slimier light.

He grins, like this is good news. Like he knew I'd know who he was, like he's some kind of steaming-hot pile of golden shit I'd be lucky to step in.

"The one and only," he says, preening as he raises his glass.

I am no longer in control of my body, covering the distance of the six barstools that separate us. This is the guy that beat the shit out of Wanda and never paid; no way in hell is he coming out of this place with both testicles.

"And my lovely date, Jessica." He beams.

And then I look at the *lovely date* and know for the first time in my life the stars have aligned. I've won the mother lode.

"Jessicunt," I say, feeling my lips curl into an evil grin. "What a pleasant surprise."

"You two know each other?" Cal asks, oblivious to the revenge story I'm plotting, which involves me flushing their ashes down a shit-filled toilet.

Jessica looks at me, and it pleases me to see that she hasn't aged well. Lines run like canyons on her face and, in an attempt to retain her youth, she wears too much foundation and has lips filled to the point of resembling a balloon animal.

"Oh yes," she says, lifting a martini—*she would drink a martini*—up to her lips. "I've known Scotty since she was trailer trash. Now I'm getting to relive our glory days as the Callahan girl plays pretend too."

Bitch. She knew—probably helped—execute whatever was done at Homecoming to Wren.

"Ben," I call, not looking away from her ugliest shit shade of brown eyes.

"Yeah?"

"You know June's number?"

"Uh. Maybe? I have Camp's for sure. Why?"

"I need you to call them. Tell them I'm sorry, but they need to come get me. I smashed my phone." He's quiet, but I don't take my eyes off Jessica. "Got it?"

"Yeah."

I turn to Cal. "Cal, I wish Wanda would have been a better killer."

He blinks, confused, but there's no time for him to say anything.

I sling my arm back and snap it forward, punching him right in the nose.

Blood spurts.

Jessicunt screams.

Ben shouts, "Jesus, Scotty!"

Cal cups his hands around his nose with a grunt and spits, "You stupid, crazy bitch."

I pick up his drink, dump it on his head, then bring the glass down to his crotch, pressing the rim into what I assume to be a pitifully small penis until he wails with pain. I increase the pressure as I lean close to him.

"Bet you won't be so keen to beat up a woman when you're a dickless eunuch."

Cal moans in pain, begging until I coolly return the glass to the bar.

"What the hell is wrong with you?" Jessica jumps to her feet, toppling her stool over. "You always were a piece of trash. Never did see what Ford saw in you."

I guffaw. "You never could handle the fact he wasn't interested in your deep throat," I snark. "And we fucked on the hood of your Camry."

Her jaw drops; I grin, jerking my arm back then sending my fist flying forward straight to her jaw, which it connects to with a crack.

"That's for fucking with Ford's kid," I grit out.

"You bitch," she spits, swinging a hand that slaps my cheek.

I stumble slightly, laugh loud, and punch her again, this time hitting her eye.

She screams.

Hurtles her body toward me.

And then . . . I black out.

FORTY-FOUR

LIGHT HURTS, SOMETHING STINKS, and this is where I've come to die.

I force my eyes open; a gritty tongue attacks me along with blinding light through a window. A bullmastiff. *Thor*. I'm at June's. On her couch. My head is throbbing. *What in the time traveling tunnels of hell is happening?*

"You're alive," June says, standing in the middle of her living room, disapproving look of a mother on her face as she folds her arms over her chest.

I sit up, moaning as the pony-sized canine invades my personal space.

"Go away, dog," I croak. The earth spins faster. "And no, I'm not." I put my elbows on my knees and drop my head into my hands. "How did I get here?"

"Ben called."

Her voice is blurry; I squeeze my eyes shut.

"Do you remember what happened?" she demands.

"I need water, Joo. And for you to lay off with the mom voice."

"*Lay off with the mom voice?*" She scoffs. "You got in a fight. In a bar. With two people!"

Right.

"Your yelling hurts"—she glares at me—"and they deserved it."

"God, Scotty!" she says in a half shout, half groan. "That's not the point!"

"Seems like a good point to me," I mutter, standing and taking slow wobbly steps to the kitchen, fumbling through her cabinets until I find a glass. "It was Jessicunt and Wanda's abusive ex-husband. I should be knighted."

"What happened?" she demands as I slam two glasses of water then dig through another cabinet on a quest from God for aspirin.

"I went to Liberty Tap." I throw the pills down my throat. "And detected two demons then performed an exorcism."

She scowls with another shout groan. "You're impossible, you know that?"

"Thank you," I say dryly. Even hungover, I know my best friend—she'll drop it when she sees I'm not talking about the Ford-sized hole in my chest that I used alcohol to fill.

"This isn't how it works, Scotty. You don't get to-to-to get in one fight and then call it quits."

I massage my forehead, leaning over the kitchen sink. *I might puke.*

"And it wasn't even with Ford," she continues. "It was with a teenager! They specialize in fighting!"

Shut. Up.

"You aren't special, you know." I splash water on my face, trying to drown her out. "You aren't the only one who's lost someone. Who-who-who knows heartache." I blot my face with a towel, seeing it covered in black when I pull it away. *How much makeup did I wear yesterday?*

"Are you even listening to me?" she demands, leaning a hip against the kitchen island next to me.

"You're hard to ignore right now," I mutter, praying for death.

"You know what," she snaps, severe edge to her voice. "Fuck you, Scotty. You think because you grew up in a trailer park with-with-with subpar parents that nobody else knows struggle? That everyone just knows how to be in healthy relationships and how to parent and life is so easy and la-ta-da-ta-da-ta?"

Her *la-ta-da* stabs my temples but the fight in her voice stops me cold. She's not letting this go.

"You think that-that you're some kind of martyr because your brother died? That you're the only woman who ever walked out of a hospital without a baby in her arms? Well guess what?" She doesn't give me time to answer. "You're not. You're not special, okay? You're human like the rest of us."

I look at her, feeling like a peeled peach with my softest, most vulnerable parts exposed.

"And," she continues, emotion filling her voice, "even though I have a family in the traditional sense, you're the one covering my walls even though you keep saying there's nobody to put on yours." I look around her house, almost entirely filled with frames, and land on one of her and I from a few years ago after we let her then-young teenage daughter put makeup all over us. We're covered in eye shadow holding wineglasses up high as we laugh. It socks me in the stomach. "And you don't call me and you don't show me your house. And it's-it's-it's mean. And it sucks. And you suck, Scotty."

She's crying now and it's because of me. If I didn't feel like a piece of shit before, seeing her tears most certainly does the trick.

I turn so my back is to the counter and slide down the cabinets until I'm on her kitchen floor; she does the same.

"I'm sorry, Joo." I sniff. "For all of it. I know I have you. I know I do." There's a long pause while I find my next words. "When Ford moved back it was like a scab ripped open I thought had healed," I admit. "Bastard went and made me fall in love with him all over again. And his kid." I start to cry. "And I ruined it."

"You didn't ruin it." She wipes her nose with the back of her hand before leaning against me. "You've just let yourself get so tangled up in your past you can't see what's right in front of you. Life is messy. For all of us. Not a damn one of us perfect. But you don't have to do it alone because you aren't alone." She interlaces her fingers with mine. "Family doesn't only mean blood, you know?"

I blow out a breath, dropping my head back against the cabinet. "I got in a fight," I say. "I *should* be alone. I'm genetically predisposed to be a disaster."

She scoffs. "Are you listening to yourself? Do you see your gene pool, Scotty?" She pauses. "You are nothing like them. Nothing," she punctuates. "I could kill you for shutting Ford out—me out—and everything that happened yesterday. But"—she angles her head to look at me, a ghost of a smile on her lips—"I'd have paid good money to see it."

I almost laugh as I let her words settle in me, unsure how they apply to me. Unsure if they even can.

"You should talk to your mom," she says.

"Be the bigger person?" I make a disagreeing grunt. "That sounds like me."

No, it does not.

"I'm serious," she urges. "All these years of you shouldering the weight of everything. How she was when you were a kid. What happened to Zeb. Your dad. I know you see her, but have you ever once had a real conversation with her?" I open my mouth to argue, but she adds, "*Really* feel?"

Talk to Glory? She knows I haven't. Glory and I talk the way Glory and I talk: in barely tolerable dark slapstick that isn't even remotely funny. I wouldn't know where to start a real conversation with her. My mind goes to Wren and her therapist. Wren telling me I ruin everything and everyone.

I cry.

Again.

"Wren hates me."

"She doesn't," June says with ease. "Kids lash out at the ones they love the most."

She can't be right; I saw the look in Wren's eyes when she shouted every horrible truth at me. How deep every word cut. *You couldn't save your brother, stop trying to save me.*

"I can't be with Ford," I tell her, sliding my eyes closed. "Not after what happened. How Wren feels about me. And when I tell him the rest . . ."

"That's for him to decide."

I open my eyes and angle my head to face her. "This is a whole human, Joo, not a game of hide the pickle."

My arm vibrates with her laugh. "I know, Scott. But it's him." She looks up at me again from her spot on my shoulder, her soothing voice a soft cushion for all my hard edges. "Tell him. Let him decide. That's how relationships work."

Guilt talons itself under my skin, but I don't have the energy to explain why I won't subject him to me. I love him too much to bring him down like this ever again. I'll tell him, and then I'll leave. It's the only way to fix this. The house is done. The Sellecks will buy Happy Endings. This was my plan all along, now it's simply execution.

"You're right," I say, wiping my thumbs under my eyes with a sniff. My fingertips are covered in black. "Jesus. How much makeup am I wearing?"

"About that." Her lips twitch as she pulls out her phone, turns on the camera and flips the screen before handing it to me.

When I look at my face, I scream; she cackles. "The hell, Joo?"

"Sorry," she says, rocking with laughter as tears roll down her face. "I let the boys use permanent marker because I was pissed."

I look back at the screen, the word fart is written about forty-three times around a single curlicue mustache above my upper lip. *Little shits.*

"You're the worst," I say before she forces us to huddle together and snaps a picture.

We stand, her still laughing as I grab a napkin and start to scrub my face over the sink.

"Why haven't you let me see your house?" she asks, mom tone back in full force.

"Because I didn't want you to tell me how perfect it was," I confess, turning off the sink. "Pump my tires full of stories of how I belong there. How I should keep it."

I wipe my face with the napkin.

"You remember what you told me when I wanted to leave Camp?" she finally asks.

I cut my eyes to her. "Stop listening to podcasts."

Her nostrils flare.

"That I can be more than one thing. You told me I could be a mom and everything else."

"Solid advice. Your point?"

"My point is," she says with a huff, "you can too."

I scoff. "Unhinged *and*?"

She grins. "Sure. Why not? You don't need permission to be happy, you know? Why can't you be what you've been through and who you are? Be you *and* have Ford? Wren? The house on the lake?"

I don't bother reminding her Wren doesn't want me and, soon enough, Ford won't either. She'll just argue, make it sound so easy in her leggings and chambray shirt, so beautifully her in the house she's made a home with toy clutter and dinged-up kitchen cabinets.

Wait.

I drop the paper towel. "Why is your kitchen old?"

"Oh." She looks at the very unrenovated kitchen and then back to me with a shrug. "I lied."

"You *what*?"

"You were acting crazy, and I needed to buy time before you went and did something stupid."

Bitch.

"I hate you."

She looks at me, knowing I don't, and I'm suddenly overwhelmed with emotion toward her. Less an A-frame house she conned me into and the fact my face looks like a bathroom stall door, her friendship has always been free. I wrap my arms around her.

"How long did you practice that speech?" I ask into her hair.

"All night while I listened to you snore."

I chuckle. "It was good."

She snorts, rocking our hug side to side.

"Does Ford know about last night?"

"Who do you think bailed you out?"

"Bailed me out?" I rear back from our hug, panicked. "I got *arrested*?"

She pauses, looking at me as shame threatens to swallow me whole. Even Jessicunt isn't worth jail.

A wide smile overtakes her face. "No."

"Bitch." I slap her arm.

She grins, proud. "But he brought the Bronco back and helped get you into the minivan."

I cringe. "How was that?"

She gives me a grim look and I jam my palms into my eyes until I see the dim imploding stars of my hangover.

I have to get out of here, erase my face ink, and get my life together. I find my coat, slipping it on.

"Sorry about last night. And everything. Again," I say as take my keys from her. "About Thanksgiving . . . I don't know. I have some turkeys but . . ."

"Uh-uh," she says, in a tone that is very final and *very* scary. "It's just us. You can do this. If you're so hellbent on selling that place and running away, we get one holiday in it." In my hesitation she adds, "Just make the turkeys, I'll bring everything else."

Reluctantly: "Fine."

"Hey, Scott," she calls when I'm almost out the door. I turn and look. "Sorry about your face."

I shrug. "Punishment fits the crime."

FORTY-FIVE

"GLORY," I CALL AS I open the door. "You in here?"

She appears from the short hall wearing a pair of grey sweatpants cinched at the waist with a white string and an oversized blue sweater. "Where the hell else would I be?" she snaps, looking all over me. "You look like shit."

"Trying to fit in," I say dryly, not moving from the doorway.

While I usually come to Glory's from work, today I'm in my Sunday best of yoga pants and a thick sweatshirt. *Looking like shit.*

"Let's sit outside."

Her eyes narrow slightly then she swipes a pack of Lucky's off the coffee table and follows me to the steps of the small porch, taking a seat on the top one next to me. A balmy breeze blows my hair and makes it difficult for her to light a cigarette.

"What's this all about? You need money?"

I almost laugh.

"It's been brought to my attention that I'm fucked up."

She scoffs. "And? You here to blame it on me or something?"

"Maybe."

The word stretches between us as she takes a long drag.

"You were a shitty mom," I tell her.

She looks at me. Opens her mouth then closes it—twice. "I was."

Her admission hits like a frying pan to my face and she notices. "God, Scotty. You lookin' at me like that lets me know how stupid you must think I am. Think I don't know what a good mama was supposed to look like?" She scoffs, taps the ash of her cigarette off the side of the porch. "Men liked me, your daddy was garbage."

She says it like that explains everything and I give her a *try again* look.

"Fine." She huffs. "My parents never liked Lyle. Told me not to marry him. I did it anyway. Not sure I ever loved him, but I loved the idea of proving 'em wrong, you know?"

I make an agreeing sound. If my mother has taught me anything, it's stubborn.

"Then he took that job on the road, gone all the time, drinking more when he came home. Angry as sin after that. I got lonely." She shrugs. "If he was gone, I was goin' too. Wasn't gonna be strapped into a life neither of us wanted." She doesn't say it to be mean, it's honest, and as much as I know the abrasiveness of that truth should hurt, it doesn't. At least not as much as I would expect. My mom got married and stayed married to the wrong man for the wrong reasons; Zeb and I were collateral damage. "I knew he was gettin' head at every truck stop from here to Tacoma sure as

I was doing the same to any man who'd buy me a vodka and tonic and flirt with me over a game of pool."

"Your inability to show up for a school function was because you were giving retaliatory blowjobs in the bathroom of the bar?" I ask dryly.

"God, Scotty Ann, for such a smart-ass you're dumb as shit," she snaps. "Do I have to spell it all out for you?"

"Apparently."

"Fine." She rolls her eyes. "People knew. Hell, everyone knew. That day at the playground when I told you not to call me mama?"

I pull my chin back, surprised she remembers.

"I heard one of the other moms talking about me. Calling me a whore. I was embarrassed. Not for me—for you. I didn't act it, but I'm no idiot. You deserved better than me. Zeb did. Thought if nobody called me mama—if I pretended not to be one—I wasn't. Convinced myself you'd be better off. Orphans." Her lips press into a flat line that feels a little remorseful. "It's easy to not show up when you think you're doing everyone a favor."

A cardinal lands in the brown grass and pecks at the ground; I wonder if it's Zeb.

"When I was pregnant with you," she continues, looking up at the sky as she exhales smoke, "I took Zeb to one of those play gyms at McDonalds. You remember those? With the ball pits?" I nod. "He was crawling around, too little to really do anything, I just needed to get out of the house. It was raining. Having kids makes you damn stir crazy. Anyway, a grandmother was there with her grandson. She noticed my belly. '*What are you having?*' she asked.

'*A girl*,' I told her. She put a hand to her heart—just like this."
Glory spreads her bony fingers wide across her chest. "Then she
said, '*You'll have a best friend for life.*' And I cried right there in
that play area at the thought of it. My best friend growing right
inside my body. It wasn't the life I wanted, but I thought I could
change. Be better. Happier."

For the first time in my life, I see tears in my mother's eyes.

"Then I cared more about myself and getting even with your
daddy than being your best friend. I've come to terms with it."
Another drag of her smoke, another shrug. "Probably why I'm so
mean to you. You have a business and a house—a whole damn life
I'm not part of, and that's on me. It's easy to be mean when being
nice stings like a bee's ass in your eye after things don't work out."

I snort a laugh. She's not wrong.

"Why didn't you try to find me when everything happened with
Zeb?"

She laughs, it's unamused.

"You ever make a mistake you didn't want to fess up to?"

I hum in agreement, thinking of Ford and what I did.

"How you think it feels to tell someone their brother is dead
because they were a piss-poor excuse for a mother?"

I look at her. Exactly the same as she always is but different. Human. The whole narrative of my life shifts slightly. *Again*. Glory,
in her own twisted way, did her best, even though it sucked. Just
like I can't escape the pile of shit I was born into, neither could she.
And she pushed us away because of it. Like I've spent my whole life
doing to anyone who tries to get close.

I swallow through the thickness in my throat as a car drives down the lane of the trailer park and Glory waves.

"And your parents?" I ask. "You married my dad and just, what, never talked to them again?" We never discussed them; she said they were worthless, and the context clues of my life never led me to believe otherwise. Never encouraged me to ask anything about them. Knowing they didn't like my dad is no surprise. Nobody did.

She stills, taking a long look at me. The kind of look like she's trying to see something or say something without doing either. Abruptly, she stands, goes inside, and returns with a stack of photos I've never seen before held together by a rubber band.

"When you get as good at lying to yourself as I am, it's easy to lie to everyone else." The ease of the words is at odds with the significance of them. "So I did. Starting with my maiden name." My jaw drops. "Told you it was Joplin because I always liked Janis Joplin."

I don't mask an ounce of my shock. "You *what*?"

She shrugs. "My parents hated Lyle from the second they met him. Said he was worthless. He wasn't at first—least it didn't seem that way. The more I saw they were right, more mad I got. More stubborn. More distance I put between them and me. They didn't control me—nobody did. You know how kids are. Either way"—she lifts her chin, eyes on the sky—"I did what I wanted. They met you once, when you were a baby. Lyle berated me to hell and back in front of them and they begged me to leave him—especially my daddy—but I refused. Never talked to them again. They weren't bad, there just wasn't space for them and my pride. I'd be damned if I was licking my wounds in front of them."

I'm speechless; she hands me the stack of faded pictures. On the first page, every bit of remaining air is squeezed out of my lungs. There, a smiling couple stands holding a faceless baby at the lake . . . in front of an A-frame. *My* A-frame.

The world stops spinning.

"Archie and Lydia?" I whisper.

She smiles, and it's sad. "Wasn't a Joplin, Scotty Ann. I was a Watkins."

The tablecloth of my life is snatched right out from the dirty dishes stacked on top of it. *Archie Watkins was my grandfather.*

"I made my choice, you paid the price." We sit in the enormity of that for seconds or minutes or hours. "You and Zeb both."

Archie was my grandfather, and Lydia my grandmother. Her behavior at his cremation. The A-frame. Bailing Zeb out. All of it there, making sense, clear as a sunny summer day. I press a hand to my chest as if I need to feel my own beating heart to know this is real. As robbed as I was from years I never knew them, there's a wave of relief. A feeling of being loved out of nowhere. Archie didn't show up to watch Wanda remove metal pins and hips, he was there for me. Because he cared. Because we were family.

Another cardinal lands, this time, I wonder if it's Archie. If all of them have been.

"One of these months I expect you'll stop showing up here," Glory says, matter-of-fact. "Wouldn't blame you."

It's the closest to an apology I'll ever get from my mother, and I take it.

"I've thought of it," I admit, glancing at her sideways. "But why deprive myself of the warm, fuzzy feelings you give me?"

She snorts a laugh, takes another drag.

"You ever think of talking to your parents after Dad died?"

She shrugs. "Made too many mistakes at this point. Wouldn't even know where to begin."

Another car drives down the trailer park lane and I feel her flawed mentality rattle my bones. A bullseye mark of my very own thoughts.

"Archie was pretty incredible," I tell her.

She makes an agreeing sound. "You still planning on selling that house and moving west?"

I blow out a long breath. Before right now, as much as I had grown to love it, it was just a house. That simplicity has been shattered. It's not just some house on a lake anymore; it's a family house on a lake. From my grandparents I never knew about. Selling is wrong; staying is complicated.

In my silence she adds, "You still seeing the Callahan boy?"

"The one who's only with me because he felt guilty?" I raise my eyebrows, and her lips twitch. "His kid hates me, and I got in a bar fight last night. Not sure how well that fares with a cop."

She looks at me with what I would dare call admiration. "You win?"

"Can't remember."

Her eyes dart around my face. "Probably means you won."

A laugh tickles my chest but doesn't meet my lips. We sit long enough for her to smoke another entire cigarette, in silence.

"You really were a shitty mom."

"Meh," she says, looking at me with a small smile. "You didn't turn out half bad though."

On the side of the road where the bridge starts over Crow Creek, I park the Bronco. For the first time in twenty years, I squat in front of the abandoned cross, pulling at tangled vines, which have long since wrapped around the near rotted wood. *RIP Lyle Armstrong* is all that's written in faded and chipped white paint.

My dad drove off the bridge, my brother washed away forever. Lyle got a funeral, a headstone, and a cross memorializing his stupidity; Zeb got erased. Staring at the cross, it strikes me that maybe it's why my records are his, my car is his, my job is his. Everything I've done in the last twenty years . . . it's been to remember him because nobody else will.

Except now I know: Ford has. In his own way, he's lived and breathed Zeb's loss as much as I have.

With a sniff, I wrap my hands around the arms of the cross and tug. The earth releases it easy, like it never wanted it to begin with.

I walk to the bridge and watch the water rush under it, the current steady and swift around the boulders. The trees on the bank are bare now; they would have been thick and bright green that spring twenty years ago. Swap Shop was probably on the radio. The box holding Zeb was probably in the passenger seat. My dad was probably smoking a cigarette. I'll never know if he was drunk because he'd lost a son or if he was drunk because that's simply who he was.

"Dad," I say, hoisting the cross up to the guardrail. "I wish you would have loved us better."

Before I talk myself out of it, I toss the cross over the edge and it hits the water with a splash.

It takes less than a minute for it to get swallowed by the current.

A wave of relief washes over me.

And then, I cry.

FORTY-SIX

"I'm Scotty, and I'm addicted to being a pain in the ass."

I laugh softly as I face the sea of Ledger's Ledgers, a few of them chuckling, subpar coffee in hand. Mel raises her eyebrows as she stands next to me at the podium.

"Right," I continue. "The truth is, I didn't know why I started showing up to these meetings. Mel told me once I'm addicted to being unhappy. She probably wasn't wrong." A few more chuckles, Mel's included. I clear my throat. "My parents weren't around much when I was growing up, which was for the best, but I had my brother. He was an idiot." I laugh softly, thinking about all the stunts we pulled in that trailer park as kids. Him as a teenager getting into trouble, Ford laughing from the sidelines. "He knew how to make the best sugar toast for breakfast when we were kids. He'd drop two slices of Wonder Bread into the toaster—he had to hold the button down because the toaster was broken. It would start to burn—that's how we'd know it was done—then he'd coat it with enough butter and sugar to give a healthy man diabetes just by looking at it. We could eat a whole loaf of that damn stuff." I smile at the memory; I can almost smell it. Almost taste it on my tongue like candy. "Zeb was his name. He died of a drug overdose twenty years ago. Twenty years and seven months ago, really."

I pause to let the wave of emotion come and go.

"When he died, I blamed myself for it. And the world. And God. Grief is confusing like that. The targets change depending on the day. Who you hate and what you fight for. And then somewhere along the way I just became that one part of my life. That one horrible event of my brother dying became my whole identity. My job. My house. The music I listened to and the car I drove." I chuckle softly and think of Wren pointing that out. "There was who I was and what I wanted before he died, and what I became after. But"—my voice cracks—"I accidentally fell in love with someone. Someone good. Someone so good it makes me wish I would've been born someone different just to get to love him right, you know?"

A few people nod and my heart aches. They get it, of course they do. We might be on opposite sides of the story, but the pages between are filled with the same ugly words.

"He has a kid, a teenager who might hate me, but it's like she can see me clearer than anyone else. Like she was born with some kind of annoying bullshit detector." A few people chuckle. "She's not mine—I wasn't carved from the right material for that job—but God I see myself in her. Her hurts and mine are different, but not really . . ." The second Wren said she wondered if she could have changed what her mom did, she became my twin flame. She's smarter than me, she'll heal faster and do better things with her life, but I see it when I least expect it. How startled she is when I ask her opinion on things. How uncomfortable she is with my rare displays of affection. And it goes both ways. Her reaction is mine, mine is hers. Even if she hates me—even if I run to the ends of the earth to save her from me—I'll never shake our likeness.

Mel clears her throat, making me realize I've gone silent.

"Sorry." I shift my weight between my feet. "Anyway, I guess what I'm up here to say is thank you. For sharing. For putting up with me. For letting me ask questions that really have nothing to do with you and everything to do with me." I look around at all the vulnerable faces staring back at me. All of us marred with different-shaped bruises. "I wish my mom would've come to the classroom parties. I wish she would've cheered in the bleachers when I graduated high school or helped me with homework. I wish my dad would have drunk less and asked about my day more. I wish my brother . . . I wish." I swallow around the prickly pear–sized lump in my throat. "I guess what I'm trying to say is, I think it's good you're here. I think Mel"—I look at her, a slight smile lifting my lips and hers—"is a pain in the ass but is also helping." A few people laugh. "And I think even if you stumble—even if you watch the video of the nude maid when you don't want to"—I do not look at Gary—"or fall victim to whatever thing you don't want to do, the people around you will appreciate it if you keep trying. People around you want you. Even if you're broken." At the back row, there's an empty seat; I wish Zeb would have sat in it just once. All these people are doing it because they want to change; he never did. At least not enough to still be flesh and bones. I could have dragged him into this room, but he wouldn't have stayed. He would have blown me off. Blown the problem off. I cared more than he did—so did Ford. And even Archie for bailing him out. We never could have fixed him. *I* never could have. Accepting that truth causes my next breath to feel like the first full one I've taken in twenty years. "Maybe even if it never gets easier for you, being here will let people you love live lives that aren't filled with ghosts."

Someone coughs, a phone dings, a chair slides.

In the awkward silence, I add, "The end."

As a hushed applause washes over the crowd, I look at Mel, grinning as I whisper, "And I didn't even tell anyone to fuck off."

She gives a reluctant chuckle before she turns to the room and says, "Thank you, Scotty. Who would like to share next?"

Instead of June's minivan parked next to my Bronco, it's Ford's truck, him leaning against the bumper with a cup of coffee in hand and one ankle crossed over the other. The sight of him in worn blue jeans and a Ledger sweatshirt makes me stop right in the middle of the parking lot before walking the rest of the way to him.

He's a sight for my weary eyes.

"Where's June?"

He hands me the coffee.

"Said she had to go."

I take a sip, less out of wanting coffee and more to keep myself busy. Being so close to him for the first time since the fight with Wren, I'm buzzing. Want. Dread. Confusion. Sadness. Hope. I can't decide if I should lean into him or build a nine-mile-high wall between us. If I should stay in Ledger and figure out a new way of life in this town or hightail it across the country. I was hellbent on leaving right up until the second Glory told me about Archie. His name on that house formed a sentimental tether I never expected. One I'm not sure I'll ever be able to sever. Ever *want* to sever.

But even if I stay, Ford doesn't fit. Wren doesn't want me to fit. And I can't blame either of them. She's his priority, as she should be, and I won't be the reckless thing to ruin what they've worked hard to build. I'll tell him everything and let him cut me loose. Whether I stay or go, I need to figure out what comes next without his intoxicating influence.

"And," he says, "she wanted me to tell you that your speech needed work."

I chuckle softly around another sip of coffee. "You listen?"

He shrugs.

He did.

Damn him.

"You know I was a Watkins?"

He looks at me a long time.

He did.

"Archie told me when I moved back," he says, squinting toward the sun. "He wasn't sure how to tell you, so he never did."

"Guess keeping secrets runs in the family," I say, a shake in my voice as a cinderblock forms in my gut. "You have time for a drive?

I park outside the two-story house in the cookie-cutter subdivision and cut the engine. Merritt is unloading groceries and Blue helps, carrying four bags on each arm at a time and teetering with a laugh. He's handsome. I always knew he would be.

"When I went on that hike in college," I start, not looking away from the mom and son through the windshield, "there was this couple. He was twenty-one, she was twenty. They were just married. The hike was their honeymoon. I thought they were the dumbest pair of dipshits I'd ever heard of. Married so young?" I scoff. "What was the point? But over those two weeks I watched them. How adoring he was of her. Helping her with her backpack. Always putting her sleeping bag down first. When she got tired, he sat with her on a log. And I just thought, *God, he reminds me of Ford*. I thought it over and over. Thought it until I went crazy missing you."

In the passenger seat, Ford's grey sweatshirt makes his blue eyes look like the winter water of Lake Ledger as they bounce from the house to me. I pick my fingernails.

"I knew on that trip I was going to come out of those woods and ask you to marry me." His eyes stop on me and go wide. If I wasn't so focused on not vomiting, I'd laugh. "I couldn't not. I'd spent years refusing to be your girlfriend because I was stubborn, but the more time I spent away from you, the more I knew I never wanted to again. I could make a different life than where I came from. With you. I felt it."

Ford swallows slowly, dropping his forearms to the dash and leaning forward in his seat, eyes on me.

"And then I came back, and not only was half my family dead, but you were gone. Every morning I woke up without you felt like being stabbed in the gut. But grief has a way of moving time in strange ways. Makes things hazy as a fever dream. Somehow, a month passed, two months . . . I realized I hadn't had a period in a while. Figured it was the stress of it all." Ford's mouth opens slightly, understanding making him still as a statue. "But then I just knew—the way a mother does, I guess—I was pregnant. Two months already on that hike, four when I found out."

At Ford's shocked expression, I glance out the window; Merritt sees me and waves. I do the same.

"Your mom saw me in the grocery store once. She told me at Orchard Fest she never told you. My belly was so big there was no denying I was pregnant. She just stared at me and she knew. You were gone and I couldn't raise a kid on my own. Wouldn't put a kid through the disaster of my life. I had no degree, only just started working at the crematorium, and you made your decision when you left. I put the baby up for adoption with three conditions: I'd pick the family, the name, and always know where he lived."

Emotion fills my voice as I look back to Ford. "I had a baby, Ford. A boy. And when he came out and I held him for those first few minutes, he looked just like you." The shock on Ford's face morphs to something heavier—sadder. His eyes dart back to the window, tracking Blue. His son. "I wanted to keep him but knew if I did, I'd miss you every day for the rest of my life. I'd miss you so much I'd never get out of bed. He deserved better than that. Better than anything I could have given him."

I sniff. Ford stares. Silence fills the Bronco.

"I named him Blue Callahan—his last name is Billings. That's him." I point to the house. Merritt's gone; Blue's outside on his phone laughing as he talks and paces around the driveway, oblivious to us. He's smiling a lot; I wonder if it's a girl. "Pieces of us all grown up."

"Ours," Ford finally says. One word meaning a million.

"He's nineteen," I fill in. "Played sports in high school. I went to some of his games. He got good grades. Goes to community college now. I know the parents but have never met him. Not sure I'd know what to say."

Ford's eyes stay on Blue.

I clear my throat. "Anyway, after I got the infection, the doctors told me there was too much damage to ever carry another baby. Which was fine, I never wanted to have another one. Seemed poetic." I remember the doctor telling me the prognosis like it was yesterday; I didn't even react. I simply said, *okay*. "I had one baby with the only man I'd ever love."

I wonder if Ford notices that Blue walks like him or has my hair. If he can hear his laugh and recognizes it as his own.

When Ford's eyes find mine, I brace myself for what comes next. Ford will end it, he has to, and I will let him. I'll let him—because he and Wren deserve better than anything I can give—then I'll fall apart, pick myself back up, and figure out what comes next.

"I hate that you went through this alone," he says, clenching and unclenching his fists in his lap. "Hate that I didn't know. But . . ." I suck in a breath. "I wouldn't change it."

My breath releases in a stunned gush. "You *what*?"

His eyes swing between Blue and I. "I hate in our story I left. Hate that we missed him and each other. But even if I came back, we were in no condition to raise a baby, Scotty." There's no arguing with him, he's right. "I might not have seen it then, but I sure as hell do now. And if life would've turned out any differently, I wouldn't have Wren. Things happen the way they're supposed to, you know?"

At his calm perspective, I am utterly gobsmacked.

"You aren't mad?"

He laughs through a puff of air. "At who?"

"*At who*?" I almost yell. "At me!"

Ford chuckles and reaches his hand to my face, dragging his knuckles down my cheek. My arm. Finding my hand and kissing my thumb.

"God, no. I'm a million things but definitely not mad. I'm shocked. I'm . . . I don't know, a little hurt I didn't help make the decision, but I'm also the one that ran away first. Plus—" He pauses, watching Blue a few seconds. "He looks happy. I guess that makes me a little . . . okay."

"*Okay?!*"

This is . . . unexpected.

"I had a baby, Ford," I snap. "Yours."

His lips roll inward between his teeth before he exhales and drops his head back on the headrest. "I know."

"You know?" I repeat.

His brows pinch. "You just told me."

Jokes?

I scoff. Pick my fingernails more aggressively.

"What do you expect me to say?" he asks through an almost laugh. "It was twenty years ago. A lot happened. You made a choice. Probably the right one. We weren't ready. He looks happy."

"Wren show you the cuts?" I demand.

"She did."

"I knew about them," I bite out. "And didn't tell you."

"Mm," he says, considering. "I didn't love that, but Wren explained everything. I get it. You did what I asked you to do. She said you were checking her every day."

Irritation starts grating my skin away. He isn't yelling. He's . . . what the hell is he? Fine?

"She hates me." I'm fully pissed.

He's calm. "She doesn't."

"She does," I argue. "She all but said those exact words."

"She doesn't. My mom told us what happened at Orchard Fest." He raises his eyebrows, lips fighting a smile. "And exactly what you said to the Letts girl."

Charlene—full of surprises.

I don't dwell on that.

"And my flying fists of fury at Liberty Tap?"

A smile tugs at his lips. "Guess we won't know the fallout until Monday. I told Jessica if she didn't press charges, I wouldn't go to the school and get her daughter expelled for what she did to Wren."

He's making this impossible.

"You're a cop."

At this, he laughs. "And?"

"And we can't be together!" I shout, punctuating each word with a smack of the steering wheel. "I meant it when I told you we were done. We are."

"Ahhh," he says, grotesquely calm. "I thought that's what this was."

"What *what* was?"

"Scotty." He pushes one hand across my face and into my hair. "You and Wren got in a fight. She used her tongue as a teenage weapon of mass destruction—which reminds me of someone else I know." A smile whispers across his lips "You told me you never want to see me again. After you told me you loved me. Which you confirmed to everyone at the LL meeting." I open my mouth, but this moron doesn't stop talking. "You take me out here and tell me about Blue—which I have a lot of big feelings about—but I wonder if you were thinking I couldn't take it."

Damn him.

"And it won't work."

"Why?" I huff. "Have you not been paying attention to how at the drop of a hat I turn into a human wrecking ball that chews out kids and punches their mothers?"

"I like that about you."

"You don't," I snap.

"And if I say no? If I say you don't get to push me away? That I'm going to be the one to show up, no matter what?"

My gaze cuts to him. "You can't say no, that's not how this works."

"It is. We actually specifically said, '*no pushing away.*'"

We did say that.

"But I'm giving you an out," I argue. "And Wren."

He laughs. "We don't want an out. We love you."

I suck in a sharp breath; this makes no sense.

"I still might sell the house," I persevere. "And move to the desert. And I ruined Wren's Homecoming. I got drunk and acted like some kind of wannabe superhero trying to clean up the streets of Gotham. And I had a kid. By you. That I never told you about!" My blood is boiling now. He's making this harder than it needs to be. Impossible even. Blind to the fact that this kind of crazy is just who I am. "Just let this go. Let me go. Let *us* go."

His mouth tugs to one side. "No can do, Scotty."

"No can do?" I echo with a groan, struggling to get the key in the ignition. Not sure when or why I took it out to begin with. "It's not an option."

"I'm not going to let you do this." He relaxes back into his seat like the decision has been made. "Go ahead. Throw a tantrum. Let the viper come out to play. But it won't work. I left once because I was scared. I'm not letting you go now because you're feeling the same thing."

I glare at him as I peel onto the highway with a squeal of the tires. Fuck him for making this so hard. If he wants to prove some kind of point with a game he'll most certainly lose, I'll play. "Fine. Try. You won't win this."

I ignore the very *very* small part of me hoping he does.

"And when I convince you that you're wrong, you'll propose to me."

"I'll what?!" I slam on the brakes, jerking us both forward. He doesn't react.

"That's what you just told me you wanted to do twenty years ago—why not now?"

Asshole.

"Fine," I grit out, accelerating again.

Over my dead body.

I have gone from loving this man to hating him in the span of fifteen minutes.

At a stop sign, I glare at Ford, who smiles smugly, then punch the gas—purposefully driving over the speed limit.

The entire time, I'm seething.

"Ooh!" he says, angling his head to see out the windshield as I drive. "Think that was a pileated woodpecker."

He smiles, his face all warm eyes and smile lines that makes me want to shove him right out into the road and run over him.

By the time we get to the church parking lot, I'm a powder keg ready to explode.

He unbuckles his seatbelt, leans across the center console, and kisses me on the mouth. Then, cooler than the November breeze blowing outside, he pulls away, winks, and says, "Thank you for telling me about Blue. We did good. You did." In my silence he adds, "Tell me something real."

"We're over," I bark. "How's that for real?"

He chuckles, gets out of the Bronco and into his truck—like I didn't just tell him he had a son he never knew about—and drives away.

I must still be drunk.

At my window, a tap makes me jump.

"Jesus, Mel." I gasp, bringing a hand to my chest as I roll the window down. "You almost scared me to death."

"Failed again," she says with a slight lift of her lips as she taps a cigarette out of the box and sticks it in her mouth without lighting it. "What are you still doing here?"

"Well, I was just showing Ford his bastard child and telling him to pound sand, but that asshole is too stupid for his own good."

She looks at me, unlit cigarette still hanging out of her mouth.

"That's a lot to unpack."

I frown.

"Now what are you going to do?"

"About what?"

"Life!" she cries, making the cigarette bobble on her lips. "Love! All of it!"

"Why would I do anything?"

"Scotty." She plucks the cigarette from her mouth. "Your skull must be the thickest matter on earth. Didn't you hear yourself today?"

My eyes narrow.

"You just told a whole room that you wished people would have showed up for you."

"So . . . ?"

She barks out a laugh and looks at Ford's truck pulling out of the lot. "So let them show up for you for God's sake. Just because your parents never did doesn't mean people can't do it now. You'd be a special kind of stupid not to be with Ford because you're on some mission to be miserable. He knows what you are. You're so damn loud, we all do."

Her point knocks me sideways. I think of June throwing my own advice back in my face. Be me with them.

"I don't think—"

"What you think," she says over me, "and what is are two entirely different things." She puts the cigarette back into the box. "I'm trying to quit," she mutters when she catches me watching. "Read an article just putting the damn things in your mouth helps."

"Does it?"

"I don't know." She shrugs, slight smile pulling at her lips. "Does you telling Ford you don't want to be with him make you love him any less?"

Bitch.

Forty-Seven

"HEARD YOU HAD QUITE a weekend, honey," Wanda says with a wide smile, falling into step behind me as I head toward my office. "Heard you almost castrated Cal right in front of everyone at Liberty Tap."

"I have no idea what you're talking about," I mutter, tossing my purse on the floor then sliding into the chair behind my desk. Wanda's wearing fifty shades and patterns of brown, looking like some kind of sexy safari guide. "Don't think I've ever seen so much brown."

She pops a shoulder. "Thanksgiving's next week. I'm channeling my inner Pilgrim."

Her inner Pilgrim would make a real Pilgrim stroke out.

"Festive."

"Tell me what happened with Cal already?" Her voice is high-pitched and giddy. "How'd you know it was him?"

"I'm not talking about this."

"Oh phooey." She sticks her tongue out at me. "Bet Ford thought it was hot as hell his woman was out there goin' all Xena, Warrior Princess."

I move the mouse of the computer and start clicking through my emails, not looking at her. "Ford and I are over."

She gasps and takes the empty seat across from my desk. Uninvited. "Because of Cal?"

I fold my hands on my desk and look at her. "Because of me. Anything else?"

"You're grumpy."

"Anything else?"

A door opens and closes down the hall and footsteps follow.

"The Dondinator has arrived," Dondi says with a gappy grin as he steps into my office. "And he is here to serve the woman who took down his beloved's previous captor." He takes a deep bow, one hand holding a piece of paper over his chest, the other sweeping dramatically into the air above him.

Fuck me.

"Dondi," I mutter, starting to thumb through a stack of papers.

"Don't mind her, honey buns. She's grumpy," Wanda says.

I roll my eyes.

"Anything on the schedule I should know about?"

Dondi shakes his head, dropping the paper he's holding on my desk before crossing his arms over his chest and leaning in the doorway.

"Sellecks are champing at the bit to buy this place again, but otherwise, it's all copacetic and a piece of respectfully handled corpse cake."

The Sellecks' timing might finally be right so I can start weighing my options and figure out what to do next.

I unfold the paper from Dondi. "What's this?"

He shrugs. "It was taped to the door."

Some of the world's best people
Overdo it on the swear words but
Really know how to make a convict's kid
Really know she's loved
Yet sometimes kids are idiots. I'm sorry.

I read it. Twice. *Wren*. I chew my lip and fold the paper back up. The words linger and bounce into each other, rattling my brain. She wrote a poem. Apologizing. After I acted like a Tasmanian devil.

Sometime last night as I stared at the point of the roof from bed, I decided to sell the house. Archie wanted me to have it to make my life better; selling it would do that. I told myself it wouldn't change the fact he's my grandfather. If anything, the money from the sale would make me feel more connected to him. More grateful for the fresh start. For the space to breathe—away from Ford and Wren—and figure out what comes next. If I didn't move to the desert, I thought about going back to the crematorium apartment.

Then I remembered Wanda and Dondi were bumping uglies in my bed every night, and I hated that visual almost as much as I hated the thought of kicking Wanda out.

It was nearly two a.m. when I decided I'd figure it out later. All I knew, I was listing it, then I was going to call Lydia and tell her.

But now, Wren's note is an annoying relief that makes me doubt every late-night declaration I made to myself just hours ago.

"Wanda," I start, pressing the crease of the paper. "What do you want to do with your life?"

Her eyes narrow. "Like marriage?"

Dondi straightens.

"Like career. What's your—your passion? Where do you see yourself in ten years?"

She looks at me like I'm crazy.

"Here, honey. I loved the salon, but"—she gestures to my office—"you're the best boss I've ever had in my few short years on this planet." She pauses to purse her lips. "And these clients don't complain. And, Scotty . . ." She hesitates, eyes widening slightly. "You've done something beautiful here. Took what happened to your brother and made it good. Made it . . . worth it. Gave me and Dondi a chance when nobody else would. See people nobody else wants to look at." She swallows. "You change lives and let someone like me be part of it. Why would I ever want anything else?"

My gaze stays on her and I sit with what she's said. *Took what happened to your brother and made it good.* As many times as I've heard a version of that, I've never once let myself believe it, but the look on Wanda's face tells me I should. Tells me it's true. Zeb's death was ugly and lonely; what we do here is anything but.

I clear my throat. "Dondi?"

He glances at Wanda, lovestruck look on his face as he opens his mouth.

"*Not* about Wanda."

"Well, no offense, Scotty," he says slightly guarded. "I love driving the Ice Pop, but I want to open a float shop someday."

"A float shop?"

"A float shop." He grins, gap-toothed and proud. "See, it's a shop—on the lake—on pontoons"—he raises his eyebrows—"where you can get anything that floats. Tubes, kayaks, boats." He snaps his fingers then sweeps his hands through the air, repeating in a theatrical voice, "Float Shop."

Of course.

"Interesting. You been saving?"

"Have three thousand." He chuckles. "Need about twenty more."

I tap my fingers on the desk, brain buzzing like a radio tuned in to every station at once. Whatever I do or don't do with the house, I'm done. I feel it. This job has been good, but I don't love it. I'm sick of death. Sick of constantly being reminded of everything that's gone wrong. Everything that was and wasn't meant to be swallowing me up only to spit me back out.

Wanda would keep doing what I've done here. Honoring death in the most unexpected of ways. After hearing what she's just said, I wouldn't even have to ask.

I tap my fingers on the desk.

Snap the rubber band around my wrist.

Shift in my chair.

And shock us all when I finally say, "Let's call the Sellecks."

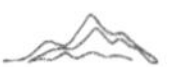

"You lost?"

Wren's familiar blue-eyed gaze meets mine as I climb the steps of the porch.

"Depends. This Monday Night RAW?"

I give her a flat look as I unlock the door. "Days away from me and you're already less funny."

She follows me inside and sheds her coat, Molly running straight to her. We stand in a tense silence, both of us waiting for the other to speak.

Finally, she does. "I should have listened about Becca."

I chew my lip. Ford's conditioned her to apologize freely, I'll give him that.

"Well. I probably shouldn't have told Becca that her mom was a dick eater," I admit.

She snorts a laugh but says nothing, petting Molly on the head.

"Your dad put you up to this?"

"No." She scoffs. "Why?"

"I broke up with him twice and he's not listening."

She scuffs the toe of her tennis shoe on the rug. "You break up because of me?"

I take my heels off with an *ahh!* and rub my toes. "I broke up with him," I explain, "because I think he's been sleeping around with the sparrows."

"Rigghtt," she drawls with a roll of her eyes.

"He tell you I had a baby?"

"Yep."

"And what do you think about that?"

She drags her fingers across the back of the purple velvet chair in the living room.

"I think you would have been a great mom but maybe not then."

Another loaded silence follows. That is such a Ford thing to say, and I hate it as much as the rash this whole conversation is giving me.

I fold my arms over my chest. "I guess your shitty poetry makes us friends again?"

She shrugs one shoulder. "Depends."

I lift my chin.

"You done using me for free child labor?"

"You barely did enough to earn your paycheck."

We *almost* smile before dropping onto the couch and propping our feet on the coffee table, Molly curling in between us.

"And Luke?" I ask, scrubbing the dog between the ears. "He okay with dating a convict's kid with ties to Ledger's Most Wanted?"

She grins, wide, Ford's big blue eyes bright as the midday sun on her delicate face, hurting my heart. "He thinks it's badass."

I snort a laugh. "I knew keeping me around had its perks."

Another silence.

She looks around the house.

"You still selling after Thanksgiving?"

"Why do you care?"

"I don't."

I squint at her. "I don't know what I'm doing. But—" A noise outside pulls me from the couch; Ford backs down the driveway in his truck. It's irritating and impacts the speed of my pulse. "My annoying neighbors are making the decision easy." I swing the door open. "What the hell are you doing here?"

Ford's nose is red from the cold; he's wearing gym clothes and a misplaced grin. "Tending my flock."

From the porch, I scowl. "Are you deaf? I told you we're done."

He pours seed into a feeder before strolling over to me. "And I said we aren't. Guess we're at an impasse." He kisses me—long enough to make me feel like melted wax but fast enough I forget to slap him.

"This is trespassing," I argue.

"No," he says. "This is me not letting you look away."

I glare at him; Wren walks onto the porch.

"Hey, Dad."

He grins. "Wrenny." A gust of wind slices the air and he shivers, rubbing his hands together for warmth. "Cold out here."

"We should get a fire going in the woodstove," Wren says, hugging herself. "Scotty hasn't used it."

"No thank you," I say flatly.

"Let's do it." Ford cups his hands around his mouth and blows into them, a cloud from his breath floating around his face. "Get some sticks. Archie kept firewood behind the shed."

"Hello!" I shout. "This is my house. I don't want a damn fire. Or guests."

They ignore me, marching around like fire-building ants collecting flammable debris.

"I don't want a fire," I repeat, softer, unmoving as I watch them.

Ford's already inside with the door to the woodstove open, stacking sticks and balled-up newspaper before striking a match. Wren stacks logs on the floor and Molly sprawls out at their feet.

Traitor.

When a fire is glowing and dancing through the glass, they give each other a high five. In the middle of my house. Without my permission. And, damn them both, I love the sight of it. The butterflies it sends fluttering through me and how perfect they look here in this ridiculously shaped house. The fact that even though I had a public display of apeshit, here they are. Writing me poems, building me fires, and feeding my birds.

The Sellecks made me an offer I couldn't refuse, but I told them I wanted to think about it. Wanted to make sure I could really live in a life doing something different. Now, standing here, I see there's nothing to think about. I don't want the crematorium. I don't want the past. I might not even want to leave.

And yet, I say nothing. The words are not in my lexicon to tell them that if they're willing to take a chance on me, I might be okay with staying with them.

"I have to get going," Ford says, giving Wren a peck on the forehead. "Scotty, can you bring Wren to the gym?"

I frown.

"He's introducing me to his minions after class today," she fills in.

I stand there, legs like concrete, unable to process what he's doing or the shift that's happening in me as he does it.

He strolls over to me, tilts my chin. "Thanks. Love you." There's a smug smirk on his face when he pecks me on the lips.

Then he walks out the door, leaving my house and heart warmer than I'll ever admit.

Damn him.

"You coming in?" Wren asks, as I follow her out of the Bronco.

"Your dad's launching some kind of psychological warfare on me. Of course I'm coming in."

The truth: I'm going in because I love him and looking at him even though I don't know how to tell him.

The gravel crunches beneath our feet until we stop at the propped door.

"I'm proud of you for doing this."

"Secret's out now." She shrugs. "No point in not talking about it with other kids it might help."

She opens the door to Fight Club, but my eyes catch on the For Sale sign still taped to the unoccupied side of the building.

"You go in, I'll be right there."

At the window, I cup my hands around my eyes and look inside. It's one big room, much like Fight Club, but it's completely empty. The ceilings are high, the floors are concrete, and there's dust everywhere. It's nothing that could be anything. I linger a minute, imagining what it could be. It reminds me of the A-frame, a potential diamond in the rough.

In the gym, Wren's already with Ford, him introducing her to his sweaty group of boys on a mat between hitting bags. I watch them, smiling together, the boys doing the same. Wren mock punches Ford in the gut and he reacts dramatically, doubling over with a grin.

One man changing the lives of seven, over and over.

"Why you crying?" the meatball behind the counter asks.

"Because it smells like crusty balls in here," I snap, thumbing moisture from my eyes.

He grunts as the phone rings, delivering a rough, "Fight Club."

Across the gym, Ford's eyes hook with mine. He lifts his chin; I mirror the movement. His gaze on mine holds like a Chinese finger trap: The more I fight it, the tighter it grabs.

Even with all the stress fractures on our lives and hearts and histories—even as insufferably destructive as I can be sometimes—maybe June was right. Maybe everyone was.

Jimmy, the kid whose sister died, laughs at something Ford says as he takes a gloved swing at him. Full-blown, no worries, laughing. Even with a dead sister.

Across the room, Ford mouths, *I love you* to me and it face-plants me into my universal truth: I want this. Him. Right now.

Forever.

Scotty

I got a new phone.

What if I stayed with Ford?

I've never killed anyone, you know? Maybe I'm not that bad.

And Wren doesn't even care that I attacked Jessicunt in public.

And Ford keeps feeding my birds.

And I *like* him feeding my birds.

Despite what Sweaty Vince says, I read December is the worst month to list a house . . .

Where are you?

Is this that thing you do where you don't answer and let me talk myself into figuring out what you already know?

Since you're ignoring me, I guess you won't care that I came to an agreement with the Sellecks and I'm at House of Ink.

June

On my way.

Forty-Eight

The hours I've spent in the kitchen have led me to one conclusion: Turkeys can go fuck themselves with a baster.

I push one sleeve of my green sweater up my arm as I check the bird—the last one I ever want to make for the rest of my life—and it's still not done. Ford would laugh.

No.

Ford is tomorrow's problem.

I slide the turkey back into the oven, closing the door with my hip as I toss the oven mitts on the counter. I need to get through today, enjoy June and her family, and make up for being such a hemorrhoid, then I'll figure out a way to eat crow to Ford.

The last few days have been a whirlwind of work—of me flipping every piece of my life over to figure out where I want to go from here. I've been so busy I haven't seen Ford or Wren—haven't spoken to them once in two days—but I know they've been here.

The birds have been fed and firewood stacked by the door both nights when I get home.

I've been waiting for everything to get ironed out—to find the right words to explain if they still want me, I want them. Tomorrow, I'll know what to say. And if I don't . . . that's tomorrow's problem.

Out of nowhere, I'm at the trailhead twenty years ago, ready to tell Ford I loved him only to find him not there.

Then a month ago, him getting shot.

Anxiety tightens my chest like a tourniquet.

What if I wait until tomorrow only to find all of this gone? *Him* gone.

I reach for my phone and punch his number; no answer.

My pulse picks up in my throat. I can't wait. I need to—

The front door swings open, and Molly barks as June appears in the doorway in a chunky turtleneck, rosy cheeks, and two armfuls of groceries.

My eyes narrow. "You're early."

She smiles and shuffles across the room like it's familiar, dropping the bags in the kitchen. She does a double take of the living room. "You moved the chair again—I liked it better on the other side." She looks back to the kitchen, assessing then rolling her eyes when she catches my face. "Oh stop. You think my best friend gets a lake house and I'm not going to figure out a way to see it?"

"You've been coming here?" I gasp, once again violated by her invasion of my privacy. "Inside?"

"A key under the mat?" She gives me a look, like *amateur*. "Anyway, hi. Happy Thanksgiving." She hugs me. "Don't get mad—and it was all Ford's idea." His name gives relief amidst my confusion. I set the phone I'm still holding on the counter. "If you're going to hate anyone it's him." She bends over and pulls boxes of plasticware and tablecloths covered in cornucopias out of the bag as I stand, watching her dumbfounded. "How many chairs do you have?"

"Uh . . ." My eyes narrow. "Six?"

"Right." She pulls out her phone. "Camp. Hey. Yeah. All the chairs too. Mhm. She's glaring but fine. Love you."

What the hell?

"Listen to me. It's all taken care of."

"What is?"

"Mom?" a voice calls.

My head whips to the door.

"Lyra. Excellent."

June's home-from-college daughter stands in the doorway, more bags in her arms and a big smile on her face.

"Aunt Scotty!" Lyra cries. "This place is awesome!" She sets the bags down and hugs me. "Great sweater!" She tugs at the sleeve of said sweater, talking and moving too fast for me to respond. "Oh, and I have this." She pulls a framed picture out of the bag. Her and I from her graduation over the summer. In it, she's sticking out her tongue in her cap and gown and I'm smiling wide, wearing a shirt with her face on it.

To her mom: "Okay, what's the plan?"

"The plan?" I look at June.

"Right. Camp's coming with tables, there will be one for the photos. Lyra, let's set them up there. Scotty, you're hosting Thanksgiving."

"Yeah . . ."

"Like really hosting it. And it's all Ford." She makes an apologetic wince. "Mostly all Ford."

What?

A gift bag appears in her hands. "Before everyone gets here, this is for you."

Brows pinched, I reach into the bag, pulling a small frame out that sends emotion shooting through me so fast I go dizzy. It's me, nearly twenty years ago, in a hospital gown with a baby in my arms. Me the day I had Blue; the only picture that exists of us together. I look at her, her eyes wet as she smiles. I can't speak.

"There's one more," she says.

I reach in, feeling something bigger. It's a canvas. A large photograph of the lake, cut in half with a band of light. Across its entirety, a murmuration of starlings form a breathtaking shape as they fly across it. It's stunning.

"It was Ford's idea," she fills in. "Again."

In my belly, every wing in the photo flaps.

"What's going on, Joo?" I whisper with a sniff.

"We're filling your walls, and Ford's . . ." She looks through the wall of windows to the flat-watered lake. "Sweeping you off your feet."

Before I can argue or demand more information, she gives me a quick hug then turns to the kitchen and claps her hands. "This is going to be so fun!"

I don't move—I can't.

The door swings open and in walks Wren, smiling wide, another bag in her hand. "June, Dad's outside—hey, Scotty."

"Wren?" She shouldn't be here.

Wren sets the bag on the counter which June immediately digs through, then steps next to me and hands me a frame. Her and I fill it with the picture she took for the homecoming slideshow, both of us smiling post-pumpkin stabbing.

I don't know what's going on or why she's here, but when she gives me a slight shrug, I wrap my arms around her.

And then, I cry.

FORTY-NINE

THE TRIANGLE IN THE woods is pure pandemonium. June, Lyra, and Wren buzz around the kitchen, shuffling pans in and out of the oven and around burners of the stove. Every outlet has a crockpot plugged into it.

I try to help, but since I might be in shock, I opt to stand in the way.

A muffled shout from outside grabs my attention. There, a literal team of boys is unloading folding chairs and tables from the back of Camp's truck as Ford and Camp stand off to the side directing the boys around the yard.

Ford smiles and waves like this isn't at all shocking. Like I have a damn clue as to what's happening.

"So," June says, stepping next to me on the porch. "There are people coming."

"No shit, people are coming. Why is my yard covered in teenage boys?"

"They're helping." She smiles with all her teeth before disappearing.

Four long tables get set up in the yard, surrounded by metal folding chairs, and two more tables go on the porch, which immediately get filled with crockpots that are plugged into extension cords. Off to the side, one lone table.

Ford strolls over to me. "Hi."

Despite how handsome he looks in his dark jacket and subtle layer of scruff on his jaw, I scowl. "What the hell?"

His lips twitch then he leans in to kiss me. "I love you, Scotty, but you're stubborn as hell." He kisses me again. "I told you I'm not letting you push me away."

All I can manage: "Doubt that."

He chuckles, kisses me again. "Mm. I've missed you." And again. "And I can tell you have too by the way you're gripping on to my shirt."

I am, in fact, clinging on to him for dear life.

Damn him.

A car pulls up and he pulls away, taking my hand. "They're here."

I look; *his parents?*

Charlene and Earl get out, stacks of pies in hand and smiles on their faces. Ford doesn't look at me, just walks me over to them. His mom hands the pies to him . . . and hugs me. "Scotty," she says as she pulls away, looking at me square in the eyes. "It seems you're sticking around."

My chin jerks back as she chuckles and looks at Ford. "Put me to work, son."

"Inside. Fair warning, June's a drill sergeant."

Charlene looks back to me and reaches into her purse, pulling out two framed pictures. "For you."

Despite my confusion, I take them from her, and my breath catches. In the first one, me, June, and Wren are mid-laugh as we dance at Orchard Fest. In the second, me, Ford, and Zeb stand in the middle of their orchard with teenage faces. Zeb's wearing a T-shirt that says *No Fear* while holding up a peace sign with one hand. I'm leaning on Ford's shoulder smiling. Ford's looking at me. It cracks my heart in two.

Charlene and I look at each other, a small smile pulling at our lips before she goes to help June.

Lyra swoops in from seemingly out of nowhere. "I'll take these," she says, swiping the pictures out of my hands and taking them to the table at the edge of the yard, propping them up next to the one she brought.

Ford's next to me again, squeezing my hand in his. I look up at him. "What's happening?"

"I can't let you leave, Scotty," he says, kissing my thumb. "Can't live anymore of us not being us. So"—he looks around at the chaos happening around us—"I'm fighting like hell to keep you here."

I should say something. Argue. Tell him I've made up my mind and this is ridiculous.

But I don't.

Because I can't.

Because inside of my body, every single piece of me is being taken apart before being remade.

And then, Thanksgiving day unfolds like a dream I didn't know to have.

The cars keep coming.

Wanda and Dondi arrive, carrying two casserole dishes. Dondi is wearing a ridiculous plaid suit, Wanda is wrapped in shades of brown and orange with turkeys dangling from her ears. She hands me a framed photo, a selfie of her and Dondi. "Never would have met the man of my dreams if you didn't believe in us, honey," she says as she hugs me. "I'll miss your face every single day."

Then Mel, carrying a large bowl of cranberry sauce. She's wearing a sweater dress and gold earrings—she looks beautiful. When she steps up to me, she hands Ford the dish and hands me a photo. It's her and I standing outside of the church by the LL sign, looking at each other with half smiles on our faces. "Your friend took it," she says. "Thought it suited us."

I open my mouth only to once again find nothing. She shows mercy. "You're not so bad for a pain in the ass."

I laugh. It's borderline watery.

Three of Ford's boys from the boxing gym show up with bags of premade rolls and a picture of them with Ford at Fight Club.

Gary shows up with his wife, Deb, and a sponge cake and picture of the two of them from Halloween. She's wearing a maid costume. "Thanks for the idea," Gary says with a sheepish grin. I will scrub that visual out of my mind later.

Vince the real estate agent comes with his family; he's wearing a coat and sweating as he gives me a picture of him and Archie—the grandpa he was friends with—fishing from a few years ago. "We could have made a fortune on this one." It was the same thing he said to me when I called him yesterday and told him I wasn't selling.

I laugh and he shrugs.

June's parents bring yams and a picture of me and June from her wedding.

Camp's parents arrive with a crate of rosé and a picture of me, June, Camp, and Ford outside of the gym before senior prom.

Ben and his girlfriend show up with ingredients for Moscow Mules and two pictures. The first is of me, June, and Ford the night they hauled my ass out of Liberty Tap. Ford is holding me like a child in his arms; there's a drunk smile on my face. The second one is Ben and another man wearing leather jackets standing in front of motorcycles—*his brother*. He gives me a knowing look; tears in my eyes, I hug him tight.

Hank and Ty proudly present me with a picture of them drawing all over my face as I'm passed out on their couch, making me laugh, long and hard.

"Ford, what's happening?" I whisper again, watching the lone table fill with pictures as the rest fill with bodies. Laughter bubbles up as people gather. He wraps an arm around my shoulders and squeezes as yet another unrecognizable vehicle arrives. When Merritt, Joel, and Blue get out, tears fall straight down my face. I can barely speak. "Ford?"

He looks at me, eyes so bright they're almost golden. Just like him. "Scotty," he says, "you've changed the life of every single person here. You've made their lives better by simply existing on this planet. By growing up in a trailer. By getting in bar fights and having a mouth of a viper." He dusts a kiss on my lips. "By having a baby and giving him away. You're selfless and you have the biggest heart ever made. You denying it doesn't make it any less true."

"Scotty?" Merritt says with a warm smile as she approaches. "Hope it's okay we're here." She gestures to the casserole dish in her husband's hands. "We brought carrots."

I sniff and wipe my eyes, unable to stop looking at Blue. Other than when I held him as a baby, I've never seen him so close. He has freckles. My nose. "I'm very happy you're here."

Ford's hand squeezes mine.

"Sorry," I sniff. "I'm all emotional. Joel." I smile at Blue's dad. "It's good to see you again. Happy Thanksgiving."

"Scotty." He shakes Ford's hand as they exchange introductions. My eyes stay on Blue.

Merritt clears her throat. "Blue, this is your birth mom. Scotty."

He and I look at each other like we're newly discovered life-forms. A small smile tugs at his lips. "Hey."

"Hi," I say, clearing my throat. "And this is your"—I look at Ford—"sperm donor. Ford Callahan." Ford chuckles as Blue's eyes double in size. "I named you after his eyes and his last name. I'm creative like that." I laugh awkwardly.

He and Ford look at each other; Ford shakes his hand. "Blue."

Blue studies him, and I wonder if he's seeing the same pieces of himself I do.

"I didn't know how to be a mom," I blurt, desperate to explain myself in the silence. Like if I don't tell him he'll slip through my fingers like sand in the wind. I'm watching Blue intensely enough to notice his eyes narrow *just* slightly. "I didn't want you to think you were a demon baby I had to get rid of or something. Or that you were unwanted. Or unloved. I picked your parents out because they didn't look like serial killers or cult leaders."

Blue's lips twitch. "Yeah," he says. "You did good. They raised me cult- and killer-free."

I chuckle, relieved, and when I look at Ford, my own pride reflects in his eyes. *We did good.*

"Your friend asked us to bring a picture in a frame," Merritt chimes in, almost unsure. "But I made you an album. Blue over the years." She offers it to me. "If you'd like it."

I take it in my hands, fresh surge of emotion swelling in me. "I'd love that."

She and I look at each other, an unspoken bond of motherhood traveling between us. Her appreciation for the life I gave her, and my appreciation for the life she gave him. The one I was too young and broken to have ever given.

Wren appears, introduces herself, and looks at Blue. "I guess we're kind of siblings."

Blue's taken aback but he also smiles. "I guess so."

"Alright, people," June shouts from the steps of the porch with her hands cupped around her mouth. "Let's eat already!"

Blue and I exchange one last smile, then everyone moves toward June, forming lines at the food tables and filling the chairs. I stay behind, my whole world tripling in size by being in the presence of all these people.

Wren props the front door open and puts a record on—a Lindsey Stirling one I bought to surprise her—and flicks me a half smile.

My legs won't budge, so I just watch. Every beautiful piece of it.

June bosses Ford and Camp around; they obediently listen to every word.

Blue sits next to Lyra and Wren; Lyra instantly makes them both laugh.

When every seat is nearly filled, a blue SUV parks at the street and nearly makes me collapse. In a bright floral skirt and yellow sweater: Glory.

I watch her until she's next to me and I blink back tears. My mother has never once showed up for a holiday outside of the ones we had in that trailer before it all went to shit.

"You didn't buy me any ingredients to cook with," she says without heat, gesturing to the bag in her hand. "I brought a bottle of wine and some scratch offs."

I snort a laugh. "I'd expect nothing less."

Her eyes linger on me, then she and Ford wave at each other across the yard.

"Don't let that one go, Scotty Ann."

I watch him, heart expanding in my chest with every passing second. "Not sure I have a choice."

June sees Glory next to me and her eyes nearly pop out of her head. I swallow my laugh. "Go eat," I tell her.

She pulls a framed picture out of the bag. It's the one of me, her, Zeb, and my dad from the beach that always hung in the hall. "You deserve the good memories."

In my hands, it feels heavy. My eyes burn with tears I've seemingly carried around for twenty years.

"Mama," I call, the word clunky on my tongue as she starts to walk away. She pauses, surprise filling her features as she looks back at me. "Thanks for coming."

She half smiles, half shrugs. "Not like I had anything else going on."

Instead of walking toward the tables, her attention goes over my shoulder, morphing her expression to one of shock. I turn and follow her gaze . . . to Lydia.

The three of us stand staring at each other—three generations of women who've known heartache and loss—silent. Taking in the bigness of the moment as our dinged-up histories fill the spaces between us.

It is the heaviest silence of my entire life.

Lydia reaches her arms out with a slight tremble and pulls Glory and me to her chest. "Stubborn women raise stubborn women," she says, watery laugh in her shaky voice. "But I should have fought harder for both of you girls." She sniffs. "Should have done better."

I pull back, wiping my eyes as the sentiment washes over me like a tidal wave. After a lifetime of feeling like nobody in my family could show up for me, could stick around when I needed them, here they are, just on a different schedule. Their timelines intersecting with mine a little later, albeit annoyingly so, than I hoped.

"Archie would probably tell me the past is a good thing to set on fire," I say, smiling as a bright-red cardinal lands on a branch of bare shrub near us. "We could always start now."

She smiles and squeezes my hand. "We could." Then to Glory, "Will that work for you, Glory?"

My mother's eyes are wet. She hesitates, smirks, and in a flippant tone: "Guess I have time."

Lydia shakes her head, but there's a smile on her lined face as she hands me a frame from her purse. It's gold and detailed, bordering her and Archie on their wedding day. His smile is wide, her dress is stunning. She looks from the picture to the house. "He would have loved seeing you here, Scotty," she says. "Having you home."

I smile, hug her again. Molly runs up to her and she chuckles, petting her on the head gingerly. I have so much to say, so many questions, but not now. Not today. There's time. I'm not going anywhere.

She and my mom walk toward the tables of food, close but not touching, quiet but not scowling. *Home*. Lydia's right. I guess part of me has known it all along. Felt its comforting pull from the second I stepped inside and smelled the mothballs.

June fills the now vacant spot next to me, buzzing with joy.

"I hate you," I say with a sniff.

"I know you don't." She bumps my shoulder with hers. "But you do have enough food to feed an army and enough pictures to fill every wall in your beautiful house."

Ford's eyes meet mine across the people filling plates in the middle of my yard.

"He's the worst," I tell June.

She chuckles next to me and hooks her arm through mine. "Then you aren't going to like what's next."

In perfect timing, Ford, the only one standing at the end of one table, clinks his glass bottle of Coke from Mexico until everyone falls silent.

"Happy Thanksgiving," he says warmly, everyone responding with a murmured *Happy Thanksgiving*. "We celebrate today to give thanks. We gather with gratitude. The Pilgrims, they say, did it to celebrate surviving. I'd venture to say we aren't so different sitting here. We made it—some of us against all odds." Ford looks at me and winks. "But what really binds us together today—the silent thread that's been woven into our lives without even meaning to—is our beautiful host, Scotty Armstrong."

When he pauses, these idiots clap. Especially June who screams *woo!* in my ear. I elbow her and glare at Ford.

He grins.

"And while I considered making everyone go around and say how Scotty has changed each of our lives"—I level him with a look, making him chuckle—"I know better. Your presence is enough. The photos you've brought to fill her walls. The food. The company."

He raises his bottle of Coke. "To old faces and new," he says. "And to the woman that's had my heart since I was seventeen, Scotty Armstrong."

When everyone echoes, "To Scotty," I flip him off.

Like it always goes with him, he smiles.

So do I.

FIFTY

The food—even the turkey—is delicious. A celebration in the truest sense. Wren, Lyra, and Blue play every record and June's boys end up in the lake with Molly. It's loud and chaotic.

Ford and I stand off to the side. June was right; Ford swept me clear off my feet. At the table of photos, my heart is so full it might pop. Me in some of them, people I know and love in all of them. Even Gary and his maid, in some weird way, is endearing.

Ford hooks a pinkie through mine. "Tell me something real," he says so only I can hear.

I swallow slowly, tightening my pinkie around his. "I've been working on a good speech to give you tomorrow pouring my heart out and you ruined it."

He chuckles. "You done pushing me?"

I look at him, lips twitching as I fight a smile. "You think anyone will notice if we sneak away for a few?" I ask.

He bites his bottom lip. "I'm going to need more than a few."

"That's not what I'm talking about," I tell him as I slap his chest. "Entirely."

He chuckles and nods toward his truck.

"Where to?" he asks as he turns the key.

"Fight Club."

He gives me a confused look but doesn't argue, driving us the few minutes it takes to get there.

He follows me to the building—empty because of the holiday—and I slip a key out of my pocket, unlocking the door to the vacant side. Our footsteps echo as we walk in, and the door slams behind us.

"Do I need to be worried?" he asks, hint of amusement in his voice.

"Probably," I say with a smirk, taking his hands in mine and walking him to the center of the room. "It occurred to me in your annoying mission to keep me with you that me and you aren't the only things I want to change about the rest of my life."

"Oh really?" he asks. "What else?"

"For one," I say, "I came to an agreement with the Sellecks this week to sell the crematorium to them."

His eyes widen.

"I had terms, of course. Wanda and Dondi stay on with Wanda in charge. And, contingent on everything going through, I bought this building."

A breath wooshes out of him. "You what?"

"And Fight Club."

His eyes bulge. "What?"

"I didn't stutter, Officer," I say, taking a step toward him. "I want to turn this into whatever you want to turn it into. I want this to be my what's next. My now to forever. With you."

He rubs a hand over his face, which is covered in a half-shocked, half-ecstatic expression.

"You sure about this?" he asks, looking around the dusty walls and high ceilings.

"No," I admit, lifting our connected hands and kissing both of his thumbs. "But I still want to do it."

I knew I did. Even without a vision or a plan. Even if it's reckless, this is my step in the next direction, and I don't want to take it without him. Ford is showing up and I'm damn well going to let him. I'm done hiding. Done running. Done carrying heavy things.

Wrapping his arms around my waist, he kisses me, squeezing me tight and lifting me off the ground. "I love you, Scotty," he says against my mouth.

I pull away from him slightly and slip a black rubber ring out of my back pocket and drop it into his palm. His lips tug to one side as he stares at it.

"Call it whatever you want," I say.

He wraps his fingers around it, smiling wide. "What are you calling it?"

"A promise ring."

"A promise ring?" he says coyly. "And what are you promising?"

"That I'll fuck up any woman who looks at you."

He barks out a laugh and slips it on his finger, knuckles moving along my jaw. "And if one day I want to buy you a ring?"

"I'll do you one better, Golden Boy." I bite my lip and yank up the sleeve of my sweater, revealing a freshly inked murmuration of starlings flying up the length of my arm, seven of them outlined in blue and standing out bolder than the rest.

He looks from the branded birds on my skin to my face, so much adoration in his eyes I can barely stand it. Then he kisses me like he's trying to drown in me—the familiarity of it something I'll never quite get enough of.

"You know," I murmur into his mouth, "every new business venture needs a good christening."

He laughs against me, but he's already moving us toward the door that connects to Fight Club. I fumble to get the key in the lock while refusing to pull my mouth from his.

We make it—barely. And in the middle of the boxing ring with the only man I've ever loved, that's exactly what we do.

He looks at me, I look at him, and then I tell him I love him.

EPILOGUE

ONE YEAR LATER

"You think they'll do a cavity search?" I ask Wren as one guard pats me down while the other examines the contents of the manila envelope—the only item we were permitted to bring—in a bin off to the side. "I wore my best undies."

Nobody laughs.

Losers.

The guard looking through the envelope gives it to Wren before guiding us into a large room with stainless-steel tables and chairs, gesturing to the table by the window. "That one," he says with a gruff tone. "Break the rules and you're out."

At the table, a woman is already waiting.

Except, it's not just a woman, it's Riley. Next to me, Wren's face goes ashen.

I grab her hand, stopping her in the middle of the room between tables of other prisoners visiting their loved ones. "You got this," I tell her, rounding my spine so our eyes meet. "No matter what she says, that's on her, not you. We don't have to be our mothers." I know that one from experience. "We can be better. We can be . . . someone else's mother," I joke.

She nods, almost smiling as her eyes ping around before taking the final steps across the room.

We sit across from Riley, the three of us looking at each other in silence. Even in an orange prison uniform, no makeup, and the dark roots of her hair grown out to the blonde tips, she's pretty. Outside of a cage, she'd probably be beautiful.

"I'm surprised to see you," she finally says to Wren. Looking at me: "Who's this?"

Wren clears her throat. "Scotty." She puts the envelope of photos on the table.

I smile slightly and offer a greeting Riley ignores.

"I wanted to come here so you know I'm fine," Wren tells her. "In case you ever wondered. And I wanted to see if you were fine, because I do wonder."

Riley remains silent; I stay out of it like I promised Wren on the drive. *"None of your colorful language,"* Wren said about forty-nine times. I told her I'd stay quiet, but it's a struggle. Under the table, my knee bounces and I snap the shit out of my wrist with a rubber band; Wren threw hers away months ago.

"I'm friends with the mom of the girl you killed." Wren's voice teeters just slightly. "And she's"—a breath comes out of her in a gust—"incredible."

Riley's eyes widen slightly, but she says nothing. I wish Mel were here to witness it.

"Anyway." Wren slides the envelope toward her. "I have some pictures. Of me, if you want them. And there's some paperwork in there I'd like you to sign. I brought a pen."

My eyebrows pinch—I only knew about the photos. Riley wordlessly empties the envelope onto the table, picking up the papers first and skimming them. Her eyes flick to us as she flips a page. To me: "Who are you again?"

"Uh." My chin pulls back. "I'm Ford's . . ." My eyes swing to Wren. "Person."

"She's my best friend," Wren says in the wake of my lame answer. "She took me to therapy when I started cutting myself after you went away." I stop bouncing and snapping; my jaw drops. Riley stares at her. "She helped me talk to a boy. My boyfriend now. Luke. She kept me out of trouble. She took me shopping. She bought me a record. Lots of records, actually." Wren laughs softly. "She let me pick out furniture for her house. Our house." She looks at me; I don't argue. Six months ago, she and Ford stayed the night at the A-frame and never left. "She defended me when kids at school made me feel ashamed. She helps me do my homework even though she's really bad at it. She's teaching me to drive even though I'm not sure anything she does is legal. She loves my dad, and he loves her so much it's disgusting."

At my recited resumé of skills, I bite back a proud smile.

Riley eyes me before picking up the pen, hovering it over the papers. "You got any other kids?"

I look at Wren. *What the hell?*

"Uh—"

"She does," Wren says to Riley, voice strong. "A son. She was a selfless mother to him." She glances at me. "And that's why I want you to sign over your rights. So she can adopt me."

My jaw drops.

Wren adds, "If she'll have me."

I press my tongue into the back of my teeth to keep from crying, swallowing twice. Three times. Finally, I look at Riley. "I could probably do that."

Wren's lips twitch, amused brightness in her eyes. *Little shit.*

Riley doesn't hesitate; she scribbles her name on the papers and slides them across the table. "I never wanted to be a mom," she says to Wren, the familiarity of them to what Glory said smacking me across the face. "You were a mistake." Under the table, my hand grips Wren's. Tight. "But you seemed to have turned out okay." Her gaze flicks to me. "Ford kept a picture of you in his house. You're the one with the brother, right?"

At her words, I understand why prison shanks are a thing. I hate this bitch.

I clear my throat and nod. "I'm sure a lot of people have brothers, but yes, I *had* a brother."

She thumbs through the pictures Wren brought—her at various stages of life—then haphazardly tosses them onto the envelope, looking at her daughter again. "Anything else?"

"That's it," Wren says, indifferent as she shuffles everything her mom doesn't want back into the envelope. I open my mouth to tell this woman that she can go fuck a rusty razor blade, but Wren stops me, standing abruptly and taking a moral high ground I loathe. "I hope you have a nice life."

Wren looks toward the guard and gestures we're done. We leave—without looking back. The visit is over. Deep down I think it will be the last time Wren will ever see her.

The conversation replays in my head—what Wren must be thinking. Feeling. Me adopting her—Ford must know. Everything jumbles together like dice in a cup.

At my Bronco—a brand-new one that's fire-engine red and fully loaded—she opens the door. I sit without starting it. Without moving or speaking. Heart galloping in my chest.

When I look at her, I expect to see tears, but instead, she's . . . fine.

"You okay?" I ask.

"She's exactly how I remember," she says with a slight shrug. "She never wanted kids—guess I can't blame her for not caring."

My chest swells with pride as my phone vibrates with a text from June. *Unhinged* and *a mom. Welcome to the dark side.* I smile to myself; of course she already knows.

"You know," I say to Wren, putting the key in the ignition and looking at her sideways. "I expect to be called Mommy."

At this, Wren laughs, and violins scream in the speakers as we take off down the highway.

I wave at Ford across the gym, wide smile on his face. Next to him, Blue lifts a gloved hand my way.

I grin; twins born twenty years apart.

After the deal with the Sellecks went through, Ford, after twenty years of trying to save people the way neither of us could save my brother, retired from the police department. We are now the proud owners of Fight Club . . . where Blue is a member with the family discount.

"How'd it go?" Ford asks, pinching off his gloves as he approaches me, knowing look on his face.

I raise my eyebrows. "How do you think it went when your daughter announced she wanted me to adopt her in the middle of a prison visit?"

"She wanted to surprise you," he says, working his teeth over his bottom lip. *Sexy bastard.* "You going to?"

"Eh." I shrug. "The dad might be a deal-breaker."

He chuckles, smacking me on the ass as we head next door. Where we opened . . . a birding store.

Ford made the case for it being a necessity for anyone who goes through an intense round of sparring to also need a new bird feeder and bag of seed. I laughed when he said it—thought it was the most ridiculous thing I'd ever heard of—but it didn't take long for the idea to grow wings inside of me and soar. Because he loved it so much. Because I wanted to be wherever he was with that smile on his face. And because ultimately, the birds were kind of growing on me.

We named the bird store Pecker Heads.

Believe it or not, that was all me.

At the end of the aisles of bird feeders, bird baths, birdseed, and more books about birds than I ever care to read, Glory stands behind the counter wearing a T-shirt covered in woodpeckers, slight scowl on her lips.

Along with seeing her and Lydia for regular Sunday dinners, she's here a few days a week when she works in the store. She's almost bearable.

"About time you showed up," she barks, untying her apron. "I can't be on my feet so long, Scotty Ann." She doesn't bother asking me how it went before marching outside to light a Lucky. *Some things never change.*

I chuckle, leaning a hip behind the register, Ford mirroring my movement and running his fingers through my hair, blue eyes smiling bright.

"You know," he says, lowering his hands to mine and bringing my thumb to his lips. "Probably wouldn't be too good for Wren to grow up in a home with an unwed mother."

I fight a smile.

"Who am I to stand in the way of what's best for the youth of the nation?"

"Yeah?" he asks, coy. Like he hasn't known I was theirs all along.

I lean into him, angling my head so our eyes meet. "I'm not getting rid of you. What do I care if you want to be legally obligated to be my on-demand sure thing?"

He booms a laugh, vibrating all of me as his arms wrap around my waist and he presses his lips to mine.

It turns out, I'm not as doomed as I once thought. My grandpa Archie was right, there are a lot more things in this world than bodies to set on fire. Even though my brother is still gone. Even though my life had a starting point I wouldn't wish on anyone except Jessicunt.

Wanda was on to something when she told me about her choice of living in the now to forever. In my now, I choose this. Ford. Wren. June. Hell, maybe even Glory. Over and over again.

"A man and a viper," he says against my mouth. "Isn't there a book about that?"

I smile—wide. There most definitely is.

ACKNOWLEDGMENTS

I GREW UP IN the time of commercials on tube televisions showing eggs frying in a pan, *This is your brain on drugs* stamped across the pixelated screen. It sums up all I knew about the subject for the first few decades of my life. Do drugs, turn into a fried egg. Seemed pretty straightforward.

But life has a way of muddying the waters and teaching us hard lessons we're never quite prepared to learn. It wasn't until I was well into adulthood that I found out being in the presence of addiction is just like Scotty said: a ripple leading to a tsunami that ends in a hellscape. There are no people on the outside; everyone exposed is collateral damage. Even the ones who never touch a single pill, needle, or grain of powder feel the aching wrath if they're close enough to the ones who do.

And caring doesn't do much. At least nowhere near as much as we hope.

This other side of addiction is where Scotty's story started for me. The helplessness, the worry, and the desperation that comes hand in hand with loving someone who can't quite love themselves. Who can't quite hear your pleas. At least not until they're ready.

To my first readers—you are the stars of the Scotty Armstrong show. Whitney, Monique, Tamisha, Sonia, Morgann, Lindsay from Canada, Mallory, Andrea, Shelly, Lisa, and my favorite cult leader, Meagan . . . Scotty wouldn't be who she became without y'all. Thanks for the laughs and brutal honesty.

As always, to Kevin, who believes in me more than I believe in myself, and knows more about birds than I ever care to discuss. To my darling children, Oak and Vale, who I'm starting to believe the real reason they cheer for me while I'm writing is because it means they get extra screen time.

Big thanks to Kristin Monza and her band of medical professionals who helped me with Wren, and my friends in law enforcement, Shelly and Nicole, who answered questions about Ford and helped keep him from being completely unethical.

And, of course, to my wonderful editors. Victoria Straw who helped me shift through the shit to find the story, Kaitlin Slowik who helped me find the right words, and Ciara Lewis who made sure it was reader ready.

And, you know, to whoever is reading this. Thanks for that. You're the best.

Sorry about all the swear words.

Kind of.

Ashley Manley is a current writer and former just about everything else. When she isn't stringing words together on her computer, you can find her chasing her kids, reheating her coffee, or dreaming of her next grand adventure under tall trees. While she's lived a little bit of everywhere, North Carolina will always feel like home. To connect with Ashley, visit ashleymanleywrites.com or find her on Instagram @ashleymanleywrites.

<u>Other books by Ashley</u>

Every Beautiful Mile
When Wildflowers Bloom

<u>Life on the Ledge Duet</u>

Forever and Back (June's book)
Now to Forever (Scotty's book)